Praise for *Tiny Imperfections*

"Frank and Youmans pack their debut with drama . . . The glitzy, high-stakes world and gossipy narrative voice will put readers in mind of *Crazy Rich Asians*."

—*Publishers Weekly*

"Frank and Youmans' humorous and touching debut novel explores how being a Black woman affects their protagonist's personal and professional experiences in a tale that will resonate with readers of all demographic backgrounds."

—*Booklist*

"Offers a delightful view inside the cutthroat world of private school admissions that is hilarious, cringeworthy, and all too relevant in today's ultracompetitive educational landscape. I ate this book up like a box of candy; you will too."

—Tara Conklin, author of *The Last Romantics*

"*Tiny Imperfections* is a funny, heartwarming take on finding love in a most unexpected place."

—Anissa Gray, author of
The Care and Feeding of Ravenously Hungry Girls

"Parents and anyone who's ever been to school will love this peek into the turbulent world of private school, from two women who have worked in it for more than twenty years. Get to know three generations of Black women in San Francisco as they navigate that universe, along with their relationships, motivations, and a heaping helping of drama."

—*Good Housekeeping*

"Youmans and Frank manage to tackle a woman's journey through work, race, and motherhood beautifully in their debut. *Tiny Imperfections* is laugh-out-loud funny and full of heart. I can't wait to see what they bring us next!"

—Alexa Martin, author of *Fumbled*

"Overeager parents are just one of the many things heroine Josie Bordelon has to deal with as head of admissions for a tawny private school in San Francisco. These two authors are brave enough to expose the insanity and hilarity that happen during application season . . . A really funny read."

—Laurie Gelman, author of *Class Mom*

"Humor, charm, and intriguing drama combine in this novel—written by a best friend author duo—about the competitive world of private education."

—*Woman's World*

"Youmans and Frank's deep dive into private school culture sets the stage for a dishy, charming story of West Coast elitism and parenting at its pushiest. But it's the characters, especially the marvelous Bordelon women, who give this delightful novel its heart and humor—and who make you long to be part of the family even after the last page."

—Amy Poeppel, author of *Small Admissions* and *Limelight*

"Perfectly captures the absurdist bubble of San Francisco's tech upper class. A rollicking good read that reminds us that money, power, and influence will never be enough to make someone truly happy."

—Jo Piazza, author of *Charlotte Walsh Likes to Win*

"With a heroine to cheer for and laugh-out-loud delicacies on every page, *Tiny Imperfections* is perfect entertainment! You're in for such a fun ride. I loved it!"

—Lisa Patton, bestselling author of *Rush*

Never Meant to Meet You

OTHER TITLES BY
ALLI FRANK AND ASHA YOUMANS

Tiny Imperfections

Never Meant to Meet You

a novel

Alli Frank & Asha Youmans

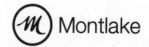 Montlake

Published by Montlake, Seattle

www.apub.com

Amazon, the Amazon logo, and Montlake are trademarks of Amazon.com, Inc., or its affiliates.

ISBN-13: 9781542034104
ISBN-10: 1542034108

Cover design by Jarrod Taylor

Printed in the United States of America

For Jared, Michael, Lila, and Lexi.
Choose Joy.

CHAPTER ONE

I tug at my tights, struggling to get my phone out of the too-small hip pocket.

Judy 7:18 PM

> 12,018 steps so far today, looking to hit 15K. Be by in five.

> "Whether you think you can or think you can't— you're probably right." —Henry Ford

I should have never given Judy a Fitbit as a retirement gift. Or that book of inspirational quotes. My audiobook is queued up, and I'm all set for the narrator's velvety voice to deliver me to the climax of the paranormal romance I've power walked my way through these last two weeks. I've been dying to find out before school starts if the priestess of the city's witch coven is going to get it on with the alpha of the local werewolf pack. I was sure tonight was going to be the night, but Judy just cockblocked the lead canine.

"Darius, you seen my sneakers?" I yell at my son, who's in the hall closet getting the lightweight cashmere-blend sweaters, label maker, and kid-friendly stationery I store between Memorial and Labor Day. I smell a funk all the way in my kitchen that tells me Darius did not shower after playing three on three this afternoon. Now his hummin' hands are touching on my school clothes. "Darius! You hear me?"

I need a hit of protein with a side of scrolling my phone before I head out to meet Judy for a walk. *You don't have any PersonalPoints, go get some!* my Weight Watchers app urges me, cutting through my thoughts like a smug mean girl I'm paying $44.95 per month to be my friend even though I hate her. When Judy suggested we join Weight Watchers last spring, I agreed in a weak moment, wondering how I would survive life at the Houghton School without her. She wanted to get healthy in retirement, and I wanted to make sure we kept a weekly date to see each other. Threesomes never work in friendships, but still I walked right into this one with Judy and the app lady.

I'm going, I'm going, I will myself.

I lick clean my spoonful of peanut butter and then dunk it in a mug of sitting water at the kitchen sink. Soon enough my nights will be filled with lesson planning and answering the same anxious parental questions I've been fielding going on twenty years. The extra nudge to take advantage of the last few carefree summer evenings I have is probably a good thing. If Judy and I walk at a crisp clip, I won't bother tracking the peanut butter points.

Judy 7:24 PM

> I'm outside stepping in place waiting on you. AGAIN.

I head down the hall, cursing the day AirPods hit the market; I know Darius hasn't heard me yelling after him the past two minutes. He's deep in the closet with his back to me, so I hike his basketball shorts up from half-mast to command his attention.

"Ma!" Darius freaks, pulling them back down before I can get out a chuckle. "Quit playin'!" I knew inciting a teen-fashion faux pas, even in the privacy of our own home, would flip his switch.

"I've been yelling for you since last year, but you can't hear me with that noise bangin' so loud in your ears. And *oowwee*, son. I swear to God you are funky as a donkey." My assessment of his aroma is met with a practiced eye roll. "Do you know where my sneakers are?"

Darius leans over, attacking me in an enveloping hug, knowing my head is going right in his armpit. I never pushed away his hugs when he was little, but as mother to a teenage son, the hormones meeting high heat is too much. I wriggle away for self-preservation, but he holds tighter, laughing at my lockdown. "What?" Darius feigns innocence. "You're always saying I don't show you enough affection."

I swat his behind and repeat my question. "Have you seen my sneakers or not?"

"Yeah, they're right outside the back door. You left them there after weeding yesterday."

"When you finish pulling down my sweaters, hose out the compost bin in the kitchen; it smells almost as bad as you." I wink at Darius, the great love of my life, and head down the hall and out the back door.

There my sneakers are, right where Darius remembers I left them. I've been at war all summer with the slugs in my vegetable garden. I'm locked in brutal battle in the dark underbelly of gardening, struggling to protect my turf and my turnips. Some nights I'm out here at midnight, headlamp on, drowning the slugs in a concoction of Budweiser and salt when they least expect it. The internet swears it will work, and I'm not going to stop the beerboarding until it does. I peek in my Nikes to make sure none of those nasty wigglers have crawled inside.

Lacing up my shoes, I see Judy has moved three houses down and is talking someone's ear off, so I take the few extra minutes I gained to pull my recycle and trash bins to the edge of my driveway for tomorrow's pickup. Jiggering them into their proper place in an effort not to block the sidewalk, I see my newish neighbor, Noa Abrams, seated on her front porch next door.

My grandma Birdie used to call me "Nose-Retta," a not-so-subtle hint at my tendency to always be underfoot, in the mix, overstepping my bounds, and on her last nerve. "Curiosity ain't got a chance to kill the cat," she would say, exasperated. "Marjette is always around as a witness."

When the Abramses moved in a little less than a year ago, I fought my lifelong impulse to immediately sniff out their story and friend up. You don't become a kindergarten teacher by being aloof and uninterested in other people's business. You become a teacher because people *are* your business. To say it's been a concerted, if wholly unnatural, effort to mind my own affairs when it comes to the Abramses would be an understatement, but I'm holding firm to my conviction.

At first glance, the day the moving truck arrived, I had no reason to dislike the Abramses. I didn't know them from any other professional-looking, White starter family fresh from living in San Francisco. So many of them were moving across the Bay Bridge to Oakland in search of more space. Just like my grandmother warned me not to be nosy, she also warned me not to become friends with people too quickly because most likely I wouldn't end up liking them later, and then I'd be stuck. And White people as friends . . . Well, that was never a likely scenario given Birdie's experience in rural Oklahoma. Not surprisingly, my grandmother didn't have many friends. Besides, these days, every White woman is dying to find herself a Black friend. It's like we're this decade's must-have accessory. Every lady might be clamoring for a brown-skinned bestie, but I've never been one to submit to trends.

Also, I'd been burned by my previous neighbor. Being a collector of people and self-appointed fixer of their woes, I failed to heed Birdie's lesson over and over but had always been able to untangle myself from some awkward friendship if it slid south. That streak came to an end two years ago. Turns out it's hard to distance yourself from a friendship gone sour when all that separates you is a too-narrow driveway between similar 1930s bungalows.

Layla Garcia and I weren't the standing "Thursday-night margaritas to complain about our kids" kind of close, but we were close enough that I knew her life story and we held each other's spare keys. While Layla and her husband were all sorts of fun, hosting neighborhood potlucks and outdoing every other house on our street with Halloween decorations, domestic caretaking did not rank high on their to-do list. Here and there, I would kindly drop suggestions about repairs to their house and maintenance for the lawn that would increase their property value (and mine). For a handful of years, Layla never seemed to take any of my recommendations seriously until one Saturday afternoon, hallelujah, a yard service showed up. Layla and her family were out of town for the weekend, and I figured the service got their dates mixed up when they came knocking on my door. I didn't want the handymen to postpone or for Layla to have to reschedule for fear she wouldn't follow through. I let the eager gentlemen into the backyard to get started. I even showed them the most troubled spot of overgrown shrubs pushing against the fence, causing it to lean into my property. They assured me after they thinned the bushes they would right my fence at no expense to me.

Feeling proud for urging my neighbor in a direction that would serve the common good of the whole community, I was confident that when Layla returned to see how beautiful her yard looked, my counsel would spawn a waterfall of pride and continued home improvements. Instead, coming back from dinner at Judy's, I grew queasy seeing the circle of neighbors congregated on Layla's front lawn. I whipped into my driveway, told Darius to stay buckled, and sprinted next door to find out what the neighbors knew.

Turns out that was no lawn service I had let into Layla's backyard; it was a full-fledged theft ring that had been posing as gardeners, breaking into homes, and robbing people throughout the East Bay. Only they didn't break into Layla's home; I walked them right into the garage with my spare key and great enthusiasm for their assumed skill with trimming shears. Once Layla returned home, her weekend away cut short by crime, I cooperated with her and the police to get all the details right for the report. The back-and-forth took a few days, and after that Layla wanted no part of me or my opinion on her domestic upkeep. She didn't even say goodbye when she and her husband sold the house to the Abramses and moved an hour north.

For the past year I've been playing the role of indifferent neighbor while observing the flawless Noa Abrams. In passing, she's never struck me as a woman I would be interested in getting to know. Her story is obvious from twenty feet away and without having to scratch an inch below the surface. Women like Noa Abrams roll through life getting everything they want. It probably takes a little bit of effort and a pinch of hard work, but the goal—whether it be a coveted project at work or an annual exotic beach vacation—is always easily in her reach. She has the type of body that screams, *I get up at five o'clock to interval train while you waste precious calorie-burning hours sleeping.* Hair that strawberry blonde in your forties only comes in an expensive bottle, and from what I can tell Noa hits the bottle hard. And every morning, when we both pull out of our driveways at about the same time, Noa Abrams's Tesla serves as a reminder of the life I could have had if Booker hadn't left me—sleek and enviable with all the high-end extras.

As I do a few hamstring stretches and wait for Judy to tie up her conversation, I give Noa a kindly half wave and quick smile from the sidewalk. I may not feel compelled to be her friend, but when you grow up as a Southern Baptist, manners are drilled into you, and I'm not rude.

"You still giving that neighbor of yours the cold shoulder?" Judy asks, creeping up on me in her blindingly white sneakers. She can tell I'm eyeing her at the ankles and takes a step back so I can admire her new kicks.

"I'm not giving her the cold shoulder. I'm just keeping my distance," I answer and again look Noa's way, expecting acknowledgment of my greeting.

"Well, you can spend our walk explaining the difference, and I'll pretend to care. Let's go."

My wave is not reciprocated, so Judy and I push off toward the Cal Berkeley stadium.

Since it's seven thirty, any potential families who might be joining my kindergarten class next week are tucked in their homes for their five-year-olds' bedtime routines. This ensures, at least for a few more hours, I'm spared any chance of the parent-educator chitchat that is the foundation of a teacher's life.

The combination of walking and listening to Judy talk about everything and nothing, an unusually humid Oakland night, and fifteen extra pounds I've been half-heartedly trying to shed since I ate my way through Darius's middle school years leaves my body aching for water. A sweaty puddle, I skip to get back in step with Judy as we turn left onto my street.

"Well, isn't that nice; that neighbor of yours is still perched outside, waiting for you to get home," Judy cackles, playing with her Fitbit to get an accurate step count. "I'll see you tomorrow morning at our meeting. You're buying coffee 'cause I'm getting another five-pound charm."

I blow Judy an air-kiss, not wanting to mix facial sweat, and wish her good night. I need to figure out how to drop at least a few ounces between now and ten o'clock tomorrow morning.

Noa's rigid, sitting outside her house, still staring me down as I walk toward my front door. Her face doesn't crack when a passing car's muffler backfires.

I wave again since I know this close there's no way she can miss me. No response. Not a muscle moved. Maybe Noa didn't see me when I headed out an hour earlier, but not waving twice to your neighbor? That's downright ill mannered, and I've done nothing wrong. Mrs.

Abrams needs a little educating on what it means to be friendly on her no-longer-new street.

I wipe the sweat dripping from my brow and head across Noa's lawn to insist she acknowledge my presence. She doesn't have to want to get to know me either, but she's not going to treat me like the hired help I've watched creep in and out of her house. Midcharge I pump my brakes. Upon closer inspection, Noa looks ravaged. Her skin's the color of graying Elmer's glue my students peel off their palms, and her eyes look purplish from lack of sleep, too much crying, or both. I can see she's not right in her mind. I take a deep breath and walk the last steps to her front porch. I keep a few feet's distance from Noa, not wanting to crowd a woman who looks on the edge. It's obvious now that it's not that Noa didn't see me both times I waved; Noa's not seeing anything in front of her. She holds a stare that's distant, in another world. Now that I, too, have stopped moving, the air's heavy between us. The only action on the front porch is Noa's aggressive pulling of each knuckle in anxious repetition.

I clear my throat to announce my presence. I rest my hand over the hip pocket of my exercise tights, ready to draw my phone and call someone or 911 to help this woman.

"Can I get you anything, honey? Get your husband for you, maybe?" I stumble over my tongue trying to remember her husband's name. I'm drawing a blank. My plan is to help Noa connect with someone she really needs, and then I'll be on my way, minding my own business from here on out. I don't need to know what's going on; I just need to get my neighbor some support and get back home. I'm treading into territory I promised Judy I would never go. Also, I told myself after my walk that I would get out my Welcome to Kindergarten letters before I was allowed a hit of Netflix. This situation looks like it might cut into my TV time.

No response. I listen for the daughter I've seen playing out front from time to time. If she's around I can ask her to get her father. There's no noise coming from the house, so I try again with Noa. "Honey, let me get a hold of your man for you." I tap Noa ever so lightly on her knee, signaling I'm still there, waiting for her to come to. "Doesn't seem like he's home, but I can call him. Got my phone right here, just give me his number. I can't leave you out here alone like this. You need your husband."

Expressionless, Noa announces, "Charlie's dead." That's his name.

Grandma Birdie pops in my head, sweeping her uneven porch. Apron on, bony hands gripping the broom, I can hear her accuse, "I told you to leave White folks alone. You never did believe fat meat is greasy." Words that cut were my late grandmother's favorite weapon of discipline, and though she used them repeatedly to break my nosy habits, it never worked.

CHAPTER TWO

"Last night I was shaping my eyebrows in the magnifying mirror Charlie installed about a month ago." Noa's voice begins shaky but evens out, determined to relay a story I didn't ask to hear. "You know, the kind that lets you see too much up close." I manage an uncomfortable smile and nod. Every woman knows that mirror. "Charlie came up from behind and hugged me. I knew what he wanted, but I didn't turn. I needed to focus. I had a big meeting this morning at nine with people flying in from Atlanta, and I wanted to look fresh." Noa stares at me, searching for solidarity in her commitment to her beauty regime, but I'm rendered speechless, rare for a woman who talks for a living.

In the face of tragedy, Noa's demeanor is alarmingly flat while she recounts the specifics of her husband's death less than twenty-four hours ago. I shift my weight to my back foot and slide my front foot to meet it. Now there's a more comfortable distance between the two of us in case Noa becomes unhinged and I need to run for the cut between houses.

"Maybe if I had turned around when he was copping a feel, Charlie would still be alive. I could have caught him. I could have seen his face one more time. But it all happened so fast. One second, he was feeling me up, the next he was trembling, and boom"—Noa smacks her hands together for emphasis—"he stopped cold and dropped to the floor. I didn't have time to act. A few jagged breaths and he was gone."

Our eyes mutually drift to the half-empty bottle of Jim Beam and ravaged bag of OREO cookies on the outdoor bistro table. Up until this moment, having only observed Noa from my house, I would have never pegged her for a store-bought cookies kind of woman. I would have assumed a preservative hadn't ever passed through her front door. Noa lifts her chin in acknowledgment of the familiar blue package, a kind offering from a shell-shocked wife. I shake my head, though I see they're Double Stuf, and one OREO would stave off my growing hunger.

Noa grabs the bottle of Beam and swigs. I cringe and hope she's too distracted to read the *Whoa, this is extra, even for me* expression broadcast across my face. "We were going to Mexico in two weeks to celebrate our twelfth anniversary. Going to do it right. First-class plane tickets, a suite at the resort, full breakfast buffet, *and* spa credits." Noa holds up her phone calendar and shakes it at me to serve as evidence of her vacation and beauty commitment. "Instead, I'm planning a shiva call for this weekend when I'm supposed to be making scuba-diving reservations."

I look over my shoulder, still hopeful someone more appropriate is coming to step in for me—a mother, a sister, a friend, someone to care for Noa. Nope, alone here. I'm searching for the right next thing to say to help this woman I really don't know in her time of need. I take a beat to think about what I would want if the tables were turned and Noa was staring me down at my lowest moment.

"Would you like me to help you even up your brows?" I ask. "Promise I'm a pro with a Tweezerman." I know it sounds tacky given the circumstances, but if the tables were turned and I had my husband's funeral to attend, I'd want someone watching my back making sure I didn't show up looking busted.

"What in the *what*? You don't even know this woman. How'd you start off with the fact that her husband's dead? Go from the beginning and don't leave nothin' out," Judy insists under her breath, so it sounds more like a subtle threat. She doesn't care that our Weight Watchers meeting has started and Carole, our cheerful leader dressed in a denim power suit, is staring us down with her *Star Trek*–turquoise contacts.

While Carole is talking to us about having compassion for ourselves when we slip and fall into a vat of potato chips, Judy is fake listening while leaning into me to rummage through her purse on the floor. Carole receives several oohs and aahs when she shares her necklace with two charms, one a cake and one a turtle. She wears the necklace daily, she tells us, to remind herself that when she face plants into her preferred red velvet cake, it will take her forever to lose the gain, her metabolism being slow like a turtle. That must have been one deeply reflective moment Carole had on a Thursday evening shopping for herself at Pandora.

Judy pulls out a scrap piece of paper and pen from her purse and shows them to me in elated victory, her archaeological dig complete. She writes down, "How'd he die?" and passes the note to me like we aren't touching shoulders sitting side by side and I wasn't watching what she was writing. Her demand for deets about Charlie's death is disturbingly dark given the fact we are seated in this windowless church basement to receive the holy grail to living healthier, happier, longer lives. Every Saturday for thirty minutes we fill our cups with a watered-down version of "stop feeding your piehole and move your ass."

"LATER," I write back and gesture to our fearless Queen of Points Counting. Judy sticks her tongue out at me like we're five. As a teacher, I believe in giving another teacher respect. *You go on, Carole. I got you.*

Once she settles in, Judy actually listens at our meetings, whereas my favorite part is staring at the people I'm beginning to feel a kinship with on Saturday mornings. For instance, Priya was a beauty queen in India back in the day. Next month she's going to New Delhi for the first time in twenty years, and she doesn't want her friends and family to see the damage her intimate relationship with In-N-Out Burger has done. Marie comes to the meetings in a black negligee and midcalf puffy jacket every week. A month into our group, I straight up asked her why. Turns out at weigh-in Marie strips down to her negligee because it's the lightest thing she owns. And then she gave me the pro tip to never wear underwear or an underwire for weigh-ins—best to show up as light as possible. I immediately asked the staff if they wipe down the metal folding chairs after every meeting. I'm convinced Gary's only here to find a third wife, and Paul's got his eyes set on Gary for his first husband. As Carole talks, I let my mind wander about the lives of my fellow Weight Watchers attendees beyond the meetings. My curiosity is never enough to invite them over for a zero-point dinner, but my interest consumes the thirty minutes nonetheless.

The last order of business before Judy and I can head to Peet's for coffee is Carole soliciting suggestions to give our Saturday-morning group a permanent name. I get that a core group of attendees—about twelve women and two men—have been loyal to Carole and her week-end meeting going on ten years, but for those of us who are newer and hoping not to be in it for the long haul, I'm not convinced we need to celebrate our collective relationship with a hokey moniker.

"Shrinking Violets," Denise, who always wears some shade of purple and whose favorite season is spring, is first to suggest.

"Through Thick and Thin," says Kurt, who shares he's been both several times. A few members chuff in unity with that truth.

"Thick and Tired," I whisper in Judy's ear and signal to grab our coats and go. I'm over this brainstorming activity and ready for the caffeinated portion of our morning agenda.

Peet's Coffee is packed with screaming children being bribed with blueberry muffins to shut up long enough to allow their exhausted parents a moment of peace to mainline their java. Standing in line, I offer to rock a stroller for one mama with howling twin baby girls so she can wolf down half a bagel and a shot of espresso. I think I've ensured her survival until nap time. Judy, who is over children after forty years working in schools taking care of other people's kids, pretends to be interested in the travel mug display.

The young mother thanks me profusely, admitting mom brain is real and that's why she's back in line for a second time, having forgotten her husband's order. I'm happy to help. I love babies, toddlers, children, you name it. Growing up, my siblings referred to my babysitting business as an "empire." My reputation had spread wide among Tulsa parents, and they were willing to pay me double the going fourteen-year-old rate because my imaginary play and tidying skills were at the top of the childcare game. I went to college with a larger checking account than my older brother, who had been in the workforce for almost four years. Unfortunately, these days, every time I encounter a struggling mama with multiple children, the ache of what should have been my life churns my insides.

Judy took a chance and hired me, a newly minted Sooner graduate from the University of Oklahoma. I was barely twenty-two years old, with an incomplete teaching certificate, but an impeccable list of summer nannying references. The intentional hint I dropped about being a minister's daughter might have punted me over the finish line to a kindergarten teaching offer I was in no way qualified for. It was at the foot of my father's shrewd evangelizing that I learned when to wield that nugget of personal history to my advantage. Everyone trusts a church kid. Plus, Judy wasn't fooling me. I'm pretty sure she was tired of being the lone Black polka dot in the faculty lounge at Houghton and needed another brown face to keep her company. It didn't matter that I was closer in age to the students she administered over than to Judy herself.

Newly employed and recently engaged, right after graduation, my college sweetheart, Booker Lewis, and I packed my used red Jetta with 120,000 miles on it and moved from Oklahoma to the Bay Area. Booker started medical school at University of California, San Francisco, and

I started working to keep a roof over our heads and our credit intact, hustling to pay Booker's loans on time. Our plan was set in stone: medical school in San Francisco, then back to my family and my church in Tulsa for residency and establishing his practice. I could do anything for four years.

Though I excelled throughout school, the job I knew I most wanted was mother. That was not happening at twenty-two years old with a husband in his first year of medical school, so I decided to become what I believed was the next best thing to occupy my time until Booker was into an established medical practice: an elementary schoolteacher. I knew it was going to be a long haul between medical school and fellowships until I could start filling my lap with babies and be home to take care of our family, but I was down for the cause. I wanted a big house filled with five children, and Booker had promised if I steered our ship while he sailed through medical school, he would make bank and we could make all the babies I wanted. Until then, teaching was a solid job that would pay our bills and guarantee we wouldn't lose our apartment, since Booker's Regents Scholarship only covered partial tuition. And each year I'd have new students to read to, count with, and lead in silly songs. My lap would get plenty of practice before I had mini-Sooners of my own.

Darius was an oops baby, born in Booker's third year of medical school and long before we had meticulously (or so we thought) planned. Though he was supposed to come later, he was not supposed to be my one and only. Darius was meant to be the first in a long line of Lewis children and destined for a southern upbringing. Every August, when Darius turned a year older, I told Booker that our baby boy needed a permanent playdate, a lifelong ride-or-die by his side like we both had coming from large families.

Booker always had a reason at the ready to delay having more kids and our heading back to Oklahoma. Residency, moving into our first house in Oakland, fellowship, private practice opportunities, and not wanting to step off our family plan, again. He never went so far as to accuse me of purposely getting pregnant with Darius, though I suspected he considered it. I spent years convincing myself, Judy, and my family that after Darius was born and had a colicky first year of life full of ear infections and digestive issues, Booker was even more stressed and exhausted. I continued to rationalize that he didn't want to grow our family until he could be totally present, which, after our experience with Darius, we would need if we were going to have all those children. Still alive at the time, Birdie repeated often what I already knew: if we were back in Tulsa, we could be having all the kids we wanted with so many hands on deck to help.

While I'm struggling to peel myself away from the borrowed twins at Peet's, Judy orders our Americanos and puts her hand out for my credit card per our post-weigh-in rule: she who loses the least weight buys the coffee. Our Q1 score is 1–10, and this home team is getting her plump ass kicked. I nudge Judy down toward the pickup station. While we wait, I casually mention what I know she's been itching to hear all morning: "My neighbor's husband died copping a feel."

"He died trying to get busy?" We look at each other and bust out laughing. Inappropriate, we know. "So, what'd you do?" Judy asks, wistfully gazing at a twentysomething gazelle glide by with her supersize whipped caffeinated drink that is kissing cousins to a chocolate milkshake.

"I offered to shape up her eyebrows. They were a mess," I share, blowing on my steaming cup of energy.

"NO, YOU DIDN'T!" Judy blurts, like I just confessed to being the one who killed Charlie. "Marjette, now that is too bold for words. What makes you think she even wanted your help?"

"No woman wants to walk around with crooked brows on their forehead, Judy. Trust me, it was the right thing to do. She has a memorial to attend, and her face was already jacked up enough from crying. I did her a favor." Judy gives me a skeptical side-eye. "And please, that's not all I'm doing to help this poor woman. After I'm done with you, I'm heading to the grocery store to pick up chicken to fry and take over for the shiva tomorrow after the funeral."

"Was the husband one of the smoky haired like me or just unlucky?" Judy pats her hair, acting all holy, but she likes to roll around in the dirt.

"Unlucky, I 'spect. If I had to guess, I'd say Charlie and Noa are around my age. Eh, maybe a handful of years older. Since last night was the first time I've really looked at Noa up close and she was tore up, it's tough for me to say. They have a little girl who is maybe sixish that I've seen playing out front from time to time. That's all I know. I told you, I'm done gettin' in the trenches of other people's business."

Judy puffs a blast of air out her nose at my declaration.

"I'm going to make some food, stop by the shiva tomorrow afternoon for a quick minute to pay my respects, and then I'm out on this one," I state confidently. "Though I do feel for their baby girl."

"Uh-huh." Judy raises the same eyebrow she used for twenty-five years at Houghton to tell wayward children she didn't believe for a second whatever story they were spinning. "I keep telling you to stay out of folks' business. If you don't end up bringing drama to her, she's going to bring drama to you. Don't you have enough to do without running somebody else's life?"

"Judy, you worry too much. I'm not taking over her life, I'm just taking her chicken. But"—I pause and peek at my friend beneath lowered lids—"there is one thing." Judy gives me a moment to gather myself before I share more and then waves to hurry me up.

"Okay. Please, God, don't strike me dead, but I also love the new black BMW SUV I've seen Charlie pull in and out of the garage a few times the last couple of months. It's so sharp! Kind of car I always thought Booker would buy me." I take a sip of my coffee and feel the heat rush through my core and out to my limbs. "You know I always wanted to be the fly mama in the neighborhood, but we know how that coin flipped. Wonder what she's gonna do with that car now? And before you say it, I know, I know. It's twisted that this woman just lost her husband and I'm drooling for his car."

"I'm not judging you," Judy says, though her words belie her suspicious expression, confirming that she is full-on judging and lying. "But don't ruin my hard-earned Americano by bringing Booker into my morning. I'm tired of giving that man any of our time. I've said it a hundred times: you got the house, you got the kid, you won."

Booker's with someone new who's built to the hilt—he's rich as hell with no real responsibilities to speak of—and I'm left single, getting by on a teacher's salary, raising our son practically on my own. *So no, I did not win.*

Judy has not so patiently lived every moment of the Booker saga with me. If she were my therapist, she'd be rolling in dough, and I'd be broke as a joke. When Darius was seven, I was thirty-two, and we were *still* in California. I went off the pill without telling Booker. I had been teaching for over a decade, Booker was settled in a plastic surgery private practice, we owned our beautiful four-bedroom home in the Rockridge neighborhood with ample backyard for all my dream babies, and paying our bills was, for the first time in our lives, not a primary or even secondary concern. It was a now-or-never time to have more kids; Booker just needed a little teasing and enticement.

I threatened Booker that Joe, our mailman, was starting to look sexy as hell, and I looked like Halle Berry with a case of the thickness, so I knew he couldn't keep his hands off me. Also, I was no dummy; I worked in a school where 80 percent of the teachers were women, and I had consoled one too many hopeful mamas in their mid- and late thirties who struggled fiercely to get pregnant. For some it never came to be. That was not going to be me. My path in life was to raise a starting basketball lineup. After ten years of putting Booker first, it was time to prioritize myself.

Within the year I came bounding into the kitchen one morning, jumping for joy, waving two pregnancy tests in my fists like pom-poms. Booker looked at me sideways, asking me why I was acting funny. I figured he was tired from working long days and doing back-to-back procedures. His clinic was expanding as the practice gained a reputation of excellence repairing cosmetic surgeries gone awry. Despite his grumpy attitude, I was not going to let Booker kill my moment of joy. I pretended I was going to dunk one of the pregnancy sticks in his coffee and stir. I distinctly remember laughing at my attempted prank and from the sheer giddiness of knowing I was going to be a mama again. Booker ripped the test right out of my hand and stared at it too long without a reaction. One second without a positive response was too long for me. I stopped jumping around and sought to ground myself by putting a hand on Booker's shoulder. He shrugged it off and asked me point-blank how this could have happened. I knew he wasn't asking for a lesson on the birds and the bees—he was asking how I could get pregnant if I was on the pill.

I steeled myself for whatever objection was about to come from my husband, who always claimed his number one pet peeve in people was deceit. Booker would consistently tell Darius to "man up," "play it straight," or "no excuses" when he was learning life's hard lessons, most of them on the playground. I stood in our kitchen in my pink-and-white striped pajama pants and one of Booker's undershirts I liked to sleep in and told him straight up I had taken myself off the pill nearly eight months ago. The next minute, in our California Craftsman with the September sun shining in over the kitchen sink, Booker said the second-most painful truth of my life: "Are you so hardheaded that you are really going to make me spell it out for you?"

I stared at him cluelessly.

"Don't you think if I wanted more kids with you, we would have had more kids by now? I like the way our life is. Or I did until you went off and screwed it up."

I stood stunned still. Booker pushed his kitchen chair back hard, called sharply for Darius, and before I could catch my breath, the two of them were off to our son's baseball game.

The next few weeks Booker and I avoided even entering each other's personal space. We averted our eyes in the house and made sure never to collide for fear of an explosion. Darius was in heaven because every moment that Booker was home, he swept him up to have "little-man time" so he could avoid interacting with me and talking about the baby. At a time I thought would be spent calling relatives about our expanding family, my husband minimized his communication with me and increased his patient load.

While Booker's and my relationship hadn't thawed, at least at school I got to cozy up to my students for warmth during story time. I always read to my kids after lunch recess to bring down their body heat after they'd been running around and refocus them for the rest of the afternoon. We were halfway through Harold dragging a purple crayon along a wall and I knew. I called Emma, my teaching assistant, over to finish out the chapter, and I walked straight to Judy's office and asked her if she could take me to my doctor. I didn't call Booker, and I didn't let Judy call him either. I had miscarried, and I didn't want my pain to be his relief.

Once the baby was gone, I was left to grieve on my own in the presence of Booker's indifference. I figured if I buried my feelings down to a depth I didn't know I had, then it would only take a few weeks, at most a month or two, for Booker and me to get back to normal. We had been together since the second day of our freshman year, nearly fifteen years of sticking by one another's side. We worked together to get Booker through a decade of medical training and into private practice. I had even let go of the promise of returning to Tulsa, and graciously, I might add. His turn at his career had been up first, but I always figured at some point in our partnership our priorities would flip, and it would be my turn. It seemed I figured wrong.

Now I was left to contend with the searing pain of losing a child without Booker for support, far from my family, all while praying Darius and my students would be enough. Or at least enough for another year. I tricked myself into believing maybe Booker just needed to get his medical reputation more firmly established in the greater Bay Area and then we could revisit the more kids thing when he was less stressed. I had gotten pregnant with Darius in what seemed like a minute, and while number two wasn't immediate, it was quick enough. So I told myself as I marched toward thirty-five, and the feared geriatric-pregnancy label, that my eggs would continue to hatch.

There was no more baby talk in our house. Whenever Darius, as any young child would do, teased and asked if we could buy a baby brother at the grocery store, I quickly changed the subject. Booker spent less and less of his already limited time at home, but at least when he was around, he was back to being sweet to me and helpful with the projects that befall a ninety-year-old home, even though his efforts often felt disingenuous.

On my thirty-fifth birthday Booker had to work late, but he managed to arrange for an in-home massage and takeout from my favorite restaurant for me and Darius. There were even carrot cupcakes in the fridge from a sinful bakery on Piedmont Avenue. I had been convincing myself for over a year that things between me and Booker were on the mend. After all, every marriage had hiccups and long stretches of difficult times. In the end, despite all the efforts he put into my birthday, he still wasn't home with his family. Sometimes denial is a woman's best skill and her worst enemy.

A week after my birthday, it was a Monday, Veterans Day, and I had the day off. To my surprise, Booker had taken the day off as well, and Darius had a playdate with a buddy from school. I suggested we go pick a new paint color for the living room and then head to Telegraph Avenue for pulled pork sandwiches. The perfect marriage day date. Booker had other plans for us. In the living room, while I was fluffing decorative pillows and holding up paint swatches, Booker announced he had met someone. Initially, I was more confused by *how* he met someone—he was so busy working 24-7—than by the fact that he was telling me there was another woman. He gave me some tired explanation. She was a *client* of his. I corrected him, *patient*, reminding him he wasn't going to gaslight me with bougie speak from the plastic surgery world. With a poker face, Booker declared that nine months ago she had come into his office on a recommendation from a friend. She had originally gone to a quack plastic surgeon who had botched her boob job. As he told me his mistress's tale of woe, he had the gall to look wounded, not by what he was doing to me but with the story of twisted titties he was laying across my coffee table. It had taken her two turns under his knife to do a complete reconstruction of her chest, but he had righted her desired DDs. Apparently, he had done such a good job that he desired her DDs too.

I asked if he was in love with her. He answered by telling me that he wanted Darius and me to continue to live comfortably in our house so he would move out, and he had already begun the process of making me the sole owner of our home. In his life as in his practice, snip, snip, cut, cut, Booker had removed what he did not want and constructed something new that he preferred. Of course, I screamed and called him everything but a child of God. But I did not beg. I would not beg. If Booker wanted out, he could get out.

When Booker packed his bags and walked to his car, I yelled at his back, "I will never settle for bad sex again. You hear me, Booker?" Truth is, Booker had been my first and only, so the sole comparison I had was the Booker who was in love with me for the first twelve years of our relationship and the Booker who had begun acting like sex with me was a chore the last three years of marriage. He kept walking, unfazed by my hurled insults. I worked hard in my life to temper my street with sweet, but in that moment, I wanted to throw my shoe at his head. In a fleeting moment of clarity that at least I got the house and our son, I decided it wasn't worth leaving our neighbors with their tongues wagging.

I was thirty-five, alone in a large house that was supposed to be filled with kids and located in Tulsa but instead was in Oakland and filled with only my son and my sorrow. What was supposed to be a chaotic house was quiet. What was supposed to be a team sports family of seven was now a sole coach grooming an individual competitor. I had built the House of Booker from the ground up, and then he decided he preferred something remodeled.

Ignoring my dipping into Booker territory, Judy asks me, "Why are you going to your neighbor's shiva gathering? Don't you have to be invited?" Even though she ran a school, Judy is not the most empathetic of people. She no longer has time or tolerance for folks she's not invested in, her lifetime supply of compassion having run dry by her sixth decade.

"Seriously, Judy? She lives next door. I found Noa all alone in a big fat puddle of grief last night. And I'm just guessing, but I'm not so sure she knows many people in Oakland. I think they've only lived here for about a year, and it always seems pretty quiet at the house. I can't not go."

"I thought you didn't know anything about them and were committed to keeping your nose on your side of the driveway. Sounds like you know plenty about the Abramses that you're not spillin'."

"Relax, Judy. It's not like I've been exchanging recipes with this woman and not telling you. A few months back I asked another neighbor on our block what she knew about Noa and Charlie. It was an indirect dig for information, and I got a few key nuggets out of it. It was harmless fishing for a little gossip, nothing more."

"You can put lipstick on a pig, but it's still a pig. A pig with a big snout."

Ding.

Yay, saved from Judy's farmyard comparisons.

Darius 11:48 AM

Ma, where are you, I gotta get to the DMV.

"I have to go. Darius is taking his driver's test today. Booker wanted to take him to the DMV, but I said no. I taught him to drive, I get to make sure he shows off his parallel parking skills, right?" I say, gathering my sweatshirt and purse. "Get this, girl. You are not gonna believe what he did. Booker went behind my back and told Darius he's buying my boy a car. A *car*. My baby is not getting a brand-new car when he can barely reach the gas pedal."

"You better let his father pick up the tab for Darius's car," Judy admonishes, sticking to her rule of uttering Booker's name as little as possible. "It's the least he can do given how absent he is for all the little things in that young man's life. Anyway, that so-called 'baby' of yours is over six feet and can reach the gas far better than you can. He should be the one worrying when you drive."

Instead of admitting to Judy that I don't want Darius to have a car because then what will he need his mother for, I give her a half-hearted "Ha, ha, ha."

"And speaking of gas pedals, given last night's drama, slow your roll. And sure as hell don't go crashing into your neighbor's world. Her life is not yours to fix."

"Again, all I'm fixing is fried chicken, Judy. Chill. You just mad you can't have some."

CHAPTER THREE

"Ooo, Ma! Can I get a piece?" Darius asks after his hand is already reaching for a wing. I smack it back in retreat. I haven't seen my son all afternoon, but one whiff of fried chicken and he magically appears, ready to eat. "Ouch!"

"No, you may not. I'm taking this over to the Abramses' house in a few." I throw back the last nip of whiskey left in my glass. Doesn't matter time of day, I can't fry chicken without it. I poured myself a bit more than usual given the circumstances I'm about to enter.

Darius makes like the toddler he used to be and whines, "Aw, hook me up with some yard bird, Mom. You got more than the colonel up in here!"

"I said no, but I'll make another batch this week to celebrate the start of school if that's what you want," I promise and kiss the bottom of his jaw, the only place I can reach. I don't know when this child is going to stop growing.

"Who are the Abramses anyway?" Darius wonders, rummaging through the pantry looking for something else he can devour. I set turkey slices, cheddar, sourdough bread, mustard, and a knife on the counter and elbow him. Shock registers on my son's face that I'm not going to make the sandwich for him. How Darius will ever survive in the world without me is an issue I'm going to have to take up another day. Right now I have my first ever shiva call to attend, and I've been dragging my feet getting out the door.

"You know, our neighbors to the left. Remember I told you the husband passed away suddenly the other night?"

"Yeah, sorta. Why you going? You don't know them," Darius asks, twisting the clip off the bread. I watch to see if he closes it up after he pulls out his slices. Of course he doesn't. The plastic bag and my mouth are left hanging open.

I take a deep breath to give me the patience to instill the lessons of being responsible and neighborly all in one sentence while swapping out my gold hoops for a subtler ruby stud. "When tragedy befalls a family, we show up to pay our respects, *and* we put the bread away just like we found it," I preach, looking from the orange clip to Darius and back to the clip.

"Why are you showing up with all this fried chicken? You can't just bring flowers?" Darius coaxes, ignoring the bread bag but still eyeing the crispy poultry like a stack of cash.

"Listen, you may not have been raised as diligently in the Baptist church as I was, but after the funeral is the repast where people gather to celebrate the deceased. Whenever someone dies there're tears, there're condolences, there's storytelling, and there's food. Lots and lots of food. That's universal." Darius nods like he's getting what I'm telling him. "And so is loving fried chicken."

"Ah, you just like showing off your cookin' skills. I know you," Darius calls me out.

Cramped in her second-floor apartment, my godmother, Shay, taught me to make her fried chicken when I was twelve years old. Humid Tulsa summers were unbearable without air-conditioning. To this day when I think about her apartment, my hairline breaks out in beads of sweat. Sweltering or not, I never gave up any chance I was offered to learn from Auntie Shay the skill my mother never possessed—how to cook. I would steal sideways looks at her as she slid around her kitchen, gathering everything we'd need for my next cooking lesson and sipping on whiskey from a Dixie cup.

Auntie Shay was my mother's best friend and in no way tied to me by religious duty or relation. As far as I knew, Shay never went to church like we did and was not present to witness my baptism, yet I always knew her as my godmother. The area where I grew up was not one of the rough hoods of Tulsa. We lived somewhere my brother refers to as *hood adjacent*. But still, on our block, Auntie Shay had a reputation of being "fast." I gathered she hadn't earned some Olympic gold medal or I would have heard about it from my mama, so I dismissed the cruel talk as corner gossip because Auntie Shay and I shared a deep and lasting bond. We found our greatest joy in the kitchen, together.

Lathered from her crown to her corns with Pond's Cold Cream, Auntie Shay's skin glowed. In her signature tank tops and cutoff shorts, she instructed me on how to butcher and clean a bird to get it ready for frying. Each batch of chicken in her lessons started with a whole fryer cut up, rinsed, and patted dry. Seasoning was something Auntie Shay taught me other folks didn't know much about. She would hold my index finger and thumb just right so I would pinch the correct amount of paprika, salt, garlic, onion powder, and pepper, and then I was commanded to douse the chicken in splashes of hot sauce. The tiniest dab of sugar rounded out her seasonings' secret, and then for two hours, the worked chicken would nap in the fridge while we watched Auntie Shay's favorite game shows recorded on the VCR.

Today, I fry chicken the exact same way my auntie taught me, and every batch I have ever made starts and ends with a paper bag. I throw a few cups of flour in a big sack from the grocer, add the chicken from the fridge—two pieces at a time—and shake vigorously, the last step before it hits the fryer. After a hundred afternoons frying with Auntie Shay, I know the exact sound a chicken sings when it settles in the cast-iron pot half-filled with Crisco. Too much shouting and the oil's too hot; barely bubbling and the bird's going to be greasy; just right and

I can hear myself hum whatever song is stuck in my head. When that golden-brown chicken comes out of the skillet, hot enough to burn your mouth, it's lifted onto a second layer of paper bags to drain.

"Yeah, well, have fun I guess," Darius says with a shrug, his brow furrowed like he's chasing a thought in his head.

"I don't think Mrs. Abrams is setting up a Spades tournament, Darius. I'm not going over there to have fun, son."

"I know, I know. It's just . . . that sucks, you know." Darius brightens, finally securing his thoughts. "Tell Mrs. Abrams I'm sorry for her loss. I know that's a thing you're supposed to say."

I'm proud Darius recalls his manners and touched by his concern for our neighbor. "Yes, it is, and I will tell her. What are you up to while I'm out?" That's mom code for, *I know you haven't finished your summer reading, and school starts in two days.*

"Simone's coming over to hang out," he says.

The short time I planned on staying at the shiva has now been cut in half. That's one fountain of milk chocolate I don't need my son dipping into.

"I best be seeing both of you on the couch, hands to yourselves, when I get home."

"Do I hafta hear that every time I bring up Simone? Besides, I think we're gonna go out and grab some pizza first, so you don't have to worry about what we're doing," Darius informs me, fisting his two sandwiches. I can't believe how much this boy eats. And I can't believe Simone is going to be in my house when I'm not home. I check my watch to see if I have enough time to get into it with Darius regarding my feelings about his so-called girlfriend. I don't.

"You be sure to wipe down those counters before you head out. I don't want to come home and put my hand on dried mustard you couldn't be bothered to clean up."

"Yes, ma'am." Darius salutes me, not a worry on his mind while I got plenty on mine. I've never been to a shiva before, so I'm not sure what to expect, though I have worked in a K–12 school coming up on twenty years, and I do know, too well, what to expect from raging hormones. Slipping on my shoes, I peek out the window to take in the steady stream of folks heading into the Abramses' house. Looking at who the gathering guests are, I'm pretty sure they aren't expecting who I am to arrive. I hike up my skirt to yank each leg of my SPANX to just above my knees so there's no chance of a midthigh line appearing where my skirt should be smooth. In the mirror my pixie cut is lying nice on the sides, and I make a final pop with my lips to tone down my red gloss just a bit. Quick application of hand cream and I'm now officially out of excuses not to get out the door.

Standing at the open entry to the Abrams home is a woman not much older than me dressed in too much Gucci and not enough nutrients. She hugs me without even seeing me. I awkwardly lean in, unable to return her embrace since I'm carrying five pounds of bird. I think I spy her nose scrunch at the smell. As quickly as the greeter, who I can only assume is Charlie's sister, sweeps me into her arms, she releases me and moves on to the gentleman close on my heels. She's hugging on automatic repeat.

Hoping to catch one last glance of myself before I head into the sea of strangers, I notice the entryway mirror has an ugly black blanket hanging over it. Now why would someone go redecorating Noa's house on a day like today? I set my platter down on the credenza and reach to pull the cloth down.

"I wouldn't do that if I were you," a deep, raspy voice whispers in my ear as it's passing by. "It's supposed to be like that." By the time I turn, I glimpse only the back of a well-tailored gray suit. Noted.

A crowd of people are standing around somberly in Noa's living room, speaking in hushed tones. I've never experienced a room so packed be so quiet. If I didn't know I was attending a shiva, I'd ask someone, "Who died?" it's so stifling in here. Get forty Baptists in a room to celebrate life and people are whooping and hollering, piling plates with food, trying to one-up each other with tall tales about the deceased. My childhood church family celebrated life well lived, and while some might consider dancing and drinking and enjoying oneself on the day of a loved one's homegoing tasteless, we did it anyway. Being joyful was a whole lot more comforting than crying the River Jordan. There must be something about Charlie's life that's worth rejoicing in, praising out loud, but as I scan the room, it doesn't seem like anyone is spinning a heartfelt tale.

I locate Noa across the room out on the back patio. Even from a distance I can see the dark circles under her eyes match her black dress, but I also see that Noa is holding her own in the formal role of She Who Must Keep Her Shit Together. The single job requirement for that duty includes not making a spectacle of yourself, thus not tarnishing your husband's family name.

I want to offer Noa condolences with my fried chicken in hand so I get props for being present, and so she knows I'm not one of the people only here for free food. I can tell it's going to take me a while to get to her, so I change my plan and decide to find the chicken a home first. I'll set it down, and then I'll bring her a piece, give her hands something to do. I "excuse me, excuse me" my way to the dining room to find where guests are gathered to drown their sorrows in delicacies. Leave it to White people to turn absolutely everything into a salad. Egg salad, potato salad, three-bean salad, whitefish salad. It doesn't take a trained chef to see the roast chicken holding court in the middle of the table is suffering from a lack of seasoning. I move the platter behind a tower of bagels and set my fried chicken down front and center. Grieving folks should not be subjected to unseasoned meats; I swear somewhere in the Bible it says so.

I think I see the rabbi's mouth watering, though his wife seems to be holding him back by the elbow. She's either warning him about his cholesterol or urging him to snag her a piece of my chicken so the other women in the room don't see her buckle under desire. I tuck a card under my tray with Noa's name on it. Whenever I bring a dish to someone's house, I include a note with the recipe in case the host, or in this case the widow, wants to add it to their weekly dinner rotation once the dust settles. I'm that confident in my cooking skills.

"That for the taking?" Gray Suit Guy asks as I pull away from adjusting my tray.

I look at him, confused.

"It's certainly not for decoration." In my head I can feel Judy kicking my shin for not watching my tongue.

"Well all right, then. I'm digging in." The fact that he's talking awkwardly and piling his plate with chicken makes me wonder if this dude is the one other non-Jew in the room.

I see the crowd part around Noa and realize this is my opportunity to get in, share my condolences, and get out before Darius rounds second base on my couch. I abandon the suit midbite to weave through the living room like a tiny linebacker knocking aside a few Chosen People along the way.

Noa's standing alone when I finally get close to her. We haven't seen each other since I found her hanging out on her front porch with her crew, Jim Beam and Double Stuf OREO. Eyes darting around the room, Noa issues warning glances to other guests who appear to be considering approaching her. I'm not dissuaded, but I also don't force too much eye contact. Despite the *kick rocks* look she's aiming at the gathered visitors, she's not scary enough to deter me. This is a woman who needs a tutorial on mastering the fuck-off face.

"Please don't say something like Charlie's in a better place now. It's just so . . ."

"Cliché?" I offer.

"Rude." Not the word I may have chosen, but I'll give her rude. Don't want to call a newly widowed woman out for poor choice in adjectives. "People are so uncomfortable when someone dies that they say the most ludicrous things. If you're unexpectedly dead, you're most definitely not in a better place." I don't disagree with Noa, though the church ladies back in Tulsa would have a fit and get to testifying if they heard her claim.

"What do you have there in your hand?" I ask Noa, catching her for the second time in three days keeping company with a bottle of sorrow.

"This is the last bottle of champagne left from our wedding. We'd been saving it for a special occasion. I was going to sneak it in my suitcase to Mexico, but here I am. No husband. No Mexico. No suitcase. No need to save the champagne." Noa swigs right from the bottle, the exclamation point to her declaration. I look quickly around for a piece of stemware to class this woman up at her own husband's homegoing, I mean shiva.

I get it. Noa's using liquor to get through the day and hoping that being buzzed will make this terrible moment more bearable or, better yet, make it disappear. Can't say I wouldn't do the same if I were standing in her shoes, but I'm not sure she's properly reading the mix of family members, Jewish literati, and work colleagues in the room. The regret she may feel in the morning if the booze really kicks in could add to her load of pain. I look down, considering what to do next. Noa's barefoot, pink toenails on full display. Okay then, I guess standing in her shoes is not an option.

"You can take your shoes off, too, if you want," Noa offers, wiggling her toes. I'm not sure if she's challenging me or being an inclusive hostess at the worst of parties. Noa's the last woman I would have expected to see out of her kitten heels.

"All right." I slip off my beige wedges, which are cutting into my heels, and hook them over my index and middle finger. The least I can do is help her feel a little bit less alone.

"Thank you."

"For what?" I ask, confused. Noa hasn't even seen my fried chicken.

"For not burying me in a pile of catastrophe catchphrases like most of these folks. I've attended plenty of shiva calls before; I know what

I'm supposed to do based on a historical grieve-by-numbers text handed down from the Temple Mount. Don't wear leather shoes. Check." Really, don't wear any shoes, according to Noa at this moment. "Wash your hands. Check. Cover the mirrors, sit on low stools, blah, blah, blah. I just spent two hours squatting on my daughter's bathroom sink step stool. My lower back is killing me." Noa places her palms on her hips and leans back, stretching.

"I'm following all the rituals and traditions that are meant to honor Charlie and supposed to help me, but"—Noa lowers her voice, I imagine so her mother-in-law can't hear—"I don't know. Does Charlie really want me to sit on my ass for seven days straight? He's dead, so I can't ask him," Noa states more than asks. I think I might like grieving Noa; she's turning out to be quite the widow renegade.

"You're a teacher, so teach me something." Noa sighs, pushing a piece of hair that's escaped her low ponytail out of her sight line. I stand a little straighter. I didn't expect that Noa knew I was a teacher. In my concerted effort to keep my nose out of her business, it never occurred to me she might be sniffing around the neighborhood trying to suss out mine.

"How am I supposed to help my little girl understand her daddy's gone? Not to the store. Not on a work trip. Gone for good." There's an edge to Noa's voice that betrays the simple black shift and delicate jewelry of a reserved woman. The anger boiling inside is palpable: not only does she have to hurt from the loss of her husband, but now inexplicable pain has been delivered to her daughter.

"Hell if I know. Faculty meetings are mostly full of get to know your colleague icebreakers, earthquake drills, and mini lessons on how to improve your craft. Spoiler alert: they don't help," I answer straight up. It's official, I left my filter at home. To be fair to me, I've never had a student in my class lose a parent, so truly I don't know what the right words are for her daughter. Real truth—there are no right words. Birdie would simply shake her head when death hit our family and go on with her day, repeating, "The only way to get over it is to get through it."

Noa bites her lip, and I think the tears she wasn't shedding the other night when I found her are about to fall. Maybe I should have leaned on Hallmark rather than honesty for this one.

"Ha!" Noa snorts. "I appreciate you not saying the perfectly right thing and for not treating me like I'm about to break. Everyone in here is holding their breath waiting for me to crumble." Crumble, maybe not, but the weight of the champagne bottle hanging from Noa's right hand is precariously pulling her over, and she's no longer standing steady on her two feet. "They're waiting"—Noa flings her arms around to signal what she believes the whole world is thinking, nearly clocking me with the Dom Pérignon—"even wanting me to become the crazy Widow Abrams.

"When we were first married, I used to joke with Charlie, on nights he went out with his friends, not to leave me. It took me so long to find him." Noa's getting a case of the loud slurs, and the people she was just gesturing about are starting to turn our way. Given my dicey divorce, I am all too intimate with the picture in front of me. The alcohol mixed with shock and memories is beginning to go nowhere positive, and a creeping feeling tells me we are minutes away from a public scene if I don't get Noa out of the spotlight quick.

"He always answered my plea by teasing me, 'Where would I go?'" Noa's eyes grow childishly wide. "But he did go. He really did. He promised me he wouldn't leave, but he did." A roar of anguish roils up from the place deep inside that no woman wants to discover, and Noa grabs on to my upper arm. She locks eyes with me as if begging, willing me to go out and find Charlie for her.

"I know. I know." And I really do. "All right, Mrs. Abrams, I think it's time for you to take a long nap. Let me get you down to your room." I'm a good six inches shorter than Noa, but still, I wrap my arm around her waist and take her weight.

"I can't. I don't want to. I can't." Noa drops her cheek against the side of my head. I can feel the room looking at us, assuming we're close even if they don't recognize me. "I haven't been in there since Charlie, you know."

"If you haven't been in your bedroom, how'd you get dressed for today?" I whisper, walking Noa through the crowd, acutely aware strangers are marking my every move.

"I still had this dress in the back of my car from when I picked up the dry cleaning last week. It was one of Charlie's . . ." And here we go; the tears are flooding. She Who Must Keep Her Shit Together has lost it.

"You got a TV?"

"We're going to watch TV?" Noa sniffles, wiping the snot puddling in her nose onto the back of her hand that's not slung over me. She looks at it, not sure what to do. I nod to her dress. She can take it back to the dry cleaner next week. "What about all these people? No one's even touched the whitefish salad. Charlie's mom will think it's bad manners if I disappear. Do you think it's bad manners, Marjette?" Her mother-in-law is going to think it's bad manners if Noa stays here the way she is, a sloppy drunk, but I'm touched she remembers my name.

"Trust me, it's bad manners if you stay. All these people will be fine, just fine," I assure her and steer my neighbor in the direction of the hallway and guest room where Noa points she has been camping out.

"So, you're going to stay and watch TV with me?" Noa beseeches, sounding like a little girl scared of the monsters in the dark. I've now been here twenty minutes longer than I intended to, and I'm sure Darius and Simone are doing all the things I dedicate my time to keep them from doing.

"Only if you like *Real Housewives*," I reply and pray I can see from Noa's guest bedroom into my living room.

"I've never watched it."

I deposit Noa onto the bed, and she tucks her legs up under the skirt of her dress, pulling the hemline down to her ankles, trying to make herself smaller. I can only assume Noa is more of a PBS period piece kind of viewer.

"You're missing out on one of life's great joys," I assure, patting Noa's knees.

"So, you'll stay with me until I fall asleep?"

"You mean pass out?" I chuckle under my breath. At least I'm hopeful that's the case. I'm not really in for a streaming marathon with my drunk, sad neighbor who I had never uttered more than a handful of sentences to up until a few days ago. Plus, I have a to-do list for the first day of school that runs three pages long, and I've barely made a dent in it.

Noa half smiles, not from any morsel of happiness, but I can tell from a tinge of gratitude given her supremely horrid day. "Yeah, pass out."

"No problem." I lean forward and grab the throw blanket at the foot of the bed and wrap it around her.

"Talk about the worst breakup ever," Noa declares, burying her head in her hands. "This is not how my life was supposed to go."

"I hear you, Noa." I agree more than my mourning neighbor can imagine. Falling back into the decorative pillows scattered on the bed, I pick up the remote from the side table and try to find us some women to watch who are worse off than we are.

CHAPTER FOUR

Charlie Abrams's shiva wiped out my Labor Day–weekend work plans, so now I'm even more pressed for time putting the finishing touches on my kindergarten classroom. School starts tomorrow, and I don't like feeling harried going into a new year. When my shiny crop of students shows up hanging on a parent's hand, day one of the thirteen-year journey they're about to take, I want them to feel they've entered a wonderland of opportunity run by a trustworthy queen who has everything in its place and a place for everything.

I have the classroom tables and chairs arranged in quads. Each seat is carefully assigned, a balance of boys and girls, olders and youngers, extroverts and quieter souls, and those who are artistic tucked in with those who are antsy. All this information I culled from the "Help Me Get to Know Your Child!" form I sent to parents last week to fill out and return by Friday before many headed out of town for their last summer hurrah. The form is a tool I use to help me connect with each child on the first day of school. The stacked answers inevitably include unsolicited advice from a few anxious parents on how I can best teach their child.

The worst are parents of singletons. Putting all your eggs in one basket can make a basket case out of some folks. My data shows singleton moms and dads are the most eager to showcase how their heir's talents will be best supported to shine in the kindergarten classroom (read *begin to crush the other children so as to establish early academic dominance*). For too many years, Judy and I kept a hall-of-fame journal of unsolicited advice from parents. My favorite from a few years back is still on a Post-it stuck to my monitor for entertainment value: Liam has a preference for the binary number system when studying mathematical equations given his love of computer science. If you insist on teaching the mundane Arabic system, access to graham crackers over Goldfish with a splash of orange, never apple juice, really helps him focus. Other than that, Liam is an easygoing kid. There was nothing easy about Liam nor his parents.

But I don't count out the veteran moms. In this battle of *momuppance*, they have experience on their side. This year's favorite comes from Rachel Ellis, whose reputation grows in mythical proportions with every passing school year at Houghton. I didn't have the Ellis family's older child. He was in my teaching partner across the hall, Catherine's, class. I knew I would have Rachel's second child, as it had been unofficially established by the administration—i.e., my girl Judy, as a final act of faculty preservation before her retirement—that no educator at Houghton would be subject to Rachel Ellis twice. All summer Catherine has been peppering me with inside information on how to last a full year with Rachel. Her strongest advice so far: "The best way to deliver difficult news to Rachel Ellis is, *don't.*"

I have already received a handful of emails from Rachel about her daughter, Tabitha, and Houghton parents only found out their child's primary teacher a few days ago. This gem was waiting for me in my inbox when I arrived this morning at six thirty to get a jump start on my day.

To: Marjette Lewis
From: Rachel Ellis
Subject: Insufficient headway at Houghton

Dear Marjette,

I am cautiously optimistic that Tabitha's kindergarten year with you will be a marked improvement over my first impression of the education standards Houghton touted when my son, Dalton, was in Catherine's class three years ago. It is my belief that Catherine never took the time to *really* get to know Dalton, thus his unique gifts were misunderstood. This year I'm making sure I do not have a repeat of my child being misjudged in her educational setting by only answering the basic "Get to Know Your Child" form you recently sent out to parents. Attached is a detailed report regarding Tabitha's learning style for you to study ahead of the first day of school. I'm hopeful you will pay particular attention to the chart in Index D on page 23 of the attached learning assessment where the data reflects Tabitha's exceptional dual capacity for numbers and languages. I'm going to assume that with this level of specificity you will be able to best customize in-class and recess activities for Tabitha.

Regards,

Rachel Ellis
(mother to Tabitha, age 6.5)

I met Rachel at least a half dozen times the year Dalton terrorized his entire kindergarten cohort with disturbing impressions of Venom from Spiderman. He chased the other children, growling and flicking his tongue at them, threatening to wear their skin. That kid was not misunderstood; he was missing all evidence of manners. I save Rachel's attachment to my desktop and file it away under documents I never plan to read. I do note, however, that to get an early academic leg up on her daughter's peers, mother Rachel has redshirted Tabitha. Perhaps Tabitha's $5,000 kindergarten learning assessment produced such high scores because the little darling should actually be heading into the first-grade suite, not kindergarten, to learn with all the other six-year-old children. If I have to listen to one more parent explain to me that the reason their child is not starting kindergarten until they can shave is so they can be "socially and emotionally" ready for the school environment, I'm going to toss my story-time stool. You send your kid to school at five for kindergarten so they *can start* to learn how to be socially and emotionally ready for learning. And then you know what? They learn those same lessons over and over again until senior year, when someone agrees to take them on for college, and then *buh-bye*.

I forward the email to Judy for a laugh. Though she swears she's ecstatic not to be slipping into pantyhose in the September heat to greet returning families on the first day of school, I know she is fighting a heavy heart, though the fight is being waged poolside in Napa, sipping on a Chardonnay with her sister.

Damn, I didn't realize how late it is already. Doing the online tutorial for Houghton's new report card system took longer than I thought.

Marjette 5:28 PM

Don't play with me Booker, I want my son home for dinner at 6:30. He starts school tomorrow, and I don't want him tired cause his father can't tell time.

Booker 5:29 PM

We're going for tacos. I'll have him home by 8:00.

Marjette to Darius 5:32 PM

Tell your father I want you in my house hungry for dinner at 6:30 sharp.

Darius to Marjette 5:32 PM

Ma, we're just finishing up looking at cars, can't I have dinner with Dad?

Marjette to Booker 5:33 PM

I TOLD YOU NO CAR!

Booker to Marjette 5:33 PM

You tell me lots of things . . . don't mean I gotta listen.

I dive in with determination, arranging intricate pencil boxes complete with sharpeners, glue sticks, color gel pens, and mini staplers with each child's name written in impeccable penmanship across the top. It takes me three tries to fit the name Frederique perfectly across a label, but I do it. Excessive organization is how I control my anger, and right now I'm channeling Marie Kondo. I place a red heart sticker on the upper left-hand corner of each box so every one of my students is reminded during the day that I'm here and I love them, even if I'm busy helping another child or away from the classroom. I slap the last one on my forehead to remind my head to try to lead with my heart when it comes to my was-band.

My natural-seagrass woven baskets are filled with chapter books, arranged alphabetically, and nestled into the cubbies below my cushioned window seat. My bulletin boards are covered tight with white construction paper and kelly-green scalloped borders. I love the look of a blank laminated monthly calendar, each date waiting to be filled with planned lessons and adventures. Just above it I write in purple Sharpie: ANYTHING IS POSSIBLE IN MS. LEWIS'S CLASS!

The Welcome to Kindergarten scavenger hunt is all set up to begin at eight fifteen sharp tomorrow. This hunt has served as the perfect family icebreaker throughout my time at Houghton. I have used it ever since the disaster of my first day teaching, when I had no get-to-know-you activity planned. That tearful fiasco (my tears, not the kids') spawned years of a solid game that would rival any escape room. A swell of pride expands in my chest as I give my pristine room a last once-over before the floodgates of chaos break open tomorrow morning. I enjoy the school cycle of September's fresh beginnings and June's grateful endings; I just never thought I would be living it on repeat.

～

"Ma, I'm home! Dad's out front and wants to talk to you!" Darius yells, announcing his return. "Got any ice cream?"

"I thought you just ate with your father?" I ask, then leisurely slip into my flip-flops and dab on some lip gloss so Booker is forced to wait on me a minute. After the house title was legally signed over in my name, my first action item, as ruler of my Rockridge kingdom, was to establish a no-Booker-in-the-house policy.

"We did, but I'm still hungry. Is there any mint chocolate chip left?"

"Of course, baby, help yourself." I smile and rub Darius's back as he's bending over to untie his high-tops. He may be starting the challenging junior-year high school marathon tomorrow, but my boy has been licking on mint chocolate chip since he was two. The thought makes me smile; life is moving so quickly with Darius, I relish the things that never change. I straighten up, steeling myself to go out front to hear what Booker's up to.

"Hey, you ready for your first day of school tomorrow?" Booker asks all sweet like this is a regular conversation we've had every September. The only time Booker paid attention to my first day was the year Darius came with me to start his school career in Catherine's class.

"Always am." I place my hands on my hips, feet shoulder-width apart, solid on my walkway. I'm not going to let anything Booker says get in my head with all I have going on. I glance at Noa's house. I see a few stragglers still inside finishing up the second day of shiva and feel for Noa. Mourning in public like that must be exhausting.

"What's that you got on your forehead? You need me to remove it?" Booker jokes, always looking for a way to reference his skills as a plastic surgeon.

"I don't need you for anything," I retort, quick to peel the heart I'd forgotten about off my head.

Looking down at nothing interesting on the ground, Booker starts in. "I think Darius is ready for school too." Good, back to more neutral territory. "You know he's out there sniffing around those girls, don't you?" For a guy who fondles women's lady parts for the majority of his billable hours, he sure is uncomfortable discussing his son's hormones.

"Yeah. He talks to a lot of girls." I don't want to give Simone too much credit in Darius's life. I'm hoping she's a short-term diversion, because Darius has grades to focus on and college to plan for. "And?" I'm not giving Booker the satisfaction of thinking he knows any more about our son than I do.

Darius hasn't been able to outslick me since the time he was seven and lifted a pack of Hubba Bubba from Walgreens. When we got to the house, I noticed he was walking around clasping his hands in front of him like he was the Queen of England. I pried his little sticky fingers open with the brute force of a mama who smelled no good going on. Fifteen minutes later we were back in front of the store manager promising her that Darius would never be thieving again. Darius swore up and down his short career as a criminal was over because it was *wrong*, he was terrible at it, and he understood they served lumpy food in jail. I actually made him repeat all of it, loudly, next to the saline solution and multivitamins. I wanted the patrons and employees in Walgreens to know my son was not going to be a statistic in ten to fifteen. Today, I don't need a girl like Simone tempting him to dip back into the fast lane of his no-good, candy-stealing past; for all I know she's just the type.

"I heard him talking and texting, and one girl was blowing up his phone all afternoon. I thought that boy would be more interested in a car than a girl, but I don't know. Someone's pressing hard on him, and I'm wondering if you know who?" Booker asks. His facial expression is an odd mix of concern and pride.

"Now all of a sudden you think you know everything about this family? I don't have time for you, Booker. I keep on top of what my son does; don't you worry about that. We'll be seeing you the next time it works for you and your schedule. And I'm gonna say it one more time, except now it's to your face. NO CAR." I wave Booker off like a fly I can't get to stop buzzing by my ear.

"Later, 'Jette." ARGH! He knows I hate it when he calls me that. "I'll be seeing you sooner than you know." Booker gives me his little half smile that lets me know he's up to something and I will find out about it on his timeline.

Booker didn't have this much to say when we were going through our divorce, but it's just like him trying to get the last word now. By the time Booker sat me down to wreck our family, he had already grappled with his guilt of being a cheat and moved on to accepting that he was no longer in love with me. He informed me of our separation like I was sitting across from him at his medical practice—that it was for the best for all involved if we went forward with new plans. We were still young,

Booker claimed, a whole second and third chapter ahead of us, and he was eager to get going writing his.

The big fat flaw to Booker's happy ending for all is that for a man, their maturity, ability to hold an interesting conversation, and attractiveness as a life partner don't really kick in until around thirty-five. Booker was blossoming right on time, ripe to be the perfect husband to a second wife. For a woman, however, being thirty-five with a child, an ex-husband, and a broken heart makes you heavy with baggage. I had put thirteen years of salary, no vacations, no holiday presents, and delayed additional children into building Booker's brand so the both of us could rise to our full potential with our joint bank account flush. But now he wanted out to go sell his polished gem of a self elsewhere, and I was a cast-out stone.

When Booker left, I imagined how Sisyphus felt watching that boulder roll all the way down the hill after he had pushed it so close to the top. Defeated is what I'm guessing. My burden was made up of promises offered by a man, in front of God and witnesses, who had sworn to spend eternity by my side. Reaching the pinnacle was to be my reward for years of patience and dedication to Booker. Instead, I watched it all disappear as he eased his sedan away from our home coming up on six years ago.

There's not much I'm thankful to Booker for, but I will give him credit for being smart enough not to fight me for custody of Darius. He knew I would go thirteen rounds and come out the winner. Booker easily agreed to parenting every other weekend, though it made me hurt for my son. As our first year of divorce marched on, one of the weekends a month fell into a time warp. Booker became an occasional two-day-a-month parent rather than the consistent father Darius needed. After a weekend drop-off, watching my son linger in his baseball uniform and stare at the closed door—waiting in case his dad changed his mind and returned home—was nothing short of agony. I caught myself more times than I can count, desperate to erase the despondency on Darius's face by considering Booker might come back to us. I finally knocked some sense into my head. I'm part of a club no mother wants to join. Moms who are agonized by hearing their inner saboteur say, "I would do anything for my children . . . ," but ultimately having to let the pain of divorce run its course in their child's life.

Back in my house, I take a few deep breaths to ward off a Booker hangover that I can't afford to settle into my brain and leave me restless for the night. The last things I need to do before I tuck in to get a full eight hours of sleep are cross-reference my class list with my phonics folders and finish baking the strawberry-peach scones that I make every year for the opening day of school's morning mingle. I spent almost thirty minutes in the produce section selecting the perfect strawberries and end-of-summer peaches.

The name at the top of the class list stops me. I had been writing my students' first names all day, but not paying much attention to their last names.

Esther Abrams

I didn't see any children yesterday at the shiva, but when another woman hovering around the buffet asked if there were any kids around, I did say that I overheard someone mention they were at the park. Then I offered her a crispy thigh. Though it should have, it didn't register with me that one of the kids shuffled off to play, specifically the one who lives next door, could also be in my class. When Noa asked me about how to talk to a child about a parent dying, I didn't realize she was alluding to the fact we would be doing it together.

CHAPTER FIVE

Ding.

Judy 8:00 AM

Hands off the scones!

I wish I had looked at my phone before polishing off two strawberry-peach sugar bombs with my morning trough of coffee. I wipe my fingertips on my woven-fabric desk chair to hide the evidence from Judy, even over text. I'm not tracking these points; I'm chalking them up to tradition on the first official day of kindergarten.

Marjette 8:01 AM

Why are you up so early in retirement, Sleep-In Beauty?

Judy 8:01 AM

I'm done with Houghton, but not with you. Had to check in before the day got going. I have a feeling this is going to be your best year yet.

Marjette 8:02 AM

Really?

I don't know where Judy is coming up with this prediction, considering I am now operating solo without her on campus, and my concerns are already bouncing off the inside of my skull. It's junior year for Darius, and I'm worried about his need to keep his grades up and his pecker down.

Judy 8:04 AM

As long as you don't kill Rachel Ellis.

Ugh. She had to go there and add to my angst.

Judy 8:04 AM

Or let her crush your soul.

Judy 8:04 AM

Then you'll be good. Have fun!

The scrubbed-clean faces and first-day-of-kindergarten getups slay me. I have to forcibly hold myself back from gathering into my arms every shiny baby face with pigtails or a pressed button-down. I want to squeeze them and then slip them into my satchel like a Gen Z celebrity with their omnipresent purse puppy. Who doesn't want cherubic cheeks tucked in by their side, looking up at them with awe and wonder? It's a guaranteed dopamine hit without having to sweat. Like clockwork, every Tuesday following Labor Day I'm fighting my impulse to love all over the kids before I even get to know who they are.

Parents are strolling around the room, scavenger hunt clues in hand, each trying to pry their child off their pant legs, and encouraging them to engage in the creation stations I have set up for each stop. I stand loosely at my classroom door to greet each family unit as they ceremoniously wait for their turn to introduce themselves to me in the hallway receiving line. When they step forward, we exchange pleasantries, and

I gesture for the family to pass through my threshold, now parents of kindergarteners. Tears are quickly brushed away and nervous voices are par for the introductions. The parents, mostly just the mothers, more tentative than their kids.

"Whoa!" A blur of blue tulle and red braids tears into the classroom like she's making a break from her jail warden, determined to take cover behind the wall of marble rollers. I reach out my arm and catch the budding track star across her squishy midsection, scooping her into my sphere until I can locate to whom she belongs. Her green eyes pop, and she screams like a child who has been thoroughly trained in stranger danger. When she's run out of voice, her teeth come down hard on the flesh between my thumb and pointer finger, and I drop her onto all fours. In less than ten seconds I've been taken down by a turbulent ball of scratchy ruffles. I'm already feeling a tinge of love for this pint-size bad girl.

"Where's my cheecher?" my little friend asks, bottom up, distracted by a sparkle that dislodged from her party shoes when I dropped her. Luckily, I speak toothless.

"I'm right here, sweetie. I'm Ms. Lewis."

As she looks back through the gap between her legs, I see two little brows furrow, becoming one.

"You don't look like a cheecher!" If I had a dollar for every time someone from five to fifty has paused to consider whether I really teach in a tony private school, I'd be up north with Judy right now, hanging out in a pampered palace, paying for both our rooms. This little girl is brave enough to call out her confusion.

"I don't, huh? What do you think I look like?" I always enjoy hearing the answer to this question coming from the innocent honesty of the kindergarten set. There's a long pause, and I wait while the wheels are cranking.

"Like a waitreth." *Really?* I haven't heard that one before. I usually get something more along the lines of a person who details the family car. "Your dreth doethn't look pretty with a dirty apron over it. My mommy sath firth impressions are everything; that's why she made my daddy take uth all to school in the Range Rover and pretend like they aren't getting a 'vorce. He'th parking right now," my new friend insists, proud that she's in on her parents' dirt. Straightening out her powder-blue extravaganza, she lets me know who showed up fierce for the first day of school.

Well, crap. I was so hurried with the last-minute setting up of clay and paints that I forgot to take off my splatter smock. I quickly untie the apron and toss it toward my desk. I can tell the brain between the braids is noting that tossing rather than putting things away nicely is a clear possibility in this classroom. I'll squash that pipe dream later today when we get to Ms. Lewis's community rules of conduct.

"And who do you belong to?" I inquire, reaching my hand out so I can keep this feminine ninja in my grip until someone claims her.

"Me. And her name is Tabitha. Tabitha Ellis," a woman with a sharp voice declares out the side of her mouth, a cell phone pressed to her ear. Rachel's index finger is dangerously close to my face, asking me to hold on a minute. Her manicure is flawless, but her manners not so much. I should have guessed this little one belongs to one of the rumored biggest bitches around.

Shoving her phone in her purse, Rachel introduces herself. "I'm Rachel Ellis, Tabitha's mother." She towers over me in her power pumps. At five foot two I'm physically incapable of intimidating anyone, but Rachel's presence screams proficiency, with her frightening female visage locked down. "I don't recognize you. Were you hired in the last year or two?" Of course. Rachel is one of those women who only remembers names and faces if committing them to memory will prove useful in obtaining something she may want or need at a later date.

"No, I've been here for quite some time. In fact, I was the teacher helping in Catherine's class the day we were all picking up the bins of LEGOs your son, Dalton, dumped onto the carpet during choice time."

I let the memory surface from the recesses of Rachel's mind before continuing, "When I suggested that Dalton lift a finger and help clean up like his classmates, he surely did lift a finger. His middle one. Right at me." I smile and clench my jaw to keep myself from cracking up as I recollect that day. Rachel ignores my walk down memory lane and waves to a mom she recognizes so she doesn't have to acknowledge that we both know this is not our first time at the kindergarten rodeo.

"I'm good at Legoth, Ms. Lewith," Tabitha announces, her big ears working overtime to follow our adult conversation.

"Let's go, Tabitha. I see Char over there, and I want to find out if she got the house in Martis Camp up in Tahoe." Rachel gives her daughter's hand a firm tug.

"I bet you are, Tabitha. Why don't you take your mom over to get name tags for the both of you, and get one for your dad too. When you're done, head on over to the marble rollers. I saw you eyeing them earlier," I say, winking at Tabitha. Ignoring my suggestion, Rachel pulls Tabitha in the direction of Char and Lake Tahoe updates.

I check my watch. It's nine fifteen and all the families, minus one, are busy working, a charged buzz energizing the room. There's no way the Abramses are showing up today. Charlie's funeral was only a few days ago, and from what Wikipedia told me, Noa has five more days of public grieving to do before she can wail it out in the privacy of her own home. I can't help but picture Noa sitting alone on a milking stool, waiting for someone to show up with a magic wand and make her nightmare disappear. If I have an ounce of energy left tonight, maybe I'll pop in for a quick minute and check she's not spooning with Jim Beam again.

With a two-to-one ratio of parents to kids, safety is not an immediate concern, so I step into the hallway to catch my breath and relax my face, my cheeks burning from smiling so hard the past forty-five minutes. I hear a soft, "Hi, Marjette," that startles me, and I jump. I look over my shoulder to see Noa and her daughter, Esther, sitting on the stairs that lead to the second-grade suite.

Eyes closed, Noa vigorously shakes her head and clears her throat to give her greeting a second try. "Hi, Marjette." Wearing a somber look that is strikingly similar to her mother's, Esther doesn't move from where she's tucked under Noa's arm.

Noa's outfit is one that would make any woman ripe with jealousy, but otherwise she looks so exhausted I wouldn't trade places with her for a minute. "Oh, umm, sorry, I didn't mean to scare you," she says. I put my hands up to gesture no problem, but my heart's still thumping. "This is our daughter, Esty. Well, Esther, but we, I mean, I"—Noa stumbles over her pronouns, and I can't help but wince—"I call her Esty." Esty begins to pick at something imaginary on her shirt, pretending it's supremely engrossing so she doesn't have to make eye contact with me. I try not to let the shock that Noa and Esty are actually here for the first day of school register in my body language. I scan my brain to come up with an argument to send them back home, knowing that today, these two ladies will be the only familial unit in my class down one family member. If they come back tomorrow it may still be awkward, but at least not as awkward as today, when everyone shows up, even spouses who can't stand each other, for the good of their kindergartener. Noa stands, making a move to head into my classroom.

I open my mouth to say something but then shut it, resigned to what I can tell Noa is determined to do. I squat so I'm eye level with the dark-haired beauty who will be joining my class. "Are you ready to go inside and meet some new friends? We've all been excited to meet you," I say to Esty, a bent truth mixed with a bit of encouragement.

"I don't want to," Esty informs me, looking at her mom pleadingly. Noa turns away from her daughter's gaze before Esty can break her resolve.

I rise slowly and notice Noa is gripping the handrail so tightly her wrist is vibrating. I can feel she really doesn't want to either, but life must go on. Whether you want it to or not, life marches forward, and being left behind sucks.

"Well, take your mommy's hand," I encourage Esty, more for Noa's sake than for hers. Esty reluctantly does what she's told. "May I hold your other hand?" I ask, not wanting to push too hard on a fragile child.

Please do, Noa's face begs. And I do because this woman deserves for something in her day to go right.

By nine forty-five, Noa and Esty have not left my side as I float around the classroom. When each family looks up from their child-centered activity to chat with me, I introduce them to Noa and Esty like these two are family. I really need some space to do my teacher thing, but I can't shed Noa. With every introduction to another mother, I hope she will stay and chat as I work the room, but Noa winces and says, "Nice to meet you," and moves along right beside me, Esty rolling behind as the caboose.

At the stroke of ten, I raise my voice and initiate all parents and children into the elementary school club they now belong to with the call "One, two, three, eyes on me!" More than a hundred eyes do what they're told and look toward me, waiting for whatever comes next. I wait a beat and then teach them the response that will mark every student's day for the next six years of elementary school. "One, two, eyes on you." I then give the parents the five-minute warning to head out of my classroom and on to the rest of their day, even Rachel Ellis, who is frantically texting and ignoring my closing words. It's time for me to begin teaching the children the curriculum these moms and dads are paying for. There are several *awwws* in the room from parents not ready to part with their babies, even though down deep they know the time has come. Noa is the only mother who looks relieved that she can soon escape this place where she is the wife with the freshly deceased husband and Esty is the kid at school with the dead dad, even if no one knows it yet.

Like an Oklahoma country rancher herding her cattle, I start corralling my parents toward the door and on with their lives. Several moms break free of my efforts and rush back to give their children one more kiss and a final reminder that school ends exactly at three o'clock so there's no confusion over when they will be reunited.

Noa continues to hang by my side as the parents file past us saying their goodbyes. I notice she's pulling on her knuckles just like she did the night I found her on the front porch. I gently place a hand over hers, her nervous energy making me feel panicky for no reason other than I'm picking up the vibe she's putting down. My own fingers ache when I notice that her nail beds have been gnawed to the nub.

Last to arrive to the first day of school, Noa is also the last to leave. Turning to say a firm goodbye and push Noa out my door and back home, it strikes me, given her charcoal dress and classic beige Burberry trench coat, that she doesn't look like she's heading to her house to assume the mourner's position.

"So, will I see you at pickup?" I ask, though what I really want to know is if Noa is going out to lunch at the Claremont with friends, because that's what her outfit indicates.

"The plan was that I would drop off Esty at school and Charlie"—I watch Noa swallow a grapefruit-size lump in her throat—"would pick her up." I shake my head, acknowledging what was meant to be just five days ago. "He works market hours." Noa catches her grammar again, but this time not without tears. "He worked New York market hours, so he was going to be able to pick her up. I work at Golden Gate Books, a publishing house in San Francisco, so drop-off is easy for me but pickup is impossible," Noa forces out, her voice losing its composure. Newly widowed or not, I can see one's clothing game has to be on point in the publishing world.

"I'm the lifestyles editor." That definitely explains the outfit, but not why she's going into work so soon after her husband passed.

"I know Esty will love that you can bring her to school every morning. That time is really special," I assure Noa, squeezing her forearm for added emphasis. After Booker and I divorced, I was sure everything I did was a major mom bomb. I was convinced there was no greater fail in the test of parenting mastery than not being able to keep your family intact for the sake of your child. I can only imagine how hard Noa must be beating herself up over something that is not her fault, but I know from experience the loop of what she could have done differently plays nonstop nonetheless.

"My brother, Max, is picking up Esty today. He may from time to time on other days too, but for the most part she will have to go to after care until six o'clock, when I can rush over the bridge to grab her." *That's a long workday for a five-year-old.* I know I can't reveal my thought to Noa, as it will most definitely crush her. "Max has a new bakery on College Avenue at Ashby, so it's pretty easy for him to come over here to pick up Esty. Please don't judge if he shows up a mess; that's just who he is. A good guy but kind of a disaster." I nod vigorously so Noa knows I understand and it's not a problem. "I guess we both are."

"Are you sure you can't rely on your brother to pick Esty up more than just every once in a while? Uncles are fun," I hint, hoping Noa will pick up what I'm suggesting about too long a day at school.

"Trust me, I'll be surprised if he can pull it off once in a while." Noa exhales and rolls her eyes like a woman who feels the weight of the world resting solely on her shoulders. I recognize that weight, because I've been carrying it around since Booker walked out on me and Darius. Truth be told, I never thought the burden would look so heavy on a White woman. I thought all their gurus, therapists, and life coaches made sure that weight falls right off. "Given his fickle history, I can't always rely on Max."

~

I'm exhausted. After a summer spent in quiet solitude in my garden, I'm out of practice for seven hours of nonstop talking and answering at a decibel level that—Lord as my witness—grows louder and louder each passing year. Every June after I lock up my classroom for the summer, I conveniently forget how many questions kindergarteners ask throughout a day. And then every September, I'm bombarded again and act like I'm surprised by how curious and tiring it all is. The added bonus: this year I get to do it hungry. Darn Judy and her born-again devotion to her health.

I desperately want to kick off my shoes and lie flat on my floor since most of my students are now tucked into a parent's or nanny's car, no doubt clamoring for snacks, but unfortunately there's still one left: Esty. Noa wasn't kidding when she said her brother's unreliable. I check my watch. Fifteen minutes late picking up a child on the first day of school is inexcusable. Not being on time to pick up a grieving child is downright cruel.

I look up Noa's phone number in the Houghton directory and dial to let her know that if no one is here in the next five minutes to pick up Esty, I'm going to have to take her to after care, *on the first day of school with a newly deceased dad.* Shit, the phone goes directly to voice mail. Charlie's cell phone number is also listed. I wonder what would happen if I called it. Is it dead too?

Looking at Esty, I know I'm such a fraud. Of course there's no way I'm sticking to school policy and abandoning this baby at after-school care on day one. What I am going to do is firmly establish with Esty's uncle, whenever the hell he gets here, that he's going to have to be respectful of my time on the days he picks up his niece. I don't tolerate flakes.

I'm unable to move from my desk chair I'm so wiped, but I can just barely make out Esty's play at the miniature kitchen. She's babbling to herself about baking a pie for her daddy for when he comes home. Though I'm ravenous, her imaginary baking makes me nauseated. I think back to five days ago, when I would have never even recognized my neighbors if we crossed paths at the local Trader Joe's, or if I had, I probably would have hidden by the milk. That's how committed I was to not intermix our lives. I spend my days surrounded by White folks' problems, so I know Judy's advice to keep home separate—which is code for "keep home Black"—is solid. Yet with all that conviction to not friend up to my neighbor, here I am fretting over her baby like she's one of my own.

"Where's Ms. Lewis's class?" I hear someone ask Catherine next door. Too tired, I don't get up to find out who it is. I know Catherine will direct them my way.

"Ms. Lewis?"

I put my hands out for my desk to quickly push myself up from my seat but miss entirely and almost tumble tits first onto my keyboard.

"Uncle Max!" Esty runs toward the door, her face lighting up for the first time all day.

This is fickle Uncle Max? I straighten up, hideously aware that my jaw is hanging open, but I lack the ability to close it. Uncle Max is no flour-covered dough boy. In fact, Uncle Max is no boy at all. The man who is gloriously filling out my doorway squats to catch his niece, and I can just make out his muscled quads flexing beneath linen pants. Esty flies right into his arms, and before I can stop her, she has rubbed lingering pastel chalk from her hands all over the crisp white shirt that perfectly complements her uncle's summer tan. The two of them share the same thick, dark eyebrows that protect ocean-blue eyes. Esty buries her face in her uncle's chest, and he looks up to me. Well, sort of. His squat is not far from my sight line. "This is always the best part of my day," Max says adoringly to his niece.

You must be the best part of some woman's day.

In a practiced move, Max slings Esty up onto his hip. "Sorry I'm late. I'm Max." Noa's brother offers me his hand while adjusting Esty's unicorn backpack over his shoulder. He must have a baby mama out there somewhere; he's such a natural. Usually, if a parent literally picks their kindergartener up, I gently, but directly, explain that in Ms. Lewis's class the students walk in and out of school like the big boys and girls they are. They also haul their own gear, and that includes glittery unicorn backpacks. Since it's the first day of school, I give this uncle a break, but next time we'll be having words.

"I had a meeting at the bank with a loan officer, and it ran a little long."

"Nice to meet you." I, too, put my hand out to shake.

"Actually, we've met before," Max says with a smile.

"We have?" I return politely. I hope this isn't going to be a long-winded story. I'm ready to go home and kick off my shoes. And please don't tell me this is another instance when a White man thinks all sisters look alike. There's nothing about me that someone would confuse with Beyoncé, other than our mutual age and the fact that I'm having a good hair day.

"Okay, not so much 'met' as I saved you from a horrifying slipup when you leaned in to pull the cloth off the mirror at Charlie's shiva. We Jews forgive, but we never, ever forget."

Huh? I should have paid better attention to the gray suit on Sunday. "I believe you also ate my chicken."

"I did, and I've been eating it every day since. Best fried chicken I've ever had."

Damn straight.

"Uncle Max, did you bring me a special treat from the bakery?" Esty cuts in, bored with adult conversation.

"I have an Esty-clair waiting for you in the car."

"It's called an éclair, Uncle Max!" Esty scolds but is clearly giddy that her uncle has renamed a favorite delicacy.

"That's quite a treat for your first day of kindergarten," I admit, rubbing Esty on the back, marking a decent first day of school for this little warrior.

"A chocolate-and-vanilla treat on the first day of school has to be a sign it's going to be a great school year, don't you think, Ms. Lewis?" Max asks with hope in his voice that I will take excellent care of his niece.

"A surprise treat on the first day of school certainly hints to the start of a great year."

CHAPTER SIX

It's five days into the school year and too many weeks on what Judy refers to as "our wellness adventure" but I call the "hunger games." I finished up a sci-fi thriller with Ben & Jerry's earlier this week, so I find myself crossing my fingers that the scale is on my side as I stand in line with Judy for our regular weigh-in. I look up toward heaven and hope somebody is keeping track of my afterlife points for being such a devoted friend.

"You go ahead." Judy pushes me in front of her, and I almost knock over the pyramid of Weight Watchers two-point sesame crackers on display. Something's definitely up with Judy. She always wants to weigh in first, gloat second.

"What's wrong with you?" I urge, while Judy pretends to be engrossed in the same six Zen photos of hummingbirds and fruit bowls that have been hanging on the walls since our first meeting. "That banana is not going to save you from whatever you got going on."

Judy huffs so loud I swear she's about to blow this house down. Not taking her eyes off the stock photography, she answers, "I ate my emotions this week. S'mores are the new sadness." Where's Judy roasting marshmallows?

"What did you have to be sad about up there in wine country rubbing elbows with the grapes? I see you and your tan line winking at me from the neckline of your T-shirt. Whatever it is, it can't be all that bad."

"It is bad. And I can't tell you."

"You can."

"You'll hassle me."

"I won't." I'm glad my fingers were already crossed behind my back on that one. Judy gives a head tilt to signal I need to move up the line closer to the scales.

"Maybe I shouldn't have retired," she mumbles under her breath. Well, I could have told her that. I knew she'd miss seeing me daily like we've done for the past eighteen years. "I miss the kids. I mean, I *really* miss the kids. Or at least I missed them this week. The September optimism in the air, that feeling of limitless possibility for what's to come. That's unique to schools, and you don't realize how much it's part of the cadence of your life until it's gone." It's not like Judy to be self-reflective. She's a woman who believes the answer to everything that ails you is to just. keep. going.

"I can tell you what's coming. That September euphoria turns into October reality. Frida starts in again, griping that administrators don't understand how hard teachers work because she has to be reminded, for the umpteenth time, to deliver her attendance sheets to the front office by ten every morning. When that fun kicks in, and you know I'll let you know when it does, you won't miss school."

"I won't miss Frida," Judy corrects, bending over to untie her sneakers and take off her socks for weigh-in. I was really hoping, just for today, we could skip this part of the meeting. I'm going to try rolling onto the balls of my feet; that might lighten the scale a titch.

"And Rachel Ellis is no longer your problem," I add, joining Judy in disrobing down to my tank top and leggings.

"No, she is not. She's your problem, and that, my child, is a glorious thing." I give Judy a *pul-ease* lip purse. "For me. Not for you."

"Guess who showed up on my class roster?"

Judy stands, waving her hands, encouraging me to *get on with it.* Now we're getting to the gossip that'll perk her right up out of her funk.

"Remember my neighbor I told you about?"

"Which one? You have words about all of them." Judy calls me out for the millionth time on what she believes is my unnatural interest in other people's business. It's the same thing Auntie Shay used to do when she would catch me peeping around corners, listening to grown-folks' talk. Inevitably, she would stop the conversation with whomever she was talking to and announce, just loud enough for me to hear, "Hold on a minute. I need to take care of somethin' 'cause little people have big ears in this house." That was my warning I better beat feet before I was caught, because Auntie Shay was frighteningly accurate slinging her house shoes. In my mind I wasn't being nosy. I was just seeing if someone needed my help, even if I was only seven.

During my second year teaching at Houghton, Auntie Shay passed away, and I found myself rudderless, no longer a girl, but not yet a grown-up. Blessings came my way, however, when Judy picked up Auntie Shay's baton and ran with it, not only assuming the responsibility to mentor me into adulthood but lifting me up whenever I stumbled on the road to becoming a grown-ass woman.

"To be clear, my neighborhood would have fallen apart years ago if I weren't on top of all that goes on, taking care of things others ignore. It's the ministering part of me I inherited from my daddy. And don't you dare bring up Layla and her landscaping." Judy bites her lower lip like she's not going to say a thing, but I know letting that story slide is killing her. "But, specific to this conversation, I'm talking about the Jewish family next door, the Abramses."

"Oh, this sounds like one of those old-school jokes: 'A Baptist and a Jew walk into a bar.'" Judy laughs at her unfinished comedy. The man in front of us turns. I think the mention of a bar is making him wistful for a point-heavy cocktail even though it's only 8:26 a.m.

"This is no joke. She's the one whose husband died suddenly, and then she brought her baby girl to school only five days after her daddy passed." Judy can tell from the change in my tone that this is not one of those times we're going to be clapping on a child and their hovercraft parents.

"Mom was a wreck. She wouldn't leave my side during parents' hour. Esty, the daughter, hung to herself the whole day. You know how hard it is to watch a child kick wood chips all recess and not play with the other kids."

"I do." And I know Judy does. "Did you spy a smile on her face at all on the first day?"

"Not until the very end, when her uncle Max finally arrived, late I might add, to pick her up. Then she lit up like a Christmas tree."

"I think you mean menorah."

"Seriously? You're retired. You can drop the whole religious-responsive act."

"Right, habit. So, was this Uncle Max and his wife in for the funeral?"

"From what I know, he's just opened up a bakery on College Avenue toward Berkeley and will be picking up his niece from time to time to help his sister out. His being late best be a one-off mistake."

"Sorry, did I hear you say he's single?"

"Now you know I didn't," I admonish Judy. She looks at me like she doesn't know what I'm talking about even though we both know she does. "Why are you interested in whether he's married or not? You've been off the shelf for forty years."

"Just 'cause you on a diet don't mean you can't read the menu." We both crack up. "Never mind. And I swear I'm not fishing. I'm just wondering if one Saturday it would be worth the effort to grab our coffee elsewhere. It's always nice to support new local businesses. So is he good looking?"

"There's no reason to spend our money and our points on someone else's pastries when I make the best in town, and you know it. And yes. He looked all right. He had the standard body parts." Judy is so desperate for me to find someone, she evaluates every single man who crosses my path for mating potential.

"We wouldn't be going to check out the pastries, Marjette," Judy says, disappointed in me yet again.

"First off, the guy left a newly grieving child by herself for an extra fifteen minutes on the first day of school. Uh, no thanks. And next . . ."

"She wasn't by herself. She was with you."

"Okay, try this one because how quickly you forget. He's the uncle of one of my students." Handsome I'll admit, but I have a no-dating-family-members-of-my-students policy. Actually, since Booker bolted, I've had a strict no-dating policy period. I can't imagine another male touching on me and sharing the house with me and my son. "And he's Jewish, remember. Like super Jewish; that shiva was serious stuff. Guests aren't even allowed to catch a glimpse of themselves in a mirror to check if their lipstick's straight."

"Super Jewish, is that kinda like Blackity Black?"

"Comparing eating chitlins to eating matzah is kind of like comparing apples to oranges, but you get what I'm saying. We got nothing in common but a shared concern for his niece."

"But do you get what I'm saying: *Is baby girl's uncle single?*"

⌒

To: Marjette Lewis
From: Rachel Ellis
Subject: Appropriate reading material for kindergarten students

Marjette,

Well, I did not expect to have to become the kindergarten curriculum cop so soon, yet here we are. It's like déjà vu from Dalton's abysmal first year at Houghton all over again. Tabitha came home from school yesterday sharing fearful tales of guns, violence, and killing bad guys. I couldn't get her to sleep last night; nightmares kept her lodged between me and my laptop until morning. The severity of the situation even forced me to have to talk to Roger. I'm going to assume, without question, that you will be addressing your literature selection this evening at Back-to-School night.

Let's both hope yesterday will not be representative of the rest of Tabitha's year.

With concern,
Rachel Ellis

Rachel's assessment of yesterday's story time is typical kindergarten-parent crazy, but she's not wholly wrong either. I'm just irked I have to address this issue tonight given her email, because if there's one thing I know about Rachel Ellis, it's if I don't do what she wants, she will do it herself.

The past few weeks all the kids and families have gotten into a good rhythm at morning drop-off. Parents walk their child in, help them get settled, share a word or two with me, and then they're out. Esty, however, gets a kiss outside my classroom door—I get a reserved wave but no words—before Noa scurries off and her daughter is left to settle herself in for the day. I admire the independence, but at this point I've connected face-to-face with all the parents, except Noa, on how their child's transition from home to school has progressed. I know I could cross my lawn and do it in person, but getting locked into a conversation about school during my home time is something I'd rather not do.

To my delight, yesterday the two Abrams ladies finally stepped into the classroom together. Esty did all the talking, explaining excitedly that her uncle Max gave her a new book, and since he was coming to pick her up from school today, she asked if he could come early to read it to the whole class. That's when Noa piped in with a promise, laced with concern, that she would do all she could to ensure Max showed up on time given the first-day-of-school debacle. As a rule, I don't like last-minute changes to my lesson plans. But it was nice to actually hear Noa's voice, and given Esty's continued reluctance to connect with her classmates, I knew this little girl needed a win with her peers. That's how almost two decades into this education game I made the rookie mistake of not vetting Esty's new book before Uncle Max showed up, resulting in Rachel's email littering my inbox.

There's a New Chef in Town was a riveting hit with the assembled six-and-under crowd. My class sat fixated by the metaphor of a chef representing a sheriff, his spatulas held like guns in holsters until they were drawn whenever a hot tray of chocolate chip cookies needed to be scooped from the baking sheet onto the cooling rack. *Bam! Bam! Bam!* went the chef as he flipped his cooled cookies onto the plate, drowned those bad boys in milk, and then jailed them in the chef's stomach, throwing away the key. Uncle Max read with passion, as if he had written the book himself, while I shifted uncomfortably in my seat, wondering if my unease was from his shoot-'em-up gesturing or how his biceps flexed every time he pointed his gun fingers at the kids. The book and Uncle Max did what I hoped they would do—they gave Esty some much-needed schoolyard cred, but they also got me in trouble with Rachel and most likely others in her mom squad. But it's okay;

I'm ready for it. Back-to-School night is where I hold the stage like Lena Horne at the Apollo.

I've pulled out my stacked Miu Miu heels and indigo palazzo pants that just dust the floor and lengthen my petite legs. I know my robin's-egg blue satin blouse is turning all sorts of heads, as are my hood-meets-haute hoops. I have a whole closet filled with curated clothes perfect for the country club or a nightclub, every item purchased before Booker took our checking account and ran.

Rachel is all over me with a list of literature suggestions, but at the mention of whether Roger will be joining us for the evening, she scurries over to her beehive for protection. Speaking of reinforcements, Noa glides into my classroom with her own backup, Max. Every mom in the room notices.

Spying my chocolate macaroons and shortbread, Max takes ten giant steps to my cleaned-off desk, where I have the tray meticulously arranged. Noa scurries after him.

"Mmmm. These are perfect. Might even be better than mine. Where did you get these?" Max asks, macaroon crumbs catching in the corner of his mouth. I'm about to give him a hard time for assuming I bought them, but then I remember he doesn't know my reputation at school for feeding people.

"I made them," I reply, just loud enough so the whole right half of my room can hear and realize they better step up to my plate of offerings or they'll be marked discourteous in my grade book.

"Noa, you have to try one of these things," Max insists, and when his sister opens her mouth to answer him, he shoves a whole coconut mound in her mouth, which is clever; she needs the sustenance.

While Max grabs a couple of shortbreads, Noa chews, swallows, and then apologizes, "Sorry, Marjette. Umm, my brother is, well . . ." I'm curious what Noa is going to say because so far, what I've seen is a man who is doing his best to help take care of his family.

"One of your very favorite people?" Max finishes her sentence, cracking Noa up in a fit of giggles. Hearing Noa laugh, even for a second, somehow lightens the atmosphere in the room, and from the grin across his face, I can tell Max is reveling in being the initiator of Noa's momentary levity. Score one for the little brother.

"I was going to say devoid of manners." Noa slaps Max's chest with the back of her hand. "But yes, when you're not being a total worry on my mind, you are also one of my very favorite people."

"I have to get started with my presentation, but feel free to have as many cookies as you want. Whatever you don't eat just goes home to my teenage son with an unappreciative palate. To him, a macaroon or McDonald's, it's all the same."

"You have a son?" Noa asks.

"I do. Darius."

"Sorry, I didn't know." My neighbor apologizes for the second time in five minutes. "I should have known that," Noa confesses, looking down at my industrial carpet, her momentary lightheartedness gone. I don't want her feeling any more uncomfortable than I suspect she already does having brought Max for support. Plus, nothing is more unappealing than a woman who apologizes too much. I want to like Noa as a parent in my class and as my neighbor, but weak women have never been my choice of company.

"Don't worry about it, Noa." I give my best smile of assurance. "We haven't known each other like that."

Walking across the room to grab my laptop, I brush by Rachel and overhear her whisper loudly behind her palm to her hive, "I checked. He doesn't have on a ring." *Why didn't I think to look?* Even if I'm not in the dating game, I should still possess an ounce of strategy.

Char quickly pipes in, not wanting Rachel to have all the glory nor all the intel, "Yeah, at first I thought how crude, this woman is showing up at Back-to-School night with another man, and her husband hasn't

Never Meant to Meet You

even been gone a month." The squad all nod in agreement. "But then I overheard, ohhh, what's her name—"

Taking back the conversation with this pertinent fact, Rachel interrupts: "Noa." Score two points for Rachel in this thick forest of man-hunting moms.

"Then I heard Noa refer to him as her brother." I didn't realize Noa's widow status was already common knowledge in kindergarten. "Rachel, this just might be your best school year yet!" Char trills, and the hive buzzes in mutual high hopes for their queen bee. Is there room enough in my class for us both to have a great year?

"Did anyone catch his name?" Rachel asks the group, sniffing out the final clue to their conversation.

"Max," I blurt, my teacher instinct to pounce and answer any question proving too strong.

Startled, the group turns and looks at me. "Thank you, Marjette. Aren't you full of useful information," Rachel says with bogus gratitude. Now I know my name and face will be registered in Rachel Ellis's manipulative mind forever. "Perhaps you're right, Char. This year the tuition at Houghton just might pay off."

I resist my inclination to shut Rachel down and instead think of the message sent out to the entire faculty from the head of school an hour before Back-to-School night reminding us to be on our best behavior when it comes to parents with deep pockets. Houghton has a new theater arts center to build and a lack of funds to do it. I take a deep breath and in my best teacher voice reply, "It is my hope that every parent has a rewarding year, Rachel." I continue walking to the front of my room, the kindergarten math curriculum now the last thing on my mind.

⌒

"Darius!" I call out, but all I'm met with is silence and the smell of ribs I've had in the slow cooker waiting for dinner when I got home after a fourteen-hour day. I'm proud of myself for avoiding my own treats at Back-to-School night, so an extra splash of barbecue sauce on my ribs will be my reward. "Darius!"

I check my phone. No response to the text I sent asking him to pull out the fixings for a salad and start chopping.

Marjette 7:59 PM

DARIUS!

I attempt to yell over text, my thumbs flying, in case he's in his room with those semipermanent AirPods in his ears. Nothing. And I'm starving.

I've been home for almost an hour without a word from him. I know one thing: Darius better not be somewhere huddled up under that fast-assed girl, Simone. If I find out he's had me worrying about him while he's sniffing after her, I will put a hurt on them both. I check my phone again even though I know nothing new has come in. As I'm about to call Judy and complain about my foolish son, I hear the sound of Darius's key turning the front door lock.

From the dark of night, in walks Darius, big as day, like he hasn't just had me packing his bags to go stay with Judy. "Darius Lamont Lewis, where have you been?!" I shout, the perfect ratio of fear, irritation, and hunger marking my point. "You enjoy making me go out of my mind with worry?"

Wearing a smile that suggests he enjoys everything in his life without a care in the world, Darius meets my alarm with, "Ma, chill. Why you so geeked up right now?" He holds his hand out to me, palm forward like he's warding off my verbal blows.

"You comin' in this house way too late on a school night has me geeked up, and I don't even know what that means. I asked you where you been," I repeat, but the truth is there are far too many possible scenarios that I'm not sure I really want to know. "I got home to make you a plateful of ribs thinkin' you'd be right next to me for dinner, but you ain't here and didn't think to tell me where you are." For his school-teacher mother to be dropping her *g*'s and tossing out *ain't* informs Darius this is not an average kind of trouble he's in.

"Ooooh. Is it ready?" he responds, trying to change the subject off how unacceptable it is that he didn't respond to my texts and then waltzed in like he's the king of this castle. Right now, I'm seeing a little too much Booker and not enough me in my son.

"It was ready at eight. Now it's cold waiting 'til all hours of the night for you to come home, and I'm downright starving."

"Ma. I told you I was goin' over to Rex's house to start planning out our junior-year capstone project. You want me leaving that to the last minute?" Darius explains, knowing the answer to his own question since my weakness for organization is no secret.

"I don't remember you telling me that. Why didn't you answer any of my messages?" He may have been doing schoolwork, but not answering his mother's texts remains inexcusable.

"Now see. That's the problem around here—you don't listen," Darius accuses, walking toward the kitchen to claim his dinner, ignoring my interrogation.

"Hey, I know you're not talking to me crazy. I don't pay for that fancy phone for you not to answer when I'm calling."

"Okay, okay . . . dang. Rex's mom always takes our phones when it's time for us to focus on work. She's hard core like that." Right. I forgot how much I like Rex's mom. "If you were hungry, why'd you wait so long for dinner?"

"You know I don't like to eat by myself. What's the point of having a nice meal if it's just me? Might as well microwave some popcorn and call it a night if I'm going to eat solo." My insecurities around being alone often arise at mealtime.

"You know I'm graduating next year. Whatchoo gonna do when I'm gone and you have the house to yourself?" I ignore Darius's question and get to plating. "How 'bout maybe getting out there and getting your swerve on?" he teases, elbowing me while I'm creasing two napkins.

"Don't you worry about me and what I do, young man. I got a life. Go wash up while I heat these plates so we can eat," I insist, giving my son a playful shove, letting him know we're all good or at least getting there. "I can't wait to hear all about your capstone project over dinner."

While Darius is in the bathroom, his words turn my stomach, making dinner sound less appealing. Alone in this house for the first time is a thought I ward off every time it enters my mind. So is getting my swerve on when I've been living life in a straight line.

CHAPTER SEVEN

In October, when the leaves change and the temperature falls off, so does student behavior. Every. Single. Year. It's a national phenomenon that when the longest month with no federal holiday rolls around, the shiny newness of school dulls, and kindergarteners wake up to the hard truth that they pretty much have to do this school thing for their foreseeable future. Given this fact, I always plan a field trip to the San Francisco Zoo midmonth to shake up our daily schedule and make our animal kingdom unit real. Well, as real as a giraffe living in the middle of a city by the ocean can be. I actually hate the underlying sadness of zoos—I don't like seeing God's creatures caged—but it's a crowd-pleaser and a great introduction on how to travel successfully in our class pack outside the Houghton campus.

When I was young and heading out with Auntie Shay to pick up the fixings we needed for whatever we were planning to cook, she would remind me exactly who we were representing out in the world: the family. Unbuckling in the car, Auntie Shay's final words came out as rules to live by—"Don't touch nothin'. Don't ask for nothin'. Don't even look at nothin'"—when we got in the store. "And remember: a hard head makes a soft behind." Acting up was never worth a swat or, even worse, Auntie Shay turning me out of her kitchen.

Minus the threat of corporal punishment, I have a similar speech every time I'm about to step out the classroom and onto the sidewalk with other people's children. I take my students' safety to heart; I will not lose somebody's child, nor will I let somebody's child embarrass me in public.

Huddled up on the circle-time rug, I can feel the kids itching to go, so I need to take care of reviewing our safety guidelines quickly while all eyes are on me and not the door. "Okay, class, I want to go over some of the basic things we've talked about concerning safety and staying together in public," I begin. I've already lost Naman to the fascination of the Velcro closures on his sneakers. "Imagine one of you is separated from the group. Who can remind the class what to do?"

Before I can call on him, Jonah announces, "Find a zoo worker wearing a uniform, and tell them you need help finding your teacher." A few kids look to Jonah in awe, like this is the first time they've heard this headline, oblivious to the ten other times we've talked about field trip etiquette this week.

"Excellent, Jonah! That's exactly right. Find a grown-up helper. But one thing we haven't covered is how to explain what your teacher looks like so they can find me." Knowing Jonah would answer every question if I let him, I add, "Does anyone else have some ideas?"

"You have a red jacket the same color as a fire engine," offers Drew, my dedicated junior firefighter.

"I do. That's an excellent place to start."

"You have short hair," says Cameron, who believes girls should have long hair. One look at me on the first day of school and she begged her mother to let her be in Catherine's class.

"You do really good voices when you read stories," claims Mia, totally missing the point of visual clues, but I appreciate the compliment.

Rachel and Max, today's chaperones, sneak into the classroom, alerting my intuition that it's time to tie up this conversation so we can hit the road before Rachel hits on Esty's unsuspecting uncle.

"Can anyone tell me one really big, important, obvious clue about me?" I prompt, aware that already at their young age most of these kids have been trained to believe that mentioning race is impolite. I look at Deja and Javon, my two brown students, thinking they've got my back with this answer, but they're focused on their coat zippers and not on me. What I want is for someone to say loud and strong that their teacher is a Black woman.

The time to think for themselves is over. I cave and give the final answer. "How about telling a grown-up, 'My teacher's a Black lady'?"

All jaws drop open except for Deja's and Javon's. They look up at me like, *No shit, lady.* "My mommy says that's inappropriate to say," woke Abby explains to me and the class. "You're not supposed to do racism."

I hear Rachel let out a small *oop* behind me, and Max stifles a cough.

"It's not inappropriate if it's true," I respond, knowing I should unpack that flawed logic with my students but recognizing we don't have the time. One more day of existence under the PC regime of the Bay Area won't kill these kids.

Esty's hand shoots up. I nod to her, knowing this has to be our last comment; we need to get going. "I would tell the helper person you have a big Black bottom." Esty emphasizes the details of her answer by putting her arms out wide. "If they know that, then they can find you super easy." She beams, supremely proud of herself for her attention to detail and also for her alliteration. Knowing Esty's mom, I can see how she came to her conclusion, but I'm mortified she chose to share her observation in front of her uncle Max and Rachel. The class bursts out in laughter, tipping over like bowling pins at the mention of my bottom. Tomorrow's lesson will be on tact.

After a relatively uneventful bus ride, we arrive at the zoo. While our designated zoologist leads my class around the seven continents and their species, I keep one ear turned toward my children and one toward Rachel, who, instead of watching the children, is pushing up on

Max. It's obvious to me what Rachel is doing with her light touches to Max's forearm, but what I can't read is if Max is playing hard to get or if he is genuinely interested in the penguins of Antarctica. How Rachel even worked the phone lines to find out that Noa had volunteered her brother to chaperone the field trip is next-level female strategy. I guess you don't become the founder and CEO of the Bombshell Bar without knowing how to get done what you want done all in a fabulous hairdo. But did she have to do it in front of the pandas?

The field trip is going smoothly until Esty starts hanging off her uncle's vest, complaining that her legs are tired and she doesn't want to walk anymore. I can see Max is giving it his best effort to hustle her to join our class, but she continues to lag, immune to his encouragement. I hang back to help Max out—the battle of wills with a five-year-old is one I can tell he's losing.

"Hey, Esty, how about we walk on our own two feet. We don't have much time left at the zoo, and the best has been saved for last," I say. The lions are always the highlight of the trip, so every year I request they come at the end to motivate my kids along.

"I don't want to walk anymore," Esty whines, deciding right here is where she's going to stop moving for the rest of her life.

"You don't, huh? What is it that you want to do so you can keep up with your class and finish the trip with your friends?" With this question I'm confident Esty will come to the conclusion that she will need to walk like everyone else. Offering an option with only one possible answer works every time for the lone straggler who insists on holding up the group.

"It's not fair. I want a chair with wheels like that person. No one's making him walk when he's tired," Esty insists, pointing behind me to what I know is a disabled person in a wheelchair out to enjoy a beautiful day only to have it ruined by an ignorant child. Then, at the decibel of being heard in a wind tunnel, Esty confirms her belief with, "He should share, Ms. Lewis. Go ask him to share and walk on his own two feet."

Max's eyes pop and he mouths in exaggerated silence, *"Oh my God."* Even though I was raised Baptist, I'm also a realist, and I know God can't help us here.

I take Esty's hand and head over to the gentleman in his wheelchair. Now she's walking at a crisp clip, probably because she thinks she's about to hitch a ride.

"Excuse me, sir, my name's Marjette, and I'm the teacher of this curious kindergartener, Esty. What's your name?" I can feel Max hanging back, seemingly terrified of the direction I may be taking this touchy teachable moment.

I explain to the man, who shares his name is Daniel, that Esty is wondering why he gets to enjoy the zoo on this beautiful morning in a chair but she has to walk.

"I wish my chair was built for two—then I'd share with you," Daniel kindly replies. Gripping my hand tightly, my complaining companion has gone quiet. These are the moments I cherish with my students, where they learn that the best way to educate oneself about human differences is to step up and ask, and then be open to the answers that come. At the end of the day, we are all human, and when we share, we find common ground about ourselves.

Back at school, as Max packs up an exhausted Esty to take her to his bakery until Noa can grab her, he sheepishly glances at me. He's probably as uneasy as I am about who's going to talk to Noa about Esty's behavior today. In stable family situations, prickly topics like learning challenges and classroom behavior issues are difficult enough to broach with parents who have spent the last five years convinced their child is the one human who has inexplicably escaped the imperfections that befall us all. Families with singletons are especially sensitive given this is their one shot for reproductive redemption. Add to that a kid whose father has died, and we're at next-level conversational challenge.

"We could Rochambeau for who gets to tell Noa her daughter's a budding bigot," Max offers, covering Esty's ears with his hands to make earmuffs. As a recovering eavesdropper, it always cracks me up when people think this works, but I give Max points for not dancing around the topic of Esty's expressive vocabulary today.

"Let's start with the easier one first and tell Noa that her daughter's an ableist. Today it's a wheelchair, tomorrow it'll be a Lark." Max squeezes Esty's ears harder like he can't believe what just came out of his niece's kindergarten teacher's mouth.

"What's a Lark?" Oh, thank goodness this man doesn't offend so easily.

"Electric scooter. Definitely a step up from a wheelchair. Lark makes the best ones."

"That's a random fact to know." Max laughs, releasing Esty from his vise grip.

"You have no idea the amount of random information I carry around in my head day in and day out. I can sing every song from *Frozen* all while whipping up a lasagna made with fresh rolled pasta and vegetables from my garden." I think of the conversation I overheard Rachel and Max having about Paris when I was pointing out lemurs and howler monkeys and cringe at the banality of my life compared to theirs. I make great lasagna because I have nothing better to do on a Friday night. Max makes the flakiest croissants in Northern California because he studied with masters in France.

"Anyway," I continue, letting Max go before he grows bored of me. "I'll talk to Noa. Gently crushing the hopes and plans of parents is what I do best. It's a perk of the job."

"And who gets to enjoy the perks of your cooking?" Max intones, gazing into my brown eyes. I look away first, too embarrassed to admit my son is my only regular dinner companion, and even he has had spotty attendance lately. Plus, I've never stared so deeply into blue eyes before; it's unnerving.

"Well, thank you so much for coming with us to the zoo today," my teacher speak snaps back as I gesture toward the door, letting Max and Esty know it's time to go. "It's always fun for the kids when a da—, er, I mean uncles come along."

"Yeah, Uncle Max, can you come every time?" Esty pipes in because of course she's been listening all along. *From your lips to every kindergarten mother's ears, Esty Abrams.*

⌒

At the end of a long day, shedding the stiff fabrics of my work wear is one of the best aspects of stepping in my house and closing the front door. I strip off my jeans that, frankly, aren't any looser since the school year began and my nightly walks went by the wayside, and I slip into the comfort of my jersey cotton joggers and Sooners sweatshirt. I called Noa on my drive home to set up a time to meet to talk about Esty, but my call went straight to voice mail. I didn't leave a message. The discussion of a child's errant behavior needs to be handled in person, not squeezed into a forty-five-second recording. Leaning over my kitchen sink, I can see out the window that Noa's car is in the driveway and the living room lights are on. Knowing that catching Noa at drop-off is near impossible, as she's always rushing to the office, I make the conscious decision to blur the professional and personal lines I have so clearly drawn and pay her a home visit, in my sweats. There's no way I'm putting hard pants back on.

To soften the bitter news with some sugar, and to have something to focus on other than Esty's behavior, I grab the sweet potato pie I made early this morning that's sitting on my kitchen counter covered by a tea towel. It's my specialty, and my personal downfall. This pie is what got me through my divorce from Booker, so maybe it will offer a little comfort for Noa, whose fragility is about to receive another crack.

The pie in my hands, I ring the doorbell. The familiar words of "I'll get it" are muffled by the walls. Noa opens the door looking like she's about to head out for a night at a Michelin star restaurant, to my night on the couch caressing the remote. Clearly, she's not a woman who needs to nestle into loose comfies at the end of the day to allow the elasticity of her skin to bounce back.

"Marjette, it's nice to see you," Noa says kindly but unable to mask her confusion. "Did you need to talk to Esty?"

Here goes. "No, and I don't mean to interrupt your evening, but I actually came to chat with you for a minute if that's okay," I explain with what I know must look like an uneasy smile.

Judy's voice crowds my mind. She would tell me to "get in, get it over with, get out." "There are some issues with Esty at school that we need to discuss." And then I thrust the pie at Noa to soften the blow. So awkward.

"Uhhh, okay. Well, Esty's inside watching *SpongeBob*; is it all right with you if we sit outside and chat?" Noa inquires, gesturing to the two chairs and table where our distant neighborly relationship shifted six weeks ago. Most parents would lie and tell me their kid's busy doing Kumon flash cards or reading a chapter book, so I appreciate the honesty and the invitation. I nod and step back from the door, making way for Noa to come out. She sets the pie on the table between the two of us and sits down. I do the same.

As I'm about to launch into a lecture about teaching children not to talk about other people's bodies, a car flies past us and whips into my driveway like it didn't see the SLOW CHILDREN AT PLAY sign I spent fifteen months arguing with the Oakland city council to post. Out of the passenger seat hops my son, but not before leaning over to lay a kiss on the NASCAR driver. I watch every move Darius makes like I'm on a stakeout. That girl better not put that car in park, cut the engine, and go in my house while I'm over here at the neighbors'. Darius gives the hood of the Jeep Cherokee two knuckle bumps, and I let out a massive sigh of relief. Simone, or I assume it's Simone—my son better not be two-timing like his dad—pulls out, missing my hydrangea bush by a sliver. I'm no fan of hers, wasting my son's time that should be spent studying or helping me around the house, but no woman deserves to be stepped out on by a cheat, even if that cheat is my son.

"So, that's your son? He's quite handsome." Noa breaks our silence, her compliment cooling the flames raging in my brain.

"Yep," I answer, still distracted, not taking my eyes off Darius as he closes the front door, oblivious that I'm watching him. Once he's safely inside, I turn back to Noa and realize her expectant face is looking at me like I'm some wise oracle of parenting given I'm a full decade further into this journey called motherhood. I realize my assumed expertise may help soften the blow of Esty's choice behavior today, so I decide to let Noa know she is not alone in the struggle of single parenting. In a show of solidarity for our difficult paths, one I've been on for a while and one Noa is only starting, I begin by letting her in on a little secret.

"I married a total dickwad."

"Ha!" Noa blows up. The laughter keeps on coming, tears leaking out the sides of her eyes. Her emotional release is contagious, and I start to chuckle from my gut too.

"I was married for thirteen years on top of the four years Booker and I dated exclusively in college. I put my ex through ten years of medical training and watched him disappear for the next three as he established his plastic surgery practice. I never complained when we didn't move back to Tulsa, when he failed to ask me about my days teaching or help out at night with Darius, because I believed he was busy building the life I wanted for us." Noa is hanging on my every word. Avoiding her tragic tale and jumping into mine is allowing her a moment of respite. "Right when I thought the two of us had arrived—gorgeous house, flush with cash, time to expand our family—Booker announced it was time for him to get going, solo." Noa nods at me, acknowledgment from a woman who knows something about losing a partner.

"Even if your marriage wasn't perfect, once he left, did you ever play over and over in your head what you could have done to make him stay?"

I wish I could lie and tell this woman that *no*, when Booker left, I stood tall and waved good riddance with my middle finger, but I've never been a good liar.

"Yeah, every day for the next two years."

"I can't stop thinking about what I could have done differently the moments before Charlie left me," Noa confesses. The two of us sit in silence, gazing out at the street, contemplating a past we can't change but can't escape either.

Flashing lights off, a police car slowly rolls down our block like it's searching for a suspect. As I watch, my stomach drops, and I do a mental check reminding myself where Darius is. The police park at my curb, and an officer gets out like he knows where he's going. I panic, my body heat rising along with my heartbeat. My fists are gripped; he better not be coming for my son.

CHAPTER EIGHT

Noa looks at me, scared, but I'm practiced at not appearing to be the angry Black woman. I don't need to go off just yet.

"Good evening, ladies, I'm Officer Nichols."

"Good evening," I repeat, standing up, a mixture of self-defense and trepidation in my tone. Noa stays quiet by my side.

"I'm looking for a Noa Abrams." Oh, thank the good Lord above; my mind erupts, though I'm not giving away my relief in front of this officer.

"I'm Noa." Noa now stands to meet the officer face-to-face, pressing the crease out of the front of her skirt. She's wearing a blank expression like the fact this cop is asking after her is no big deal. This is either some White girl magic or this woman's been spinning tales and she actually killed her husband.

"Nice to meet you, ma'am," Officer Nichols replies, placing a Ziploc bag with a set of keys on the table right next to my sweet potato pie. A beautiful silver key chain with an engraved capital *M* catches my eye.

"I'm so sorry to disturb you two, but on the night of your husband's death, when the hospital returned his watch and wedding ring to you, they forgot to include these keys that I guess were in his pocket." Noa is nodding along to the officer's words, but her eyes are fixed on the key chain. "A nurse or someone just found them this morning and turned the keys in to the police. Not sure why they gave them to us instead of calling you directly, but they did, so I wanted to make sure we got them back to you as soon as possible. Hope you weren't missing them." For the second time tonight, I give thanks to the Lord above. This time it's for Darius and me not living next to a murderess.

"Thank you. I appreciate you coming by to drop off my husband's keys. That's very kind of you," Noa says tightly, swiping up the clear plastic bag and shoving it in the pocket of her sweater.

"Okay, well, you ladies have a good night. I'll leave you to it." Officer Nichols backs up, feeling Noa's discomfort more than any appreciation.

"Good night and thanks again," I throw out from the both of us, aware of always wanting to stay in the good graces of the police. I feel awash with relief, but judging from Noa's grim expression, she's feeling something wholly different.

Silence hangs heavy in the air. I'm not sure where to go next with our conversation, and Noa no longer looks open to having a difficult dialogue about her daughter. I try by testing the waters with, "It's always good to have a spare set of house keys. If you like, I could hold on to them in case you ever get locked out of your house." There's no way I'm telling Judy I put up this offer.

"Those aren't my house keys," Noa forces out, fondling the evidence in her pocket. I open my mouth to make a comment about car keys, but I catch the veins in Noa's neck flexing, and I know those keys won't start her car. *A cheating husband; now there's something we have in common.*

Noa turns and asks me point-blank, "Why did Booker leave?" picking up our conversation right where we left off before Officer Nichols derailed my agenda.

I think for a second. "The question really is, Who did he leave me for?" I answer, sitting back down. Noa, too, drops back in her chair, expecting to hear the rest of my story.

"I've always loved kids; that's why I became a kindergarten teacher. My years at Houghton were only supposed to be practice for the big family Booker and I were going to have once he became an established doctor. That's why we got that house"—I point my finger behind me—"four bedrooms up, three bath, nice community." Noa nods along. I suppose the reasons we both moved into the Rockridge neighborhood are decidedly similar. "But while I was looking after other people's children and after my own son, Booker was looking after another woman, a tall, leggy Brazilian to be exact." I spare revealing to Noa that Judy and I spitefully refer to Booker's sidepiece as the Brimbo. She might think that's tacky.

"Is he still with her?" This woman is now scratching too far below the surface of my life to a level of truth I do not like to go to. I don't answer Noa, which is all the answer she needs.

Noa's whole body begins to shake from the cocktail of nerves and fear and ugly truth that turns you cold. "I'm pretty sure Charlie was cheating on me." Noa's voice wavers at the admission. I suspect this is the first time she's made this claim out loud. "Now I can't even ask him. Or catch him."

I slip my hands into the front of my sweatshirt and pull out two forks wrapped in paper napkins. I hand one to Noa. As I unwrap my fork, I tilt my head, signaling Noa to do the same, and she follows my lead. I dig right into the middle of my sweet potato pie and hold up a heaping bite. "Girl, there are no calories in grief pie, so you go on and dig in." Noa stabs the pie like it's Charlie. It seems real estate and shitty fate have brought the two of us together.

⌁

I stay outside until Noa is tucked back in her house, and then I race walk across my driveway so I can burn up the phone line with Judy. This tea is too hot to hold on my own.

"Hello." I can hear Judy fussing with something. She is not going to want to multitask through this conversation.

"Ohhhhh . . . wait until I tell you what I just witnessed." As I predict, the fussing stops.

"Kitchen's closed, and Phil's snoring back in the bedroom, so I got all night," Judy says, hungry for some entertainment.

"You know my neighbor with the dead husband?" I wait for Judy's "Uh-huh" before I get to telling.

"The po-po rolled up tonight." I draw out "po-po" so I really know I have Judy's attention.

"Whaaaaat?!" I bet Judy's jumped to my same conclusion: Noa killed Charlie. "Get the hell out of here—what happened?"

"When the officer got out of the car and started walking toward us—"

"Wait, what do you mean he started to walk 'toward us'?" I can feel Judy judging me for going over there this evening because she thinks I was trying to friend up.

"I was talking on my neighbor's porch for a few minutes about her daughter, who, remember, is in my class, when the officer walked up. I thought he was coming for me."

"Was he?" Judy blurts as if there's some big dark secret she doesn't know about me. If only my life were that interesting.

"Nah, he was there for Noa."

"No! What'd she do?"

I fill Judy in on all the details of what transpired with the keys and end with, "Turns out Noa's husband, Charlie, was a dirty dog just like Booker." Our exchange comes to a halt. I look at my phone to see if Judy accidentally hung up on me.

"You still there, Judy?"

"Please, Marjette, not another sad story about a woman and her man." Judy's voice has shifted from interested to irritated lightning fast. "You know misery loves company, and I'm here to tell you that you don't need that kind of company. What you need is to leave that woman alone to heal and to leave Booker in the rearview. Don't go getting pulled down into that woman's sadness."

Well, this isn't as fun as I thought. I pout alone in my living room. Judy's warning is a buzzkill, and that was some good gossip I delivered.

CHAPTER NINE

My school-day ritual is many years in the making and I detour for no one. Up at six thirty to get dressed, shake my son awake, twice, and make him a breakfast that would feed a family of five. I arrive at Houghton by seven thirty to park in the last spot of the southeast corner so no newly licensed knucklehead dings my Volvo. Depending on how the previous afternoon has gone, I finish any classroom setup or lesson planning that needs to be done to guarantee the students stay entertained until three. When the clock strikes eight, I make myself a coffee from the Keurig I keep tucked deep inside my supply closet and allow myself fifteen minutes to sip, scroll, and center before I have to turn it on for the rest of my day.

This last week I haven't been able to shake Noa's situation, wondering, between the two of us, who has it worse off—her with a dead cheater husband or me with an ex one who is very much alive. Would I want Booker dead if I could have him dead? That's a tough question and one that varies from day to day just like the weather. I wish Judy were still across the courtyard to confer if it's better Booker is alive than dead. Eh, I know her answer. Yawning, I load up the Keurig to power me through the day or at least until eleven o'clock.

Ding.

Dang. There's Booker in my text feed. It's like the man can sense when I'm wishing him ill.

Booker 8:06 AM

> Checking in to make sure Darius is in a good spot for his college boards coming up. I'd ask him but he'd just tell me he has it covered. Have you signed him up for an SAT prep class yet?

Look at Booker checking up on me to find out what I'm doing, or not doing, like we're still cool like that. He needs to mind his own business on what he does or doesn't do for his son and stay out of mine, especially when I've been doing it all for Darius this whole time. My thumbs are itching as I think how to respond.

Marjette 8:08 AM

> You know about the classes, have YOU signed him up?

Of course, I know all about the SAT prep classes. I work in a school, for God's sake. Who does Booker think he's telling? I want my ex to sweat over his son's future for a minute, so I pause before I hit "Send."

Booker 8:08 AM

> I'm just trying to look out for our son's education. I know you got it handled, I'm just checking.

Never mind me, you need to handle yourself, Booker Lewis. I stew, sipping my coffee with a superior slurp.

Marjette 8:09 AM

I'm glad you're checking in on your son, he's always needed his father.

With that dig, I put my phone away in my purse. I'm going to leave it at that. But then I pull my phone back out and add to my to-do list in the Notes app: Sign Darius up for SAT class. To calm my ire, I mindlessly scroll through the pictures on my phone and land on the one of Darius as the Tin Man in his fifth-grade production of *The Wizard of Oz*. That was about the time I should have realized Booker had no heart.

"Good morning, Marjette. I brought you these," Rachel singsongs as she struts into my classroom dropping a white bakery box, from its red ribbon, into my hand. Tabitha is tripping behind her mother to catch up.

"Hi, Ms. Lewith." Tabitha falls into my legs. My cotton skirt catches her head uncomfortably close to my crotch, but I give her an enveloping good-morning hug to ease both our embarrassment. Rachel is fidgeting in her big buckle ballet flats; I can tell she's dying to tell me something.

"Why don't you go hang up your backpack, Tabitha. Mr. Bigs hasn't been fed yet today. Would you like to do it?" Without confirmation, Tabitha sprints to put her stuff away and have the honor of feeding our class's one-pound chinchilla.

"I had Max Kopelman cater my breakfast meeting yesterday, and his pastries are to die for. Talk about serendipity, your class bringing the two of us together." What Rachel better not be bringing me is her leftovers. "Anytime you need something from the Bombshell Bar, you let me know. It's the least I can do for you." I got my hair cut and eyebrows tinted over the weekend and was sure I was slaying at the Houghton faculty meeting yesterday. But from the way Rachel is giving me the top-to-toe once-over, I guess I felt wrong amid the sea of infinity scarves and Dansko clogs.

"Char, Char." Rachel beckons, waving her bestie over from a coffee-clutching mom posse. Char scurries over, eager to be in on Rachel's fuss. "I was just telling Marjette about the kismet of me and Max landing in her class together." It looks like Char's working hard to sort out what *kismet* means while Rachel's pleased with herself for throwing out some Yiddish, only, even I know *kismet* isn't Yiddish. Oy, Rachel, you can be such a schmuck.

"Didn't we have the best time when we swung by Max's bakery the other day to sample his treats? Meant to stay for five, but we were there for an hour." Rachel holds her palm up to me, spreading her five fingers. There's a pause among the three of us while it registers with Char that this is the moment she's supposed to enthusiastically agree with Rachel's assessment of their time spent with Max.

"I might even guess Max was trying to keep you there, Rachel, the way he was going on and on about how he could help you cater your event," Char recounts, spoon-feeding Rachel exactly what she wants to hear. It's all I can do not to upend Rachel's fairy tale by explaining that Max was probably trying to land a corporate account, being a new business and all.

Rachel grins approvingly at Char for adding to her narrative. "Everything was so delicious yesterday I had to stop by this morning and thank Max for his hard work." Rachel and Char glance at each other like they're holding a secret, one that takes no mental giant to figure out. Rachel did not show up at Max's bakery's doorstep this morning for the gratitude; she showed up because she's thirsty.

"I got Tabitha a croque monsieur for her lunch today and a vegetable quiche for you, Marjette. I figure you can heat it up in the faculty room microwave for lunch." I can tell Rachel wants a star sticker for her generosity.

"Thank you so much for thinking of me, Rachel. I'm glad to hear Max is treating his customers well." I dig just an inch. Rachel cocks her head, trying to figure out if I've delivered a slight or a compliment.

"Oh, Marjette, this is so ridiculous of me, going on and on in front of you about the parents in your classroom, like you would even be interested in our personal lives. If I've been talking out of turn, please forgive me, but you know how it is since you're a single woman like me."

I am nothing like her, I want noted, but opt to continue pretending to hang on Rachel's words because, in truth, the personal lives of families in my classroom are one of my favorite topics.

". . . finding someone who you like and well"—Rachel drops into a low whisper again. I guess she doesn't want Tabitha to hear her mommy's out shopping for her new daddy—"he's giving you indications the feelings are mutual. With news like that, it's hard not to broadcast it to the world. Am I right?"

I leave Rachel's verbal high five hanging in the air. I know Max did not sign up to be the unwitting uncle pulled into the kindergarten cougar lair. But what I also know is that men like Max love women like Rachel. It's their beauty and their bank account, particularly if that man's been struggling to find his path, according to his sister. Plus, I'm pretty sure Rachel's a member of Max's tribe, so they're practically doing the hora.

"Well, whatever it is you're working toward, I hope it happens for you," I muster with zero sincerity and pray Rachel can't tell. My artificial wish lands on deaf ears.

"Char, let's take the kids by the bakery Saturday after the soccer game. Three days between visits isn't too obvious, is it?" Rachel turns and asks Char, not at all interested in my take on her stalking strategy. I'm torn whether I should step in and save a fellow single mom from her stupid self or let her learn her own lessons. I opt for teaching a woman to fish by letting her flounder.

Quiche is one of my weekday meals to make, and I consider my recipe to be the gold standard, so I wasn't set to be impressed by Max's attempt at it. Only two bites into the loaded vegetable quiche and I can't shake the fact that there's something unique in Max's recipe I'm not privy to. A few more bites with my trained palate trying to figure out the hidden flavor and I'm still stumped. Not being able to suss the mystery ingredient out, I know my curiosity and competitive spirit in the kitchen will have me in Max's bakery by four, four thirty at the latest. I hurry my kids out of the classroom at three fifteen and shove twenty Family Tree and Me projects in my bag to review and comment on after dinner.

I make it to Flour + Butter a few minutes past four, but the CLOSED sign is up on the door. A picture of Max waving bye-bye as he walks away from the Eiffel Tower, his backpack overflowing with baguettes, reads FERMÉ. I'm curious what his OPEN sign looks like. I huddle out of the rain under the cornflower-blue awning of the bakery, not sure what to do with myself now that I have a free afternoon. I text Darius to see what he's up to. All I get back is:

Darius 4:03 PM

with Simone

Tap. Tap. Tap.
I jump, startling a couple passing by on the sidewalk.
Tap. Tap. Tap.
I look behind me and Max is waving from one of the shop's bay windows, where he's pulling in a tray of confections for the evening. I wave back, not sure what to do next. Does he think his niece's teacher was randomly passing by so he politely waved, or does he want me to come in? I'm frozen on the sidewalk contemplating Max's flick of his wrist.

"Would you like to come in and look around?" Max asks, pulling the door open so I can duck in from the rain. A bell rings above his head, and I take the welcoming sound as a sign.

I spy a whole row of quiches in the case behind him, so yes, I would like to come in and snoop around. "Sure, I have a minute," I reply as casually as a competitive cook can muster.

I pass by Max and take a big whiff; the smell from the tray he's holding is a nutty, chocolate, cinnamon aromatic perfection. "Would you like a rugalach?" Max winks, popping a chocolate ruga-thingy into his mouth like it's a piece of popcorn. Find me a grown woman who doesn't wish she had the metabolism of a man and could carelessly pop butter and dough and look like, well, like that. We'd all be eating the inventory too. The thick, dark, wavy hair I'm used to seeing on Max is tucked under a green knitted skullcap, a few wayward curls peeking out over his ears. There's a mole to the left of his mouth right where his cheek meets his chin. It looks like a forgotten chocolate crumb that any woman, specifically Rachel I think, would want to lick off given the chance.

I stare at the tray and do the mental math of how long it would take me to work off a thousand PersonalPoints. I lick my lips in anticipation of the chocolaty sugar explosion in my mouth but hesitate to try one, or ten.

"Don't you like what you see?" Max asks, shaking the tray, catching me in my daydream. Thank goodness Black is the best camouflage for beet red or Max would be staring at a full-blown blush. I grab one treat and pop it in my mouth to keep myself from saying something stupid.

Heaven coats my taste buds.

Max heads to the kitchen in the back of the shop with his tray, leaving me alone for a moment to chew and fixate on the quiches. I lean over the counter to see if I can spy any unusual spices sitting on the cook's island.

I'm eye level with a potato-and-leek deep-dish quiche that would definitely step up my Wednesday dinner game when Max strolls back in, taking his rightful spot behind the counter.

"Everything looks beyond tempting. I bet your customers have a hard time picking just one thing to try," I say, eyes darting between the quiches, almond croissants, and braided challah.

"If you see anything that tempts you, feel free to come behind the counter and take a bite," Max offers. Looking through the glass casement past the patisseries, I realize I'm face-to-face with his junk.

I stand abruptly. "I don't think your other customers would appreciate me nibbling on all your baked goods. Not the least bit sanitary, and I work with five-year-olds, so you know my germ awareness is deep."

"Ahh, I guess you're right," Max admits, looking disappointed. I don't want him to think I don't want two of everything in his shop, but I also don't want him to get the impression I'm only here for the free food. I can pay my own way. "Maybe there's one specific item back here I can get for you?" Max stretches, and his shirt rises above the waist of his pants, exposing a toned, hairless stomach.

Now I'm confused, or maybe I'm out of practice talking with men my age. Are we still talking about baked goods, or are we talking about something else? Looking at Max and then catching my reflection in the glass, I get a grip on myself.

"Listen, Max." I shift, back to the business of baking. "Rachel Ellis brought me one of your mini loaded-vegetable quiches for lunch today. It was so delicious I had to come by and pick up a full-size one for me and my son, Darius, to split." Nothing like the mention of a teenage son to set a conversation straight. "And hopefully find out what magic you have in there that I can't quite put my finger on. Usually, I can name a flavor in three bites or less, but you've stumped me on this one."

"Marjette, I'm surprised at you." Max laughs, shaking a finger at me like I'm in trouble. "Do you go sharing the secrets of your fried chicken with the world?" I want to tell him that in fact I do. I leave my recipe wherever I take my food, because I want the person I'm sharing my dish with to taste mine, make their own, and know mine's better.

When it comes to the kitchen, I'm Serena Williams–level competitive. This is the first time I've come across someone other than Auntie Shay who's able to best one of my recipes.

"Fine. Seems just like my kindergarteners, you don't like to share." Maybe I can appeal to Max's willingness to divulge his technique if not his ingredients. "Tell me about the basics, then; the things that aren't a secret."

"I'm left-handed, a Taurus, and I hate it when books are adapted into movies and people don't read the book first," Max says with a sexy smirk.

"I was thinking more along the lines of do you use whole milk or heavy cream as your base?"

Max grins at me, flipping the towel left on the counter over his shoulder. "Come on, Marjette, you know there's nothing better than heavy cream. It's the only way to go." I agree, but from the way Max answered my question again, I'm not sure we are talking about the same thing.

"Okay, then. What about the crust? How do you get the edges so even and neat? Every time I shape my pie edges, my fingers get stuck to the dough and ruin the scalloped pattern. How do you do it?" Without coming right out and admitting it, I have just laid out my cooking weakness, crusts. I might as well be standing here butt-ass naked.

Max leans his elbows on the counter, invading my space with his broad shoulders, causing me to retreat back a step. "Two words: wet fingers," he draws out, locking in on my eyes. "Make sure you use cold water to keep your fingers moist, and then the dough won't stick as much," Max says, punctuating his advice with a click of his tongue and a side smile.

Now I know why Rachel likes it here so much. I can barely breathe talking about pie crust. Ripe with the possibility of misinterpretation, I've got to get out of here before I embarrass myself thinking this man is talking about anything other than food.

～

Carole is cutting in on my conversation with Judy, yammering on about how hydration and sleep are two of the three pillars of weight loss. No one wants to admit that starvation is the third. Paul brags that he sleeps eight hours a night and he's lost twenty pounds. I lose weight in my sleep, too, when nothing's going into my mouth. It's the daylight hours that really trip me up.

"I gotta tell you about Max and his cooking."

"Who's Max?"

"The uncle I told you about. Remember he showed up late on the first day of school to pick up his niece with the dead dad. My neighbor's kid."

"Right, right. I remember. Whew. I thought maybe Max was a new code name for Booker," Judy says, but I see she's totally distracted from the pillars and my pursuit of happiness. "What do you think of that jacket the new woman, Nancy, has?" Judy asks, pulling off her readers so she can see distance. Lucky for us, newbie Nancy is busy reading the recipe card for curried lentil casserole, today's party favor. I look at the woman sitting next to me and wonder where she's hiding my friend Judy.

"Are we here to watch our weight or to watch people?" I tease.

"Both."

"I thought you were too busy mourning school to think about fashion. Since when did you become a woman who wears animal prints?" I demand from Judy, whose favorite color is navy.

"I had a few rough days in there missing my old life, but I'm over it, and I've moved on to the new. And new me needs to freshen up my old look." Judy gives me a little shimmy. I feel queasy.

"You don't need a fresh look," I huff, trying to imagine Judy in the leopard-print swing coat currently thrown over Nancy's substantial shoulders. "I thought when you're middle aged, you need to find a signature look and stick with it." Judy's look has always been office conservative.

Judy ignores my pissing-on-her-style parade. "I don't own any casual clothing. I can't be wearing a pantsuit to my tap classes with Phil. Savion Glover doesn't want to heel-step with a woman in a polyester-and-rayon blend."

"What are you talking about?!" I whisper, though it comes out more of a strained scream. The woman on her phone directly in front of me turns around to shame us. I give her a look that says, *Please, you're on your phone. We're each doing what we gotta do to get through these thirty minutes.*

Judy pulls the end of a shoebox out of her oversize purse so I can read the label: Capezio. "Phil and I wanted to try something new together since, for the first time in forty years, I'm not raising kids or running a school. We landed on tap lessons." Judy gives me a little ball change on the tile flooring.

"In this scenario is Phil supposed to be Savion Glover?" I ask, stifling a laugh. "Don't you come crying to me when you pull a groin doing a fan kick at your age." Judy tosses her hand at me like I don't know what I'm talking about.

"So, we're going to have to cut our coffees a bit short on Saturdays now. Phil wants us to get some practice in each week before class starts."

"Tell Mr. Bojangles that Saturdays are our time! I joined Weight Watchers with you because I knew you'd need to see me at least once a week. I'm helping you keep something the same in your retirement." Judy and Carole both give me the stink eye to lower my voice. I shrink in my seat.

"Are you sure it's not the other way around?" Judy whispers, raising her left eyebrow like she already knows the answer. "Carpe diem, Marjette. It's a new day." Judy nudges me and gives me one more chair ball change. She can't possibly be studying Latin too.

"It's our favorite time of the meeting, when we get to share our #NonScaleVictory!" Carole cheers, making an actual hashtag with the index and middle fingers of both hands. I'm pretty sure no one under forty does that. Nonscale victories are a marketing tactic to ensure that people who don't lose weight on the program still feel good about themselves and continue to pay their dues.

Judy moves to the edge of her seat and raises her hand. What's she doing? We agreed never to participate! "I'm feeling so vibrant these days, my husband and I decided to take up tap." The room erupts in golf claps, and I'm forced to reluctantly celebrate Judy's nonscale victory along with the rest of the group.

At our quick coffee after Weight Watchers, everything feels different. Judy orders her latte and tries to coax out information about Max and his bakery. Now it just feels like she's killing time with me until meeting Phil for tap practice. I know Judy is always there to talk to me about anything as long as it isn't related to Booker, but my adventures in crust making hardly seem groundbreaking next to Judy's late-in-life turn at vaudeville. I slump in my chair and pout as Judy sips her coffee across from me, not giving in to my childish behavior. She has toed this line with real children more times than either of us can count.

"Oh, Marjette, stop screwing up your face. I'm just shufflin' off to Buffalo. I'm not moving there," Judy chides.

"Same thing!" I insist to my best friend's back as she heads out the door.

CHAPTER TEN

"Clean up, clean up, everybody everywhere!" My students don't appreciate my gospel choir training from the First Baptist church in Tulsa, but they will when they get to first grade—those teachers are tone deaf. "Clean up, clean up, everybody do your share." If I got paid for every time I've sung that song, I'd be sipping cocktails in Aruba and enjoying my time-share.

The kids know when I sing the "Clean Up" song, they're supposed to stop, drop, and listen. Today's master manipulation tool to get my classroom tidied up is Clean by the Clock. If all the objects we've pulled out from the shelves are put away in five minutes or less, we will have time to play Telephone, a solid training game today for tomorrow's gossiping on the playground. What you think you heard not always being what was said is a truth every person needs to learn.

My students turn into Tasmanian devils, flying in all directions to beat the old-fashioned kitchen timer that is ticking down on my desk. Every item is being picked up quickly, but I know as soon as the end of day comes, I'm going to have to flip the books spines out, re-sort blocks by color, and check that all the markers have matching caps. Esty's dragging her feet so slowly around the room, several children almost bowl her over, but she doesn't seem to notice. Pushing in a chair appears to take all her energy, and it pains me to witness this apparent ongoing manifestation of her grief. She has fallen asleep during story time, opted out of games of tag at recess, and refused to walk at the zoo. All kids at this age live on a speed of ten, their exuberance extra for all there is to explore in their world. Since the first day of school, I don't think I have seen Esty kick it up past four.

With twenty-two seconds to spare, I declare my class winners, and we circle up for my promised prize of Telephone. We're going to have to talk quick—I hear parents gathering outside the door.

I have always told my families that when there are challenges at home and their child may be struggling, they do not need to divulge details. They can simply email or whisper, "handle with care," at drop-off and I will know, on that particular day, their child needs some extra love and attention. My newest fragile friend is Levi, so I place him on my left and Esty on my right. I turn to Levi to hear what message he's going to pass around. If I don't check first, this game always ends up rife with messages of butts and farts. Levi's lips come uncomfortably close to the side of my head. Lacking a built-in shield is an occupational hazard of a short haircut. With his spittle spraying into my ear, Levi shares behind his hand, "I want to kiss my cat." Lucky for Levi, that message works at five years old. I pray he's not whispering that same message into a woman's ear at twenty-eight and calling it foreplay.

Like clockwork, every time the message gets to Tabitha, she collapses into giggles, the words tickling her ear. I then remind her to sit back up and keep the game moving. When the message comes around the circle to Esty, she turns to me in slow-mo and whispers, "I really miss my dad."

"I want to kiss my cat," I announce to the circle. Levi looks at me in utter disbelief that his message made it around the circle intact. Knowing even on his toughest days Levi's inner competitor runs deep, I give him a nod, and he hops up to run a victory lap around his classmates. While his friends cheer him on, I put my hand on Esty's criss-crossed legs and give her a pat to acknowledge her words.

My classroom is nearly empty since most of my students have been picked up. The volume has been turned way down as only Deja and Esty remain, talking quietly while piled atop the beanbag. Deja sees her mom walk in and begins her ritual of hugging goodbye anyone still in the classroom as if she won't be back again first thing in the morning.

"Bye, Ms. Lewis, this was the best day ever!" Deja proclaims, throwing herself into my arms. Apparently today was better than yesterday, which was also her best day ever. Before bounding over to her mother, Deja runs back to Esty and hugs her by the neck, pausing to ask, "Are you leaving now too?"

Esty stiffens. "Yes, I'm just waiting for my daddy to come." Deja accepts Esty's fiction as fact. Meanwhile, my heart burns at Esty's not-so-little white lie. I know this is not uncommon for a child experiencing parental loss, but her listlessness and lack of engagement in class, topped by this latest claim that she's waiting for her dead father to come pick her up, is too much. I don't want to take this child by herself to the after-school program one more time, but I have to.

On my way home, I swing by the store for taco fixings. Esty's been consuming my thoughts, and I'm not in the mood to go gourmet tonight. I don't like putting my bad mood into my food. Pulling up to my house, I feel my attitude go from bad to real funky when I notice Simone's car parked in my spot. I honk once, my signal to Darius to come help me with the bags. I watch the door; no one's coming.

Leaving the groceries in the trunk, I head into the house and find an empty living room. There's no noise coming from the kitchen, so I know they're not rummaging through the fridge or pantry. I take off my shoes, so my footsteps aren't detectable, and follow the low hum of music down the hallway. That child better have his door wide open. It's not, not even a little. Gripping the doorframe, I suck in a deep breath through clenched teeth and pray, *Jesus take the wheel*, and don't let me kill the fast-tailed girl behind this door. I'm prepared to take down my own child, but I don't want to hurt somebody else's.

I bust in, expecting the worst, and find Simone sprawled across Darius's bed fully clothed but way too comfortable. Darius pops up out of his desk chair, his chemistry textbook tumbling to the floor. "Mom, you're home!" Darius exclaims like he's surprised to find that I live here.

"Yes, I am, and your door's closed," I point out, giving both kids an intimidating glare. "We don't have company behind closed doors in this house," I remind Darius like it's one of the Ten Commandments. "It's time to show your little friend home. And on your way back in, get the groceries out of my car."

I stand at the door as Simone gathers her books, Darius holding open her messenger bag to hustle her along. I notice she's taking AP Calc as a junior. As Darius rushes Simone past me, she sheepishly says, "Nice to see you again, Ms. Lewis."

"Mm-hmm," I respond, folding my arms. "Good night, Simone." Those kids scurry to the front door like they can feel my eyeballs burning their backs.

Darius drops the groceries on the kitchen counter; I knew he wouldn't forget. "You know the rules. Why was that door closed?"

"Nothing was happening, Ma, we were just studying," Darius attempts to explain. "Dad doesn't embarrass me when Simone comes to his house." Since when does Darius bring friends over to Booker's house? He's barely ever there. "And Simone's parents trust us."

"I don't care about the rules at anyone else's house." They should all match mine anyway; at least Booker's should. "I pay the cost to be the boss." Darius lets out a put-upon sigh like he's tired of hearing, again, about who's in charge. "Are we clear?"

Expecting a "yes, ma'am," instead I'm met with my child puffing his chest and throwing his shoulders back as if he might defy me. That's not a good idea.

Before this gets too heated, I let Darius off the hook. "Put those groceries away. I'm heading outside to check on my garden." We both need to take it down a notch.

Out here sweating while angry gardening, my brain ping-pongs back and forth between Esty and Darius. Hands deep in the soil, it hits me. I have a solution to both of today's concerns. With spring and summer baseball season over, Darius has less to do in fall and winter. And what I don't want him doing is Simone. I've been bothered by Esty's long hours at school since day one but didn't have any helpful suggestions for Noa, so I kept my mouth shut. Now I do.

A couple of days a week, I'll keep Esty in my classroom with me. I'm pretty sure holding on to one of your students is against company policy, but I'm a teacher, and we don't get fired. I'm going to ask Noa to hire Darius to babysit Esty after school a few days a week. I'll offer to go halfsies on the salary with Noa, as it's a win-win. She gets a happier child, and my son does not become a baby daddy.

After I talk to Noa, I'll inform Darius about his new arrangement. If he wants to continue to date Simone, he needs to be doing something constructive with his after-school time. If she wants to tag along it's fine with me, because taking care of a kindergartener is effective birth control. I dust my hands off and practically skip over to Noa's house, my idea so brilliant there's no better time to start than now. Darius thinks he's starting to run things around this house; we gonna see.

"Hi, Noa, I know it's almost dinnertime, so I'll make this quick," I say a bit too efficiently as the door swings open, so I soften my greeting with a broad smile.

"Dinner just went in the oven, so I've got time. Why don't you come in and have a drink?" Noa invites, leading me to her kitchen island before I can refuse. I know what White women mean when they offer a weekday drink. Rosé isn't my favorite, but I don't want to be inconsiderate.

"Only if you're having one," I agree, unsure of how comfortable I should get my first time in the Abramses' house since the shiva.

"Oh, I'm having a drink," Noa says, holding up a tumbler of whiskey. "Two fingers or three?" Surprised by Noa's choice in cocktail, I know if Auntie Shay were alive, she would definitely be making herself right at home, but Grandma Birdie would be shaking her head, *Oh no you don't.*

"How 'bout three; it's been that kind of day," I confess and pull out a counter stool, appreciating that Noa doesn't flinch. I'm also appreciating that my neighbor owns a ratty sweatshirt just like the stack I have in my closet.

"Did you go to Yeshiva University?" I ask, pointing to the logo across Noa's chest.

Noa looks down and runs her hands over her front side. "Oh, no. Charlie did." I recognize that sad-wife pining-for-the-past expression way too well. I wore Booker's University of Oklahoma Alpha Phi Alpha fraternity sweatshirt for six months straight after he left and probably would have kept on wearing it, but then he emailed and asked me to pack it in Darius's overnight bag.

"I've never heard of it. Where is it?" Working in a K–12 private school with a son about to hit the college application scene, I'm pretty well versed in what's out there, but this university is new to me.

"It's in New York City. It's like an HBCU for Jews, but not as cool." Well shock me silly. I can't believe this snowflake knows what a historically Black college is! Noa looks up from chopping celery to see if her joke landed. We both bust out laughing.

Before I can ask Noa if that's where she met Charlie, Esty barrels into the kitchen clutching a stuffed bunny and a battered book.

"Esty, look who's here," Noa says, brightly. Esty drops her toys and stares slack jawed like she's never seen me before.

I bend down to pick up the bunny and book, and Esty skeptically inquires, "What are you doing in my house?"

"Esty, Ms. Lewis is our neighbor; I've told you that," Noa reminds her daughter in that strained voice moms use when their kid has just mortified them.

"Yeah, but I didn't think she really lived there."

"Well, where did you think I live?" I ask but know the answer from years of experience.

"School," Esty huffs as if stating the obvious. Noa and I both share a laugh for the second time tonight. "I have to go read to my bunny; are you going to be here for dinner?"

"You're more than welcome to stay, Marjette. It's just the two of us," Noa offers, but this time I politely decline. I don't trust a skinny chef.

"I do want to talk to you about something, though." At the mention of grown-up talk, Esty shuffles back out of the kitchen.

"Is this about how Esty's doing in school?"

Well, it kind of is, but that's not how I'm going to present my idea to Noa. "Actually, this is more a mom-to-mom thing. It involves our kids and how we can help each other out."

"Let's hear it because God knows I need all the help I can get with Charlie gone." This is refreshing, a fellow mom admitting her shortcomings. Noa's not even attempting to hide her struggle.

"I need a way to keep my son from having sex."

"And I'm supposed to help you how?" Noa asks, taking an extra-long pull on her drink. I forgot she's not at this stage of the child-rearing process yet when you have to admit that your child's sex life may be surpassing yours.

"Darius has a girlfriend. Simone."

"Ah. And from the way you said her name, I gather you don't like her."

"It's not that I don't like her. I don't like the idea of her naked with my son. After school, they need something to occupy their time—other than each other." Noa's raised glass signals that she gets what I'm implying and why I need help. "I was thinking after school Darius could babysit Esty." I can tell Noa is thinking on it and running the numbers in her head since she's down an income. "We can split the cost of paying him since we'd both be getting something out of it."

"Wow, that's an incredible offer. I know these long days at school have been exhausting Esty," Noa admits. I'm so glad Noa can see what I didn't want to have to tell her. "When do you want to start?"

I kick back the last finger of my drink and ask Noa pointedly, "Is yesterday too soon?"

"Not for Esty—she hates having to stay late at school. Though they're only so often, Esty's best days are the ones when Max can get her." I know it's true; Esty becomes a different child when Max shows up.

"I don't want to step on anyone's toes with my plan. I see how much Esty loves her uncle's company." As do Rachel and the other members of her coffee klatch.

"Oh, my brother will adjust to a new plan just fine. He's always been a consummate single guy with all the selfishness that entails." I'm going to stay silent here and hope the whiskey will keep Noa's tongue loose about her life. "I'm not sure having your niece hang around is working well with the bachelor persona Max has so carefully curated over the years." Noa shakes her head, leading me to believe she may be fed up with her brother.

"So, has Max always been single?" I ask casually, checking my phone for an I-don't-care-either-way effect.

"Among other things. My brother's been an EMT, a trekking guide in Nepal, a rabbinical student for about a minute"—Noa's counting off Max's occupations on her fingers like she doesn't want to forget one—"and now a baker. I might have missed one or two callings in there somewhere." Noa puts *callings* in quotes to make sure I catch her sarcasm.

"He seems pretty serious about the bakery thing," I offer to give Max a little credit with his older sister, "and pretty talented at it too." I can't imagine Max is truly as noncommittal as Noa is making him out to be. Owning your own business, particularly in the food industry, is a major risk. One I'd never had the guts to take.

"Maybe. Who knows? Let's just say, if you had spent two years and all your savings on pastry school in France, not bothering to come home once, then you'd better have a plan to do something with that education, don't you think?" Noa insists, topping off her drink. "Most of my life my primary job has been supporting all of Max's dreams, and then worrying about him when they didn't work out. I adore him, everyone does, ever since we were babies, but I can't do it anymore. It was one thing when we were kids, and when Charlie was here, we would tag team so someone was always available if Max needed a hand, or bail." Noa swiftly wipes a rogue tear that's escaped her eye. "Just kidding on the bail thing. But now that I'm Esty's only stabilizing force—not to mention I'm on my own shaky foundation—I'm not sure I can continue taking care of Max also. I want to see that man grow up and settle down." I know a thing or two about a grown man acting like a child, and I'm very familiar with my child, who desperately wants to be a man.

CHAPTER ELEVEN

I'm so proud of myself. The whole time Noa and I were in her kitchen discussing babysitting arrangements, I could see the silver *M* key chain Officer Nichols delivered hanging on a hook, almost begging me to ask about it. Even though it's been a month of success in what I've dubbed Operation Population Control, with Esty as my strategically placed third wheel to Darius and Simone, I have yet to pester Noa about the keys. If Judy were in front of me, I'd do an end zone dance and cheer, "Look who's doing the changing now, Judy!"

Esty and Darius's time together has gone better than I would have ever expected. Darius, it turns out, has impressive patience with arts and crafts, and his stand-up easel skills are still strong all these years past his finger-painting days.

The night we made the mutual childcare arrangement, I asked Noa to email me a brief but formal letter, complete with her signature, stating that Darius is in fact in charge of Esty from the hours of three thirty to six thirty. Noa waved off my request with a "Don't worry about it, Marjette. I trust you and Darius. You're Esty's teacher and Darius is your son." I let Noa talk and dismiss my words as nonsense, but then I had to be straight with her about why it was necessary, and it had nothing to do with our mutual trust. It was Darius who needed something official to prove to anyone who questioned on buses, at playgrounds, in stores, or anywhere public that he was Esty's caregiver. A Black teenage boy with a White female child invites questioning looks from much of society, and those suspicions could be dangerous to both children. As I explained myself, Noa's cheeks grew more and more red, heating up with embarrassment or shame at her ignorance. I didn't want Noa to feel some type of way, but I did want her to understand that this is reality and my son's need for protection.

Darius is enjoying taking Esty to the Jewish Community Center to teach her to shoot hoops. According to Darius, when Esty is standing on his shoulders, her dunking game is on point. Extra bonus for my son, Max promised free snacks for the both of them whenever Darius is willing to bring Esty by Flour + Butter. When Max made his suggestion, I don't think he realized that food is as good as currency to a teenage boy. That man is saving me about fifteen dollars a day in groceries.

The first week into our childcare deal, Noa had to work late, so I offered to have Esty join me and Darius for dinner. Claiming she hated the idea of putting me through the extra trouble, Noa tried to refuse, but I wouldn't let her. Another child around my table to eat my food and light up the dining room is my version of bliss.

By the time Noa got home to pick Esty up, we were just sitting down to dinner, and that woman looked worn out. I could see in her hunched shoulders and drawn face that she wasn't sleeping well. Perhaps Charlie was visiting in her dreams and not in a good way. I took Noa's coat and bag and pushed her toward a seat at the table. Darius, Esty, and I kept the conversation going, but Noa didn't pick up her fork. It took all my strength to resist spoon-feeding her like a baby bird. Luckily, Esty didn't seem to notice her mother's demeanor at the table, too captivated by Darius's dead-on impersonations of Oscar the Grouch. I hoped it wasn't her worry over the letter we wrote for the kids. We had discussed our regret that our children needed a "passport" of sorts to operate freely in the world. Observing Noa now, however, her mind seemed distracted by the past, struggling to live in the present.

From that evening forward, without the need for predetermined plans, weekly dinners at my house were confirmed. Noa's acquisitions meetings at Golden Gate Books were always Thursday late afternoon and had the potential to run long, so I got dinner going for the four of us. I had to work extra hard not to be insulted by the small portions Noa pushed around her plate and to remember that some women eat their feelings while others starve them out. All in all, it felt like a gift having warm bodies in the room and a new friend to listen to me trash-talk my ex. Noa served as my sounding board after several difficult parenting exchanges with Booker that circled around the topic of Darius's budding manhood and relentless push for independence. Booker sees Darius as a man. I see my son as a boy who has some maturing to do before he ventures too far from home. After dinner, when Esty and Darius have gone off to play Sorry (exhibit A, still a boy), my re-creations of Booker's and my conversations entertain Noa, giving her a reprieve from whatever thoughts crowd her mind. On these nights I don't probe; I choose to only be here for Noa and Esty.

"Yum, what smells so delicious?" Noa calls, coming in my front door. I hear her exhale a loud sigh. My guess is she's released her feet from those impossibly high heels she runs around in all day. My feet haven't been in a pair of those since the last holiday party I attended at Booker's medical practice. Of all the things I miss as the female half of a whole couple, pinched toes are not one of them.

"Look what I brought." Noa waves hello with a bottle of Riesling. I knew eventually lady wine would make its way into one of our get-togethers. While I prefer beer with my gumbo, lucky for Noa, Riesling pairs pretty well too.

Ding.

Judy 6:32 PM

Is tonight date night? AGAIN.

Though I'd never say it to her, I think Judy's a little jealous I've been spending time getting to know Noa. Not being able to say "I told you so" with her prediction that this budding friendship would go south before it had a chance to take off is messing with Judy's head. So is not being a part of things.

Marjette 6:32 PM

Would you like to come over?

Three. Two. One. I say out loud what I know I'm about to read.

Judy 6:33 PM

I wouldn't want to impose.

Marjette 6:33 PM

Yes, you would.

Judy 6:33 PM

Read but no reply. Okay, Judy. I see how you want to play it. And I'll play along because I love you, old lady.

Marjette 6:34 PM

Come over and you can meet Noa and Esty.

Judy 6:35 PM

Be there in ten.

Today is the first day I've seen Noa's blonde hair out of a smooth ponytail, down and free flowing. Gliding through my kitchen looking for wineglasses, Noa's wearing my preferred jewel tones, an emerald-green cashmere sweater and fuchsia pleated skirt. A marked departure from her muted wardrobe of the past few months, I notice. Tired is still stamped across her face, but I'm witnessing her body starting to move with a hint of renewed energy.

While I'm finishing texting with Judy, Noa grabs a spoon out of my utensil drawer and is dipping it into my gumbo on the stove. Not that long ago, Noa couldn't lift a spoon—the weight of it seemingly too much—but today she's diving in before the dinner bell.

"How about some music, Marjette?" Noa suggests, between slurps. I'm not even going to correct her violation of Black folks' kitchen rules of not sticking your spoon in pots before the food hits your plate. That's how relieved I am to observe Noa's attempt to relax and make herself at home.

"Sure," I answer cautiously, knowing even the heightened noise of dinner-table chatter in the past has rattled her. Plus, I'm not sure I have soothing classical on my playlist.

"Do you have any Public Enemy?" Noa asks, hopeful, backing away from my pot.

Do I have any what?! I have to grab the kitchen counter to steady myself from the shock of her request. Judy has got to come quick to witness this because she certainly wouldn't believe it if I told her. I need to figure out a way to subtly confirm what I think I just heard.

"You sure you don't want to listen to the Beastie Boys?" I can't stop myself from suggesting. So much for subtle.

"Ah, I see, the Jews of rap." Noa raises her Riesling to me. "Touché. But I'd rather fight the power tonight. *Loudly.*"

Is this woman for real? "Alexa, play Public Enemy, 'Fight the Power,'" I command, giving Noa what she wants. "Volume three."

Noa looks at me like she's profoundly disappointed. "Alexa, volume eight," Noa overarticulates in the speaker's direction. Does she not remember we have neighbors?

Just as the lyrics kick in, Darius enters the kitchen, imitating hype-man moves—high kneed, pimp walking to the bass. Esty follows, trying to keep up with Darius's dance steps, but is thrown off beat by the giggles. Noa may have dialed the music up to eight, but Darius has dialed the Blackness up to ten. Soul food, rap music, and street dancing—have we laid our realness on too thick for this mainstream mom? I guess we're going to find out one way or another because it's about to be a scene.

I barely hear Judy ring the doorbell over Noa and Darius spitting bars at the tops of their lungs, neither of them actually on pitch. And how in the world does Noa know all the lyrics? I can't wait for Judy to walk in and witness this mash-up of Torah and tabernacle.

Before I can even offer to take Judy's coat, she's admonishing, "I could hear the bass before I even turned up the driveway. What're you doing to this poor woman?" Of course, Judy assumes this is my fault; no point telling her I had the music appropriately set for a doctor's waiting room. "And you have neighbors."

"Hold tight to your wig when you enter the kitchen. It's like a Pentecostal revival in here." Judy gives me a look like she's seen it all in her sixty-six years, but I'm fairly certain she hasn't seen this.

With the house thumping, Judy and I come up on Darius doing the stanky leg and Noa shaking a booty she most definitely does not have. If Reverend Avery back in Oklahoma witnessed all this secular music, body wiggling, and my son shaking the house with a Jewish woman, that would be three sins I would be damned to hell for. Good thing Reverend Avery's dead. To catch her shock, Judy focuses on what's most familiar to her, a little girl jumping around in delight. Esty bopping around in glee is about the only normal thing going on in my kitchen tonight.

Noa catches Judy out of the corner of her eye and pauses her gyrations to compose herself. I take the break in this dance party as my cue to make introductions. "Noa, this is Judy Oliphant, one of my closest friends and the past head of the Houghton School. She retired at the end of the last school year, much to my dismay."

In a way only I can tell, Noa ever so slightly pulls back into her shell at the mention of last year. "Nice to meet you, Judy. My husband and I actually met you last winter during admissions. Our daughter, Esty, is now in Marjette's class," Noa explains, not knowing that Judy's aware of every detail of her saga. Judy and I give each other a quick glance, hearing Noa slip back into the familiar pattern of speaking as if she were part of a couple. Public Enemy gave her a momentary reprieve from her real-life enemy—heartache.

The master of redirection, Judy seamlessly changes topics. "You all look like you're having fun in here. Marjette, you've never once asked me over for a dance party. I guess this is a young-folks thing." Noa gives Judy a soft laugh, but I know Judy's delivered a double dig, calling out my manners and my supposed ageism.

"Judy, we're so happy to have you here. Come on in and join us; dinner's almost ready," I say, not wanting Noa to be made uncomfortable by our teasing nature. I've never seen Noa with other mothers at Houghton. She does her best not to be pulled into conversation, so I don't know, other than my experiences with her, what her communication style is like with other women.

"Oh my gosh, Judy, you have to come sneak a taste of Marjette's gumbo. I already swiped a couple of spoonfuls from the pot," Noa compliments me and waves Judy over to the stove before she steers Esty off to wash her hands.

Judy whips her head in my direction, shooting daggers with her eyes, and hisses, "You've never once let me taste out of the pot! Why's this woman so special?"

I whisper back, "How's she supposed to know Black people's kitchen rules? I'm not going to slap her hand, are you?" Judy stands silent like she's thinking. "Anyway, you know better, so don't go touching my gumbo," I warn before Noa and Esty return from the bathroom.

Judy leans in like she's going for the pot, but then pulls back, faking me out. "Please, race has nothing to do with house manners. Obviously, you think this woman's friend material, but I'm gonna see for myself. Noa," she singsongs, brushing past me, "why don't you sit down right here for dinner." Two chairs are pulled out across from me.

"Thanks, Judy, that's nice of you. Can I get you a glass of Riesling before I do?"

"Wine with gumbo? We don't do that, right, Marjette? We always have a cold beer with our soup; that's how we do it." Judy looks at me, not expecting to break all our established social rules in one night.

"I like a beer with good comfort food like this, too, but trust me, you're going to love this wine. It's amazing." I'm impressed with how Noa finesses this touchy exchange with Judy, but why do White women always have to use the word *amazing*? It's so overplayed.

"Okay, pour me a glass, but not in that delicate stemware Marjette has," Judy compromises.

"I know, right? Two sips and you're already refilling. Since it's just us, let's split the difference and have our wine in a pint glass," Noa suggests, her eyes lighting up at her ingenious idea.

"I like your style, Noa." Judy nods and gives Noa an encouraging smile. What's going on here? I cooked the meal and nobody's asking what I want to drink. "Marjette, don't just stand there, grab the kids to sit down. I'm starving."

CHAPTER TWELVE

All of us are full—faces cracked from a whole lot of laughter and a little too much wine—when Darius excuses himself to go do homework, and Esty has settled on the couch for a hit of Disney.

"Do you think I'm ruining my kid by letting her watch TV on school nights? I normally wouldn't, but I'm achy with exhaustion by seven," Noa confesses to the two educators flanking her at the dinner table.

"Please, TV was a babysitter in my house, and no one ever died from Disney," Judy says with the wisdom of someone who has raised grown children.

I whip my head to Judy, my eyeballs screaming, *Are you serious right now? You can't say that to a widow!*

To distract from her thoughtless comment, Judy places both hands on the table authoritatively and goes in for what I suspect is the misplaced reason she showed up this evening. "Noa, Marjette tells me you have a brother named Max?"

I cut my eyes at Judy, who's expertly avoiding my gaze.

"Oh." Noa pauses and shifts in her chair like she's now in the hot seat. In the blink of an eye our night is about to get real. "Marjette must have mentioned my brother occasionally picks up Esty from school."

Noa looks to me, unsure if she should proceed. I close my eyes and hope that Judy will not humiliate me.

"Yes, she mentioned that," Judy agrees, putting her arm around the back of Noa's chair to create a sense of closeness so Noa will dish. If Judy mentions I said Max is decent looking, we'll be having words at Saturday's meeting. "She also hinted he's pretty easy on the eyes. That's what I'm here to hear about." Okay, it's time for Judy to go.

Noa responds like this isn't the first time she's been approached about her brother and his hard-to-ignore looks. "He's for sure easy on the eyes. He got our mother's dark Mediterranean coloring." Noa's eyes pop out worrying if it's okay she used the term *dark* in our company. "But he's never been easy in any woman's life, especially mine. He's a great guy, but he's been allergic to settling down."

Judy nods her head like she knows the exact type of man Noa is making her brother out to be. What I hear is there's likely more competition out there for Max's attention than Rachel Ellis even knows.

"Plus, he has a definite type," Noa continues, looking in my direction, implying I'm not it. I imagine Max's type could bike right off the Peloton app and into his bed.

"Marjette, are you dating anyone?" Noa asks casually. In a flash, we've swung off the subject of Max and on to me. Judy raises her eyebrows. She can't wait to hear how I answer Noa's question.

"Oh no, no, no. I'm not dating." I wave both my hands in front of my face at the absurd suggestion. I've had my big love. It didn't go well; I'm done.

"Oh no?" Noa pauses, looking unsure if she should probe further, but then soldiers on. "How many guys have you dated since Booker? I can't imagine you sat on the shelf long after he left."

Judy coughs out, "None!" The table falls silent. Shock registers across Noa's face, and it's clear she's not sure what to do with this information. Judy offers her diagnosis: "Instead of a season of fretting over Booker and his indiscretions and then getting back in the game,

Marjette has signed herself up for a lifetime of playing victim." I guess now I owe the table some sort of explanation.

"Booker did me wrong and is still worrying my patience stressing Darius's and my life like we need him—when we don't," I insist. "I just don't believe in the promises of men anymore. I don't have time for it, and my heart can't take another hit. Besides, my life is good the way it is." I have delivered a sound argument for my singlehood that should satisfy my dinner guests. Noa sits with my statement, but Judy's opinion is written all over her face. *Is it, really?*

"I understand how you feel," Noa empathizes. Of course she does. Noa's lost the love of her life, as I have. It's Judy, going on forty-five years of marriage with Phil, who can't comprehend the pain of loss on top of a cheating bastard of a husband. It feels good to be in the majority for once. "Charlie was the presence that filled our home. He had a way of shouting around the house that used to drive me crazy but now I miss more than anything. The man never shut up. And the mornings? I would slowly be waking up, and he would be tornadoing through the house trying to find his wallet." Noa has a little laugh at the memory, but the tears pooling in the corners of her eyes bare her true emotions.

"His absence is a presence. The house feels too big. Esty and I are the quiet ones; Charlie was the soundtrack to our family." This is the most Noa has shared with me about who Charlie was since I showed up on her doorstep with fried chicken Labor Day weekend. I never wanted to pry. Oh, who am I kidding, of course I did, but it's so hard to know how much you can grill a widow without making things worse. Maybe I should allow Noa space to remember out loud more often.

"There's no rhyme or reason to my grief," Noa offers, wiping away the tears now streaming down her cheeks. "It comes and goes at the most inconvenient times, like this."

I reach across the table and put my hand on Noa's.

"That's all right. There ain't no benefit to holding back, you gotta let pain out. Use it to heal," Judy encourages. As a head of school for twenty years, behind closed doors Judy has counseled parents and their children through incomprehensible life transitions.

"Just last week I used my tears to cut the concessions line at a 49ers game," Noa confesses. I bite the inside of my cheek not to laugh. "Charlie had always loved the hot dogs at the stadium, so I thought Esty should try one too. A lame effort to keep us connected to Charlie, but standing in a line ten deep, I lost it watching those disgusting things roll around cooking in the machine. A passing security guard asked me if everything was okay, and I admitted to a total stranger that I was a widow. I think because I don't fit the profile of a woman who has lost her partner, he didn't know what to do with me, so he marched me to the front of the line and offered to buy me my snacks."

"So being a widow isn't all bad," Judy offers. I deliver her a swift kick under the table, but Noa chuckles and as quickly as she lost it, has regained her poise.

"Anyway, one day when I'm no longer breaking down at the sight of hot dogs or playing the one voice mail I have saved from Charlie on repeat, I think I'll want to date again. I mean, not now, not this year, but someday, probably, right?" I don't know whether I'm horrified, impressed, or confused by Noa's ability to project past tomorrow. "Marjette, how long did it take for you to at least imagine yourself with someone else? What was your right timing?"

"Marjette wouldn't know the right timing or the right man if she tripped over him with her skirt wide open," Judy declares like she's the authority on my love life, but she's the one tripping if she thinks I'm truly ready to date. Or want to.

"Judy!" I gasp, making a weak attempt to swat her shoulder. "No more wine for you. Forgive her, Noa, she gets raunchy when she's tipping her cup too much."

Looking around my dinner table, I realize these two women have given me the most companionable evening I've had in a long while. Seeing Noa at a newfound ease with her joy and her pain, even if only for an hour or two, makes me happy that my reach across the driveway is turning out to be the possible beginning of an unlikely new girl group. But I also can't help but look at Noa and wonder how she's sanely and forgivingly managing such recent heartbreak when Booker is still breaking my heart.

Tonight, there were some tears, but where's the anger over Charlie cheating on her? Why isn't she enraged that she had to find out after he died so she can't even let him have it? I don't understand how, after only three months, Noa is so composed and becoming more and more so every time I see her, because, truth is, from time to time my pillow still soaks up my tears at night. Where's the vengeful woman inside? I know from experience she needs to come out if Noa ever hopes for any kind of peace.

CHAPTER THIRTEEN

People always assume Thanksgiving is my favorite holiday because of the feast of foods complete with recipes that have been in my family for generations since my grandmother Birdie got married and started writing them down. My mother's only skill in the kitchen was working a can opener, so when my grandmother decided to pass her recipes on, she walked those recipes right over to where Auntie Shay was living and handed them over. From that moment forward the cornbread dressing and smoked ham as well as everything else on the Thanksgiving Day menu were the responsibility of Auntie Shay. As soon as I could stand at the kitchen counter without a step stool, it was on me too.

But here's the turkey rub. Spending my weekends pulling fresh vegetables and herbs from my garden so I can try out new recipes and fill my house with delicious aromas? *Love.* Cooking because the calendar dictates it? Don't love at all. I could blame it on the travel time to Tulsa in the middle of the school year, but it's not just that. My entire family showing up in elastic-waistband pants, expecting I will cook the entire meal and then complaining they're too full to help clean up feels like I'm stuck in a feminist time warp. I now only visit on non-food-centered holidays, like Arbor Day.

I made the Tulsa for Turkey Day mistake a few too many years in a row, so now Darius and I go to Judy's house for Thanksgiving dinner with Phil, their three grown children, and a predictable rotation of girl-friends and boyfriends. My only responsibility is dessert, and thanks to Max's advice on how to work and pinch the dough, this year's pumpkin, cinnamon apple, and praline pies were the best to date.

Truth is, Christmas is my favorite holiday. Every year right after Halloween, I'm ready for the retailers to bring on the holiday cheer, piping Christmas carols through every store orifice. I become especially excited for Starbucks to roll out their holiday cups. From the minute trick-or-treating ends to the last day of school before winter break begins, I run myself ragged spending hours and hours shopping and agonizing over the perfect present for every one of my students. Tradition goes, I choose a common book that my kindergarteners receive to practice their reading skills over the holidays, and then a little something extra special for each child to let them know I see them for the unique and mighty superhuman that they are.

I started my holiday gift-giving tradition the year I lost my baby. I immediately supplanted the agony of not getting to dote on that baby at Christmas by doting on the babies I did have for a part of every day. Year after year, as my dream of having a big family faded, the holiday traditions in my classroom deepened. When Judy was head of school, she turned the other cheek at my classroom, which resembled a chaotic North Pole working at warp speed to get those presents on the sleigh in time. She knew my efforts came from the right place and warded off any parents undone by my intense holiday spirit with their cries of Christian privilege. We both knew no little drummer boy was going to wage a holy war. With a new head on campus, though, I don't enjoy the same protections. While I have toned the decorations way down, twenty presents are stowed under my desk, beautifully wrapped in red foil with a sprig of holly to hand to each student this afternoon as they head off for winter break.

At drop-off this morning, Noa told me Max would be picking Esty up at one thirty to make it into San Francisco to grab her from work so the three of them can head to the airport to see family in New York. Noa informed me that as a Jew, for Christmas you have to go where the best Chinese food and movie theaters are—some of the only venues open on December 25. I pointed out Chinatown was two blocks from her office, and she countered that in her humble opinion, the Chinese food in San Francisco blows compared to New York. Same goes for bagels.

It's two o'clock, and there's no sign of Max. I send my students outside for their last recess of the day but keep Esty with me in the classroom in case Max shows up. In the division of travel habits, I've always been in the camp of racing through an airport with your pants on fire versus arriving with enough time to sit down for a full meal, but even I'm starting to get nervous. I don't want to snitch on Max and add to his sister's view of his wavering responsibility, but there's no sign of him, so I cave and pick up my phone to text Noa.

"Please don't do that! She'll kill me," Max begs, flying into my classroom breathless. Rubbing his stubble, he points at my phone, where I'm mid-text, with a final plea: *"Please."* He's absolutely right; Noa will kill him. I put the phone down.

"Esty, hustle and get your backpack. We gotta go," Max commands in a gruff voice I haven't heard from him before. This is a man most definitely terrified of his sister. "Do you have plans for the holiday?" Max asks me politely but is clearly distracted by Esty's glacial pace. He urges his niece on: "Hurry!"

Wanting to please her antsy uncle, Esty does what she's told. The ambience in my classroom feels tense and not full of the warmth and holiday spirit I hope for when sending my students off for their winter break with a Ms. Lewis gift tucked in their hands.

"Darius and I are staying here," I say, and hand Esty's present to an agitated Max, since there's no way to give it to her as she wrangles with her coat. My practiced speech about love, joy, and looking forward to seeing her back on the circle-time rug after the new year goes unsaid. Holding the present uncomfortably, I guess unsure where to put it or if he should have Esty unwrap it right here, Max avoids making eye contact. He manages to mutter "Thanks" and "See ya" all together before scooping up Esty to ensure a quicker escape from school and across the Bay Bridge.

"Byyyyyeeee, Ms. Leeeeewis! Seeeee you neeeext year!" Esty yells to me, her chest bumping against her uncle's shoulder as he jogs away. I'm left unsatisfied with my inaugural gift bestowment of the holiday season and confused by Max's uneasy reaction to my having something special for Esty. Does he think it's in poor taste to give a present to all the kids? Or just the Jewish ones? Maybe he knows about a Seventh-day Adventist in my class that I don't.

I turn back to my desk and see the gift tag with Esty's name on it lying on the classroom floor.

I need to process what just happened, so I call Judy to get her take on my weird encounter with Max before my kids come pouring back in the classroom. Does Max think I got *him* a Christmas present? He couldn't possibly. I'm sure he doesn't, he can't, but then, *ahhhh*, the gift tag ripped off and I don't think I said anything about the gift being for Esty! And the box with the nineteen other presents is under my desk, so there's no evidence in sight that I would be passing one out to all my students. Yep, the more I reflect on it, I definitely didn't tell Max the now unmarked present was for Esty. I'm dying, and certain mortification is going to drive my blood pressure up and make me stroke out by Christmas Eve. Damn, Judy doesn't pick up.

Marjette 2:06 PM

NOA'S BROTHER MAX THINKS I GOT HIM A CHRISTMAS PRESENT!

Come on, come on, Judy, hit me back.

Judy 2:08 PM

Why do you have to keep acting like Santa's Black elf?! I told you to take your tinsel down now that I'm no longer at school to protect you from your out-of-control Christmas self. What'd you do?

Marjette 2:08 PM

I panicked because Max was late picking up Esty and I shoved the present in his hand with no explanation.

Judy 2:09 PM

Was he looking Christmas delicious?

Since we started Weight Watchers, Judy's always hungry.

Marjette 2:10 PM

Focus Judy, this is not about Max's looks, but my humiliation. The gift tag ripped off Esty's present, so now he's going to open the present and find The Snowy Day and Thinking Putty. What's he gonna assume?

Judy 2:10 PM

He's going to assume you're kind of freaky.

Judy's been watching too many Hallmark holiday movies in retirement. She's probably watching one right now.

Marjette 2:11 PM

I don't even want to imagine what could be freaky about Thinking Putty.

Judy 2:11 PM

Stop being a drama queen and get your head
together. Text Noa.

Duh. What was I thinking? Of course, I'll just text Noa and sort
it out. Tying up my own workshop at Houghton has me acting like a
deranged Mrs. Claus.

⌐

Saturday is a few days before Christmas, and my house is looking nothing like it's supposed to. The fall leaves are still piled in the gutter, the
icicle lights are packed in the garage, and my decorations remain in the
Christmas bins high on the garage shelf where Darius knows I can't
reach them. Our holiday preparation has always included Darius and
me, dancing around the living room to the Mariah Carey Christmas
album, creating an atmosphere that looked like Mrs. Claus herself did
the decorating. This year, my son is away from the house more often
than not, and I feel like my holiday-making partner in crime is losing
interest in our family traditions.

Today's the day we're supposed to go get our tree, and Darius is
still hanging out at Simone's. He knows our routine is to pick out our
Christmas tree the Saturday after school lets out, but he's nowhere to
be seen.

Ding-dong.

There he is! Darius must have forgotten his keys, but it's all good
because we still have time to go out and find our tree. I skip to the
front door feeling the Christmas spirit creep back in and throw it open,
cheering, "Let's go, my little elf, we need to get our tree!"

Standing on the landing is Earl from Flower Power Florist, according to what his name tag tells me. He doesn't look the least bit excited to go get a Christmas tree with me.

With indifference, Earl hands me an enormous potted chrysanthemum and turns on his heels, shuffling back to his delivery van. Door open, letting the cool December air in, I paw through the branches looking for a card.

> Thanks for the book. It happens to be a Snowy
> Day in New York.
> Merry Christmas.
> Love, Max

Did Noa tell Max about the gift mix-up? Maybe it slipped her mind. I wonder if he opened the present on the plane or once he got to New York. And what about the putty? He had to know they were for Esty. I read the card again and again. Noa warned me I'm not Max's type. But then he did write *Love, Max.* Or he told the person taking his chrysanthemum order to write *love,* so it might not have been off the cuff; or maybe it was. Hmmm. I need to marinate on this for a while. I head back into my living room and place the chrysanthemum where my tree should be.

Usually, Darius and I sit down at the computer and log in to the Houghton family portal to review his grades together, but since he's not here and I'm killing time until he gets home, I'll help myself. Darius's junior year is too important not to be on top of his academic progress. As I scroll through each subject, there's a common refrain from his teachers I haven't heard in years past: while Darius participates in class, the quality of his work is not accurately reflecting his potential.

I snatch my cell phone right away to call Booker. We need to strategize on what I should say before Darius gets home from Simone's. Despite our differences, I can count on Booker's support when it comes to Darius's education. We're on the same page with the same goal: good grades, better SATs, best college.

After three rings, Booker picks up, and I spare not one second before launching into my concerns. "Booker, we need to talk about your son."

"Well, hello to you too, 'Jette," Booker responds languidly. This time I let the name I hate go; I've got bigger issues at play.

"I just opened Darius's report card, and I am *not* happy with what I saw; not one bit. And trust me, you're going to be none too thrilled either. Do you know your son's slacking in school? His teachers used the worst report card line possible." I give Booker a second to try and guess. The end of the line is silent. "Other than your child is failing." Booker lets out an enormous sigh of relief.

"The teachers are saying he's not living up to his *potential*." I over-articulate each syllable in *potential*.

"Jesus, our son's an academic cliché," Booker barks back. I don't react because I can recognize, in this instance, Booker's bite is not aimed at me.

"And yes, I know what the problem is—that little girl he's been running around with," I tattle. "As a matter of fact, he's at her house right now when he knows he has responsibilities at home to take care of. That boy's been slacking at school *and* here at the house."

"Take a breath. Darius isn't at Simone's house." How does Booker know and since when is he on a first-name basis with that girl? "He's here, 'Jette. He came over this morning so we could make plans for after Christmas, and we've been hanging out all afternoon," he replies. Now I'm the one silent on the other end. "Promise, I didn't know he had a standing date with you or that apparently he should be studying more."

"Plans? What sort of plans do the two of you think you're making? The only plans that boy needs to be making is how he's going to get these grades back up and keep my foot outta his behind," I erupt. I do hold back from reminding Booker that Christmas is my time. He gave up Christmas when he gave up us.

"I thought it'd be fun for us to spend some time together, so we're going snowboarding at Tahoe over New Year's. Did I not mention the idea to you a while back?" Booker knows he didn't mention it to me because I would have said no. "We're going to hit the slopes and kick back for some bonding time. With Darius almost off to college, he needs to be spending more time with his father," Booker claims with the kind of sweet in his voice that gives you cavities. "He's about to be out in the world as a man on his own, and there are some lessons I need to be sure he takes with him."

"Hold on, Booker." I mute my phone and walk in tight circles, exhaling in rapid succession to keep my sanity in check. What? Now that Darius is supposedly a man, he needs his father, but as a little boy he didn't? I'm in my right mind enough to know I can't attack from all sides. I choose to focus on Darius's faltering grades, not Booker's faltering fatherhood.

"Darius should not be getting a ski trip at a time like this. We have always agreed that good grades are expected and not rewarded. Given what I read, Darius will be lucky if he gets to keep eating out of my fridge," I say, gripping my phone. And then add, so there's no room for misinterpretation, "No way, Booker. Skiing in Tahoe is not happening."

"Be reasonable, 'Jette. This trip will give me some time to talk to Darius about his future. I promise to address his grades and get him refocused on school. And I'll even throw in a conversation about not letting Simone serve as a distraction if that will make you feel better." That actually would make me feel better, but not good enough. "Though Darius told me she has her sights set on Stanford, so I'm not sure she's the problem. And besides, I want this time with my son," Booker says with a sincerity I rarely hear. "Please. Think about it."

I take the phone away from my ear to check that I haven't accidentally called another Booker in my contacts list because this person on the line is one I'm not sure I recognize. If I let Darius go with Booker, what am I going to do by myself over New Year's?

"I'm driving him home now. I hope we can talk about this again tomorrow because I'd like to leave on the twenty-ninth, and then I'll have my boy home by early evening on the second, promise."

"*My* boy. And fine, we can talk tomorrow," I concede. "I need Darius home within a half hour; we have to go get our tree." I am not letting these two ruin my Christmas.

CHAPTER FOURTEEN

After a festive Christmas with Judy, Phil, and too much eggnog, Darius and I spent three days curled up on the couch watching all the Marvel movies chronologically before he headed to Tahoe with his father. For seventy-two delicious hours I had my son all to myself because Simone was with her family in Phoenix.

If Darius is up there enjoying himself in the mountains with Booker, then I get to ring in the new year embracing the mountainous task of clearing out his room. Grandma Birdie always touted the importance of a fresh start by having a clean house going into a new year, cleanliness being next to godliness. How your year begins is how your year will be, according to the First Lady of Baptists. I figure with Darius gone, I'll finally have the chance to get in the corners of his bedroom. No matter how many dusters and sprays I leave in easy reach for him, he doesn't seem to notice. I have to remind him his bedroom is part of what's considered "under my roof" when he objects to me deep cleaning in there when he's home.

Taking in the chaos, I know this is going to be a full-evening job. Before getting started, I crack open all the windows and run the fan stored under the bed so I'm not suffocated by musty sweat and stale Doritos residue. I pick up the piles of laundry lying on the closet floor and put the first of what looks like three loads into the washer. How it doesn't occur to Darius to tidy his space before he leaves the house for school in the morning, let alone a vacation, boggles my mind. Unless he changes his ways, no woman other than me is ever going to want to live with this boy.

If I fold the clothes in Darius's bureau, he'll know I've been readjusting his things—something he has repeatedly asked me not to do. But if I don't there could be small vermin hatching in the sock drawer, and I wouldn't even know about it. The thought of Darius and me not being the only two breathing creatures living in this house tips the scales. I opt to wiggle open the stuffed drawers to refold his clothes. I need to make room for the ones I'm washing to be put away nicely.

Pulling all the socks out so I can put them together with their matches, I can tell there's something jammed up in the back. I swipe my hand through, my fingertips barely grazing the culprit. I yank on the drawer, trying to pull it all the way out, but it's definitely stuck. Tugging harder is going to jack up my shoulder, so I need a new plan. I go into the garage and get the yardstick and headlamp I use in the garden. Down on my knees, I turn on the headlamp so I can see inside, insert the yardstick, and jab around to dislodge whatever is blocking the drawer from sliding. The yardstick hooks behind the object, and I flick it hard. A silver box flies out of the dresser, landing next to me on the floor. I'm face-to-face with a Greek tragedy. It seems I've mutilated Darius's cellophane-wrapped Trojan Pleasure Pack. Happy New Year to me.

I flip the box of condoms over with my yardstick, looking to see if the cellophane is ripped open anywhere. In my moment of shock, I can't decide if I want to know if the box has been opened or if all twelve in the pack are accounted for. Though I prepared Darius for the responsibilities of having an intimate relationship someday, I wasn't prepared for someday to be *today*.

I saw Max drive up to Noa and Esty's house earlier this morning. I had planned on giving the Abramses the day to unpack and settle back home before heading over to hear about their holiday and sit with some much-needed company, but I'm jumping out of my skin with this discovery. And Judy and Phil have the nerve to be in Florida.

Marjette 4:56 PM

Happy New Year. You guys back from New York?

Though I am, I don't want to come across as desperate.

Noa 4:57 PM

Just this morning.

Marjette 4:58 PM

Can I come over for a minute?

I wait five but don't hear back from Noa. I peek outside and see all the lights still on in the house, so I know someone is home. Maybe Noa's phone died or Esty's playing a game on it. Feeling condom vibes clinging to my clothes like dust bunnies, I quickly change before I head over to Noa's house.

As I'm about to knock, the door flies open and Max runs right into me. My mouth practically munches his left nipple.

"Oh, Marjette, sorry! I thought you were Amazon Fresh." I peel my cheek off Max's solid chest and look up to receive his apology. "I was just finishing up reading a riveting story about a snowy day to Esty." He grins. The embarrassing collision has me ready to scurry back across my driveway, but I stop myself. Max might have advice on what to do about the uninvited Trojan visitors in Darius's room, but I'm not sure if I could keep the focus on parenting my son while having a sex talk with Max. I don't know him like that.

"I hear reading helps plants as well as children grow. Should I go get my chrysanthemum?" I tease to prove I can match his quick wit.

"There's only room for three on the couch. Maybe next time." Did Max just invite me to come in and sit on the couch with him, or is he referring to him, Noa, and Esty so now I should beat feet home?

"Noa's back in her bedroom resting—she's not feeling so hot—but I have massaman curry on the stove, and I know Esty would love to see her favorite teacher." Darn, this is not good timing for Noa to be sick—I need her counsel—but Max *was* talking about me on the couch, minus the potted flower! Thank the Lord, Grandma Birdie always taught me to bring my best face wherever I go, and I swiped on some mascara and smoothed my hair before I came over. Now that I'm here and putting a little thought into it, I might want to hold off on the teenager talk while Max is around. Usually, I consider Darius my best asset, but perhaps not in this moment.

"I'm Esty's only teacher," I correct Max, "and yes, I'd love to come in and wish Noa and Esty a happy New Year." I pass by him close enough that I get a whiff of cardamom and cloves.

"Don't sell yourself short. Esty's preschool teachers killed it at nap time. They could get twenty kids to fall asleep in three minutes flat. You *do* actually have some serious competition." This man continues to be quick with the verbal duel.

"Hi, Ms. Lewis," Esty mumbles, not looking up from serving tea to her two favorite stuffies and one American Girl doll with an unfortunate home haircut. "I would give you some tea, but I don't have any more cups or NILLA wafers," she explains, chomping down on a cookie she has nabbed from one of her guests' plates. I love a good tea party, so I'm going to try not to feel slighted.

"I thought I heard you out here, Marjette." I look from Esty to see Noa shuffling down the hall in her pajamas, a hand on the wall to steady herself as she walks. I look to Max, wondering what he has done with my booty-shaking buddy who was at my house wolfing down dinner not that long ago. Noa moves as if she's aged thirty years. Max looks helplessly at his sister, not sure what to do.

"Mommy, do you feel better?" Esty asks, hopeful, dropping her tea party like the pot was actually hot at the sight of her mother.

"No, no, baby, not yet, but I will," Noa croaks, cracking a pained smile, her lips looking dry and peely. "Marjette, I'm just getting an extra blanket off the couch, but I'll catch up with you later, okay?" she suggests, not looking at me but simply making her way over to the couch to retrieve the chunky knit throw. "Stay and keep Max company. He may be tired of talking to a five-year-old."

"I can do that" is all I manage to say. What I want to do is jump in and take action, but Judy's words echo loudly in my head: *Did she ask for your help?* Neither Max nor I say anything until we hear Noa's door click closed.

Screw Judy. Observing Max frozen in action, I declare, "I should go back there."

"Hey, Marjette, why don't you give Noa a little bit of time. It was a rough trip back east and we are all really missing Charlie," Max says gently. Even laced in kindness, I don't take "no" well. My friend did not just look physically sick, she looked heartsick, and I need to do something about it. Max senses my agitation and steps between me and the length of the hallway. "Why don't you help me get dinner ready? Noa's not going to be eating with us tonight, so please stay. There will definitely be enough to go around." Though Max's arms are folded across his chest, as if guarding his sister, his face brightens as he nods me toward the kitchen. "Do you have any suggestions about what I should do with the several bunches of collards that were in Noa's CSA box when we got back from New York?"

Pft. Do I know what to do with greens?!

As I'm about to lay into Max for even insinuating I wouldn't know what to do with collards, I read his body language more accurately. His question was his way of asking for help with either the greens or, since he knows his way around a kitchen, more likely Esty. Though I don't have a clue why, clearly New York did not go well.

"Of course. I'm happy to help with dinner. Let me just run Noa a glass of water, then I'll be back to get going in the kitchen," I say with as much casualness as I can.

Max grabs my hand full stop. "Marjette, I know you mean well, but leave Noa alone." This man doesn't know that I don't leave much alone.

~

Ding.

Darius 12:10 PM

> Remember I have a dentist appointment 6th period. Bring Esty to the bakery and I'll meet you there.

What dentist appointment? No matter, I thank Darius in my head for providing me a legitimate reason to stop by Flour + Butter. I haven't laid eyes on Max since New Year's Day at Noa's house, when he warned me to let his sister be. I've been heeding his warning for two weeks now, but I'm done.

Last Thursday Noa canceled on dinner at my house. I even had her favorite baked macaroni and cheese cooked up, which oddly she believes is a main dish. (Where I come from, it's most definitely a side.) I always make double the recipe so Noa and Esty have some to take home, and I usually end up seeing a serving in Esty's lunch box the next day. Esty proudly opens her thermos to show me, and I give her a little wink; it's our special thing.

This past week, though, Noa's gone from seeming sick to appearing strung out, and I'm beyond worried. I can't imagine I've befriended a suburban opioid addict who's passing drugs on the playground. Noa doesn't seem the type, but then I suppose no soccer mom looks like she has a pill-popping problem until she looks like, well, Noa. With

Darius's request, I mark this afternoon to shake down Max for the truth and for some of that delicious cheesecake he had Esty bring me her first day back at school.

The sun is working extra hard to warm up this January day, but my fingers remain frozen at recess, so I decide to play kickball with my students to warm up. When I step into line to take a turn at home plate, my kids go wild with excitement that Ms. Lewis is going to wallop the ball farther than any kindergartener possibly can. Once it's my turn, Javon, who will be rolling me the ball, signals Tabitha, Mia, and Naman in the outfield to back up. To a bunch of littles, I'm a powerful giant. My ego gets the best of me, and I give that round bouncy ball a World Cup football kick. All the kids on the grassy field go wild as I round the bases, arms stretched high, caught in the thrill of a home run, just like I've watched Darius do for years rounding the baseball diamond.

As my students jump in victory for their teacher, I'm relieved I didn't pull a groin muscle and have to be carted off the field. Hands on knees to catch a few heaving breaths, I spy Esty, by herself, all the way across the outfield at the chain-link fence, talking closely to a woman on the other side. Though I'm too far away to make out details, I can see this woman is blonde, and I know she is not either of Esty's grandmothers. Esty just saw them over winter break a few weeks ago, and both live out of town. I quickly scan the playground to see if there's an administrator out here to come with me to escort Esty away from the fence without causing alarm, and so I can threaten this stranger to beat it far from my school. Unfortunately, the only other adult out here is Catherine, so I jog over to the climbing structure and ask her to keep an eye on my kids, all while keeping my own eyes on Esty.

By the time I reach the chain-link fence, the woman is squatting face-to-face with Esty. She doesn't notice my arrival until I step between the two of them. I grab behind me to hold Esty firm in my grip and introduce myself. As I'm about to give the woman the third degree concerning her presence near the playfield, she falls back on her butt, rolls over, and runs away. She's dressed in a black wool pantsuit and a conservative heeled ankle boot, which looks awfully formal for a kidnapper. Pulling on my memory, she also kind of looks like the woman at Charlie's shiva who was asking me if there were any children around.

"Esty, do you know that woman?" I press, trying to sound unbothered as we walk back across the field hand in hand. I turn to look behind me to make sure the woman is truly gone and is not across the street lurking behind a tree for last glances at Esty.

"Not really. But you know her," Esty replies with a hint of *duh* in her voice.

"I do? How do you think I know her?" Maybe after I left the shiva Esty came home and they are familiar with each other from there. But why would the woman run off when I approached the two of them?

"She said she's a kindergarten mom. I think she looks like Harper's mommy." Harper is in Catherine's class, but I taught Harper's two older brothers years before, and that woman is most definitely not their mother. In fact, I'm positive she's not a kindergarten mom at all. It is my business to know *every* family, *every* year, at Houghton within the first week that they start at the school, if for no other reason than terrifying scenarios like this. Stranger danger is only one consideration when looking out for the students in my care. Families with estranged relationships, stalkers, and custody battles are some of the more important details teachers must be aware of when allowing adults within arm's reach of the kids.

Between Noa's change in demeanor since Christmas, Max shutting down my concerns about his sister's well-being in the face of my offers of support, and now Esty being approached by a complete stranger at school, I can no longer ignore that something distressing is gripping the Abramses' household. As Esty's teacher, her safety is my primary concern, and now that school is out for the day, my afternoon will be dedicated to finding out exactly what is going on and if Darius has any cavities.

~

"Hey, son, how was the dentist? Did you get your makeup work for last period?" I ask when he comes into the bakery. I attempt to come across relaxed even though my fingers are cramped from not having let go of Esty's hand since we stepped off the Houghton School campus.

"Ouch, Ms. Lewis. You're squeezing too hard!" Esty protests, trying to slide her hand out of my death grip. I suppose it's okay since we're inside, and the two customers Max is serving must have a collective age of at least 160, so the chances of them ditching their baguettes, nabbing Esty, and making a break for it are slim.

Darius has yet to lift his eyes from his phone and acknowledge me, the woman who gave him that phone and his life. "Darius!" I admonish, reminding him of the importance of greeting his elders, especially his mother. My son raises his head, his eyes slow to follow. He offers his knuckles to give Esty a fist bump. She pounds him hard, then wraps her arms around his waist.

"What's so important on your phone that you can't be bothered to greet your mother?" I tease, though I'm praying it's not Simone's perky boobs in a cheap push-up bra.

"Since you jammed me up getting a new car, Dad got us Warriors tickets. Center court."

"You and me?" I ask, confused why Booker would do that.

"Mom, why you playin'? 'Course not. Me and Dad. Besides, you'd never throw cash down on a Warriors game." It was a momentary lapse in reality, thinking Booker would ever pay for something nice for Darius and me to do together that he knows I cannot afford. Car, snowboarding trip to Tahoe, Warriors tickets—Booker is taking buying his child's love to a new level. Something is going on with that man, but I don't have time to sniff it out right this second. Even Easy Rawlins could only focus on one mystery at a time.

"Darius, you can let me know about the dentist later. Why don't you take Esty into the kitchen for a snack and see if there's any babka in the back for us to take home. It looks like Max may have sold out up front," I instruct, looking around the bakery. I need a loaf of babka about as much as my Weight Watchers leader, Carole, needs another rhinestone belt, but I want to get Darius and Esty out of earshot so I can talk with Max alone. His two octogenarian customers seem to have as big a crush on Max, and are as obvious about it, as Rachel. They only clue in to leave when they hear my fingernails heavily drumming on one of the glass pastry casements. I have to give it to their stellar hearing.

"Good to see you, Marjette," Max declares once the couple have left, punctuated with the snap of a tea towel in my direction. *Is it good to see me?* I wonder so loudly I'm afraid Max can hear my thoughts. "I was sure the cheesecake I sent in with Esty would lure you back here sooner, but I guess I put the wrong bait in my trap." Oh no, this is the absolute worst. When I told Judy about the cheesecake, she claimed that was Max's modern-day way of spraying male pheromones. I told Judy the only thing spraying was her spit and pushed her out of my face at last Saturday's meeting.

"That cheesecake was so good—just ask Darius. Three bites in and he snagged it right out from under me and finished it off before I could fight him for it."

"Hey, Darius," Max yells into the kitchen.

"Yeah," Darius answers, jogging to the threshold where the kitchen meets the shop.

"Hands off the presents I send home for your mother. I feed you plenty," Max says with a joking smile and puts out his palm for a hand-shake as he and Darius go through a series of motions.

Ting.

Ting.

The store bell jingles even though it's four o'clock. I wish I had turned Max's FERMÉ sign for him when I walked in. I really need to get his take on the woman who showed up at school today.

"Marjette, what in the world are you doing here?" a familiar voice behind my back inquires in mock surprise. Sweet baby Jesus, not today.

Turning, all I say is, "Hi, Rachel." No good ever comes from parents knowing too much about their child's teacher. Except for me and Noa.

Rachel maneuvers around me as if I'm a part of the bakery seating. She leans in to give Max a kiss on each cheek like she's French or something. I notice she's the one doing all the leaning. "Max, I'm in an absolute pickle, and I need you to save me," she says with a mock pout and girlish frustration in her voice. Rachel launches into her catering nightmare. "I totally forgot I agreed to host the Bay Area's most powerful fifty females under, well, you get the picture. The event is tomorrow morning, and I'm in charge of the breakfast meeting. I need you to be my knight and shining baker." Rachel can't even get the idiom right, *and* she just accidentally revealed she's well over forty. Suddenly this afternoon is turning into a whole show.

"Sure, Rachel. Let me know what you're thinking, and I'll do my best to deliver."

Rachel gives me a triumphant look over her shoulder. I think back on the times I have been either in Max's bakery or side by side cooking with him in Noa's kitchen and realize, watching Rachel in this moment, it's too easy to misconstrue what Max is saying when he references food.

"This may take a while, so maybe you want to quickly finish up with Marjette first," Rachel suggests. She's shooing me out of the shop just like I did the last two customers!

I don't want to alarm Rachel with private matters from school, so I decide to skip over getting Max's take on what happened at recess and head straight to Noa's house later this evening. Besides, I justify, in all matters of children, the mother really should be the first to know.

"Have a good afternoon," Rachel calls to me, hoping to expedite my departure. Max pretends to wipe down the counter, seeming to feel some tension between his audience of two. He needn't worry since there's no stress coming from me—I'm smart enough to know that women like Rachel Ellis always get their way.

CHAPTER FIFTEEN

To my surprise, as I'm pulling into my driveway from the bakery, Noa's outside my house dressed like a Fort Lauderdale fitness model. It's January and she looks chilly to me. Taking note of her wardrobe change, I think Judy bought a pair of tights just like hers. One of them is buying outside their age bracket. Noa waves vigorously, and I roll down the window as I put my car in park.

"What's up, Noa?" I ask curiously. I'm not sure what confuses me most, the fact it's five o'clock and Noa's home or the fact she looks like she's pulled an emotional one-eighty.

"Well, I've caught you and Judy going walking together a time or two, so I thought maybe you'd want to go with me. I took the day off work to, uh, pull myself together. Mood follows action!"

Glad to know someone's been listening to her therapist. I nod and smack my lips together to acknowledge the difficulty of Noa's last few weeks. I guess Max's advice was spot-on, and it was best I left her alone to move through her New Year hurdles.

"Sounds good, I could use a walk," I agree. "Give me five minutes to change my clothes."

"Great!" Noa claps, excited at the prospect of a walking buddy. "I'll wait outside and soak up the sunshine."

Noa walks at a more leisurely pace than Judy. Whether she just wants a chatting buddy or she's out of shape, I don't mind; at my height, keeping up with anyone is a tall order.

We trade offspring and workday complaints. For the last twenty minutes of our walk, Noa prattles on about an impossible YouTube star whose "Build Your Dream Tiny Home in Thirty Days" manual is months overdue and an actor with a cookbook launching and no interest in boiling water, which makes promotional segments on talk shows difficult.

"Well look at that, 6:04 p.m. Want to come in for a quick glass of wine before Darius drops off my little monster?"

I am thirsty, and we do still need to talk about said monster. Swapping stories and laughing through our walk was the most fun I've had in the past few weeks, and I didn't feel like spoiling our conversation with talk of a foiled child abduction.

"Would love to," I accept, and Noa grins from ear to ear opening the front door. Playing hooky looks good on her.

"Esty and I had an unusual experience at school today," I begin, then slug down half my glass of liquid courage.

"Please don't tell me she brought her terrible British accent to school. Esty spent a lot of time in New York with her Israeli cousins who live in London, and, well, I think it's fair to say my kid lacks an ear for language but embraces a love of mimicry."

"I wish. I'm kind of a sucker for an accent, good or bad." I pause to switch subjects. "Today at recess, I found Esty alone at the fence of the northeast corner of the school talking to a woman I didn't recognize and Esty claimed she didn't really know." Noa becomes stiff, as I imagined she would. As any parent would. "Don't worry, I chased her off, and as far as I could tell, the things they were chatting about were totally benign, but I'll be keeping an extra eye on Esty at recess the next couple of days." I pause again to let Noa soak it all in.

In response she swiftly grabs the key chain off the wall and slams it down in front of me.

"Remember these?" she demands. I do, but I don't say anything. Now it's Noa's turn to chug her wine. "What'd she look like?"

Funny thing, thinking on it, she kind of looked like Noa, but I don't think I should say that.

"Average height, blonde, slight, around our age. Maybe blue eyes? Dressed like she had just stepped out of a conference room," I list off, trying to remember the best I can.

"Or a courtroom?" Noa questions.

"Totally possible." Closing her eyes, Noa inhales a deep breath. I think it's to keep herself grounded.

"Wait, *what*? Are Charlie's parents trying to sue you for custody of Esty? Is that why you've been so shook up since New Year's? Max told me not to pry, but I should have asked, I knew I should have." Damn men and their emotional avoidance.

"You've been a great friend, Marjette, please don't think otherwise." Noa puts her hands over mine in a gesture of assurance. "I probably would have refused your help anyway. Not that I didn't need it, I just didn't want to need it. And Max, well, I love my brother, but he so badly wants me to be okay—like, right now—but he can't hurry my feelings along, as much as he would like to." Max and Judy should meet, sounds like they both put a time clock on feelings. "And no, Charlie's parents do not want custody of Esty. But Christmas Day was Charlie's and my anniversary. I thought I'd be okay if I was with family, but turns out I wasn't; not at all."

"I've never heard of people getting married on Christmas. Is that something Jewish people do?"

"You get your choice of venues on Christmas Day; not a lot of bridal competition."

"I'm so sorry, Noa. That must have really been rough for you."

"Between my anniversary and the holidays without Charlie, it all just hit me much harder than I expected. Eight nights of Hanukkah drag on when the candle that burns brightest in your family is gone." I can't even imagine. The first couple of Christmases without Booker were almost unbearable, and all I had to do was get over the hump of one day, let alone an extended week. "Hanukkah is not even that big of a deal in the grand scheme of Jewish celebrations, but Charlie always spent the month beforehand intensely shopping for the most inane socks to give Esty and me each night. My favorite pair from last year were bright-blue knee-highs with 'Hanukkah Ho Ho Ho' in bold white print down the side. I got that pair on Christmas Day. He made me wear them to bed that night." Noa giggles at the sweet memory, and I join her because remembering the good stuff *is* the best stuff.

"Anyway, this is going to be my first full calendar year without my husband, as a single parent, alone, one income. You name it. January first the world was celebrating a new year, and I wanted the old one back. Charlie's passing is in the past and people have moved on, as they should, but that leaves me navigating the long, slow part of grieving alone."

"You're not alone," I promise Noa. "You've got me, right over there." I point behind me in the direction of my house.

"I do, but this will always be my own rocky road to walk down one day at a time. And now, apparently, I also have this." Noa picks up the keys and jiggles them in my face. The sun streaming through the window catches the pendant with the *M* engraved on it, creating a prism on the wall. I'm confused, and I can tell Noa is searching for courage and the right words.

"The *M* is for Monica. Monica Jensen," she says. I nod; here we go. "Monica was also the visitor at the fence, I suspect." Noa gives us both a large repour. "Before me, Charlie was madly in love."

"With Monica Jensen," I hesitantly confirm. Noa raises her glass to signal *bingo*.

"They wanted to spend their lives together, but Monica isn't Jewish, and Charlie's family are devout conservative Jews. All three of the Abrams children were expected to marry Jewish. About the time he should have been proposing, instead he broke up with Monica, destroying them both. Charlie promptly moved to California. I'm pretty sure to gain distance between the two of them so he wouldn't be tempted to get back together with her."

This is a lot, and not where I was expecting this evening to go, but I'm here for it all. Tonight, the widow dam is breaking wide open.

"Six years passed between his breakup with Monica and when Charlie and I met. We had a whirlwind romance, and since we were older, we married within the year, so happy to have found each other and both eager to start a family."

"I know all about wanting to start a family" falls out of my mouth without my even thinking about it.

"I know you do," Noa responds with the kindest smile even though she's the one unearthing tragic facts. "Charlie never even mentioned Monica until after we were married. That's how much he had moved on, or so I thought. He treated his life with her like a distant memory."

Okay, this part of the story sounds shady to me. I'm not sure I could trust a guy who waits to tell me he's loved another until after he's put a ring on my finger.

"I've never doubted that Charlie loved me. We had real love; I know we did." Noa takes a moment to look out the window. I pray that Darius doesn't return with Esty anytime soon. This is a conversation for grown folks' ears. "Our first two years of marriage were 'practice' getting pregnant, but we had no luck; not even a maybe. Years three and four were consumed with doctors' appointments, multiple rounds of IVF, and more stress than a newish marriage should have to take on. Year five was marriage counseling and interviewing surrogates."

"Did you ever consider adoption?" I ask, hoping it isn't rude, but I'm curious nonetheless since Noa and Charlie seemed to have explored every other option.

"I was open to adoption, but Charlie wanted our baby to be ours. He needed the baby to be religiously Jewish, and most important to him, Jewish by lineage, and that means the mother," Noa says, pointing to herself, "must be Jewish."

"What does it matter where a child comes from as long as it's healthy? There are so many kids who need loving parents," I counter, sounding judgy as hell.

"I know it sounds selfish, but when you're a devout Jew, there's an acute awareness that we're a dying breed, and reproduction can feel like a heavy burden. The first five years, Charlie was the rock in our marriage. He doted on me, he cried with me every month when my period came, and when I wanted to give up, Charlie remained steadfast in his belief that we were meant to have a family." The next logical question is, *So where the heck did Esty come from?* But I hold back. That said, if Noa tells me Monica became their surrogate, I'm getting up from my stool and calling Hollywood because this needs to be a show.

"At forty-two, to the shock of everyone—doctors, family, me—I became pregnant with Esty. Charlie was the only one not surprised, because he always had faith. We were overwhelmed with happiness, and then I became overcome with singular attention toward delivering a healthy baby. Since Esty was the only child I was going to have, my prebirth attention morphed into a laser focus as she grew from a baby into a toddler and now the little girl you see today."

I can't believe this woman has been living next to me for over a year and a half, sharing a similar motherhood outcome to mine, and I didn't even know, or bother to ask. The fact that neither of us considered crossing over our driveways to talk now seems completely ridiculous.

"In our new dynamic of three, Esty thrived, but our marriage suffered. Between being a late-in-life first-time mom, working full-time, and nurturing Esty every waking moment I wasn't at the office, I had nothing left for Charlie. The irony is the first five years of our marriage, when we couldn't get what we wanted, we were an indomitable team. Once we got what we wanted, we drifted apart. The anniversary trip we were taking to Mexico would have been the first time since Esty was born that we would have been away from her, together."

"You and Charlie had never left Esty?" I pipe up, shocked.

"Charlie traveled quite a bit for work, but no, I've never been away from her," Noa says, averting her eyes.

"Not even to visit Max in Paris?"

"Not even then, which I know, thinking back on it now, sounds crazy, but I was so afraid that if I left Esty and something happened to her, well, I could never forgive myself. Nor could Charlie."

"That's a lot of pressure to put on yourself as a mother, Noa."

"I know. That's why, since Esty was entering kindergarten and not going to break, I decided to finally wake up and press reset on my marriage. But it turns out, I was too late." Noa sighs, heavy with remorse. "The kids should be home soon. Give me a minute to throw these enchiladas in the oven, and I'll tell you the rest of my sorry story. I want it out of my system before my baby gets home."

Listening to Noa's confession of being a mother consumed by her child, balancing work and home life while her marriage took a back seat, is a walk down memory lane I am none too thrilled to recognize. I was the work widow in my marriage, wasn't I? I had no other choice than to concentrate all my efforts on Darius and teaching since, due to Booker's decision to keep us in California, the cost of living was high compared to Oklahoma, and I had no family around to help me with my son. Booker could have spent more time with us if he wanted to. Or like Charlie, did he stay away because he felt like there was little room for him at home?

In my recounting, the dissolution of our marriage has always fallen squarely on Booker's work habits and dedication to his clients over family, over me. But after listening to Noa, was it not all Booker's fault? Maybe I didn't cheat on Booker with another grown man, but maybe Booker felt second best after our little man was born. Was Booker trying to tell me he didn't want to move further down my priority list by adding more kids to the mix? The idea of changing the narrative of my last five years leaves me itching in my skin and wanting to take cover back on my couch.

CHAPTER SIXTEEN

"Mrs. Abrams! Ma! Esty wants to learn to skateboard!" Darius blows into Noa's kitchen trailed by Esty. And Simone. Have I not scared that girl off yet? Noa and I look at each other. Uh. No, skateboarding is not happening.

Reading our faces, Darius has a persuasive argument at the ready. "Simone and I will each be on one side of her. The parking lot a few blocks over is flat. I have Esty's bike helmet right here, and we stopped by Simone's to pick up knee and elbow pads from her little sister and a beginner board." As Darius lists the collected items, Simone and Esty hold up what they have in their hands. This is not going to be an easy argument to shut down, but I'm up to the task.

"Darius, how many times do I have to tell you it's okay to call me Noa?" Noa mock reprimands while hunting for salsa in the fridge. One look from me and Darius knows, *Don't you dare.*

"I taught both my sisters, Mrs. Abrams. I promise I won't let anything happen to Esty." Simone speaks up with a confidence not typical of a sixteen-year-old girl getting the stink eye from her boyfriend's mother.

"Okay then, sounds great," Noa says, too flippant for my safety-first self, and drops the avocados for fresh guacamole on the counter.

"Yay!" Esty screams. "Ms. Lewis, don't tell everyone at school tomorrow, I want to tell them!"

"Oh, I won't, Esty," I assure her. I don't need my class heading home, sharing with their parents that Ms. Lewis thinks they should learn to skateboard in kindergarten, and, bonus, her teenage son and his questionable girlfriend will teach them.

Once the kids have bounded out the door, I stare down Noa.

"What?" she asks. "Now that Charlie's gone I have to stop being such a worrywart parent. With one set of hands, it's my only choice." In my parenting handbook, one set of hands means you double down on the overprotection, not cut it in half. "Plus, since when has worrying ever stopped bad things from happening? Case in point: Charlie's dead. I probably could have solved climate change with the wasted time and brainpower I've spent fretting over things of which I have zero control." It's true but hard as hell to implement. Case in point in the Lewis house: my stressing over Darius not making me a premature grandmother and getting advice on adolescence from Judy did not keep condoms out of his dresser drawer.

Noa peeks out the living room window to make sure the kids are heading off to start the skate lesson. I follow to make sure Darius knows how to properly put knee and elbow pads on a girl. I can worry a little.

"Anyway, you bored with my story yet?" Noa huffs, blowing an errant hair out of her eyes.

"Not in the least." I smile and take another sip of wine for the home-stretch. All our dinners together, I'm usually the one running my mouth keeping the conversation going while Noa follows along, encouraging me to continue amid Darius and Esty's table antics. Tonight, the roles have reversed, and I sit captivated as Noa plays the part of raconteur.

"The past couple of years I have had a nagging suspicion that Charlie might be stepping outside our marriage." Well, that's one way to lay it out nicely that your husband's a low-down cheat.

"Just so we're clear, that *is not* how a Black woman would call out her husband cheating on her."

"Oh no?"

"Uh, no. If I had suspected Booker of being out in the streets, I wish I would have caught him hugged up with some other woman. It'd be the last hug either one of them would ever get. They're lucky I never caught them."

"The past two years I had a nagging suspicion Charlie had a side-piece. Is that better?"

"Much. Keep going."

"I know this is going to sound so weak, but every time I thought about confronting Charlie, I was too tired to take it on. A toddler in your midforties is no joke. So rather than confront him, I set my sights on getting back in shape, getting Esty off to kindergarten, and then fixing our marriage once our girl was comfortably in school. And trust me"—Noa points a paring knife at me—"I know I sound like a text-book middle-age suburban cliché."

"Yes, you do. But if it helps at all, I could tell your body was bangin' from my front window."

"Thanks. It doesn't," Noa says with a wry grin. "The night you were over here and the officer showed up, my worst nightmare was confirmed. Not only did I have to face the fact that Charlie was cheating on me, but it became a worse betrayal when I saw the *M* on this key chain." Again, Noa picks up the keys, this time holding them by the *M* medallion as if they reek like Darius's socks.

Oh no. That nice policeman delivered an already-devastated widow the proof of her husband's infidelity with an ex-girlfriend that evening. That is a whole 'nother level of cold as hell.

"I thought she lives back east?" I defend my lack of understanding, repeating back to Noa the details she told me.

"She did. Boston to be exact. But a few years ago, Charlie casually mentioned that she had moved out here. A common buddy from their

Boston days filled him in. I asked Charlie if they had been in contact, and he swore up and down he had only had lunch with her twice. And I chose to believe him, because I loved him." Noa buries her head in her hands and muffles, "I'm such an idiot."

"No, you're not. I would have wanted to believe Booker too; I really would have. If you can't believe the people you love, then who can you believe?" I peel Noa's hands off her face, now streaked with tears. I pull my jacket sleeve over my fist and wipe across her cheeks.

"The night Charlie died, when he told me he was out having drinks with buddies, he was obviously with Monica. I thought he was having an affair with a junior associate from his office. He traveled so much. I convinced myself he was only hooking up; it didn't really mean anything. But that wasn't the case, was it? That last person Charlie was with, really with, the night he died, was Monica."

I can't help but be pissed off on Noa's behalf that after being with Monica, Charlie came home and tried to put the moves on her. I'm not going to say anything, but that has to have crossed her mind.

"So here I am, a forty-seven-year-old widow still desperately in love with a dead man who cheated on his wife with his first love. What am I supposed to do with all this, this . . ."

"Mess?"

"Yes, mess! I need to figure out how to move on."

"Yes, you do," I say to Noa, one eyebrow raised along with my wineglass. And I know how. We move on by finding Monica.

~

The past week I've been slammed during my time outside school prepping for parent-teacher conferences, so Darius's chore list, on top of taking care of Esty, has grown long. In a couple of weeks baseball season starts, and Darius's time will become impossibly limited between practice and schoolwork, so there are a ton of things around the house he needs to take care of before I'm buying him new cleats. Noa and I are going to have to change up a schedule that's been working beautifully, adding angst to a rhythm that has run smoothly for all of us for the past several months.

"Hey, hey, Marjette," Max sings loudly, bounding into my classroom right at the stroke of end of day. The moms in the room are thrilled to see Max, every inch of him perfectly filling out his original Levi's 501s. He's also got a sneaker and hat game going that's usually reserved for brothers. A side of him I'm surprised to see.

"What are you doing here? I thought today was a Darius day. Should I text him and Noa and let them know you're taking Esty this afternoon?"

Esty's big ears catch wind of the change of plans, and she runs over to us. "I don't want to go with Uncle Max. I want to go with Darius and Simone!"

"I'd want to go with Darius and Simone, too, if I were you, Esty; they're pretty great," Max says, swooping his niece into a big hug. Man, Noa can't stop talking about how much Esty likes Simone. Booker has let me know on more than one occasion that he gives her the thumbs-up, but I always considered his opinion coming from a man whose taste gets poorer as he ages. Now Max is giving her a positive endorsement. Am I the only one on Team Kick Simone to the Curb? "No, you're still going with Darius and Simone. I just have a favor to ask this lady." I look around my classroom to see all the other moms have cleared out, so I'm actually the lady Max is here to see.

"How can I help you?" I ask with a curiosity I wish were laced more with confidence.

"No laughing at me, okay?" Max waggles a finger at me. Esty starts to laugh. "Truly, Marjette." That sends Esty into howls.

"No laughing, I promise." I cross my heart with my fingers.

"I got a big catering gig for a fiftieth wedding anniversary this weekend. A couple that Darius and Esty met at the JCC if you can believe it," Max starts in. "Turns out your son and my niece have been selling Flour + Butter hard after school. Darius is the best word of mouth a guy can have."

"He owes you for how much you feed him," I say, but inside I'm filling up with pride that my boy has put into practice the lessons of kindness and paying it forward I've drilled into him.

"Mr. Greenberg loves brisket above all else. His wife doesn't let him eat it because of his three stents, but she's willing to make an exception for their anniversary. Problem is, I'm terrible at cooking meats, and I really don't have the patience for brisket."

Max reads my face perfectly. "Yes, the irony is not lost on me that as a chef and a Jew I can't make a cornerstone dish of my people." I shake my head—yep, that's exactly what I was thinking. "But let's be real, brisket and barbecue are siblings, so I was thinking, maybe you could come to the bakery and help me make it?" Max grins with all teeth showing like a little boy asking his parents to stay up another hour past bedtime.

"Hmmm. I smell a racial stereotype cooking here. How do you know I can make barbecue?" I inquire, perhaps having taken it a sentence too far. Please don't let me have killed our vibe with a social justice joke.

"Educated guess after eating your fried chicken. And you're from Oklahoma, where the cookouts are legit. I'm just saying . . ." Damn, this man even knows we call our Sunday afternoon picnics *cookouts*.

"You just so happen to be right when it comes to my brisket, but don't get used to it," I tease. "And I'm not sure about two cooks working in a kitchen that small for that long."

"It'll get too hot?" Max throws back boldly.

I suck in my breath. "I was going to say it'll get too dirty."

"I like dirty." Max tips his chin at me. "Let's get it going tomorrow after school, at my bakery. You in, Marjette?"

"I'm in," I agree, and for the first time let myself look at Max as more than an uncle.

When I get home around seven o'clock the house is dark and not one item on Darius's to-do list has been done. Including putting the baked ziti in the oven at 350 degrees. And I'm starving. All there is in the way of explanation is a note on the counter in Darius's handwriting that says, "Call Dad." It's the last thing I feel like doing, but "getting over the bad to get on with the good" has always been an Auntie Shay mantra I try my best to live by.

Booker picks up on the first ring, which surprises me. I'm used to him letting my calls go to voice mail.

"Hey, 'Jette." I like the sound of my name coming out of Max's mouth better.

"I have a note here from Darius to call you," I say, keeping it to business and hopefully short. I'm bone tired from five back-to-back parent-teacher conferences after my visit from Max.

"Thanks for calling. I don't want to take up your time," Booker starts. Clearly, he does or there wouldn't have been a note for me to call him. "But I have a few things I need to discuss, or really to share with you."

"If I've told you once, I've told you a hundred times, Booker, there's nothing about Darius I don't know, so spit out what you think you know, and then let's get on with our evenings."

"This call isn't just about Darius; it's also about me."

My stomach sinks and Auntie Shay pops back in my mind clear as day. The last time I saw her healthy was when she was just a few years older than Booker and I are now; six months later she died of cancer. I brace myself, realizing all those times I wished him dead, I really didn't.

"I'm getting married, and we're having twins."

My stomach sinks through the floor. The Brimbo is getting my husband, and Booker is getting my big family. I don't say anything but listen to the rustle of Booker's ill ease on the other end of the line.

"And what is it you wanted to share about my son?" I demand as if brushing off his words makes them not true. He said it; he knows I heard it. It's an exercise in maintaining my pride by leaving it at that. When Booker told me about the Brimbo the first time, minutes before he pulled out of our driveway, I intentionally chose dignity and denied my need to confront this homewrecker over the havoc she caused my family. The only time I have actually laid eyes on her is scrolling through pictures on Darius's phone. But now this woman has stolen my happy ending, and feelings I thought buried are once again scorching my insides.

"Also, Darius wants to come live with us." Though his voice is clear, this time I'm not sure I heard Booker correctly.

"What did you say?"

"Darius would like to live with us."

CHAPTER SEVENTEEN

Noa has informed me that my denim game is dated, and she wants to take me shopping. I need to get my mind off Booker's claim yesterday that Darius wants to move in with him and his soon-to-be expanded family, so I agree to go. I don't believe Booker for a minute that my son would rather live with him and the Brimbo, but I'm happy Darius spent last night with a friend, giving me space to figure out how I will be having the *over-my-pile-of-ashes* conversation with my son and his delusional father.

Thumbing through a rack of jeans that are stiff with no stretch, I recognize it's been a minute since I've jumped into the high-end shopping pool. About the same time I had to start paying my own credit card bills. It's all coming back to me—the higher the price point, the less comfortable the clothes.

"I've looked. I don't see anything I like," I announce loud enough for Noa to hear, but not so loud I've insulted the saleswoman dripping in labels carried by the store. I don't want to have to admit to Noa that shops like this stop two sizes below where I begin and don't even pretend to serve curves like mine.

"We've been here three minutes." Noa ignores my declaration of defeat and pulls multiple pairs of jeans off the rack. Ohhh . . . I kind of like the pair of light-wash ones she flings my direction. "Here, go try these on." She thrusts a final six hangers into my chest and grabs the coffee cup out of my hand, stealing my shopping security blanket. "And try this lavender sweater too—the color will be amazing on you." Since I don't have a free hand, the sweater is tossed over my shoulder as Noa bullies me toward the fitting room, picking up two more shirts and a belt for me to try as we make our way to the back of the store. The saleswoman is eyeing Noa like, *You're hired!* Little does she know there will be no sales today.

"I take it you don't approve of my casual wear?" I probe, closing the dressing room door behind me.

"Contrary to popular belief, yoga pants are not for every occasion." Noa raises her voice so I can hear her sermon through the slats of the dressing room door. I open my mouth to protest, but Noa beats me to it. "Not even when they're paired with a trendy sweatshirt and the right sneakers." Noa has reviewed my weekend outfit in full and given it a failing grade. "You're too young to throw in the towel, and trust me, leggings are for quitters." I release the huge sigh I've been holding since I agreed to this escapade; she really is not going to let me out of this. "And I'm not just talking about fashion. I'm also talking about men."

I poke my head out of the dressing room. "Baby steps," I warn.

Noa puts her hands up in surrender, but I'm educated enough to know that Jews, just like Blacks, have a history of persevering by finding clever solutions to thrive and get what they want—and apparently Noa wants me to have style *and* sex.

I hold up the first pair of jeans and know I'm never going to get them over my hips. Standing in line for coffee, I pinkie promised I'd come out of the dressing room and show Noa everything I try on because I was sure I would find nothing. I figured I would be the one sitting in the comfy chair designated for reluctant husbands, sipping away on my Americano, while Noa paraded in front of me wondering if she needed a smaller size. How did I end up the one staring at myself in beige cotton briefs under fluorescent lighting?

Miraculously, I get the first pair of jeans zipped. Unfortunately, though, since I'm short, the fashionable high waist is well past my belly button and is practically kissing my underwire. I turn around in the three-way mirror and can't help but laugh out loud at what looks like a porn star's denim corset. "No fair laughing alone! Let me see, let me see," Noa whines from the other side of my door. "You promised!"

"Is anyone out there with you?" I whisper, having to bend flat backed at my hips to slip on my shoes since the waistband is digging into my upper ribs. Is it possible to get acute appendicitis from a pair of pants?

"Nope, just me," Noa confirms, anticipation in her voice. I'm about to take our relationship to another level and hope Noa can handle it. If she can, friendship bracelets are in our future. I adjust my plain Maidenform bra, which is about as old as Darius, and tie the lavender sweater over my shoulders Hamptons-style. With confidence, I strut out the dressing room like I'm heading onto the store floor, boobs leading the way over the waistband of the jeans. Noa rolls off the seat howling as I stride by like a woman on a mission. I catch a glimpse of myself in the full-length mirror: my sneakers look good with these jeans.

"Is this what you had in mind instead of yoga pants?" I ask innocently over my shoulder as I turn and pose.

"Are you heading out to find yourself a crop top?" Noa tries to ask seriously but busts up all over again. I have to hold back from joining her because the pressure over my diaphragm will rupture the zipper wide open, and I'll be out a couple hundred bucks.

"You're right, though—lavender is my color," I concur, holding one of the sweater's sleeves up to my face. I give Noa a wink before scurrying back into the dressing room when I hear the saleswoman's mules flip-flopping our way. Still giggling with Noa through the louvered door, I peel off the jeans and do a little happy dance. They may not have been my style, but they were my size. I grab another pair off the hanger and hope they land on my hips.

Riding the postshopping buzz, bags hanging heavy in my hands, I offer to treat Noa to lunch for elevating my tired weekend look. I may even entertain her suggestions about my nonexistent dating life, I'm in that good of a mood. Behind her menu I can tell Noa is gearing up to pepper me with questions. Lately, I've suspected Noa has joined Team Judy in working to kick me out of the safety of singlehood and into the world of highly anticipated first dates that tumble into the hell of bad second marriages. I'm not an idiot, I know how it goes. I'm a skilled eavesdropper when I hear Houghton mothers congregating to gossip on the playground.

In a rigid voice coming from behind her menu, Noa inquires, "What's new?" Even I know that's not how you lead into a conversation that ends with "you need to get laid." I immediately snatch the menu out of her hand. If Noa wants to talk about sex, she has to woman up and look me in the eye. We aren't thirteen.

"What do you mean by, 'What's new?'" I'm withholding Cobb salad until I get a direct answer.

"I don't know." Noa flutters her right hand by her ear, trying to brush away her question and mine like it's no big deal. Is Noa a total prude or is there something specific she's too troubled to spit out? "Making small talk, that's all." Noa looks around the restaurant for our waiter so she doesn't have to look at me. I see him first and shoot him a look that reads, *Don't even think about stepping foot over here.* He quickly spins on his heels and heads the opposite direction. Noa turns back to me. "I really wanted an iced tea." I show a complete lack of concern for her need to hydrate. "Okay fine. Have you talked to Booker lately?" Noa reaches out to grab her menu back, but I pull it an inch out of her grasp.

"What aren't you saying to me, Noa?" I cross my arms in front of my chest, hugging our menus. "And whatever you're not saying, that's the thing you better say real quick."

"I'm getting to it." Noa straightens up, so even sitting she towers over me on the other side of our tiny two top. "Has Booker talked to you about Darius?"

Oh no. Wait a minute, hold up. How does Noa know my family business before I've shared it with her?

"Talked to me about Darius concerning what exactly?" I am not giving up my family matters quite so easily.

"About, you know," Noa hints uncomfortably, reading from my reaction we are on the same page, but she doesn't want to be the first one to spit the truth out loud.

"Do I?" Like a cat chasing a mouse, I'm making Noa work for it.

"Fine, but don't shoot the messenger." Noa exhales deeply and pushes her chair back a foot so she's out of striking distance. "I know Darius is thinking about moving in with Booker." She says it in a way that makes it sound like Darius has any sort of choice in the matter of whose house he lays his head in.

"And how are you in on that piece of nonsense? Which, by the way, is not true." I don't want Noa to think she's ahead of me in knowing what's going on with my son.

Her face softens toward me, or maybe on behalf of Darius.

"It's no big deal, Marjette. From time to time Darius and I chat, and he told me he's been thinking about it." I lock down my jaw to control my heart, which is racing to catch up to the temperature rising under my sweatshirt. "I promised him I wouldn't say anything."

I'm not sure why Noa waited until now to say something versus hightailing it to my house the minute Darius mentioned it, but I suspect it's because no working mother wants to rock the precarious child-care boat. "When do you and Darius 'chat' about his living under my roof?" I use air quotes, the universal signal of a pissed-off woman.

"Please don't be mad at me or Darius. You may be small, but you're kinda scary," Noa begs, not wanting to ruin what, up until this moment, has been a five-star female field trip. It's looking like she's about to drop tears of fear, so I relax my shoulders so she'll continue. "Sometimes, when I'm home starting dinner and Darius is cleaning up from playing with Esty, I ask him about his day. Usually, he just shrugs, but other times he opens up. I promise you, if he ever told me anything where I thought he was in real danger, I would immediately tell you."

I nod my head on the imminent-danger front.

"I ask him about his life, too, but the answer is never, 'A'right, I'm thinking about moving out of my childhood home.' And he ought to be using his manners and asking you about your day like he's got a mama." Truth is, when I push Darius, the sentence usually starts and stops at *a'right*.

"Relax, Marjette, he does ask how I'm doing," Noa assures, offering me some relief. "He never specifically told me he wants to move out. Only that he gets to be more of a kid at his dad's house, not so many responsibilities piled on top of schoolwork, taking care of Esty, and baseball coming up. That, maybe, things are stricter at your house than at Booker's." Once the words fall out of Noa's mouth, I can see she wants to collect them up and stuff them back in.

"Strict?! That kid's got it better than I ever had it. I've provided so much for him that I hope I come back as my own child in my next life. I grew up a minister's daughter; he hasn't seen strict with binoculars." I hate to think my son is ungrateful for all I've done for him, but for right now, maybe this is a sore spot it's time to put a salve on.

"Turns out he wants to live with his dad; at least that's what Booker tells me," I share, hating the sound of it as it comes out my mouth. "Makes me feel like the Brimbo is going to take my place in more than just Booker's heart, maybe in Darius's life too."

"Please, Marjette, you know there's no way that's true. You're a fabulous mom. The kind they write up as a case study in those guilt-inducing parenting books I skim."

"Thank you. I think."

"You could stand to lighten up on Simone, but other than that, you're a true role model for me on how to raise a great kid all on your own."

"I'm going to chalk up that Simone comment to the fact that Esty is only in kindergarten. Trust, when she's in high school and boys are sniffing around your house, I'm going to bring you right back to this conversation."

"Okay, okay, that's fair. I'm big enough to admit what I don't know." Noa falls silent, and I'm glad we're moving off the Simone topic.

"But I do like Simone," Noa slips in quickly and smiles before taking a sip of water. "Now, back to Darius. What'd he say when you asked him about living with his father?"

"That's on for later today. He's been at a friend's house overnight. Can't say I'm looking forward to it." I sigh and hand Noa back her menu but swat at her fingers, playfully punishing her for almost ruining my first carefree shopping day in a long while. "Before we order, you have any other big reveals that may make me lose my appetite?"

Noa leans over the table, her menu shielding us from the rest of the restaurant, and whispers like she's Israeli intelligence, "I found out where Monica works."

⁓

I'm curled up in my well-worn leather chair where I like to read, the afghan Auntie Shay knit me for high school graduation thrown across my lap. My favorite mug Darius made in third grade is steaming with chamomile. I'm not sure if the glaze he used contains lead, but it might benefit Darius if it killed me before he shows up. I've been thinking on Booker informing me that Darius wants to live with him, and I can't decide if my feelings are hurt, if I'm mad as hell, or who the hell I'm mad at. The list is long.

Darius should be home any minute. I've cataloged, deep in my brain, the reasons why moving in with his father is a terrible idea. A few key points may have slipped my mind between the dressing room and preparing to dress Darius down, but I know when we get to talking, they'll come back to me.

Number one reason Darius isn't going anywhere: no one will ever love my son the way I do. Ever. It's not even worth giving breath to that argument. And then there's straight-up reality, starting with, my boy needs special laundry soap because he has sensitive skin. Any ole Bounce sheets in the dryer won't work for him; they must be fragrance-free. Neither Booker or Darius knows that. Plus, I always have a ridiculous supply of Cheez-Its in the cupboard, but not the extra cheesy kind. Darius only likes the plain ones that come in an oversize plastic bin from Costco. And then *I know* his father is clueless that Darius will only wear three-quarter-length socks, never a crew or a no show, and they have to be white and prewashed in the fragrance-free detergent. These are only a few of the basics necessary to get my son through a day. Add to those simple details that Booker doesn't know who Darius's pediatrician or his dentist is, and he could never get past the second line of a health history form. Who's going to save my son's life if he gets airlifted to a trauma center? Not Booker.

I hear Darius drop his bag and kick off his shoes at the front door.

"Hey, Ma, why's it so dark in here?" Darius asks, looking into the kitchen. "And I don't smell any dinner. Are we ordering out tonight?"

"No, there's some leftovers in the fridge you can pull out if you want. I'm not hungry."

"Okay." Darius hesitates, seeing me curled up under my childhood blanket. "You feelin' all right?"

"I'm feelin' as well as can be expected after speaking to your father yesterday," I answer as calmly as if I'm talking to my financial adviser. "He tells me you two have some plans."

"Oh," Darius says, shoulders curling in, chin dropping closer to his chest like I knew it would. "So, I guess he mentioned that." Typical boy, thinking without thinking of the consequences. Of course Booker told me. Did Darius think he was just going to move all his shit out in the middle of the night?

"Yes, he mentioned it to me. The question is, why didn't you? We don't keep things from one another, Darius. At least we didn't used to."

"Ummm, because of this." Darius points back and forth between the two of us. "You sittin' in the dark looking all scary like a serial killer." That's the second time I've been called scary in one day. Never underestimate the reaction of a vexed mother.

"Serial killers don't drink chamomile."

I purposely go quiet after that. My tactic is working as Darius shifts uncomfortably from one leg to the other, realizing moving out is another one of the harebrained ideas he has not thought through. Kind of like keeping condoms in his sock drawer. At tonight's fight, Darius is not going to make it past the first round.

"Ma, you don't understand," Darius accuses. Apparently, the bell has rung, and Darius has come out swinging with an all-too-familiar jab.

"You tell me what I don't understand."

"Well . . ." Darius hesitates.

"Well, *what*? I changed your diapers. I was sleep deprived for three years before you decided to make it through the night in your own bed. I've gone to every single baseball game all over the state of California, and I read the entire Harry Potter series out loud to you, and there's only one Black student in all of Hogwarts. Only one!"

"I know, Ma, but all moms do that stuff."

Ohhhhhh, my child; no they do not. Now I'm hot like fish grease on an Oklahoma Friday night.

"But do all those moms you think you know so much about do that 'stuff' alone?"

Darius drops onto the couch, a first sign of defeat. He knows he can't trump the single motherhood card. It's not even worth trying.

"Mom, I know you've done a good job taking care of me."

"No. You take care of a plant," I correct. "I've done a good job raising you."

"Yeah, yeah I know, but what I don't know is what happens next for me, and Dad does."

"Please. I work in a school. I know what happens next for kids." Who does this boy think he is? I've been working with children for almost two decades—there's nothing about them I don't know. The only kids Booker comes across are Darius and occasionally Simone.

"I'm not talking about graduating first grade, Mom. Or high school. I'm talking about moving on to being a man."

"What's the dif—"

Darius cuts me right off. "Who do you think bought me my first athletic cup for baseball? It wasn't you. Do you think I told you about my first armpit hairs? I didn't, but Dad reassured me I wasn't turning into a werewolf, that they'd stop sprouting before I was covered in body hair. And what, Mom, you want to hear about my morning wood? Do you?"

Yeah, umm, I don't, I really don't. "If you needed to talk to a man, I would've asked Phil to come over. He would have been happy to do it. He loves you like a son. You know that."

"I don't want to talk to Judy's husband, Mom. I have my own father, and he's done a pretty good job lately," Darius huffs, locking eyes with me in defense of his dad.

I cannot as easily erase the first fifteen years of Darius's life when Booker was sporadically invested in his son.

"Oh, he has, huh? Is it because he lets that little girlfriend of yours come over?" My gloves have come off and now we're in hand-to-hand combat.

169

"No, it's because he lets me enjoy being a kid. He treats me like I'm sixteen, not forty-six."

"What does that even mean? You've always been my kid."

"It means why am I the one on the couch keeping you company every night? That should be somebody else's job. A grown man's job. Not mine."

I open my mouth to tell him to keep his nose out of my business, but nothing comes out.

"That's what I thought."

"Well, you thought wrong."

"Come on, you know I'm right." We're silent in a game of standoff for several minutes. Self-satisfied that I have been rendered speechless by his words, Darius collects his overnight bag and heads to his room.

I can't believe he dared dismiss my prioritizing him over any other man in my life. Everything I have done was to keep Darius safe so he can grow into the right kind of man. All that work I have put into his upbringing, and he feels put out by my efforts at making sure we maintain a close bond.

Alone, back in the quiet of the dark, I realize I have been knocked out, and there's a new reigning champion in this house. At least for tonight.

CHAPTER EIGHTEEN

"Do you think Frances is polyamorous?" Judy speculates, unfortunately out loud, as three fellow WW members take seats directly across from us. I gag a little hearing Judy use the word *polyamorous*.

"What in the world would make you think that?" I ask, wondering if I've misread Frances's public librarian persona for what it really is, a cover-up for urban kink.

"Look at the way Gary and Paul are flanking her, vying for her attention. They both plopped down in the chairs on either side of her. This is Valentine's Day week, and love is in the air."

"Those were the only two chairs left in the room," I point out, looking around the packed basement. Our Saturday-morning meeting has been humming with newbies since New Year's. I give it until mid-March when attendance, along with motivation, begins to wane.

"I don't know, Killjoy Cupid, they're both looking at her hungry with desire. I know that look, trust me. Since I retired, Phil's been rubbing up on me all hours of the night and day. When you're feeling fit and no longer working, eleven-o'clock sex is on the table. And I mean on. the. table. #NonScaleVictory! It's like we're back in our twenties touchin' and groovin' and—"

"Ahhhhhh enough!" I put my hands over my ears. We're close, but not like that. I do not want to know what Judy uses her whisk for. You talk about your sex life with your sister or girlfriends in your generation, but not with the friend who reminds you of a member of the deaconess board at Sunday service.

"What? You can't tolerate me talking about a little bump and grind?" Judy starts moving around in her chair like she's thinking about getting her sexy on right next to me. Maybe I should call Gary over.

"What do you have against Valentine's Day this year? It's party time at school. Don't tell me you haven't been planning your kindergarten Valentine's Day dance for weeks. I know you."

Judy's right, at least she has been every other year of my teaching career. My class honors Martin Luther King Jr. Day by focusing on his message that hate cannot drive out hate, only love can. Then we ride the reverend's words right into our own celebration of love brought to life with my legendary Valentine's Day dance. Many parents hope their kid is assigned my class for the minicotillion that goes down every February fourteenth. For weeks prior to the fourteenth, my students work on their manners in class, learn to waltz with their PE teacher, and are exposed to Bach and Beethoven in music. Then when the actual day of love rolls around, my kids dress up in their finest threads, dance like their social lives depend on it, and enjoy the finger foods and punch I provide. I know right about now Judy's missing my red velvet cupcakes with cream cheese frosting.

The purpose of the event is to have some fun in the doldrums of winter and embrace learning the ins and outs of polite conversation and party manners. I like to sprinkle a healthy dose of southern etiquette over the laid-back ways of these Californian children. I consider the entire event a success if I can get my students to chew with their mouths closed. After the dance, the kids go home jacked up on sugar, their fancy duds wrinkled and stained, and I go home assured I've done my small part to encourage a civil society.

This year, however, I'm having trouble rallying. Between the Monica revelation, the Booker pregnancy surprise, and Darius's claim he wants to live with his father, I'm not feeling a lot of love in my heart. I'm wondering if there's a revenge holiday we can pivot to instead.

Parents of my students are expected to participate in my lovefest not with their creativity, only their compliance. Year after year I have the dance details covered. All I need is a handful of foot soldiers to carry out my orders on the designated day. Not one parent has ever stepped out of their lane with my party planning, until this year.

"I got this email from Rachel yesterday." I put my phone in Judy's face to get her mind off doing the dirty with Phil. Judy pushes it back so she can read. "Classic passive-aggressive parent move, sending me an email late on a Friday night. That woman knows the school has a 'no emailing over the weekend' policy."

"That's your 'don't go there' move," Judy responds, aghast. Then smiles, letting me know she's faking it.

"It's *our* 'don't go there' move. Who do you think I learned it from?" I remind Judy. She bows her head in acknowledgment of our master-student relationship.

To: Marjette Lewis
From: Rachel Ellis
Subject: My arrangements for the Valentine's Day dance

Marjette,

I was thinking, after doing the exact same thing for the Valentine's Day dance year after year, it might be a tad tired, particularly for parents who have been through it before. With the tuition we're paying there's no room for repeats. I've arranged for three makeup artists from the Bombshell Bar to come to the classroom and do face painting,

I have a photographer to capture all the rainbow cheeks and handlebar mustaches, and to really take the event up a notch I've hired Flour + Butter to cater the party.

Amazing right? No need to thank me. It's my pleasure.

Rachel

"I can't, catch my, breath, I can't . . ." Judy is howling so hard she's crossed her legs so she doesn't pee a little. Carole, who's been busy lining up the new Weight Watchers products to sell us on, wants in on what's so funny. "Rachel's beating you at your own game," Judy ekes out, wiping the sides of her eyes, trying to compose herself.

"What game is that?" I insist on knowing, only so I can prove Judy wrong.

"Ultimate control." The chuckles are building back up again, I can see it. "Rachel's having your dance catered. That is bold!" I get up, leaving Judy to howl it out at my expense, to text Max to find out if it's true.

I contemplate whether I should start my text saying it's Marjette. I don't know if Max has my number in his phone or not. I have his because there is nowhere my son goes where I can't get ahold of the adult in charge. From years of Little League, I have about fourteen baseball coaches on speed dial.

Marjette 9:02 AM

Hey Max, it's Marjette, quick question for you. Did you let Rachel hire you to cater my Valentine's Day dance?

The mechanics are spot-on, but my tone is a little too blamey. Erase.

Marjette 9:03 AM

Hey Max, it's Marjette, quick question for you.

Wait, is Max going to be on the other end exasperated and wondering why I didn't just spit out my question in the first place?

Marjette 9:03 AM

Rumor has it we'll be having a bake-off at my Valentine's Day dance. Just letting you know you have some stiff competition, and I don't like to lose.

That's good. "Send."

Max 9:04 AM

Neither do I. And my competition's pretty stiff too.

Did he really just write that? Flushed, I hurry back into the meeting to have Judy dissect this text with me since her mind's already in the gutter.

⌒

Max arrives twenty minutes before the dance starts to find out where he should arrange his party platters. He looks around my room, confused. The buffet table is already fully stocked with mini cucumber sandwiches, pigs in a blanket accompanied by multiple dipping sauces, impeccably iced heart-shaped sugar cookies, and of course my signature red velvet cupcakes. I point to the small counter by the industrial sink where he can put down his efforts. Max gives me a sly grin, conceding before the competition has even begun, and questions, "I'm still going to get paid, right?" before heading to the far corner of the room.

This morning when Rachel brought Tabitha into class, she was wearing an outfit that elevated her already high-fashion sensibilities. If I could have ripped those burgundy suede pants off her, I would have. Rachel informed me she had to run down to Palo Alto for an investors meeting but would be back in plenty of time to greet the face painters coming from her Oakland shop as well as the photographer to ensure they set up properly. And of course, the caterer she hired. Rachel made it clear she would be staying for the afternoon to connect with Max personally. I pretended to care she would be back on campus in four short hours, and then the second she left I stepped outside my door and called Judy to tell her where my hide-a-key is. I needed her to go get my apple-red wrap dress and matching red-soled Christian Louboutin heels. No one shows me up in my classroom. The irony that I would be changing into one of Booker's favorite outfits on Valentine's Day was not lost on me, but desperate times, desperate measures. I'm not only competitive with my cooking.

Knowing my students would ask a million questions about my midday outfit change, I was ten steps ahead of them with a last-minute lesson on how Clark Kent went about turning into Superman. I would have preferred to go with Wonder Woman's tactics, but I knew the kids would call me out on a technicality because Wonder Woman spins superfast in place and comes out in her armor. Clark Kent can change anywhere he wants, including an elementary school bathroom. It's near impossible to best a superhero conversation with a kindergartener, but I've been practicing for this exact exchange for more years than many of these kids can count.

"This looks tasty," Max says, picking up one of my red velvet cupcakes and biting off half. Oh man, now my presentation plate is off-balance before the parents have arrived to pay me the compliments I deserve. I restrain myself from doing a quick reshuffle. "You do too," Max adds, devouring the second half. I open my mouth, hoping not to say something too careless, but before I can get out a safe "thank you," I'm interrupted by a shrill bellow.

"Max! I can't believe you beat me here," Rachel teases and reprimands at the same time. "We talked about meeting out front at twelve forty-five so we could go to the dance together." From my core, I'm cringing in embarrassment for Rachel. Did she not hear the desperate scolding she just issued Max? Perhaps she's reliving a past middle school trauma and therefore not thinking through her words. As much as I would like to push this woman into a junior high locker, my mind goes to our head of school, who casually stopped by my classroom today at lunch to repeat his year-long capital campaign speech. Boiled down, it goes something like this: "Don't piss off parents dripping with cash," otherwise known as Rachel Ellis. We are only halfway to our new state-of-the-art Houghton theater.

"Oh my goodness, Max, you absolutely outdid yourself with these perfectly decorated sugar cookies. You have such a steady hand!" Rachel gushes, inspecting my table. I look at Max, eyebrows raised, the epitome of smug.

"Aren't you so happy I hired him?" Rachel straightens from breathing all over my cookies and rubs her hand across Max's chest, claiming ownership of her idea and of Max. "It's so nice to have a professional working this event." I'm unclear if Rachel's referring to herself or her hired help, but Max has about three seconds to give credit where credit is due.

"I wish I could claim the cookies, Rachel, but those are all—"

"Oh look, there's Char! Max, we have to go hear the outcome of the story Char was telling us at your bakery the other day. I bet it's unbelievable. Kind of like you." Rachel flutters, grabbing Max by the hand, much like I've seen her do with Tabitha. Captor and captive make a break for it. I know I haven't dated since Booker, but even I know that's not how you do it. Despite the heavy-handedness, Max is happily tripping along with Rachel to catch up on Char's apparently thrilling escapades. Maybe dominating women truly are his thing, as Noa alluded to at dinner when she said, in not so many words, I was not Max's type.

"Ms. Lewis! Ms. Lewis!" Esty runs over to me, her voice raised louder than I have ever heard. I like hearing Esty assert herself after five months in my classroom. It makes me feel like I'm doing my job well. Regardless of age, agency is what it's all about.

Unable to slow her momentum before she gets to me, I bend down to catch Esty in my arms, the slit of my wrap dress exposing my upper thigh, a reminder why this dress is for a club, not a classroom. "Tabitha's on the dance floor crying. Can you come help her?" Esty's eyelids are peeled wide open, letting me know this is more a statement than a question.

"Absolutely, let me get her mom," I tell my little helper, moving in Rachel's direction. Esty steps down hard on my foot, stopping me in my tracks. "Ow!" This emerging tyrant better not have scuffed my Louboutins.

"She doesn't want her mommy—she wants you." I look across the room at Rachel, her back to the children on the dance floor, hanging on Max's every word as well as on his arm. She's practically pulling his sleeve off with her body weight.

Esty leads me over to her friend Tabitha, who's squatting on the dance floor, her voluminous skirt forming a wide berth around her, hiding whatever's underneath. I squat too, knowing that to get the most out of a child you have to meet them at their level. No one likes to be talked down to.

"What's going on here?" I ask Tabitha, a clear guess in my mind. Tabitha purses her lips, locking her answer in tight.

"I saw you and Esty enjoying my sparkling strawberry punch. I made it just for you because I know strawberry is your favorite flavor." Tabitha's jaw drops, believing I made the punch for the whole class because strawberries are her favorite, not because they're red and it's

Valentine's Day. "Did you gulp yours all down?" I ask, suggesting what I already know. Tabitha nods her head.

"And oooowwweeee, I was watching you, Tabitha. You have yourself some serious dance moves! Do you take hip-hop with Esty on Thursday afternoons at the JCC?" Darius has shown me videos of Esty in her hip-hop class. He can't get enough of her trying to do the Humpty Dance, or as Esty calls it, the Humpty Dumpty. Tabitha's a little more skilled at it than our girl E.

"Did you maybe get a little too excited bending those knees to get down into it like your dance teacher shows you?" Tabitha's lower lip begins to quiver. I have a handful of seconds before she erupts. "On the count of three you're going to stand super quick, I'm going to throw this hand towel I grabbed under your skirt, and you're going to plop back down and sit on it. Got it?" Tabitha nods her head, and Esty watches in rapture like I'm about to pull off a magic trick.

"One. Two. Three." Up goes Tabitha, down goes the towel, thump goes her butt onto the floor. "Okay, now wiggle your bottom around to get it all cleaned up." Fear turns to fun as both girls start moving their bums. I have perfected the art of not touching children's bodily fluids.

"All done, Ms. Lewith," Tabitha whispers. "Now what?"

"You get up and walk into the bathroom like you own the place. Under the sink is a pink mesh bag, and inside is a fresh pair of underwear. Put them on and put your damp ones back in the bag and under the sink. Esty will stand guard outside the bathroom door because that's what girlfriends do for each other, right, Esty? We take care of one another."

"Right, Ms. Lewis, just like you take care of my mommy."

"That's right; us queens should always adjust each other's crowns."

Tabitha pulls herself up off the floor and waddles wide legged toward the bathroom, Esty following behind to guard her wet spot. Oh, if these girls only knew how many times they may be doing this exact walk for one another throughout puberty.

I look toward Rachel to see if she's noticed what just went down with her daughter, but she remains engrossed in her own agenda, holding court. I stretch my toe out to swish the towel around for a final wipe with the fanciest shoes that will ever grace this damp kindergarten dance floor.

Hand tucked into Max's elbow, Rachel's attention finally turns. "Marjette? What are you doing on the dance floor all alone?" Her audience of mothers and Max follow suit to witness me standing by myself.

Well, if this moment isn't a metaphor for my life, I don't know what is.

CHAPTER NINETEEN

I count how many sugar cookies I have left (1) and red velvet cupcakes (0) to Max's madeleines (4) and profiteroles (6). Even my finger sandwiches have been decimated. It's official; I've won. And because I look so good today, I'm going to take this opportunity to preen.

"Kids don't like food they can't pronounce. Don't take it personally; you didn't know," I say in mock sympathy, empty trays in my hands, my smile a little too big.

"You do know the first rule of business is location, location, location, right? Nothing looks appetizing sitting next to drying paintbrushes and Comet." Max grabs the sole remaining sugar cookie and bites down. "It's all right for a free cookie," he teases.

I grab the other half out of his mouth. "Then you won't mind if I have this?" I can tell Max is contemplating which he wants more, to win this debate or finish the cookie.

"Ahhhh, so you don't think I have cooties?"

I stuff the rest of the cookie in my mouth to give it something to do while my mind spins.

Eyes brimming with water, Esty slogs over to us, dragging her backpack behind her, too tired to pick it up after an afternoon of hard partying. Max and Esty are the last two in my room, and if her uncle doesn't take her home soon, she's going to curl up under my desk and go to sleep. While I finish chewing, I point my finger behind my palm to signal to Max, *Thanks for staying to help clean up, but you gotta go.*

Max picks Esty up and puts her on his hip, an action I have let go of for this year's practice at independence since Esty is possibly missing having Charlie at home enveloping her in his arms. She wiggles in to get comfortable. I'm with her. I can imagine wiggling in there would feel mighty good.

"Ow, what's this?" Esty whines, unable to get her body draped in the right position over Max's chest. She pulls a beautifully wrapped blush-pink box out of his shirt pocket.

"Ah, those are for your teacher. Would you like to give them to her as a thank-you present for planning such a fun Valentine's Day for you and your friends?" Max suggests. Esty turns the box around in her hands, not sure she wants to part with something so pretty. Max plucks it from her palm and hands it to me. The smell of rich, deep chocolate wafts through the thick cardboard. I open the box to find four pristine truffles lined in a row. Heaven.

"Do you like chocolate, Ms. Lewis?" Esty asks, perking up. For a child, dessert preference is riveting intel.

"Oh, I do. I really, really do. And not just on Valentine's Day, on all days." Except the days Judy calls to make sure I'm tracking my food points. She can knock the taste out of anything.

"Uncle Max does too. Especially chocolate cake with vanilla ice cream on his birthday. Right, Uncle Max?" I can see Esty's brain working overtime, perking her back up.

"Of course. Who doesn't like chocolate?" Max questions as if it's the most absurd possibility in the whole world.

"Then maybe you should ask Ms. Lewis out on a date because she's not married. You can have dessert for dinner!" Esty lights up with energy like this is the best idea she's ever had and how is it that her uncle Max hasn't thought of it on his own?

Max gives a hearty laugh to gloss over my failed love life being summed up in one sentence by his niece. I on the other hand am used to my students' fascination with my personal life or lack thereof. It's a favorite subject of a kindergartener.

Max plants a kiss on Esty's cheek, purposely not making eye contact with me. "You silly goose, you know I can't do that, right? Marjette's your teacher. School rules. And we always follow school rules."

"But you just called her Marjette, and the school rule is you have to call her Ms. Lewis. You broke a rule, and now you have to apologize."

Max does as he's been told. "I'm sorry, Ms. Lewis. I didn't mean to—"

I cut Max off to protect myself from further rejection and humiliation in the usual comfort of my classroom. "Thanks for thinking of me, Esty, but I don't have time to date. I'm too busy taking care of Darius, you, and everyone else in our kindergarten class. All you kids keep me so busy that by the time I get home I'm ready for bed," I say, blowing out a big puff of air to indicate exhaustion. I put the lid back on the truffles to signal the end of this conversation, the end of this day, and the end of yet another sucky Valentine's. I guess I'll be heading home to my side of the bed, as promised to Esty.

Judy has texted twice and called once to find out about this year's updated dance with all of Rachel's trimmings, but I know if I pick up she will want to know if I have Valentine's Day plans. I decide to take Esty's suggestion to heart and treat myself and Darius to dessert before our evening meal. The last few days under my roof have been tenuous after I told Darius I needed some time to consider his proposal to move in with his father, or more accurately how to talk Darius out of it. My hope is with baseball season having started today, the real estate in Darius's mind that was occupied by thoughts of moving out will now be dominated by hopes of home runs. Having grown up with brothers and now being the mother of a boy, I know the male brain only runs on one track at a time.

I put my sweet potato pie in the oven and grab my phone to text Darius that I'm running out to buy some milk, his preferred drink with my specialty, and for him to be home by six thirty for us to dig in. After the time I've had, I do not want to be eating alone on Valentine's Day, but just before I hit "Send," I remember Darius has plans with Simone and erase the whole message with one big heaving sigh.

Ding.

Come on, Judy, leave me alone. I'll holla back at you when I'm ready.

Max 5:48 PM

> Are you really too busy with your kindergarten-ers to date or was that your subtle way of telling me you prefer much younger men?

I look behind both shoulders for I don't know what. Maybe Judy needling me since I'm not answering her texts?

Marjette 5:49 PM

> I don't like my men that short.

My fingers are vibrating with nerves or more likely disbelief. It takes me three times to spell *short* correctly. "Send."

Max 5:50 PM

> Good thing I'm 6′ 2″.

Typical man, they always measure.

Marjette 5:51 PM

> Why are you asking me what type of man I like to date?
> School rules remember.

Max 5:51 PM

> Despite what I told Esty, some rules are made to be broken.

This feels a step beyond our usual friendly banter. This feels like legit flirting. I pour myself a glass of wine, kick off my slippers, and hop onto my kitchen counter. This is the best Valentine's Day I've had in years.

Marjette 5:53 PM

> What rule are you about to break Mr. Kopelman?

Max 5:53 PM

> Brother code. A guy's not supposed to date his sister's friends.

Marjette 5:54 PM

> Don't tell me you haven't broken that rule before.

Max 5:55 PM

> Okay, I've done it and I've never been caught so I'm willing to do it again.

Huh, I hadn't considered keeping my indirect flirting with Max a secret from Noa, but I certainly wasn't thinking about mentioning it to her either. Now that going on a date is on the table, intentionally holding back from my friend is too. I don't want to jeopardize our relationship as neighbors—I don't intend to make that mistake again—but more importantly I'm wary of doing anything to threaten our friendship. Noa needs me more than ever right now given the

Monica situation, and since she has been in on the Booker and Darius dilemma, I need her support as well.

Max 5:56 PM

So, how about it Ms. Lewis, dinner?

It's only dinner, really nothing to tell. I guess Noa doesn't have to know everything, yet.

Marjette 5:57 PM

Okay, when did you have in mind?

Max 5:57 PM

30 minutes.

I fly off my kitchen counter.

As I prepare to go out to dinner with Max, I'm grateful for Noa's insistence that I upgrade my jeans. I pull out my Louboutins for a second time today for a sexy high-low effect and to bring us a little closer in height. I pair my earrings with the wide gold bracelet that Darius refers to as my shero accessory. My hope is it will give me nerves of steel to make it through my first date since freshman year of college.

Booker proudly hails from one of a handful of Black cattle-ranching families in Oklahoma who had survived enslavement, Jim Crow, and government land theft, so it was no surprise our first date was at a restaurant called What's Your Beef? and I didn't dare order chicken. We had our burgers, and, out from under my father's watchful eye, I had my first kiss. From that moment on I had a boyfriend, who soon turned into a husband. At forty-one, I'm about to go on my second first date ever. It seemed more absurd than impossible, or both, but better late than never, I suppose. Really, I don't know; I'm so damn nervous.

For the first time all year, I'm thankful for Simone and her insistence that she and Darius spend Valentine's Day together, so when Max shows up there will be no room for awkward error. On time, I grab my purse, ready to head out to Max's car. To my horror, my ear catches the purr of a motorcycle curbside with my date astride. Before he can walk up to my door, I skip down my driveway to ensure a quick getaway before Noa catches on to any commotion outside her front door.

"Nice to see you again." Max winks and hands me a shiny white helmet. I steal a glance over Noa's way to make sure she isn't peeking out her blinds. Obviously, Max knows nothing about Black women and their hair, which, if there is a second date, will have to change. I slide the helmet on, doing my best not to disturb my style. "Hold on around my waist," Max instructs. I wrap my arms around Max's midsection, but there's nothing to hold on to, his abs firm for a dough boy. I spread my hands wide to get as much of a feel as I possibly can.

We arrive at the restaurant, and I hobble in, my feet frozen blocks of ice from the February air. While I start shaking them for circulation, Max slips his hands under the table, takes off my shoes, and begins to warm my feet under the veil of a floor-length tablecloth. The tingling as I thaw is euphoric, not to mention sexy as hell, but I certainly hope Max is going to wash his hands before the appetizers arrive.

Max babbles enthusiastically about great early reviews he had read of the chef and owner, who's a classmate of his from their cooking-school days. I'm assured the drinks are free so I should order with abandon.

Our banter flows freely, Max sipping on his Kir Royale since he has to steer me back home on his death cycle. I opt for one and then two glasses of champagne for a hit of conversational courage, which it turns out I don't need. My questions about Max's time in Paris are endless.

After mediocre moules marinières and pomme frites, Max leans across the table and motions for me to lean in too. I brace, unable to do as I'm asked. I'm not at all ready for Max to kiss me, though given our conversation I can't imagine he's the type to do so in the middle of a restaurant. While the forward, flirty language of Parisian men is a keen skill Max picked up during his time in France, he claims to detest cigarettes and man sandals.

"This food is terrible. How hard is it to crisp a fry in a French restaurant?"

I giggle like one of my students and relax that my lips aren't being put on Front Street.

"Let's ditch this place and go to Barney's Gourmet and get a burger. I know they don't screw up their french fries. Have you been?"

I don't tell Max I have been there a thousand times with Darius, only that I love their battered pickle chips. He beams at my willingness to change course, checks that I have my shoes on, and hands me back my helmet. Even though I do not want to get back on that bike, I also don't want my date to end, so when Max grabs my hand and says, "Let's do this," I do.

CHAPTER TWENTY

Over lunch on our denim shopping date, Noa mentioned—in a hushed tone like she was confessing to a bank heist—that she had dug around a little and found out that Charlie's ex worked at Kref, Levy, and Johnson, a bicoastal law firm. I pretended to be shocked by her audacity. While Noa and I have gotten to know each other working through her first year of widowhood and my nagging family troubles, so far I've kept to myself my tendency to stick my nose in other people's affairs. An admission like that can tend to be a turnoff until you know someone loves you unconditionally, like Judy. That said, if it weren't for my meddlesome ways, Noa and I may not have discovered all that we have in common. A trait Noa refers to as our Blewishness when we rap Hamilton lyrics like our hometown boy, Daveed Diggs. Noa is remarkably quick lipped.

After learning Noa had discovered Monica's employer, I assumed she would reveal more clues for us to follow at our Thursday-night dinners, but no scraps were ever thrown my way.

Riding a high from my date with Max, but exhausted from flexing my dormant feminine wiles, I returned home and tucked myself into bed with my laptop for some mindless retail therapy. Disappointed there's nothing new on my favorite websites, my mind wanders to the whole Monica, Charlie, Noa love-triangle-and-key-chain debacle.

Within an hour, I collect a dossier on Monica Jensen to peruse with Noa when she's ready for closure. First topic will be Charlie's Nordic type—tall, blonde, blue eyed, slender—and that we are going to have to give the guy credit for finding himself a Jewish replica in Noa. Not an easy feat in an ethnicity dominated by dark-haired beauties. Second will be the lack of images and details online that point to Monica having any other substantial relationships since dating Charlie forever ago. No children, no husband, no dog, not even pictures of gentlemen escorts to law firm parties. And I'm the goddess of googling.

I did not need any more pieces to put together the puzzle that for too long, Monica must have been calculating every step to climb the partner ladder professionally as well as personally, regardless how steep. Monica surely had plans to get Charlie back only to have his death deliver a second blow to her heart. I almost feel sorry for her until, after studying her partner photo on the Kref, Levy, and Johnson website, I realize she was definitely the woman at Charlie's shiva questioning if there were any children around. She actually had the nerve to step into Noa's house. The mystery I want answered is how she slid past Charlie's sister guarding the front door with her factory-line hugging. It's possible she was invited right in, it being kosher she was there to pay her respects and no longer a threat to the Abrams lineage. I want so badly to tell Noa that Monica was in her house, taking in her pain, asking after her daughter, but decide sharing that information could come across as mean spirited, so I let it go.

I may have been waiting for Noa to deliver all the dirty details on Monica, but so far, since the afternoon when the secret of who the *M* key chain belonged to was revealed, she hasn't seemed interested in where Charlie had been the night he died. I was impatient to find out where he had been the last couple of years of Noa and Charlie's marriage. It obviously wasn't next to Noa. But where was Noa's anger? Where were her hot tears? It was clear to me that in order for Noa to move past Charlie's indiscretions she would need to confront Monica and get some answers. Or punch her in the face. Widow's choice. I just need a little more time to figure out how to bring Noa around to my line of thinking.

At our next Weight Watchers meeting, I pick up Judy's name tag at the entry table and slap it on her chest. You would think after ten months of perfect attendance we would be awarded laminated clip-on tags, not these cheapies that leave glue on your jacket. Plus, I'm pretty sure Carole knows who we are by now.

"Ouch," Judy yelps.

"Just making sure it sticks," I answer, looping my arm through hers, steering us toward our seats.

"Why you walkin' around all chipper like you're wearing a smaller size?" Judy wonders with suspicion, checking out my lower half.

"I'm definitely down two pounds and up a first date."

Violet gets wind of my confession and turns. "Are you dating someone new?"

"We'll let you know when we have news for you, Violet." Judy twirls her finger in the air, directing Violet to face front in her chair. Then she turns to me. "Are you dating?" Judy demands as if after all these years of asking it can't finally be true.

"I am." I pause. Never having known me as a woman on the prowl, Judy needs to absorb this unexpected breaking news. "Well, I had a first date and right after this meeting I kind of have a second date, so you'll have to buy me my Americano another time."

"If that's the case then next week let's skip getting coffee and go straight to shopping for lingerie."

"What about tap lessons?"

"I'm the best student in the class, and if I'm gone Phil will get some extra attention from the teacher. Which he needs."

"Is the lingerie for me? Or for you, or really for Phil? 'Cause sorry, Max and I aren't there yet."

"Noa's brother, Max?" Judy starts bouncing in her chair, a little too giddy.

"Pump your brakes. I'm only heading back to my house to cook up some navy bean and corn chowder soups to take over to Flour + Butter for his customers. Max loved my brisket so much he's been asking to taste what else I have to offer." I know all Judy's picturing is me and Max getting busy in the pantry. Safety guidelines set by the Food and Drug Administration are no concern of hers.

"I've cooked a time or two for Max this last week, and it turns out my soups are selling out. I might swap out my tomato bisque for the corn chowder today." From the way Judy's fluttering her eyelids, like her contact is stuck or something, I know she couldn't care less about my soup selection.

"Max is sounding more and more like someone I might approve of. How long has this been going on behind my back?" Judy inquires coyly like the thought hadn't crossed her mind from the minute she heard about him over dinner at my house. "And don't go skipping details."

"You'll be the first to know when I have something to share, I promise." My answer gives Judy little satisfaction.

"Does Noa know?"

"What, am I supposed to say to my new friend, 'I like you. And I *really* like your brother'?" My snipping at Judy momentarily replaces my guilt over keeping a secret from Noa.

Ignoring me, Judy decides, "You should bring him over to meet Phil."

"You mean I should bring him over to meet you?"

"That too," Judy agrees, straightening in her chair and turning to give her full attention to Carole. I know that posture; in Judy's mind she's already dusting off her mother's china for tea.

That week, after Thursday-night dinner at my house, Darius takes Esty home to get her ready for bed and do his homework while Noa stays to watch a couple of episodes of the newly released season of *Real Housewives of Atlanta* with me. Apparently, I unleashed a reality TV–viewing monster at Charlie's shiva when I lulled Noa to sleep with on-screen bitch slapping. In a nod to my southern roots and dedication as my friend, Noa's totally caught up on the first ten seasons of my Georgian women and is anxious to get started on the newest installment. I want Noa to stay so I can pester her with questions about her brother, but it turns out she's a bossy TV companion and relegates any information mining to bathroom breaks and wine refills. All I'm able to get out of our binge-watching session is that Noa has formed an unhealthy attachment to one of the housewives who suspects her husband is having an affair with his first wife (she's number three), and that Max seems happier than usual. Noa suspects he's getting laid by a Houghton mother.

I want to tell Noa, Max isn't getting laid by any Houghton mom but is being laid out by my cooking and my company, but I don't. I'm not ready to know what she thinks of the idea of me and Max dating, when my own brain is still processing it, so instead I act shocked and tell Noa to fill me in right away if she finds out it's Rachel. To my surprise, Noa gives me a look of indifference at the idea of Rachel sleeping with her brother. Then she turns up the TV volume to drown me out.

After two weeks of my cooking navy bean soup, tomato bisque, and corn chowder at home in the evenings, only to then drop the soup off to Max the next morning before arriving at school, he has informed me that while sneaking behind Noa's back may be low risk, cooking food for lunch service out of my house is high risk. I need to step into his commercial-grade kitchen to keep the growing Flour + Butter lunch crowd coming back and the health inspectors at bay. I agreed that's probably best, though I hope the invitation is as much to see me first thing in the morning as it is to keep his bakery doors open.

Max is taking a noticeably long time tying my apron around my backside, and I know slow tying; I endure kindergarteners putting on their shoes. I don't mind Max's lingering as long as he's admiring what he sees. It's pitch dark at six o'clock, and the mood in the bakery's kitchen is intimate, the two of us alone, warmed by the heat of the oven. It feels like we're the only two people awake in the world.

"Can I get you a coffee or espresso?" Max whispers in my ear as he pulls my bow tight. I've never actually had a man make my morning coffee. During my whole marriage Booker would make enough coffee to fill his thermos before heading into the hospital or the office, and then leave an empty pot with grinds in it for me to add more water if I chose. He was so entrenched in our morning routine that even on weekends, Booker only made enough fuel for one.

"How do you like it?" Max asks, reaching across me to grab an apron. I check myself. It's dawn and as far as I know, Max is only talking about coffee.

"First thing in the morning I prefer it black," I answer businesslike, running my fingers through the colander of navy beans to give them a good washing before I pick through them to remove any stones.

"Me too." Max holds my gaze. Oh, Jesus Lord above, I'm starting to believe this man is talking about more than coffee.

"Cheers." Max clinks my oversize mug before he gets to rolling out his croissant dough. Though we've only been hanging out for two weeks, and the daughter of a God-fearing father in me has not yet let Max past my front door, there's an ease standing beside him and working in his kitchen that's unexpected. Up until this moment I believed comfort like this was reserved for couples who have been together forever and can finish each other's sentences, but here it is between the two of us. While I'm sure there was a period of time I felt this connected with Booker, I no longer remember it. I do, however, miss feeling in sync with my son.

"Can I ask you something?" I hate it when women ask for permission to talk, but here I am doing it.

"Always, Marjette." My name sounds decidedly warm and relaxed coming out of Max's mouth, almost like it's been on the tip of his tongue for quite some time.

"Remember I told you about Darius wanting to move in with his father," I begin cautiously. Talking out my parenting woes with Max may be relationship suicide, particularly for a guy who shies from commitment, according to his sister, but I'm in need of some male advice. I know Judy would be hurt that I didn't go to Phil, but recently Max has gotten to know teenage Darius, so he may have something useful to say. For Phil, Darius will eternally be six and in need of having his steak cut. He just about reached over and did it last week.

"I do." Max puts down his rolling pin to give me his full attention. His small act of focus makes my concerns feel important and my trepidation disappear.

"Well, I think I'm big enough to admit that maybe Darius needs to be spending more time with his father now than in the past since, you know, since . . ." I don't want to say it out loud.

"He's becoming a man," Max fills in my blank.

"Ew! Why does everyone keep saying that? Including Darius." I roll my eyes in pseudo disgust at what I don't want to admit is the truth.

"Is being in the company of men so bad?" Max inquires, biting his lower lip.

"If you're suggesting my son is a full-fledged man with distracting thoughts about Simone," I reprimand, wagging my finger back and forth between the two of us, "that is something I'm not ready for."

"Hey, Simone's a good kid; Darius could do worse. Did you know she has an internship lined up this summer at Berkeley Lab? I love talking with her and Darius when they bring Esty in. Those two are on top of what's going on in the world." Why is it that everyone's a fan of Simone? Does no one other than me see how she's distracting my son? I was so sure baseball season would slow their roll, but all it's done is push Simone's hours at my house later into the evening.

I look at my watch. I have to get these soups finished up and take off for school in a half hour, so I better get to it. "Do you think I should let Darius move in with his father?" I can hear my mind begging Max to give me the answer I want.

Max puts the tray of croissants in the oven, sitting on my question for a minute. I can't help but tap my foot, waiting impatiently for his answer. "I think maybe the two of you should work on getting through the rest of the school year together. I don't know that making a big change in the middle of junior year is the best idea." Well, there it is. Max and I are definitely made for each other, and yes, it's because he agrees with me. "But I think letting Darius try out living with his father over the summer may be a solid idea."

Excuse me?! "You think leaving a sixteen-year-old boy—sorry, 'man'—at home, alone in his father's house during the open-ended hours and days of summer is a good idea? Do you remember nothing from being a teenager?"

"I remember, regardless of what my parents did or did not do, I was still going to do what I wanted to. Besides, Simone will be tied up with her internship, and Darius will be playing summer ball. When he's not at practice, he can work for me delivering catering orders." I would like Darius to have a solid summer job and start saving up for college. His father may be able to afford tuition and board, but my son will be paying for the bonus social life I know he's planning on having. "I could use the help. Rachel and all her pals have built my catering business up to a point that I think I'll need to bring on some additional hands. Plus, Darius told me his dad's getting him a car."

Argh! I thought I had killed the car conversation this fall. We manage just fine with one car between the two of us. I guess a car of your own is part of all the extra freedom of living with your father. And what is Rachel up to with all her catering orders? I've been in a Bombshell Bar a handful of times, and those women haven't touched a pastry since the early aughts.

"Yeah, but . . ." I'm trying to pull my protest together but tripping over my own words searching for an airtight defense.

"I'm not saying you have to do it, Marjette. I'm just saying think about it. Or better yet, ask Darius what he thinks about living with his dad starting after school ends. Then you can revisit the living situation in August before school starts back up. You have a solid kid for sure, so maybe it's time to loosen the reins a little bit and let yourself focus elsewhere."

"Where?" I spit out, a knee-jerk reaction to the sixteen-year singular commitment of being Darius's mother. And then it clicks. I may be inexperienced, but I'm not stupid. "Oh, here. Don't worry, I won't screw up your soups, though by summer I'm not sure your patrons will want something hot. We might have to rethink the lunch special." Whoa, that was a little presumptuous of me to assume Max will still want me around in three months. I hope my calendaring slid right past him. "Either way, I'm a pro at cooking and kvetching." Score one for my expanding Yiddish vocabulary thanks to listening to Noa bitch, I mean kvetch, about her twenty-four-year-old assistant who can't be bothered to show up at the office two out of five days a week. Apparently a UTI, IBS, and a misplaced IUD are now legitimate reasons to skip work.

"No, I mean right here." Max steps between me and the kitchen island, his broad chest allowing me no other view than the chef's coat standing before me.

Hands on my hips, in one swift movement Max lifts me up onto the stainless-steel countertop, slipping his body between my legs. "Marjette Lewis, when you are not teaching my niece or overparenting your son—" I raise my index finger, warning Max to watch himself. In response, Max grabs my hips a second time and pulls me in closer, showing me he's in charge of this kitchen.

"Will you be my sous-chef?" Max cradles my jaw, tilting my head up toward him. My knees roll in, holding Max's thighs firmly in place as he leans over to give me one hell of a good-morning kiss. I take in Max's faint smell of sweet pastry dough and feel an electric hit of morning energy as his mouth rolls over mine. For several seconds I let Max's lips find their momentum as he kisses me for the first time, but then I pull back, leaving this gorgeous man confused but grinning from ear to ear.

"Let me make one thing clear: I'm nobody's sous-chef."

CHAPTER TWENTY-ONE

"Noa's tripping out," Max said with a shake of his head as he walked me to the front door of his bakery this morning. "Maybe you could keep an extra eye on Esty the next few days." He didn't know why, Max admitted, and, if my experience with the men in my life was any indication, he was likely too afraid of the answer to ask. He requested I not say anything to Noa. I was hustling to avoid being late to school—our make-out session over simmering beans leaving me only a handful of minutes to get to Houghton—so I promised to keep my lips zipped, but I don't like being in the middle of family issues. Loose as they may be, I do have boundaries when it comes to meddling.

Several times while writing the morning message on the classroom whiteboard, I forgot what I was supposed to be doing. My mind was tangled up with thoughts of Max and what might have happened if my life were not dictated by a school bell. As my students were being dropped off, a girlie voice in my head kept repeating, *I was gettin' busy while you were gettin' your socks on!* Thankfully not one parent called me out on my slanting penmanship. Not even Noa noticed a difference in my demeanor, though she did point out my lipstick was janky.

The promise I made to Max stuck with me all day, but not enough to stop me from thinking about how to circumvent it. If I can help a struggling friend, I'm going to do it. I finally convinced myself that stopping by to say *Hi* when Noa got home wouldn't send up any red flags.

While I'm sorting construction paper after school, my phone starts blowing up. Abandoning sunshine yellow, I stumble across my room to grab my lifeline, hoping for a little afternoon sexy texting. It had taken all my self-restraint not to text Max at lunch while my kids were dissecting their cheese sandwiches for hidden lettuce. I even had the perfect flirty words at the ready: *Kissing is like cooking; do it well or don't do it at all. Turns out we're both pretty skilled in the kitchen* . . . But then I thought of sitting on Grandma Birdie's couch between her and Auntie Shay, clutching sweating Coca-Colas, watching *The Young and the Restless* because Shemar Moore was the hottest Black actor on daytime television. Since all my dating advice came from Grandma Birdie's religious teachings and Auntie Shay's sexual freedom, as a young girl the messaging could get confusing. Today, Grandma Birdie's advice, *Don't go chasing men, let them chase you,* rang louder, so my phone stayed in my purse.

Ding.

Darius 3:42 PM

You coming to my game @ 4?

Lately we've been walking in circles around each other at home to avoid issues we need to discuss, and I had forgotten about Darius's opening game. Glad it's on campus and I can finish closing my classroom and be over there in fifteen minutes to catch the opening pitch.

Darius 3:42 PM

BTW Dad's coming.

Curious as it is, I'm going to let that one slide. Booker hasn't made it to one opening-day game in Darius's whole baseball career, but now he's going to turn up? This best not be the day the Brimbo decides to take up the all-American pastime as well. I've made it six years not meeting her in person, never trusting what I might do if I were to find us face-to-face. I certainly don't need it to happen now, because she's got all the feels of a step–baby mama. I may be small in stature, but I'm big enough to carry an enormous grudge.

Noa 3:43 PM

> I haven't gone to the movies in forever. Simone says she'll watch Esty tomorrow night. Want to go? Warning though, I don't share my Raisinets or SweeTarts with anyone. Don't even try 😅

Marjette 3:44 PM

> I only like popcorn so we might be all right.

Judy 3:43 PM

> I won't be able to make our meeting on Saturday. Phil and I have our spring tap recital. Sorry to make you go solo.

This news is too good not to warrant an immediate response.

Marjette 3:44 PM

> Oh, I'm coming to your performance Shirley Temple.

Judy 3:45 PM

> You're not invited.

Marjette 3:45 PM

I'm inviting myself. Tell your Gregory Hines I'll see him there.

I save my first text from Max for last so I can soak it all in without the pressure of others waiting to hear from me.

Max 3:42 PM

Your soups disappeared way too fast today. And so did you. Can I see you tonight?

Marjette 3:45 PM

Absofuckinglutely.

I hear you, Grandma Birdie, I hear you. Too much. Erase.

Marjette 3:46 PM

Not tonight. I have Darius's baseball game and then my son and I need to have a serious talk with his father. I suspect it's going to be a late night.

Max 3:47 PM

You do realize a "serious talk" with a teenage boy takes five minutes, less if they're hungry. But I get it. How about Friday night?

Damn trigger finger responding to Noa before reading Max's text. Regardless, I know the golden rule of female friendship: you don't bail for a male.

Marjette 3:47 PM

I just agreed to go to the movies with your sister on Friday.

Max 3:48 PM

Well, if you can wait until Saturday to see me . . .

I actually can't. I've taken to counting the minutes since last night and to when I will get to see Max next.

Marjette 3:48 PM

How do you feel about dance recitals?

Judy's going to love this.

I let Darius ride home from the game with Booker so I could swing by my classroom and grab a few binders. They must be picking up something to eat, because I beat them home by ten minutes. As they walk up the driveway with matching grease-stained bags, I feel ready to have the conversation with Booker about Darius possibly moving in with him. Who knows, maybe with a bit more free time, I might actually give this whole dating thing a solid try. Even Judy's taken up tap dancing, so I imagine if I really lean into it, there are a million things I may want to explore in addition to Max's body. I've seen people kite-boarding in the Bay. I could do that if I didn't have to deal with cold water. Or sea lions.

Feeling a chill rolling in, I stand on the front porch and hurriedly wave Darius and Booker into the house.

Pointing to himself, Booker signals, *Me too?* I nod, and he cautiously steps across the threshold, possibly waiting for me to trip him. Not only was my morning kiss a confidence booster, but mashing faces has left me in a more than generous mood toward my ex.

"I'm going to go eat mine in my room. I have a physics lab to write up," Darius announces, opening up his backpack. I'm about to insist Darius sit himself down to be part of our conversation, but then reconsider. Perhaps the decision about where a growing boy should live is best decided by the grown-ups in the room.

I nod at Darius, giving him permission to excuse himself. "I love you, son. Nice opener today," I say to send Darius off to work on a positive note.

"Catch you later, Pops." Since when did Darius develop an affectionate name for Booker? He's always been referred to as "your father" or "your dad" in this house.

"Sure, my man, go ahead and start your homework. Your mother and I have some things to sort out." I already excused Darius, so what's Booker doing handing out directions?

We sit down at the dining room table, and Booker unwraps his meal. One sandwich. One serving of fries. One empty bag.

"Where's my food? I gotta eat too," I say, admittedly ruining Booker's first bite just a little.

"Sorry, 'Jette, I didn't even think about it," he says with his mouth full but his head empty.

"That's okay, you eat your food." I don't know why he would have thought of me; he never did when we were married.

While his mouth is occupied, I start the conversation to move us quickly through tonight's agenda so Booker can move on out my front door and I can move on to checking for more texts from Max. Shoulders tense, I'm realizing no kiss can erase how much I don't like having Booker in here, eating in the seat where he always sat. I should have kept him relegated to the front porch.

"I've given a lot of thought to the idea of Darius spending more time with you."

"And Giselle." I've also put in effort to never hear that woman's Christian name. Swallowing hard, Booker then asks, "What are your thoughts?"

"My first thought is, do you even know how to take care of your son long term?" Or at least for a summer, if I follow Max's line of thinking.

"How hard can it be taking care of a sixteen-year-old boy?" Booker asks as he gets up and heads to my fridge, rummaging around for something to drink. "He mostly takes care of himself. I just need to feed him. You saw how happy he was with that burger." Popping the top on a can of soda, Booker shrugs and takes a long sip, seemingly pleased that he just equated our son with a feral cat. "And I'm pretty sure he's too old for a bedtime."

That's it. I'm not sending Darius to go live with this man. I invited Booker into my house to discuss Darius's future, and like no time has passed, he's helping himself to what's in my fridge like he still lives here.

"Instead of telling me that you know how to take care of your son, you give me examples of why you don't have to take care of him. How is that supposed to reassure me, Booker?" I demand, feeling a sense of déjà vu dealing with my ex-husband. Answering with nonanswers being one of Booker's go-to communication strategies.

"Giselle and I'll figure it out." Booker thumps his chest to let out a burp into his palm.

"Uh, no, you won't. You two are going to be too overwhelmed with your newborns to be figuring anything out for your firstborn." Intellectually I understand there may be things that a boy can only learn from his father, but right now I don't give a damn. Darius can learn them from Phil or even Max if things go well. Right now, I don't want to give Booker what he wants. "Darius will be staying here with me. Gather up your trash and take it out to the curb with the rest of you."

"I see your mood can still go from zero to ten for no good reason." Booker heaves a loud sigh like he's heard it all from me before.

"Yeah well, these hands can go just as quickly from zero to life in prison, so let me save you a trip to the hospital and tell you my reason: I don't want my son turning out like you."

—

Making our way into the theater, Noa begins to turn right toward the front, but I issue a loud *pssst!* With her attention, I cock my head to the back of the theater and start walking, giving Noa no choice but to follow.

"Why are we sitting all the way back here?" Noa asks as I side shuffle into the last row. I roll my eyes.

"We're sitting back here so we can talk."

"Oh. Did you not actually want to see this movie?"

"Yeah, I do, but we're sitting back here so we can talk at the movie and during it too."

"Really? Isn't that super disruptive?"

I'm about to give my friend an epic lesson in entertainment etiquette. "Have you never been to the movies with Black folks?"

"I don't know. It's always so dark in here," Noa deadpans.

"Oh, you don't need to see it, you hear it."

Noa gives me a *whatevs* smirk, pops a SweeTART in her mouth, and plops down in her seat. I check mine for gum. I had a bad experience once.

"I'm double fisting sugary snacks tonight so I can stay awake through the show." Noa holds up her SweeTARTS and Raisinets but doesn't offer me any, true to her warning.

"What's up, you not sleeping well?"

"Going to sleep used to be the best part of my days, because Charlie would visit me in my dreams even if only to remind me to update my car tabs." I hand Noa one of my napkins covered in artificial butter in case this is going to be one of those moments she becomes unexpectedly weepy. "Now, though, Charlie hasn't been visiting me as frequently, but when he does someone else is with him. I know it's a woman. I suspect it's Monica, but I can never quite see her face. Being frustrated in your dreams is exhausting. I want helpful Charlie back." Ahhhh, this is why Noa's spinning: terrible REM.

The lights dim, signaling the start of the movie is moments away. I turn ninety degrees, so my face is inches from Noa's. This is the perfect time for me to tell her what she needs to do to put this Monica thing to rest, because unlike me, she's too polite to talk in a theater.

"Girl, you know that's Monica invading your dreams. It's time for you to confront her face-to-face so you can get the full story about Charlie, and then get her out of your head for good."

"You want me to what?!" I guess it's not only Black people who shout in theaters.

It was going to be too difficult for me to lay out the plan I'd been hatching on behalf of Noa with Dolby surround sound interrupting us, so I suggested we duck out of the movie early and into a Mexican cantina across the street. A margarita can make anything more digestible.

"How is it that you see this happening, again? I could only catch every third word inside the theater," Noa asks warily, licking her lime. "I can't believe I paid eighteen bucks and don't get to find out how that movie ends."

"The accountant decides to follow his dreams to become a bass player in a jazz trio. Epic fail. Did you not read the book?" I solve the mystery for Noa so we can get on with it.

Though I know Noa trusts me, I can tell she's dubious that any plan I have might work. I, however, have been training my whole life for a moment like this. Nosy people live for intrigue. It's going to be so easy, I think. "You know how Rachel Ellis owns the Bombshell Bar?"

"She does? I didn't know that. I assumed she's a tennis and blowout mom like the rest of her crew."

"No, she's actually a working divorcée just like me. Her hair is a perk of the job." Whoa. I can't believe I just claimed to have one thing in common with Rachel. "How could you not know? Her daughter, Tabitha, is good buddies with Esty." I would have thought if Noa considered Rachel a decent match for Max, she would have gathered a little more information on her as a potential sister-in-law.

"Since Charlie died, I often feel like Esty has gone from having two parents to half a mom. I've swung from all my attention on Esty to half listening, half paying attention, half-assing everything. I don't need those women seeing it and judging me for it. It's one of the reasons I send Max into school so much instead of me showing up. Besides, no one knows how to talk to a widow. It just ends up being uncomfortable for everyone all around."

My heart hurts for Noa's skewed assessment of herself as a mother, but we are not going down a therapy rabbit hole right now. I have an agenda. I pat Noa's hand, letting her know she's going to be all right, and continue, "Yes, Rachel owns the Bombshell Bar. And Monica happens to have the Kref, Levy, and Johnson founders party coming up in a few weeks at the Palace Hotel in San Francisco. No woman working hard to climb the partner ladder would show up to that shindig not having visited a Bombshell Bar to get her look tight for the event."

"Okay, that's enough. I don't want to know any more." Noa covers her ears. "No, wait, maybe I do. How do you know all this detailed information about Monica? That's all I want to know. I think. Yes, that's it." Watching Noa in deliberation would be kind of entertaining if she weren't also looking at me like she's caught me doing something illicit.

"I have mad research skills."

"You mean stalking?"

"Same but different. Do you want to do this or not?" I wave my hands in the air, not wanting Noa to get caught up in the semantics of my private investigation strategies.

"Fine, fine, as long as you don't tell me the specifics until it's go time. Anticipation gives me ulcers." I cross my heart to save Noa's stomach. "And I'm only going forward with whatever this is on one condition," Noa says with an edge to her voice that sounds like she's readying herself for a negotiation. Moving our empty glasses out from between the two of us, Noa scoots her chair in close. What condition could this woman possibly have? I'm doing her a huge favor. A bouquet of flowers for my efforts would be nice, not a condition.

"If you're pushing me to deal with what's haunting my dreams, then you have to promise to face what's hampering your days. You gotta deal now so you can be done with Booker. The clock's run out."

Before I can refuse, Noa reaches out and takes hold of both my hands. "That's it. Those are my terms. There's another man out there in the wings who will love you, Marjette. I know there is. But he can't as long as you're still letting Booker stand in his way."

"I am not letting Booker do anything!"

"Really?" Noa circles her finger at me, and I shrink in my seat. "Marjette, still, after all this time it seems what Booker says or doesn't say, does or doesn't do, determines what kind of day you have. No man should have that much of a hold on you."

I mull over Noa's words for a few minutes to decide how much I'm going to reveal in this moment of negotiation. "It's not so much Booker's words that have such a strong hold on me," I share, lowering my eyes. Noa bends closer, our foreheads practically touching. I'm working up to divulging one of the most private details of my life, but it's not easy. It's one I've not admitted out loud, even to Judy. "I've never been intimate with anyone other than Booker. Even though he's an ass, he's the only ass I've ever known, and I have no idea how to be with someone who isn't him. I don't know if I can."

"Never?" Noa whispers in disbelief.

"Ever," I confirm.

CHAPTER TWENTY-TWO

It's been two weeks since Noa and I watched half a movie and I got her to commit to confronting Monica. Now I have to manage to pull it off. To get the ball rolling, I need a moment alone with Rachel. She's been in Seattle the past week expanding the Bombshell brand, so I've yet to corner her, and time is ticking. This weekend is the Kref, Levy, and Johnson shindig.

Since before I arrived at Houghton, there has been some version of an Earth Day assembly touting the merits of reduce, reuse, recycle to the community at large. Each grade gets two minutes and thirty seconds in front of the whole school to creatively pressure the audience to alter their ways because, well, climate change. There's nothing like preaching to a sea of parents cradling Starbucks cups.

Time's run out. I'm tired of dancing around environmental topics with cutesy skits, so this year my class is taking it up a notch, transforming into One Use Warriors. This month we have been learning the haka, aligning the vigorous movements with our call to ban single-use plastic, all thanks to Mia's father, who played inside center for the All Blacks rugby team. No one is going to cry cultural appropriation on the daughter of a New Zealand national treasure. In our black clothing and eye black borrowed from the athletic director, who is also the football coach, our goal is to intimidate folks into heeding our call. In rehearsals, we're pretty ferocious up until the lion's breath. My mini-Māori warriors can't escape the giggles at the idea of sticking their tongues out at the entire school.

Before our performance even starts, our fierceness falters. One by one, my warriors abandon the class line to run and hug their moms and dads as we march onto the stage to kick off this year's celebration. Twenty sets of legs spread in ready position, hands on thighs, faces slack. Javon and Esty step out front of the rest of the class to emerge as the performance leaders. Esty stomps back and forth onstage assessing whether the audience is worthy of the sage counsel my kindergarten class is about to impart. These two are the only students left in my class whose teeth are intact; therefore when they enunciate, understanding them is actually possible. Hurtling toward the end of kindergarten, a full grill of teeth becomes a numbers game.

"Refuse!" Esty yells, bugging her eyes out at the audience, not blinking.

"Single-use plastics!" her backup warriors respond at the top of their lungs, holding up Ziploc sandwich bags that held the apple slices and Goldfish crackers packed by their parents. A gym full of proud parents gasp and then look down at their feet in dishonor. The only thing worse than peer pressure is public shaming from one's offspring.

"Why?" Enraged, Esty puts her fist on her hip just like I taught her and scans the audience for any nonbelievers.

"To save our planet!" Behind Esty, in unison, thirty-six hands slap their thighs for emphasis or fear. You're welcome, Mother Earth. Ms. Lewis's kindergarten class has got your back.

After the all-school meeting, I tail Rachel and Char across campus to the bike rack where their new electric bikes sit unscathed. As Char motors off to pick up her Range Rover at the mechanic's, I approach Rachel. She's snapping on her helmet while yelling into her phone at someone who apparently ordered the space-gray rather than rose-gold hair wands. I release a cleansing breath and remember Judy's impassioned plea that the best life to live is one in the service of others, particularly if you're getting paid squat. I'm serving this one up for my girl Noa.

"Hey, Rachel," I utter in a low tone, not wanting to startle her as she hangs up her confrontational call over hair tools. "Is Tabitha not going home with you today?" For some reason Rachel looks surprised to see me standing there, at school.

"Roger is taking her for ice cream. He finally decided to show up for a school event. Other than the first day of school, he hasn't been here once. And he only came then because I agreed to have Tabitha for a whole month so he could go diving in Belize." Rachel throws her ex under the school bus. "Couldn't even be bothered to come to her midyear parent-teacher conference, remember? I believe his exact words to me were, 'Text me if her teacher has earth-shattering commentary on how Tabitha holds a pencil.'" That's extra for sure. Seeing Roger's presence on campus has rattled Rachel, I feel for her. Even Booker showed up for a school conference or two.

"Anyway, exes, right?" Rachel flits her hands, waving annoyances, small or big, into the blue sky. "Is there something I can do for you?"

I had rehearsed a hundred times in my head how I was going to approach Rachel, but now that the opportunity's right in front of me, my feet want to run. "I need a favor. A pretty big one, honestly. And I need it to stay between us." Now interested, Rachel stops fiddling with her bike lock. There's no turning back.

"Okay, I'm listening. And I'm intrigued to say the least."

Here goes. I'm about to tarnish the reputation of kind, upstanding kindergarten teachers everywhere who choose to live by high moral standards, unlike me. "I'm wondering if you'd be willing to search the Bombshell Bar database to find if a certain woman has an appointment coming up?"

"That's it? You just want to know if a friend of yours is getting her hair and makeup done?" Rachel looks at me in mock horror. She's going to make me spell it out for her.

"I don't just want to know if there is an appointment; I also want to know when and which salon." My body tenses with my ask, my discomfort obvious to Rachel.

"Ahhhh" is all I get in response. "Are you planning some sort of surprise for this friend?"

"You could say that." I don't want to give away any more information than I have to. Without speaking, Rachel examines me and then logs her password into her phone.

"What's the name?"

"Monica Jensen."

Rachel slowly types the letters like she's stewing on something else at the same time. After some scrolling, she looks back at me with the steely stare of a seasoned CEO. "If I do this for you, there's something I need in return." It hadn't crossed my mind there may be something, anything, Rachel might need from me.

"Sure," I agree, a little too quickly. "Something you need for Tabitha?" Probably should have pressed pause on my eagerness a bit.

"No, no, Tabitha's fine. The favor's for me. Bombshell Bar turns ten next month and I'm hosting a huge blowout birthday party. Pun intended," Rachel says, giving a hearty laugh to her own joke. I have to wonder how many times she's used that one. "I, well . . . don't want to go alone." Now Rachel's the one shifting foot to foot, looking supremely uncomfortable. "It doesn't feel appropriate, me being the CEO and all." I hope Rachel isn't asking me to be her date to Bombshell's birthday party. Wouldn't Char be more appropriate?

"I've noticed you and Max have developed kind of a friendship over the school year. I'm sure it's rooted in supporting Esty in this difficult time since her mother's absent." There's nothing I dislike more than one mom passing judgment on another's parenting. To do it about Noa in front of me makes my bile rise, and I remind myself Rachel knows nothing of Noa's and my friendship. She's just plain awful.

"Poor Esty aside, I've noticed you and Max talking from time to time." Ohhhhhhh, I'm feeling where this is going, and I'm not liking it one bit. "I was wondering if you would ask Max if he'd be interested in being my date for the party." Here we are again, back in junior high. "I mean, don't make it weird or anything, kind of feel him out, see if he's interested, then let me know." Oh, it's weird all right.

"You want me to ask Max to be your date to Bombshell's tenth birthday party, is that correct?" I inquire, hoping if I say it slowly enough Rachel will realize how ludicrous she sounds.

"Well, don't make it sound so sordid, Marjette. We're simply exchanging services. You need something from me, and I need something from you. Besides, I've had a hunch since the zoo field trip that Max likes me. I don't want to be the one to make the first move, so the whole thing should really be pretty easy on your end." I can't fault Rachel for not wanting to make the first move seeing as I've been raised the same way. But easy? No. Nothing about this is going to be easy.

"But you are making the first move."

"No, you are"—Rachel smiles, shaking her phone in my direction—"if you want the details on Monica Jensen's appointment."

⌒

I give Noa the full top-to-toe once-over. I told her she doesn't need to wash her hair but she should put on her best boss-bitch outfit. She slides into my car in stilettos, leather pants, and a greasy top knot. It's an unusually warm late-April afternoon, so wearing leather pants is a real commitment. "Okay, I've done as you asked with zero questions, but I'm not closing the car door until you tell me specifically where we're going and what in God's name we're going to do once we get there."

Noa's legs are stretched out straight to hold the door open. Either that or she can't bend in those pants.

"Monica has a five thirty appointment at the Filmore Street Bombshell Bar in San Francisco for hair and makeup." Noa's mouth hangs agape, saying either *So what?* or *Oh fuck!* It's a little difficult to read. I suspect the night of the movies Noa never imagined I would actually follow through. "You'll be getting your hair done in the next basin over. I'm gonna be upping my look with some lash extensions." I bat my eyes to punctuate the need for our appointments.

"I'm assuming I don't want to know what you had to do to obtain this information."

"No, you really don't," I assure her.

"So, your plan is I'll take Monica down while she's getting her scalp massaged? Or is it better if I attack during the conditioning treatment?"

"First"—I count off my index finger—"you don't look like you know a thing about taking out your earrings and Vaselineing up for a fight," I observe, watching Noa sip on her Perrier bottle.

"Please. I spent the summer between my freshman and sophomore year of college on my Birthright Israel trip. I know Krav Maga." Noa round kicks her leg into the car. It's not cute. "Okay fine, I spent most of the time harvesting vegetables on a kibbutz near the Dead Sea, but I'm tougher than I look."

"I haven't worked out the details yet, but I do think we should have a little regard for Monica." I hold up my thumb and index finger about an inch. "She does have to go to her company party after we rough her up, so let's get in there before her face gets done. After we have our way with her, then the makeup artist can fix her. I'm not a total monster."

"To clarify, by 'rough her up' you mean just ask her about Charlie and if she'll be staying in the Bay Area long term. Then we get to go to dinner, right? I'm craving Vietnamese."

By six thirty Noa's hair has been cemented into beachy waves and my eyelids look like Charlotte and her web have taken up residence.

Noa's shopped the binder of hairstyling options front to back a handful of times accompanied by a stream of commentary on which one she'll try next if she ever comes back. I can tell by her nervous chatter that she's losing her conviction to confront Charlie's ex. Working to keep my eyelids open, I saunter to the front-desk receptionist and ask if she has a Monica Jensen on the books who was supposed to be here at five thirty. The receptionist clutches the reservation iPad to her chest like I'm asking for social security numbers.

"I'm sorry, Noa. Rachel told me Monica had an appointment here to get the Shell Supreme. I really thought this was a foolproof plan to find her, call her out on her nasty behavior in front of a room full of strangers, and then be on our way looking stunning. I don't know what happened."

"If I've learned anything in this last year, it's that no plan is foolproof." Noa sighs, patting her hair, laying out one of many unfairnesses of adulthood. "But it's okay. To be honest, I was more excited to get dressed up and go do something other than make buttered noodles for Esty than I ever was about taking on Monica. I'm not convinced confronting her would make me feel better anyway. Monica didn't take Charlie's love away from me. Charlie did that. If it hadn't been her, it may have been someone else, who knows."

"Seriously? You are way too forgiving, Noa. I can't believe that woman is getting away with what she's done. I'm not sure I could stand for it if I were in your shoes." Truth is I have stood for it, for six years.

"Well, I can't believe you roped Rachel into this whole scheme of yours, just to help me out." Noa elbows me. She also wouldn't believe what I had to do in exchange.

"It was a plan."

"Sure, keep telling yourself that." Noa smiles. "Word choice aside, it's really nice of you—especially for a neighbor who gave me the cold shoulder the first year we lived next to each other."

"I did not." Noa gives me the *yeah right* side-eye. "You noticed, huh?"

"Of course I did. I just figured you thought our house was cursed or something because of the big robbery." Noa lowers her voice. "I heard it was one of the neighbors who let the thieves right into the house. Gave them the keys and everything. Can you believe that?"

"That's not quite how I remember it. But you know neighbors, always spouting off nonsense, sticking their noses in other people's business."

"Doesn't matter. Here we are, and I appreciate the effort." Noa shakes her head. "Nicest thing anyone's done for me since Charlie died. A little crazy, but nice." I clench my jaw, alarm registering across my face.

"I didn't mean you were crazy; obviously you're not. Right?" Noa probes, her hand covering her mouth so the assistant repouring us water doesn't hear. "And just so I know, you didn't do anything illegal to make this happen, did you?" I don't confirm or deny, my gaze fixated on the front door of the salon.

"What are you looking at, Marjette? You're white as a ghost. Hold on, can I say that about Black people? What do you say when a person with brown skin looks terrified, or like they're going to throw up? Because that's *exactly* what you look like."

"Hush, Noa." I shush my friend and point to the figure filling out the front door.

CHAPTER
TWENTY-THREE

While Noa was claiming to have lost interest in our potential tag team interrogation of Monica, a familiar-looking woman checking in with the receptionist caught my eye. I studied her as she took off her coat and noticed she was about to pop, heavy into her pregnancy. Racking my brain, I couldn't come up with anyone I knew who was expecting, but I thought I knew this woman.

Unable to place her, I asked Noa if she recognized the woman from Houghton. Maybe she had an older child who had been in Catherine's class. Barely giving her a glance, Noa reminded me she has made a point to steer clear of the mom mob at Houghton, but she commented that she never looked that good pushing her due date. For me it was T-shirts and sweats all the way at that point in the game. As Noa babbled on, I tried to place the about-to-be mama. Did I know her from Christmas or Easter services at church? Since Booker's departure, Darius and I don't go too often anymore. Those church ladies will talk about your divorce in the pew behind you during service, then hunt you down for their single sons faster than you can say *hallelujah*, but it was a possibility.

The shop door flew open, and the mystery was solved. "I actually found a parking spot right out front!" Booker announced to the salon triumphantly, convenient parking in San Francisco being as rare as a bald Black man showing up for a blowout.

I am stunned still. The nightmare I had avoided for six years was right in front of me, and there was only one way out of the Bombshell Bar.

Even though Booker told me Giselle was pregnant with twins, if I didn't have to see it and Darius knew not to talk about it, it wasn't totally real. But right then, what was supposed to be my life is on full display and about to get her hair braided before giving birth. The truth hits me harder than a train. It's not that Booker didn't want more kids; he didn't want them with me, and I finally know how it is. Booker has outdone me, three kids to my one.

The challenge still stands that I have to pass by the two of them to get on with my night, as ruined as it is, and I need Noa to pick up her shit and go. With me. *Now.* Tonight was supposed to be about closure for Noa, not reopening old wounds for me.

I try to shuffle by unnoticed but instead hear Booker call out, "Hey, Marjette." I see how it is; now that Booker's in front of Giselle, he's not using familiar nicknames with me.

I tighten up my smile and turn to face the two of them head-on. "Surprising to see you in the city, Booker."

"Yeah, our doula's over this way. We just had our last birth plan meeting before the twins arrive." *Are you kidding me?* Booker barely slowed the car to drop me off for appointments when I was pregnant with Darius.

"Marjette, it's so nice to finally meet you." I'm surprised by how smooth Giselle's words come out, not a hint of nerves meeting her man's first wife. "Darius talks about you all the time. I hope my boys love me the way Darius loves you," Giselle says kindly, rubbing her hands across her belly for emphasis. I notice Booker place his palm on the small of her back at the mention of his future sons. That's where Booker used to rest his hand when we were together. Same habit, different woman.

"Darius is going to be a great example for our boys," Booker says proudly, beaming at Giselle. I've disliked the idea of this woman for as long as I've known about her, but it's hard to hate a pregnant lady. She's just building a family, spreading unconditional love like all the other mamas, including me, in the world. My stomach churns at the thought of what I am about to do next.

"Congratulations, Giselle. There's no greater joy than being the mother of a son. You are one lucky woman." I turn to acknowledge Booker and move on with my evening. "You two have a nice night." He tips his head to me as I leave the salon, Noa on my heels at the ready to pick up my pieces. Once we hit the sidewalk Noa hooks her arm through mine to hold me up.

"Well, that wasn't pretty," Noa confesses, shivering in the evening fog. "I know a great bar just around the corner; it's across the street from the apartment Charlie and I lived in before we moved to Oakland. Let's go drown our, well, your feelings." By the looks of me, Noa assumes I'm in no position to be directing our next move. She might be right, but I know I want as far away from this salon as possible.

"Let's go home. I need a bridge between me and those two." Though my hands are shaking, my voice is steady.

"Really? That's it? You sure you don't want to take out your earrings and go back in there and throw a punch?"

"That's it." After six long years that was all I had to say.

"You got it," Noa agrees, busy on her phone. "I texted Judy for backup. She'll be waiting at your house by the time we get there. Give me your keys."

It's seven fifteen, and Judy's pacing on my front porch as if she's waiting on a child late for curfew. I forgot to ask Noa how she even had Judy's number to text, but seeing my old friend, I'm glad she did.

"I took my hair bonnet off to come over here. Don't leave nothin' out." Judy picks up both our hands, quickly walking us inside.

"You've been wanting to let Booker have it for years. Did you finally give him what he deserved?" Judy demands as the three of us get comfortable around my dining room table.

"I thought I was going to see my first housewives' catfight in real life; I really did. Turns out, if you had been there, you would have been proud of Marjette," Noa offers in support of my restraint. Judy looks to Noa like she's not so sure.

"I did talk to Booker," I admit, "but I didn't let on how pressed I was running into him and Giselle."

"You've been talking south about those two all these years, and when you finally had the opportunity to have your say, you didn't take it?" Judy shifts in her seat, confused by this turn of events.

"If I would have gone in on them, Giselle would have birthed both babies right there on the shop floor. The receptionist did not look trained in bringing newborns into the world," I defend. "Besides, you can't cuss out a pregnant lady in public. I'm not that ratchet." Both friends nod their heads at the sanctity of pregnancy. They know it's true. "From what I saw, Giselle's not the only one packing on pounds; Booker's looking thick in the middle. He needs to tighten that up."

"Listen." Judy softens her tone, forcing Noa and me to strain to hear. "Marjette, we've talked in circles about this before, but this is the very last time. I want you to hear me right down in the depth of your soul where the truths of life live." Two hands are laid on top of mine, either for comfort or to ensure I don't run. "Speaking as your friend with considerable years on you, if you keep going on the path you've been on, twenty years from now you'll look back and realize you wasted all this time in the prime of your womanhood. Let me tell you, life's too short to be thinking about somebody who ain't thinking about you." I guess when you're retired you have a lot of time to sit around and come up with bumper sticker slogans.

"You know where I'm coming from, right, Noa? If we had run into Monica, how would you have felt?" Judy hasn't been betrayed by her man like Noa and I have. We carry a shared experience not all women can understand.

Noa drops her chin in her palm, giving my question deep consideration. "Sure, I want to hate Monica, and there's a part of me that's curious to know the real story behind her and Charlie." I raise my eyebrows at Noa. "Okay fine. And to find out if I'm prettier than she is, but I can't let their affair ruin all the good memories I shared with Charlie, because there aren't going to be any more. Trust me, it's a struggle every day, but I have to forgive Charlie because I see his face in our daughter. Carrying the weight of anger on top of my grief is too heavy a burden. Esty would only suffer more than she already has."

"Marjette, it's always easier to be the victim than it is to forgive. People make whole lives out of playing the wronged person, and you know where it gets them? Nowhere," Judy preaches, then gets up to grab us some cold water. I need something stronger than water to wash down Judy's words.

"I know you don't want to hear this from me, but I agree with Judy." Our two against one has shifted—Noa has stepped right over me to Judy's side of righteousness, and I don't like being left standing alone. Tonight was supposed to be about saving Noa, not me.

"I listen to you lay a lot of blame on Booker for what he did to you, Simone for taking Darius's attention away from you, and Darius for not doing all the things you tell him to do." Noa is starting to speak out of turn, and I look to Judy to step in and quiet her down, but she doesn't. "When things go wrong is it really always everyone else's fault? Crap happens to everyone, I'm exhibit A, but you have to figure out a way to dust yourself off and keep going."

"I have tried to forgive Booker, to move on!" I insist. Neither Judy nor Noa look like they believe me. "But I can't. If I forgive him then he's going to get all kinds of satisfaction from the fact I'm no longer angry at him."

"Like I just said," Judy said, exasperation heavy in her voice. "Booker doesn't care what you're feeling about him. He moved on long ago. You're the one frozen in time."

"Marjette, forgiving Booker isn't about absolving him of what he's done. It's about not taking what he did so personally. He was a stupid man thinking with the wrong head. Fair or not it happens all the time." Noa sounds like she's reciting a mantra she's often repeated to herself.

"Appealing to your petty side"—Judy knows how to grab my attention—"you're not letting him get away with what he did. It's about getting your freedom back. Drop the emotional baggage, because you know what? Booker isn't suffering. Giselle isn't suffering. You are the one who's been suffering. You and Darius." Judy naming my son is sobering. "And I would venture to guess part of Darius wanting to move out of your house and in with his father is because he wants to live where there's lightness, not where things always feel heavy."

"You know about Darius wanting to move in with Booker?" I question Judy, my voice cracking. I know I have told Judy many things over the past few weeks, but I haven't told her about that.

"Darius talked with Phil."

The crack turns into a crevasse splitting me wide open.

"So, Darius sought counsel in Booker, Phil, Noa, and Max before he ever talked to me about how he was feeling living under my roof?" The tears I had been holding back since the Bombshell Bar have nowhere to go but down.

I look at both my friends, who I fear believe I'm stronger than I really am. "It's scary to let go of my feelings toward Booker, because if I do, then I have to deal with my own feelings about my life. What does that even look like? Then what?"

"*Then what* can be an exciting place to begin," Judy offers, pulling a Kleenex packet out of her purse and handing it to me.

"Noa, do you really forgive Charlie, or is it just something you heard you should do from some wellness hack with a podcast?"

"Fair enough, I do love a good podcast." Noa laughs. Every time I get in her car some new voice is blabbing on about manifesting your highest self, as if anyone knows who that person even is.

"And why are you so invested in if I forgive Booker or not? Judy has history in this game, but you are fairly new to the scene." Okay, that was a little harsh. "Sorry, Noa, that was the tears talking." Thankfully, Noa isn't rattled by my direct question.

"Just like Judy said, there's something exciting out there waiting for you, Marjette; I know there is. You just need to get out of your own way so you can see the truth as clearly as Judy and I do."

"Jesus, you Jews are smart." I blow a snot bubble in the midst of my first chuckle all night.

"Well, you know, we had a lot of time wandering the desert to come up with this stuff."

"Hey, what about me? I've been saying some version of tonight's sermon longer than I want to remember, but Noa's the smart one?!" Judy pipes up, incredulous.

"You're the wise one."

"You mean old." No one refutes Judy's claim.

I excuse myself from the table, but Judy and Noa barely notice. They've moved on to chatting about our neighbor on the north corner whose flamingo lawn art has multiplied this spring.

Being a person of integrity is exhausting, but I have two strong role models taking all the oxygen in my dining room, and I heard what they had to say. I grab my phone and head to the bathroom for privacy.

Marjette 8:52 PM

We need to talk.

CHAPTER
TWENTY-FOUR

"This is for lease; what do you think?" Max exclaims excitedly, bouncing on his toes as he steers me by the shoulders through the empty shop next to Flour + Butter.

At the mention of *for lease*, I can't believe I'm about to tell this gorgeous, oblivious man that I have offered him up for rent.

"What do I think of this for what?" When I texted Max last night that we needed to talk, I wasn't intending it to be about real estate.

"I'm thinking of expanding beyond the few tables and chairs I have in the bakery and opening up a proper bistro." Max watches me closely for signs of encouragement. I give him a double thumbs-up and cheesy billboard smile. I look ridiculous, but the gesture is enough for Max to continue painting his vision for the future. "The landlord said he's fine if I tear down the wall between the shops so traffic can flow freely between the two spaces. I can have construction done by end of June, and then *boom*! By July we will have this place open!" Did Max just say *we*? "Your soups, my breads. Your meats, my breads. Your salads—"

"Your breads?" It's sounding like I would be doing most of the work. It also sounds like a dream come true for me and Auntie Shay.

"Your savory, my sweet." Max pulls me into his embrace, planting a kiss on my lips that radiates with anticipation of limitless possibilities. "It may take a few weeks to catch on, but by September we're going to be on fire. I know it!"

By September I will be knee-deep in a brand-new class of kindergarteners and their nervous parents, but the "we" fantasy is charming to contemplate. I can definitely see the potential of this property, but the risk, that's another thing I rarely choose to take. In moments of frustration with her brother, Noa has told me that neither risk nor reality has played a part in Max's decision-making, hence his lifetime succession of passion projects. Every time she has said it, I wanted to believe that was the overprotective older sister talking, but now I'm seeing where she might be coming from. While it feels good to be included in Max's excitement, it's also unsettling.

"How are you going to pay for it?" The second it's out of my mouth I want it back, back, back. Max's finances are none of my business, and there's nothing less attractive than a woman nagging over money. But really, where is he going to get the cash? Flour + Butter has been open less than a year.

"Don't worry about that, I have an investor." Max doesn't offer any more, and I don't know why but I have a sneaking suspicion that Rachel has figured out a way to weasel herself into Max's world professionally, and now she has used me to get into his space personally. I bet she never even looked up Monica Jensen for me! She probably just picked a random store and time and called it good believing I would never fail to deliver on my end of the arrangement.

"Which should I tell Noa about first, my new café or my new girlfriend?" Max asks, bending to my ear as he encircles my waist from behind. I run my hands along his forearms, muscular from kneading dough. Max continues talking but I'm not really listening, too consumed by my piecing together Rachel's cunning ways, while also hanging on the word *girlfriend*, which I heard loud and clear. Of all the days for Max to throw out *girlfriend* for the first time, today is the worst.

I turn in his loose embrace and raise my eyebrows to Max.

"What?" He shrugs innocently. "Is it the possibility of me telling Noa about the café, or telling her about us, or me calling you my girlfriend that has you giving me the *what* face?"

I'm pretty sure Noa doesn't want to hear about any of it.

For the past month, Max and I have been increasing our time spent together cooking side by side in his kitchen as well as out trying new eateries as they pop up all over Oakland. Max has easily moved at my pace, happy to hold hands and steal kisses in public. I know he senses my shyness, and his patience is as sexy as it is endearing. I even make him pick me up a few houses down so Noa doesn't hear his motorcycle coming and look for it pulling into her driveway, not mine. Or at least that's what I allowed Max to believe are my primary concerns.

Really, it's me that needs to ease into standing side by side with a new man. I'm used to looking up to see a Black man holding my door, holding my hand, holding my thoughts. Growing up, I never knew of anyone being with someone outside my religion, let alone outside my race. As an adult, I've always worked in a White world, but I've kept my home life Black. I don't even know what life would look like multihued, let alone interfaith. I think I'm ready to find out for myself, but I do worry what the rest of the world will think, particularly my world back in Tulsa.

Listening to Noa complain about Max disappearing at odd times cracks me up, but I keep to our secret. While Max and I have been dating, without directly saying it to one another, we share a mutual understanding that not telling Noa about us is a good thing. I suspect neither one of us wants to know what Noa thinks of Max having a Baptist girlfriend. I may be a lapsed Baptist, but I'm still far from Jewish. Given the centrality religion played in Noa's marriage, I could not imagine what her response would be to Max and me dating. If I had to guess, given the bliss of our last month, I don't think Max has wanted to know any more than I do.

"Max, we need to talk." I sigh.

"You don't want me to be your boyfriend?" Max asks confidently, like there's no chance of that possibility.

"I'm not saying I don't want you to be my boyfriend; you . . ." I hesitate. Oh, how do I say this without sounding out of my mind, let alone risking celibacy for six more years? "You can't be my boyfriend right now."

Max drops his hands from around my waist, taking a step back from me in surprise.

"What? Why?" he demands. "Are you dating someone else?" The look on Max's face hurts, mostly because his concern couldn't be further from the truth. I blow out a big breath, steadying myself to continue.

"Not at all," I insist, desperation in my voice. Where to start, where to start. "I kinda promised Rachel Ellis I would set you up with her." Hearing myself say it out loud, it sounds exactly as horrific as I thought it would, but when I was a child Grandma Birdie recited Ecclesiastes 5:4–7 about keeping promises to me ad nauseum, so now I'm a brow-beaten woman of my word.

"Uh, what do you mean 'kinda'?" Max asks, a cold edge to his tone. No good deed goes unpunished.

"Well, I promised Rachel Ellis I would set you up with her for the Bombshell Bar's tenth birthday party this coming weekend. Turns out a Houghton tuition gets you a teacher and a matchmaker." I try the humor route, but Max isn't laughing.

"Why me?" Max asks, looking genuinely confused. Men are so clueless.

"For starters you're definitely excellent party eye candy, and second, Rachel seems to think the two of you get along. She wants a date she's comfortable with at her own shindig." I stop short before spilling the beans that Queen Rachel has a king-size crush on Max. "It's going to be in the Ferry Building. Guaranteed good food and drinks, I'm sure. Just go, make some polite chitchat so Rachel feels good, fake a headache, and leave." That's some sound strategy right there, but still Max's tightened body language tells me he doesn't see it as easy as all that. He takes a step back from me.

"Marjette, I don't understand. I'm trying to imagine what could possibly have happened that would lead to you hooking me up with Rachel." Max folds his arms across his chest, blocking me from reaching out for his hand as I struggle to avoid offering all the details. In return, I'd like to ask him what could have possibly transpired for him to take Rachel on as an investor in his café aspirations. My response reflects an inflated sense of my ability to fix other people's problems.

"Would you believe me if I told you I did it for Noa?"

"Noa would never ask you to do such a thing."

"No, she wouldn't," I agree, dropping my head. "But please know it was all done with the best of intentions. I had a debt to repay, and this was the cost. After you told me Noa was a hot mess, I wanted to help her feel better."

"I asked you not to say anything."

"But you didn't say I couldn't do anything." Even I know the hole I'm digging is looking more and more like a grave.

"Oh, so now we're arguing semantics? That's what we're doing?" Max stares longingly toward the door, and I'm left wondering if he wants me to leave. "You're lucky I know you're not playing me right now. I can feel how you feel about me even if you won't own it yet."

"What does that mean?" I ask, wide eyed at the idea that he knows just how much he flips my switch.

"It means I can feel your attraction to me," he says, stubble grazing the side of my neck, just below the jawline where my pulse has picked up. "I will let you set me up one time because I have to believe anything my niece's kindergarten teacher does *is* with the best of intentions." I reach my hands up to cup Max's face, but he grabs my wrists midway. "But no more games after this. We're done playing around. You hear me?" he asks, softening back up.

"I do," I whisper, relieved Max is willing to go to the party.

"Do I even want to know what you did in exchange on behalf of my sister?"

"No, you really don't. Trust me."

Max kisses the top of my head, lifting the cloud around us a little.

"Well, I hope it was worth it." Max wags a finger at me. "And that my sister had some fun; she deserves it."

"Oh, she had herself a new experience all right," I promise Max.

"If you're out there making deals on my behalf, then I want you to consider making a deal with me." What is it with these Kopelmans always having counterdemands? Max lifts my chin so I'm looking into his eyes. "I want you to consider coming to work with me in the café once school is over."

"For the summer?"

"For forever." Yep. Noa is 100 percent right. Her brother lives heavy on risk, light on reality.

"If I do that then everyone will know about us," I joke so I don't have to point out the obvious to Max, that I'm a mother who needs to earn a steady salary and being a kindergarten teacher is how I do it. Cooking together before the sun comes up has worked out well for me so far. In fact, it's the best two hours of my day, but it's not what I do, it's not who I am.

"And that's the second part of the deal. There's less than six weeks left in the school year. Once it's over, we go public. I'm willing to wait until then, but not one day after."

"Well, I only asked you to shower and shave for one night of canapés and painful conversation with strangers; you're asking me to serve myself up to the Houghton tabloids."

"Yeah, well, too bad. I'm worth it. I'm getting the short end of the deal in this thing anyway. Rachel Ellis is so not my type," Max declares, running his hand through his hair, struggling to accept his Saturday-night fate on behalf of me and his sister. "Those are my terms, Marjette."

I ignore Max's terms in favor of getting to the bottom of what is Max's type. "Really? I always assumed Rachel would be perfect for you."

"Why would you assume that?" Max looks at me like he's shocked by my assumption.

"Well, she's pretty, successful, Jewish . . . Why wouldn't Rachel be your type?"

"Because you are." Max winks at me and comes in for a full, wet kiss, erasing my concerns.

Ding.

Ding.

Ding.

Ding.

Breaking up a moment I'm in no way ready to have over, Max grabs his phone out of his back pocket. "Four texts from Noa." Max's brow furrows. "What's so urgent on a Sunday afternoon?" I shrug, hoping to reconvene kissing, but before I can snuggle back into Max's fold, his phone rings. "It's Noa. Does she know you're here?" I shake my head but look around for somewhere to hide anyway. Max puts a finger up to his lips as he answers the call.

"Hey, Noa. You're at the office catching up on work? Esty's at the JCC with Simone? Okay, I'm going there right now. See you soon." Max hangs up, his face having transformed from flush to fear.

"What's wrong?" I ask, not feeling as nervous as Max looks. I know Esty's in good hands because wherever Simone is on the weekends, so is Darius. Four eyes on one kid have got it covered.

"There's been a bomb threat at the JCC. I gotta go. Noa's leaving her office in the city, and I need to go try and get the kids." Where does Max think he's going to put a couple of kids on his bike?

"Not without me, you won't." I panic, swiping my purse off the island.

"You don't need to come, Marjette, I got this covered," Max insists, hustling me out the door.

"Oh yes I do, my son's in there."

231

CHAPTER TWENTY-FIVE

"Marjette, are you okay?" Noa hands me a lemonade and then twists her hair up in a bun. I keep turning my head to double-check that Darius, Simone, and Esty are truly safe in the backyard. Adrenaline sweat continues to bead at my hairline, and I don't even care if Max sees me tore up. I had never seen so many cop cars surrounding a building in my life, not even on TV, and that was not a comfortable feeling when my son was involved. Luckily, when Max and I arrived at the JCC, the SWAT team had all the people who were in the building evacuated across the street, lined up, and accounted for. Max didn't have to hold me back from jumping into the fray. Darius had Esty on his hip and was holding on to Simone's hand. My boy was being a man.

"The question is, why are you okay?" I ask pointedly to Noa. "And you too." I look at Max scrolling through his phone, presumably hunting for news. "Why are you two so calm? Because I'm shocked as hell at what just happened."

"Don't let this White skin fool you, Marjette," Max stresses. "When you grow up in America and visit family in England and Israel, you become accustomed to threats against Jews. The possibility is something you learn to live with; it comes with the territory of being born into thousands of years of persecution, and it hasn't let up," he explains like he's telling me how to ride the subway. I catch Noa's eyes, sure she's appalled by her brother's exaggeration.

"What? You think it's pure chance we've turned out to be friends, Marjette? Please. One of the reasons we get along so well is you're Black, I'm Jewish, and White supremacists are after us both. It's a tale as old as time, though we've got several centuries on your people when it comes to hatred." I don't know quite how to react. I think of Jewish people as White folks of a different religion. Their daily struggle is real too. I guess I should just be thankful everyone is safe.

"I also love your mac and cheese." Noa plants a kiss on the top of my head and calls the kids in to get the hot nachos she's taking out of the oven. Like the vultures they are, they grab the entire plate, leaving nothing for us, and head back outside. It's okay; I'm too sick to my stomach to eat anyway. Max heads out to join them; apparently antisemitism makes him hungry.

Ding-dong.

"Marjette, do you mind answering that? I want to scrub the burned cheese off this cookie sheet before it sets," Noa says, already running the pan under hot water. Annoyed at the interruption, I was hoping we would get a chance to align on how we're going to talk to our kids tonight about today's event. Of all the things I recognize that have brought Noa and me together—neighborhood, children at Houghton, cheating husbands, my exemplary cooking—racial discrimination was not on the list. I wipe my forehead on my sleeve and head to the door. Hopefully, it's just UPS dropping a package and we can get back on the topic of this afternoon. Noa has taken to widowhood retail therapy like Tom Brady to football.

"Hi. Is Noa Abrams here?"

Well, if today's incident at the JCC did not surprise Noa, this definitely will.

"Marjette, you want to swap your lemonade for a glass of wine?" Noa yells from the kitchen. Well, now I can't lie to Monica and say Noa's not home.

"Can I help you?" I ask in a tone that sends a clear message that I have no intention of doing so.

"I'm sorry. Is this not the Abramses' house?" Monica inquires, trying to peek past me into the foyer. "I was sure this is the one." Though I recognize her, I realize Monica doesn't recognize me from Charlie's shiva or the Houghton fence. She likely hasn't spent time staring at my professional photo online like I have hers.

After the Bombshell Bar debacle, and given Noa's subsequent admission that she doesn't need answers from Monica to be able to move on without Charlie, I want to get this woman off Noa's front doorstep quick. I'm blocking the entryway with my best *beat it* body language, but Monica shows no signs of retreat, so I'm going to have to spell it out for her.

"Listen, I know who you are," I tell her. Monica questioningly cocks her head at me. "At Charlie's shiva you asked me about any children running around, and then we met again at the Houghton playfield, where you had no reason to be."

"Ah." Monica nods in recognition of our meeting, but my continued body blocking her from entering the house is still not dissuading her efforts. "I just need five minutes of Noa's time. That's all, I promise. Can you please get her for me?"

"I'm not going to do anything for you."

"Marjette, who's at the door? I ordered Thai, but I can't imagine it's showed up this quick," Noa says while she hands me my glass of wine. Opening the front door wider with her free hand, Noa's now face-to-face with her doppelgänger.

Mouth tight, Noa looks at Monica disbelievingly. I speak up to assure her: "Monica was just leaving."

"I need to talk to you about Ch—" Monica speeds up quickly to spew out her intent. I manage to almost get the door closed in her face when Noa stops it with her foot.

"It's okay, Marjette. I want to hear her out," Noa asserts, to set the tone that she's calm and in total control of the situation that's about to transpire in the warm May evening. Grabbing my hand, Noa tucks our entwined fingers behind her hip. Ahh, that's where all her rage is going, right into crushing my knuckles.

"But you said at the Bombshell Bar you were fine and . . ."

"I know what I said, and I didn't mean a word of it."

"And then at my house?"

"Lies, all lies. Except the parts about you being done with Booker. I just didn't want you to feel bad about our botched evening."

I knew there was no way Noa could be that evolved and forgiving when her dirty dead husband had done her wrong!

"See what a nice person Noa is, Monica? Charlie had a nice wife. I hope that doesn't make you feel better." I may have risen above the situation with Booker and Giselle, but it doesn't mean I don't know how to be petty when it's called for. Monica releases the breath she's been holding but still hesitates to speak. She needs to get on with it before Max and the kids come out here to join the adultery party.

"Say what you're gonna say, and then be on your way," I continue. Noa nods, her wrath bearing down even more into our clasped hands, turning my brown skin beige. I really hope this conversation is quick.

"I saw you through the window of the Bombshell Bar before I walked in, so I left." Okay, points for Rachel, she didn't purposely lie to me to get to Max. Monica shifts her body to an angle, so her back is partially to me, but her full attention is on Noa. I lean my body weight into Noa, pushing her a few steps left so Monica has to address me too.

"I'm moving back to Boston tomorrow, but I wanted to explain something to you before I go. I know I should have done this months ago, but I was too scared. Now I leave in twenty-four hours, and I don't want to carry it with me any longer," Monica confesses, only making eye contact with Noa.

"So, you've been sitting on information about Noa's husband, and you're just now getting around to telling us about it so you can feel better? You're not even supposed to be here," I accuse, tapping Monica on the shoulder, letting her know I'm still there if she's planning on hurting my friend with her words.

"Thank you for telling me you're leaving," Noa offers pointedly, then shuts up, waiting to hear if there's more.

"The thing is," Monica trails off, no doubt searching for the right words to explain her sins. Good Lord, there is always a thing with every woman. "After Charlie, I never married. I never had children. I never found love again like I'd once had with him." Noa falters a little bit hearing Charlie's name come out of Monica's mouth. I flex my arm to catch her with my grip.

"When my law firm asked if I would be willing to come to California to work in the San Francisco office, I jumped at the chance. I was lonely, and I somehow rationalized that the job offer was a sign that I was supposed to go out west and reconnect with Charlie. Maybe without a country or his parents between us, we could be together. I moved because I was determined to get him back."

I bug my eyes out at Noa to make sure she is catching every single word Monica is laying at her feet. If there were ever a time for Noa to pull out her novice Krav Maga skills, this would be it.

"Did you know Charlie had a wife? That he had a family?" Noa's response punctures the air, tight and crisp.

"I knew about you when I moved, but I didn't learn about Esty until I met with Charlie."

"Noa, should I go get Max? He can remove this woman off your property immediately." I take Noa's eye roll as a no.

"So, you knew about me and still moved to the Bay Area. And then you learned about Esty from Charlie. Exactly how many times did you have dinner with my husband?" For a woman who claimed she didn't need closure, Noa sure is going for the specifics.

"It was only a few times—two, maybe three."

"You really expect me to believe you moved all the way across the country to rekindle I don't know what, and the two of you only saw each other a handful of times? I may look worn down, but I know I do not look dumb," Noa insists, taking a step closer into Monica's space, dropping my hand. My friend is ready to cross the finish line on this confrontation alone. "Marjette, go get the keys in the top drawer of my kitchen desk."

Monica barely gets out, "I swear to you it's true," before I'm back with keys in hand. I don't want to miss a thing. "When I had dinner with Charlie, every time he made it clear that he loved you, Noa. So much. That he loved Esty. That he loved his life with the two of you, and there would never be room for me in it."

Noa's face reveals nothing, so neither does mine.

"Turns out the love I hoped to recapture had already been given to you. Completely and fully."

I melt a little. That may be one of the sweetest things I have ever heard a mistress say about a wife, and Noa and I watch a lot of *Real Housewives*. My body relaxes, taking in what Monica has to say, but Noa doesn't look like she's buying it one bit.

"If you weren't having an affair with Charlie, then why were these on him the night he died?" Noa grabs the keys out of my hand and waves the girlie cursive *M* medallion in Monica's face. The smoking gun to falsify Monica's story.

"I've never seen those keys before in my life, Noa. They don't even look like something I would own." Taking in Monica's plain blouse, nondescript jeans, and Birkenstocks, it's true. Edwardian script doesn't seem like it would be her signature font of choice.

"Listen, Noa, I haven't seen Charlie in two years, I swear. I heard about his passing from a mutual friend in Boston. I never meant to disrupt your life and certainly not Esty's."

"Then why come to Charlie's shiva? And then to see Esty at Houghton?" I jump in. These are the answers I want.

"I don't say this to hurt you, Noa, but Charlie was the great love of my life too. He was over me, but I have never been able to let him go. I needed to go to his shiva so I could properly mourn the only man I ever loved. I went to say goodbye according to his faith, the faith he chose over me." Tears are streaming down Monica's face, and she's wiping them away as quickly as they come so she can push through. "I would have never gone to see Esty at school, but when I asked after her at the shiva, she wasn't there. I was told her uncle had her over at her new school to check out the playground. I couldn't believe Charlie was going to miss his daughter's first day of school."

"And why did you need to see Esty? Why would my daughter be any of your concern?" Noa is squeezing every ounce of information out of Monica now that she has her on her home turf.

"I needed to see both of you. The daughter Charlie adored and the woman he chose to spend his life with. I knew I once made him happy, but you are the two people who made him happiest until the day he died."

Strong and assured, Noa hooks her hands on Monica's forearms. "I can promise you Charlie died happy in our home. Very happy."

CHAPTER
TWENTY-SIX

It's a nice tale she's telling, but it's time for Monica to go. Noa, on the other hand, has empathy for days. A few tears shed by the ex-girlfriend and Noa offers one of Charlie's beloved Red Sox T-shirts to her to mark their time together in Boston, ketchup stains and all. I can't help but wonder if this is the beginning of Noa finally clearing some of Charlie's belongings out of her bedroom. Though each of their relationships with Charlie began years apart, both Noa and Monica lost the great love of their lives. That hole is now another thing they have in common. At least, that's how Noa explains it to me after she shuts the door and I hit her with a look that asks, *What the hell?*

This day has felt like a year. Hungry, I head back toward the kitchen to see if Noa has anything I can snack on until the Thai food arrives. Behind me, the aching wail I've been expecting for months erupts from the depths of my friend's belly. Frozen, I don't glance back at Noa, wanting to give her pain some privacy. Instead, I wait for the agony to ease and Noa's voice to quiet before I turn and wrap my arms around her. A second primal roar follows on the heels of the first. Noa grabs the back of my shirt, and we puddle onto the floor alongside one another. Just as I'm thinking I could use a roll of toilet paper for the buckets of tears I know are coming, Noa breaks into hysterical laughter, her whole body shaking in concert. Not the gut-wrenching exorcism I was expecting; Noa looks more like she's about to orgasm.

"Oh my God! *Oh my God!*" Noa's screaming, clapping, and pounding her feet like an epic toddler tantrum before she releases herself prone on the hardwood floor, gasping for air.

Since I'm not God, I timidly ask, "Yeah?" wary of Noa's next move. I feel transported back to Noa's front porch, the day after Charlie died, trying to figure out how best to approach my distressed neighbor. Locked onto the ground with Noa, I scan the house for someone better suited to help Noa out, like a pharmacist or Max, but he's out back working on Darius's pitching arm. Again, it's just me.

"Charlie loved me! You heard her, right, Marjette? Monica said he never cheated on me!" Noa's maniacal laughter just as quickly dissolves into sobs of relief. "He always loved me; he really did." Curling into the fetal position, Noa buries her face in my lap, and I can feel the heaviness of her whole-body collapse.

I sweep away the hair glued to her cheeks by tears, lean over, and whisper into her ear, "He sure did, Noa. You are one of the lucky ones."

"Noa, are you okay?" Max runs in from the backyard, finding us in a tangle on the floor.

Noa nods, unable to speak.

"Noa's just having a moment remembering how much Charlie loved her," I answer.

Max kneels down by his sister. "Of course Charlie loved you. And Esty. And me. Damn, I miss that guy like a brother."

Noa nods a second time, giving Max a brief smile.

Other than my stomach rumble, I don't move because there's nowhere more important for me and Max to be. Allowing Noa to heave and sob and rest and start the cycle all over again is a cathartic moment for all of us. My own quiet tears of relief that our children are safe from the evils of hate, at least for today, and that some husbands do stay true to their wives, begin to fall. Love stories are real and there can be happiness after inconceivable loss. I'm not naive. I know Noa's journey back to her full self will continue for some time, and I may be wiping more of her tears along the way, but as time passes, her joyful days will surely outnumber the anguished ones.

Sitting here on the cool hardwood, I also know I trash-talk Booker far more than I should and for far longer than I should have. We had a love story too. It was a young one full of unrealistic expectations, all-consuming passion, and illusions of invincibility. We had sky-high hopes and dreams, but at the end of the day, not the same ones, so our fairy tale ran its course. For too long, I've been grading our time as a couple based on the difficulties of the last three years of our marriage and its ultimate dissolution, not on the success of the first fourteen years of our union.

Noa and Charlie had far more wins than losses. They loved each other and eventually had Esty before the universe cut their time short. Booker and I, too, had more wins than losses. Both having never traveled outside the south, we came to California for an adventure. We grew up together and we made an outstanding kid. But all great adventures eventually conclude, and for too many years I've been focusing on the ending, not the journey.

Huddling together, I'm searching for the perfect words to honor the finality of the Monica chapter. For Noa's sake it deserves to be acknowledged. Problem is, my ability to string those perfect words together is being curtailed by a lingering question that won't go away: *If Monica was telling the truth about Charlie, then what's up with those damn keys?*

CHAPTER
TWENTY-SEVEN

The Monday after Max escorted Rachel to the Bombshell soiree, I arrive at Flour + Butter at six o'clock with a couple of new lighter soup recipes for May. I have no doubt Max is going to love my gazpacho. Getting those done by seven thirty will be no problem. Flattering the Saturday-night details out of Max is going to be the morning's challenge, but I am up for it with my peek-a-boo push-up bra and low buttoned blouse. I threw a boatneck T-shirt in my bag to change into when I got to school to transform myself from Marjette to Ms. Lewis.

That early in the morning it's always easy to pull right in front of the bakery to park, and when I do, the storefront is pitch black. I check my watch to make sure I'm right on time. Then I check my texts. No communication from Max since Sunday morning, when I showed up with two espressos to make sure he was in his own bed. He either forgot to set his weekday alarm or is deep in the pantry and didn't turn the front lights on for me. I shoot Max a text letting him know I'm sitting out front in my car waiting on his sleepy behind.

I sit there scrolling through my phone for thirty minutes, and then I go to school. By eight o'clock I have ordered a pair of flip-flops making the rounds on TikTok, blown right by my one cup of coffee before eight o'clock limit, and checked my texts well over fifty times. Reluctantly storing my phone, I open my classroom doors for the day. At 8:14 a.m. I get a muffled *ding* from my desk drawer. I stub my toe lunging to snatch my cell, giving Tabitha and Deja the giggle of their lives as they put away their matching unicorn backpacks.

Max 8:14 AM

> Sorry for the last-minute change in plans, I decided to do salads this week. See you at pickup today, I'm on Esty duty.

It seems like the second hand on the classroom clock is running slow that day; I nearly call the facilities manager to come check it out. I'm not sure which was worse, time crawling slowly to three o'clock, leaving my mind way too many minutes to imagine Rachel wrapped in Max's arms, or too quickly and being confronted with the two of them on my turf.

For the first time this school year Max arrives right at three o'clock, when my classroom is at capacity with parents and my attention is most divided. Happy to see his smile and his wave, I give him the signal to wait one minute while I inform a mother that the marker on her son's forearm is in fact permanent ink and it may take a few turns in the tub to come off. I've had this same conversation with her so many times this year, I've basically prepared her for a child who will be heavily tattooed by twenty-five. When I turn around to catch up with Max, he and Esty are gone, but a single meringue rests on my desk. It looks as alone as I feel.

A few nights later Max takes me out to dinner to apologize for the café mix-up, but where he's usually the one leading the conversation, that night he is inexplicably subdued. Max and I may have been seeing each other for only three months, and this was all my doing, but I have to know if he has any interest in dating Rachel. It feels like Max might be torn, and I've already been burned by a man with a woman on the side. I have no interest ending up another man's discard.

When he turns off his motorcycle, I plan to ask Max to come in for a drink, but instead, like a teenage drama queen, blurt out what has been bugging me all night. "What's up with you and Rachel?"

"What do you mean what's up with me and Rachel?" Max responds with an undertone of irritation.

"I mean, are you interested in her?" I push back. In my childhood, if Sundays were for Grandma Birdie and the Baptist church saving me from being a sinner, Saturdays were for Auntie Shay preaching on how to save me from myself. Waiting on something baking in the oven, Auntie Shay would stub out her Kool, hold my eyes, and direct, "Don't go needing a man more than he needs you." I know I'm being the needy woman Auntie Shay warned me not to be, but in that moment, I can't help myself.

"Nah, I'm pretty sure I've made it clear I'm interested in you." Max crosses his arms, creating a barrier between us. "In fact, I know I have. Do you think I'm dropping off goodies to women all over Oakland?" I purse my lips and look at him like, *I don't know,* even though down deep I do. That was the wrong response. Max drops his head, blows out a weighty sigh, and finishes with, "What I'm not clear on is where *I* stand with *you.*"

I stand as tall as my petite frame will allow to assuage any doubt with a directness I'm not comfortable applying but that feels necessary given our spiraling situation. "Max, you know I like you."

"Do I?" Max questions me. "Because in my view, when you're falling for someone, you don't set them up with somebody else."

I defensively jump on him because he has the story all wrong. "That's not what I meant to do!"

"But it's what you did, and I'm a grown man, looking for a grown woman. I don't play little-kid games anymore." My catty self wants to retort, *That's not what Noa says,* but I have enough self-restraint not to say anything at all.

One foot on the pavement and unsure what's left to say to one another, Max leans off his bike and places a platonic kiss on my check. With a final sigh laced with defeat, Max revs his engine, mutters "Good night, Marjette," and is gone.

It most certainly is not a good night.

⌒

"This Saturday, if Carole tells me one more time I can do hard things, she's going to feel a hard thing up her—"

"Someone got a little too cozy with candy this evening," I scold. When Judy calls after nine p.m., it's always for a food confession. That woman does not do well on sugar; think wicked witch of the East Bay.

"I can no longer handle living with his narrow behind. Phil and I are over. I'm trying to make my goal by summer, and he keeps bringing tempting treats into the house with no regard for my efforts. He just leaves 'em sittin' there on the kitchen counter calling my name."

"Ah. Phil brought home a family-size bag of M&M's, had a handful, and you polished off the rest. Is that where this story is going?"

"It was a king-size Twix, but yes. And women have divorced for less." I can hear Judy pop something in her mouth. I bet it's not sugar-free. "I hate people who practice moderation, it's not natural. I don't know how you spend all that time cooking alongside Max at Flour + Butter without sampling the product. I couldn't do it."

"I can't either. I'm up five pounds of exactly that, flour plus butter."

"But you're also up one big hunk of protein," Judy goads, ready to switch subjects. My head drops.

"I may have blown it already, Judy."

"'Cause you're out of practice? Don't worry, girl, it's just like riding a bike. Promise."

"Ew. I'm not talking about that, Judy. Maybe you need to go burn off some calories with Phil."

"Pft. This candy shop's closed for the night." I can hear Judy settle back in the couch, crossing her legs to get cozy. "Punishment for his sins."

"I think Max is punishing me."

"What are you talking about? We've worked too hard to get here. What'd you do? And please tell me it can be undone."

"What do you mean 'we've worked too hard'? You have a husband. Even if he's misbehaving, you don't get another," I tease but also make clear Judy's not invited to the live Marjette and Max show.

"I'm talking the collective *we* as in you and me. Having to hear about your love life all these years, which has consisted of absolutely nothing worth repeating, I've earned the right to an opinion. But forget it, you know how I get. My mind's not right from all the sugar." Oh, I do. A few years back after a generous slice of German chocolate cake for the robotics teacher's birthday, Judy attempted to ride a scooter she borrowed from a freshman boy. She nearly broke her neck. And her reputation. "What happened? I thought everything was going according to plan?"

There has never been a plan with Max. I'm not that calculated.

"Come on, Marjette, I've got to know how you threw water on this fire." How fast Judy has flipped from *we* to *me* when things start to go left.

"I set Max up with Rachel Ellis."

"I'm not tryna hear that. Now what on God's green earth would you possess you to do such a thing?!" Judy says in a tone that lets me know if she could reach through my phone and strangle me, I'd be gasping for air right about now.

"Rachel helped me out with something I needed to do for Noa, and in return she asked me to set her up with Max. I had to follow through."

"Noa actually asked you to do that? Trade her brother for a favor?" Judy asks, sounding very confused. One dinner and Judy thinks she knows what kind of woman Noa is, even though she's right.

"No, she didn't ask me. I just knew it had to be done. And it was only one night, a party for Rachel's company, and she didn't want to go to it alone. I get it." And I kind of did. I've been third wheel to Judy and Phil too many times to Houghton fundraisers to count.

"It's never for one night when it comes to women like Rachel wanting to get their hands on a man like Max." Judy's right, again. After our first date I was counting the minutes until I got to see Max next. "How many times do I have to tell you that you don't have to do nothing you don't want to do? I can't believe you offered Max up to this woman. It's okay to hook up a friend like Noa, but you never invite another woman into your love life."

"I'm not sure I even have a love life anymore."

"Well, that's on you. Does Noa have any idea you sold out her brother on her behalf?"

"You know I can't tell her something like that."

"Yeah, you better not," Judy agrees under her breath. "So, what are you going to do now?"

"I have no clue. It's been kinda weird between Max and me since his night with Rachel. I feel like he's bumped me down from budding bae to casual acquaintance. It's all awkward half glances between us, and that's from across the room. Then there's Rachel, who's been spending way too much time hanging around in my classroom at the end of the day to see if Max shows for school pickup. Rachel claims it's so she can go over the catering details for a Houghton party she's throwing at her house this Friday, but I have thoughts otherwise." I knock my phone against my head one, two, three times. I can't believe I ever agreed to set Rachel up with Max. I'm such an idiot, and whenever I try to ask Max about the Bombshell anniversary party without coming across as jealous, he only discloses, "It was nice."

And nice is exactly how Max has been with me the last twelve days. It's been awful.

I need to get myself off the subject of Max, so I wade into school territory Judy's all too familiar with. "The head of school asked Rachel to host an end-of-the-year party to raise the final funds for the theater capital campaign, and she jumped at the chance. Just a chunk of change more and we're across the finish line. As you can imagine, the head and Ernie are thrilled by Rachel's generosity, her house, and her cash, but I'm dreading it."

"Cut Ernie some slack. Too many years directing high school musicals in a dingy auditorium, Ernie's allowed to wave his jazz hands over a new theater."

"Oh, he's jazzed all right. That Bob Fosse wannabe leaped at the chance to volunteer our faculty a cappella group to sing a few numbers to sweeten the evening. Without asking any of us first."

"Okay, I can see an issue there, but you sang at my retirement party last spring, and everybody loved you."

"Of course they did. We're great, and I'm church trained and solo ready. But just because we can doesn't mean I want to. Besides, that was your party, and this is Rachel's."

"It's not Rachel's party, Marjette, it's for the school, for the kids." I already bend backward for my kids. By the end of May, every teacher's back hurts. "At minimum, do it for Ernie—that guy has jumped your car battery in the school parking lot more times than you can count."

"Oh, it's Rachel's party all right. Check your email, I forwarded you something."

"'Kay. Give. Me. A. Second. To read." I can visualize Judy searching for the readers atop her head so she can scan the email as quickly as she can while talking to me.

To: Marjette Lewis
From: Rachel Ellis
Subject: Entertainment at the Ellis Soiree

Dear Marjette,

Bless his heart, Ernie Stern is over here at my house right now setting up risers for your musical number tomorrow evening. Max and I have been in constant contact over the menu and decided it should pair nicely with the entertainment, so we will be serving fresh mussels, salmon pâté, and oysters on the half shell. The perfect complement to your number from *South Pacific*!

Between Ernie, Max, and me, I know this party is going to peel parents' wallets wide open. I wanted to let you know the attire for the evening is cocktail-party chic, but since you will just be stopping by to sing a number or two, you don't need to go to great lengths to dress up on my behalf. I'm just so appreciative you're willing to work the event.

Anyway, I'm writing this email really to say thank you again for nudging Max my way. My feet still hurt from all the dancing!

Tomorrow night, be prepared for the best Houghton party ever!

Rachel

"Bless his heart? I didn't know Rachel's from the south," Judy marvels at the wrong tidbit of information.

"She's culturally appropriating. Or would it be regionally appropriating? Either way, she's from Bel Air. Can we please focus less on her origin story and more on her words, specifically the ones that reference me 'working the event' and her 'dancing the night away' with Max?" I beg, pulling us back to the issues at hand.

"Rachel Ellis can make champagne hard to swallow. And at her own party. Okay, new plan. Go, sing your numbers, chat with a couple of moms, maybe one dad, then get out of there. Enough said, you will have done your part for the school, and you can face the Max situation another day."

"And leave Max there with Rachel? Ugh. This is yet another example of the Rachel Ellis types of the world always getting what they want. When's it going to be my turn?"

"You want a turn, you got to step up to the plate," Judy says, chaffing on the other end of the line. She's on the backside of her sugar high and not reading between my words. Now that Rachel has gone out with Max, I don't have home field advantage. "Has Ernie let you know what you're singing?"

"If I could choose, I'd be singing, 'And I Am Telling You I'm Not Going' from *Dreamgirls*," I snip.

"Marjette, you're gonna have to shift your attitude on this one." I ignore Judy's advice.

"Ernie's selected 'Some Enchanted Evening' from *South Pacific*. More like one horrific evening."

CHAPTER
TWENTY-EIGHT

There was one piece of pertinent information Rachel left out of her email yesterday and Ernie conveniently failed to mention. When I came back from taking my kids to the library this afternoon, Ernie had draped a white sailor suit with navy trim over my desk chair. One he pulled from the Houghton costume storage closet. A note with too many exclamation points was pinned to the waistband of the pants, encouraging me to give the uniform a good press before tonight's festivities. The whole thing reeked of mothballs and pandering.

"I hate the water," I declare as Noa examines the Popeye ensemble. In the light of my bedroom, the crisp white of the costume has yellowed from use, upping the nastiness factor. There is no way this material is touching my skin.

Taking a long drink on her pilsner, Noa looks at me, probably unsure whether this is a Black joke or in reference to the uniform my a cappella group is supposed to sport for our numbers from *South Pacific*. "If I wear that I'll look like I just stepped off the Cracker Jack box," I whine. Noa picks up the accompanying white Dixie-cup hat to hand to me, and I give her a firm headshake. *Hard pass*. Not on this head, not on this body.

"You're clearly no cracker, Marjette." We bust up laughing and cheers that truth, enjoying our preparty of two. "But you can't exactly go in your robe either," Noa asserts, circling her index finger at me. I convinced her to go to Rachel's party with me by promising she only had to stay for the time I was going to be there, approximately twenty-two minutes. She claimed she had no money to spare for the cause, as Esty has a budding interest in Girl Scouts and those cookies are going to bankrupt her. She also has no desire to talk to invited guests she has nothing in common with. I informed her of the obvious: she does have something in common with them—she has a kid at Houghton. For the health of Esty's social life and general childhood development, after a year of hiding out, Noa has to show up and make some friends—every kid needs playdates over the summer. Darius can't be relied on for Esty's entertainment, given his baseball schedule and part-time job making bakery deliveries. That is, if Max is still willing to have him. And apparently Simone will be spending her days studying living systems to shift the American reliance on energy with UC Berkeley's finest brains. I'm beginning to think that girl's too smart for my son.

"Oh, I most definitely am not going in my robe." I toss the sailor suit in the corner and point to a dress bag resting flat on the bench at the foot of my bed. "I've been saving this outfit for when I need to dress to impress. The last time I wore it was when Booker and I met up at our mediator's office to sign the divorce papers. I was a bit overdressed, but I wanted to leave him with a reminder of what he was walking away from." I'm not showing up to Rachel's party in character. The most I'm willing to do is honor Ernie's nautical theme with my white off-the-shoulder bias-cut dress with suede royal-blue strappy sandals. Me in this dress could launch a thousand ships.

"Ooh la la! There are going to be some tongues wagging tonight," Noa says, pulling my dress out of the bag. I only need one.

"I hope so—now get dressed. You dragging your feet is making us late."

"I was hoping you wouldn't notice."

When Noa steps out of my bathroom in the plum halter dress she brought over to change into, she whistles a catcall at me better than any sailor on leave. I shake a little shimmy, feeling myself. The dress is zipped, and I know I look good. Thank you, Carole.

"You look beautiful too, Noa." Ignoring me, Noa's turning and yanking at the side buttons of her dress like a dog chasing its tail. Seeing the rich color against her pale skin and how flawlessly the skirt swishes over her hips makes it one of the more elegant dresses I've ever seen. With Noa still struggling, I step in to help close the bodice or we'll be here all night. "Did you hear me? I said you look beautiful."

Noa blushes. "Thanks. I haven't heard that since Charlie died." I get a shimmy back, Noa accepting the inevitability and potential fun of this evening. "Charlie gave me this dress for our trip to Mexico. I hid it in Esty's room after the officer came by that night, thinking at the time the dress was a gift given to me out of guilt, but I wanted to wear it for tonight. Charlie loved the theater. And he loved me." A giggle follows. Noa has taken to affirming out loud Charlie's love for her often, and I don't mind one bit if it helps my friend walk upright and confidently through the world.

"Let's get a move on, Golde," I direct, grabbing my purse and pointing her out of my bedroom.

"I'll take 'Jewish theater trivia' for two hundred," Noa jokes, but I can tell she's impressed I pulled a *Fiddler on the Roof* reference out of nowhere. I take the compliment and swat her behind out the door.

Rachel's house is a glass jewel box that sits tippy top of the Oakland Hills. At the end of a cul-de-sac, there are views of the Bay Bridge and San Francisco available from three out of four sides. The high ceilings and open floor plan may be challenging for tonight's acoustics, but the white minimalist decor looks straight out of *Architectural Digest*. In fact, I think it may have been a featured home in the magazine a few years back when Rachel's son, Dalton, was in kindergarten. We are so high up I feel a sense of vertigo coming on, but then the canapés distract me. I can't pass up anything served atop a puff pastry.

I send Noa off to get us a couple of drinks so I can walk the house intentionally trying to look casual when I run into Max. My hope is that as Noa forges through the Houghton crowd, she'll bump into someone and be forced to make small talk. I'm not allowing her to tail me around the party all night like she did the first day of school. Noa's been gone for a handful of minutes, which surprises me but also fills me with pride—she's making strides to navigate the inimitable microcosm of private school parents with my loving but firm encouragement.

Ding.

Judy 7:36 PM

> I always wanted in that house but never got to go. What's it like?

Marjette 7:37 PM

> We could be here whispering together if you hadn't left me alone at Houghton.

Judy 7:38 PM

> Get over it already, school's almost over, and you survived. Come on, tell me, is it tasteful or too much? I know you're going to explore every room.

It's definitely too much of something. I take in the 270-degree view. It all feels so staged and sterile. I can't imagine how a fireball like Tabitha lives here, though it does seem fitting for the CEO of a company dedicated to illusions of beauty.

Lost in my thoughts, I'm startled by laughter echoing off the glass and decide to follow Judy's advice to be social and to be seen. I set off toward a group of moms who, from afar, seem to be talking loudly and enjoying themselves. Since Noa's yet to deliver my drink, I snag a Chardonnay off a passing server's tray. I need something to do with my hands.

As I approach the group, Rachel's voice rises from the circle, and I veer right, changing course. There's nothing entertaining enough to make me join that crowd.

"Marjette, Marjette!" Rachel aggressively waves me over. Sweet Jesus, I've been spotted. I smile and wave back, hoping that's enough of a connection for one evening. "Come join us," she insists, pushing Char aside to make room for me in their Houghton huddle. *Smooth out your smile and give Rachel five minutes. It's for the children.*

"Ladies, you all look lovely tonight. Are we ready to build ourselves a theater or what?" I ask, pumping up the group. I may not like to work a room, but I know how to do it.

"We certainly are, and I guarantee the kindergarten parents are going to lead the way." Rachel scans her group, indicating her expectation that each woman present is required to dig deep into her pocketbook. "Of course, you're off the hook tonight, Marjette, since you work at Houghton. You give enough."

"You're right, I do a lot. And I still give back to my school community as a teacher and as a parent. The theater is going to benefit Darius too." A mom I recognize from Catherine's class is coveting my shoes, no doubt wondering how I can afford them on a teacher's salary. I want to tell her I paid for these shoes the same way half the people in the room paid for the items they can't afford—alimony.

"Is Darius your son? I've seen him pick up Max's niece." Rachel claps, congratulating herself for being in the know as I nod. "We are so looking forward to hearing you sing tonight," she says for the whole group. "What a treat. Darius is interested in the arts too?"

"He's the athlete of the family. I've always loved to sing, but we both appreciate all Ernie's effort on behalf of the theater program. Houghton students are very lucky." I wish the head of school could hear how I'm selling this campaign. I deserve a cut.

"Well, between us girls"—Rachel finally drops her voice a few decibels—"I've heard you're the star of the a cappella group." The women in the circle nod in unison. They haven't heard wrong. "What with the venue, the entertainment, and Max as our caterer . . ."

As if on cue, I see Max for the first time tonight as he rounds the corner out of the kitchen carrying a bucket of ice I assume is for the bar. Trailing closely behind is Noa with a garnish refill for the signature cocktails. Seeing me, she smiles, clearly proud she has found someone to talk to. Back at my house, I should have established that chatting it up with her brother or offering herself as a member of the waitstaff does not count as mingling.

After Noa elbows her brother, Max follows her gaze, spotting me in the crowd. I raise my wineglass and nod to say hello. Obviously, I knew Max was here somewhere, but now that I see him in Rachel's house, I feel hesitant, unsure where I stand.

Max's gaze drops to the floor, I guess not wanting to make eye contact with me. Then ever so slowly, the long eyelashes that hide his flirtatious eyes sweep from the floor to my hips and from there to my shoulders, taking me in. I watch Max watch me, a growing grin of appreciation for what he sees spreading across his face. Landing on my eyes, he bites his lower lip just like he does every time I send him home wanting more at the end of a date.

I see you seeing me. With a hint of self-satisfaction, I cock my hip Max's way. The smooth, heavy satin of my dress has done its job. Knowing I've caught him admiring this view, Max throws his head back with a hearty chuckle and drops the ice bin behind the bar.

"Speaking of Max, he's looking this way, Rachel," Char squeals and turns to me, placing a hand on my exposed upper arm. "Aren't you a doll for making sure Max and Rachel got together? We all knew they were destined, but sometimes men need a little push in the right direction."

"Us unmarried women have to help each other out with the men in our lives, right, Marjette? You married ladies don't know how it is." Rachel loops her arm through mine in single-lady solidarity. Fuck, I'm trapped.

"Do you have a man in your life?" Before I can answer her question with a *Yes, and he's standing at your bar*, Rachel launches back in: "I just can't stop thinking about how magical my company's anniversary party was." She lures the group, knowing someone will fish for more details. I never imagined I would be the first one to take the bait.

"I know Max was happy to do you a favor," I reply. Snarky, I know, but someone must establish that the Bombshell Bar party was not a date; it was a courtesy.

Dropping me from her grip, Rachel brushes off my version of the truth. "Oh, it was more than a favor—it was fate."

I don't notice Ernie hovering at Rachel's shoulder until the conversation pauses and he announces to the group, "Just wanted to thank everyone for coming tonight and share that we go on in five." He looks directly to me, making sure I've heard him and that I know he's disappointed in my lack of team spirit by punting on the costume. "Does that work for you, Rachel?" It may work for Rachel, but I won't be going on until I hear the rest of this story.

"Great, I'll be ready, Ernie. Go let the others know." I shoo off the interloper. "Continue, Rachel, you were telling us about your evening at the Ferry Building."

"You're right, I was." Rachel grins, thrilled to be returned to the center of attention. "I don't know if any of you were in the city that night, but it was a rare warm San Francisco evening, no hint of fog. After I gave my remarks and toasted the attendees, Max and I stood out by the water for what felt like hours. The two of us passed the night taking in the Bay Bridge and taking in each other. Now everybody at corporate can't stop talking about what a stunning couple we are."

I remain composed, shaken by her portrayal of the evening but not wanting anyone to sense it. Rachel referred to the evening as "magical"; Max called it "nice." The truth has to lie somewhere in the middle. Before anyone can notice I've gone quiet, one of the other women hoping to elevate her standing in the group jumps in, "Have you gone on a date since?" *Have you?* I'm desperate to find out, holding my breath waiting on the answer.

"You know we are both stretched so thin as business owners that so far our schedules have not aligned." Heads bow in acknowledgment of how hard this queen bee works. "I'm constantly shooting him possible dates, so I know we'll land on one soon."

"How are you going to make it happen?" Char buzzes, anticipating a happy ending.

"I can assure you of one thing, ladies," Rachel carries on in a hushed tone, so the group is forced to pitch forward in rapture. "Max will be the last to leave tonight. Or maybe tomorrow morning."

When something *big* is about to go down in my classroom, I always tell my students to pay close attention, they don't want to miss a moment. I catch a glance at my watch as I adjust my dress. "Ladies, this has been an enlightening conversation and one I will not soon forget. You might want to keep your eyes on me. The show's about to start."

That's it. *That is it!* Locking in on Max at the bar, I stride with purpose across the living room, undeterred by curious glances as I pass by. I'm over other women staking a claim on my man and letting it go without fighting for what's mine. My apologies to the head of school and to Ernie, but church Marjette has hung up her robe.

Noa's still hovering close to Max's side, but I don't let that stop me. I wedge myself between brother and sister. Right in Max's face I hold my index finger up over my shoulder. "Excuse me, Noa, I need your brother for a second." Noa takes a step back out of fear or to allow me a little more room. Either works.

Max raises his eyebrows questioningly, and I have the answer I know he's been searching for. "From here on out you're mine."

"I am, am I?" Max asks, entertained by my declaration but, I can tell, not convinced one bit.

"And I want everyone to know." Claiming what I came for, I grab two fistfuls of chef's coat and pull Max in tight. Head angled, I wrap his mouth in one long searing kiss until I know there is not one person in this room unclear about who Max Kopelman is dating. Especially Max.

CHAPTER
TWENTY-NINE

I'm pretty sure I've dropped a couple of pounds given all the work Max and I put in last night . . . and up until twenty minutes ago. From Max's house I didn't have time to go home, shower off the scent of sex, and make it to meet Judy at Weight Watchers. Still wearing last night's body-skimming dress, I'm finally putting Marie's advice into practice by showing up for the scale in the bare minimum. My panties are in my purse.

Like a long bike ride, marathon sex leaves you sore. As it turns out, though, even after a six-year drought, I still have great endurance, and I know Auntie Shay is smoking a Kool and cheering me on in heaven. That said, given my age, if Max and I keep this up, I'm going to have to increase my electrolytes. I'm limping up to our meeting with a wicked calf cramp.

I see Judy's car parked out front with Judy still in it, which is odd because we always meet inside. Her head is turned to the passenger seat like she's talking to someone. Maybe Phil's taking the car to be washed while we're in our meeting. As I get closer, Judy must feel my presence, because she turns around and lowers the driver's-side window, looking like she's getting ready to let me have it. "Well, well, well. Look who showed up ready to roll this morning. Did we miss the party in the parking lot?" She raises an eyebrow, taking me in floor to crown and back down. "Get in."

"Yeah, get in." Over Judy's shoulder Noa's head pops out, smiling from the passenger side and killing Judy's bad-cop vibe.

Seated outside at Peet's, my two friends courteously allow me a few sips of my Americano so I can get my head straight. Judy suggested I get an extra shot of espresso because we were about to cover a lot of territory and I didn't look like I'd seen much sleep last night.

"So, you two have a whole secret friendship I don't know anything about, is that what I'm seeing? When did this start?" I decide to take the conversational reins early so I can control the narrative on how these two have been boxing me out.

Judy's quick to correct me on how she sees this morning going. "This is not your interrogation, Marjette, it's ours. But if you must know, the night we all had gumbo at your house, me and Noa exchanged numbers while you were starting on the dishes."

"And here I thought you two were just being unhelpful," I tease to lighten the intense energy around the table, but Judy doesn't laugh. Noa does a little but then rolls her lips together when she gets a disapproving glance from our elder.

"We were busy working out bigger concerns."

"Concerns about what?" This is feeling terrifyingly close to an intervention, and I'm starting to get hot under this already-thin fabric. Have I totally blown it, and this is when Noa is going to tell me to take ten steps back from her brother and drop off? That I'm fine for a friend, but not a potential sister-in-law? After I planted that scandalous kiss on Max, long enough to ensure every person at Rachel's party saw he was spoken for, we ran out of there, leaving chins wagging, Ernie without a soloist, and Noa fending for herself at a party she never wanted to attend in the first place.

Under the sheets, I didn't consider the damage we may have caused, but in the light of morning, I can see I really didn't think through my actions. I look from Noa to Judy and back to Noa. She doesn't seem like a woman on the verge of laying into me for ditching her at the party or for macking on her brother. Quite the opposite. Noa's bouncing in her chair, her body language reading like a woman who is riding a high, just like me.

"Concerns over how we were going to get you and my brother together!" Noa explodes like a shaken can of soda. She lunges across the table and grabs my face, planting a big kiss on me. That's a lot of lovin' not from one but two Kopelmans in less than twenty-four hours.

"Oooooo, girl, we are so happy for you." Judy's bobbing her head and stomping her feet like she's just caught the spirit of the Lord. "I thought I was gonna be retired this year, but working out how to get you over Booker and onto Max has been a full-time job! You owe me and Noa a spa day. We're tired!" They high-five at the idea of free facials.

"Hold up. Hold up." These women are moving too fast for me on no sleep. I tuck my chair in closer to the table and rub my eyes. I want to see Noa's face clearly in the daylight. "You're happy Max and I are together?" I point to Noa so she knows this is not a question for Judy.

I get an affirmative: "Yes."

"But I'm not Jewish." I can feel Judy rolling her eyes at my documented fact. "Your family. You and Charlie. I assumed you would want Max to end up with someone faith appropriate. That it would be expected he ends up with someone Jewish."

Noa's quiet for a moment, looking like she's carefully parceling out the right words to let me know that fooling around with Max is okay for right now; however, long term it's true the ethnic legacy must live on. As it had to with Charlie, it must with Max.

"Marjette, the whole having to marry Jewish . . . That's an Abrams family nonnegotiable; it's their thing. Don't get me wrong, I'm grateful every day that was the case, and that was what Charlie wanted and needed for himself as well. We built a beautiful life together." I nod; I can't deny that it's easier to be with someone who understands your origins, explanations rarely necessary. "The Kopelmans, however, we're more *Jew-ish* than Jewish."

I look at Noa blankly, not sure what she's saying. Before I can ask for clarity, she continues, "Come on, Marjette, you know what I'm talking about. We're Jew-ish like you're Bapt-ish. Major holidays, appeasing grandparents when called on, and a few favorite dishes and traditions."

"Did you just feel the earth rumble? That's my grandma Birdie rolling over in her grave." Noa's hearty laughter soars; I suspect she has her own version of a Grandma Birdie as well. "So, you wouldn't prefer Max to date Rachel than to date me?"

"Why would I prefer Rachel?" It's now Noa's turn to be confused. She really needs to start hanging around school more.

"Because she's Jewish. Or Jew-ish. I'm not totally sure—Tabitha does eat ham sandwiches for lunch every day."

"That's because Rachel's not Jewish. She's Episcopalian or Anglican or something diet Christian like that. Esty was invited over there for her first Easter. Charlie would never have let her go, but I figured how can you deprive a child of a fictitious bunny who lays chocolate eggs?" I purse my lips at Noa, not convinced. "What? You think every White brunette with an Old Testament name is Jewish? That's like me confusing you with Halle Berry because you're both Black with short haircuts."

"Being confused with Halle Berry doesn't bother me."

"Okay fine, then how about the cashier at the ampm?"

"You've made your point."

"But even if Rachel were Jewish, that woman could offer me a lifetime punch card for blowouts, and I'd still choose you every . . . single . . . time."

I always assumed Judaism was a fundamental piece of the equation for a mate for Max. He and I were having so much fun that I didn't want to consider that one day he may have to pick between me and his sister. Or worse, that I would have to choose between Noa and him. In my early flirtations with him, I'd pushed those questions to the far recesses of my mind. The one consideration that never surfaced was that maybe not being Jewish didn't factor into the perfect match for Max at all.

"The night you and Judy met at my house, you said that Max has a type," I challenge, wanting Noa to realize what she just said to me does not track back to our conversation over gumbo and Riesling.

"He does have a type, always has. You. Or more broadly, Black women. You should see pictures of the woman he dated in Paris," Noa clarifies, punctuating herself with a whistle. Uh, no thank you.

"That night I was positive you were telling me I wasn't your brother's type."

"Just the opposite. I was hinting that you *were* his type. I didn't want to be totally transparent and make my brother seem desperate. Such a turnoff." Max may be many things, but desperate for a woman's attention is not one of them. That's another thing Noa would know if she hung out more at school. "But if you weren't sure what I meant, why didn't you ask?"

"Seriously, Marjette," Judy pipes in, slapping the table. "Of all the times not to be sticking your nose in where it doesn't belong! You could have saved the two of us a whole lot of effort!"

"Maybe. Though even if I had found out I was Max's type, it didn't mean he was going to choose me. Just because Max likes Black women doesn't mean any ole one in Oakland will do. You know that, Judy. It's like saying, 'Hey! You're single. I know someone else who's single. You two should meet. You'll have a ton in common.'"

"You think we were going to foist you on Max and run the risk of you embarrassing yourself your first time out after an interminable man drought?" *Please, girl* is written all over Judy's face. "If I had done that and it had gone sour, I'd be spending every Saturday at Weight Watchers with you until the end of time. Trust me, I have no plans on doing that. I've been protecting you going on twenty years; I would never let you play the fool." It's true—Judy's always held my best interest, even if it's been delivered with a heavy hand.

"From the first pickup, Max was all over me about you." Noa blushes even though she's talking about me. "In the first week of school, I got more calls from him asking about you than I got the entire two years he lived in Paris. It was constant, but it was cute."

Now I'm the one blushing. "He was?" I think back on the first day of school, trying to recall if I was wearing a particularly good outfit, and all I can remember is Tabitha calling me out on greeting people in a messy smock.

"Yeah, says he was a goner the second you almost boob bumped your keyboard getting up from your desk to meet him." I drop my head in my hands, horrified. I can't believe he caught that or that it's what caught him. "Your fried chicken helped too. My brother falls in love through his stomach."

"I lured Phil in through food too," Judy confesses in solidarity.

"And Max hasn't left me alone about you since, pestering me to figure out ways he could see you. He claimed his love life would distract me from my heartache. And he was right." If it were me, I'm not sure I could help another person find new love when I had just lost my enduring one, even if that person was my brother.

"He was really asking after me that much?" My ego can't help but dig for a little more.

"You've heard me talk about how hyperfocused I'd been on Esty. Do you really think her first year of school I would willingly be *that* absent? Sure, I didn't want to get cornered by busybody moms wanting to know my backstory, but I certainly would have joined a field trip or two, made a couple of Halloween goody bags. But Max begged me to let him go in my place. Did you know he's allergic to animal fur? He was hopped up on a box of Zyrtec so he could make it through ninety minutes at the zoo." I cannot believe what my ears are hearing.

"How'd you get roped into all this?" I ask Judy, curious about her part in what is increasingly coming across as a calculated ruse.

"I was brought in as a consultant to work on the unforeseen six-year Booker hangover." Judy straightens, ready to claim her part. "At Back-to-School night Max noticed you weren't weighted down by a ring, but what he and Noa didn't know at the time is that you were weighted down by an ex-husband." So, when I was trying to work out if Max was flirting with me in his bakery, he was trying to weigh where I stood on the collected-baggage scale.

"And I knew we had to consider Darius in setting you up for a successful relationship with Max, but you did that work for us. When you came up with the plan of Darius looking after Esty, it was easy to put Max in charge of snacks. Max thought plying the kids with Flour + Butter treats was brilliant. He could get to know Darius on his own terms, man to man, without you getting involved trying to control it." As Judy spins her part, Noa's eyes are dancing. I expect she's been itching to unveil this whole story for quite some time.

"Darius even told me one night when he was over watching a Warriors game with Phil that he wished you and Max would date so he could step in and do more of the heavy lifting he's been carrying for years. That sure enough is true. Darius is sick of doing all the man jobs." I go to protest, but Judy holds up her hand. "Ah, ah, ah. I don't wanna hear it, and you know it's true. Anybody can see you made that boy the man of the house at far too young an age."

"I can see where you're comin' from, but you could have told me this years ago," I say, trying to pass some of my potential missteps raising Darius onto Judy's shoulders.

"Yeah right; you weren't open to hearing me. Seems your ears are open now." I give Judy a little nod to indicate *maybe*. "Now, you bringing Max to my tap recital, besides having the nerve, you also put me and Max in the awkward position of acting like we didn't know each other."

"You've met Max?" This caper is getting out of control.

"You think one night of bingeing on TWIX is what's keeping me from reaching my goal weight? I went in once to Flour + Butter to meet

Max and suss out if he was good enough for you. I've been back at least a dozen times since for those damn almond croissants. I would have quit Weight Watchers weeks ago and put my $44.95 toward something tastier if it weren't for my sheer determination to rid you of Booker."

Done waiting for the conversation to return back to her, Noa jumps in, "Then the whole going to the Bombshell Bar on Filmore to confront Monica but running into Giselle and Booker . . . Judy and I couldn't have thought that up if we tried. Your conniving mind did the work for us. All I had to do was remain in the background reminding Max that going slow, following your lead, would be worth the prize of being with you in the end. I swear that man was ready to marry you after the Christmas present mix-up, but for once he listened to me. Oh, and by the way, I was touched you wore the jeans we bought together on your first date."

"You saw that?!"

"Of course I did. I made Max text me before he arrived. I want you to know I told him not to bring the bike, that he should borrow a friend's car. But he wouldn't listen to me."

"So, you know how Black girls feel about their hair," I state, thankful Noa is in on the most familiar stereotype of Black women. If Max likes Black women so much, how is it that this is something he's clueless on? If we're going to go the distance, Max is going to have to make other plans for the bike.

"Please, no woman wants her hair destroyed by a helmet on a first date. I pleaded with Max, but he swore he's sexy as hell on his bike, and he wanted to lock you down." It's true, he was.

"The unexpected blow to our efforts came out of left field when you pimped Max out to Rachel for the Bombshell Bar party. That one threw us. And Max."

Not wanting to relive that mistake, I skip right over Noa's declaration of my messy reality. "Max was in on all of this the whole time, for real?" I'm struggling to accept the monumental efforts of Noa and Judy to help me find my way to Max.

"He sure was. And he was on board with the slow-and-steady strategy in hopes that it would all pay off and the two of you would be together. From the minute he saw you at Charlie's shiva, to tasting your fried chicken, and then Esty being in your class, Max saw it all as one big . . ."

"Coincidence?"

"Universal sign," Noa says with a warm smile that starts to fade. "But I want you to know setting Max up with Rachel did come at a cost."

I knew it. I knew last night was too good to be true. Even with my lack of experience in the dating game, I'm worldly enough to realize that one night of pleasure is not enough evidence for a man that a woman isn't playing games.

"While I think you laying on the PDA last night was unexpected, you still have work to do to convince my brother that you are in it with him the way he wants to be in it with you. The whole thing with Rachel left him confused."

"I don't think he's confused anymore after last night."

"When it comes to men, don't mix up being willing to have sex and forgiveness. A man will happily do the first without a woman knowing if the second's guaranteed." Judy shakes her finger at me, letting me know I am not off the hook with Max's feelings.

"You setting him up with Rachel really threw Max after he asked you to join him in opening the café," Noa says, not letting up on the *Marjette, you've really blown it* scenario.

"You know about that too?"

"Of course—I know all about it. Have you not been listening? I've been in on all of it from the beginning."

"And I've been Noa's official Black-up when it comes to dealing with you," Judy adds, demanding full credit.

"Don't you mean *backup*?" Noa corrects, assuming Judy's confused her words.

"I said what I said."

CHAPTER THIRTY

"I know you'll sort it out with Max, Marjette. You have to. I consider you guys finding your way to each other a death benefit," Noa insists.

"A *what*?!" Judy and I yelp, mutually horrified.

"You know, a death benefit. A positive that came out of Charlie dying."

"I didn't know that was a thing." I cringe. And I don't want it to be a thing because I certainly don't want my kid thinking about how if I kick it, he gets my Craftsman.

"I'm not sure it is, but I have to believe Charlie's spirit is out there somewhere spreading some goodness into my world. I consider our friendship a death ben—"

"Don't say it." I put up my palm in protest. "I'd like to believe we would have found our way to becoming friends without Charlie having to die. It's Judy's fault it didn't happen sooner."

"How do you figure that?" Judy exclaims, leaning back in her chair like she has no idea what I'm talking about.

"Ever since the unintended outcome of me helping Layla get her lawn in order, you've been on my back about staying in my lane."

"*You're* the neighbor that walked the theft ring into my house? No way!" Noa slaps the table, causing it to rattle.

Judy confirms, "Oh, that was her."

"Well, that's a story from my past I don't need to relive. Moving on." I have no interest in stopping at this conversational detour.

"I'll let you off the hook right now, but you can believe you walking a theft ring right into my house will be the Thursday-night topic du jour."

"I have one last question for you, Noa, and then I have to get home and hunker down to write my end-of-the-year report cards."

"You could use a shower and change of clothes too," Judy adds, like I don't know. Darius is with Booker, Giselle, and his new brothers for the weekend. When he gets home tomorrow, I want to have all my loose ends tidied up so I can spend some quality time with him, since he may be moving in with his father in two weeks, when summer vacation starts.

"If you wanted us to be spending time together, how come you bad-mouthed Max to me? Talking about how he's flaky, unreliable, skipping around to different professions like he was skipping rocks. I believe you even said he had career ADD."

"That sounds like me," Noa admits. "I may also have said it was true with women too, sorry about that. I was just making conversation, but probably not the best way to sell you on my brother."

I wave it away like it's no big thing. "If you've been that sure about the two of us, how come you never once asked if Max could join us on a Thursday night for dinner?"

"As long as we're asking that question, how come you never invite me for Thursday-night dinners?" Judy presses, putting me in the hot seat.

"Uhhh, I think we just established why. One dinner and you become Oz of my life."

"What I think we've established is that your life needed it." Given the all-nighter Max and I pulled, she's right, it did. I'm not telling her that, though.

Fiddling with the lid of her coffee cup, Noa remains concentrated on my question. "Remember when I told you that I was so focused on Esty and my career that I didn't have time for Charlie, and I neglected our relationship?" I nod, remembering every word of that conversation.

"Charlie wasn't the only thing I neglected. Friendships too. And boy did that become obvious once Charlie was gone. I wasn't just hopeful for you and my brother to get together; I was hopeful for us too."

"But it's only silly Thursday dinners."

"It wasn't only dinner to me, Marjette. It was those two hours I hung the rest of my week on. My one respite from being alone in my heartbreak. And parenting alone." My cooking is good, but even I know it's not that good. "I also needed those dinners, because, well, I've been lying to you about something all year."

"About more than playing me like a puppet so I would land on my back in your brother's bed?" I joke, trying to lighten a darkening mood around the table. Noa dabs at the sides of her eyes with a cocktail-size napkin.

"You know how I told you I have my Golden Gate Books acquisitions team meeting on Thursdays at four and that's what makes me late to your house for dinner?" Of course I do. We're six months into our routine of me and the kids getting dinner on the table and Noa blowing in hot and flustered. "The meetings are actually Tuesdays at ten."

"It's okay if you've been showing up late because you need to catch up on email toward the end of the week, I get it. Honestly, Noa, I hope you haven't been wasting time sweating over that." I cover Noa's hands, which are shredding her napkin. I don't know why she's fretting so hard over having to do what she has to do to cover the mortgage and put food on the table.

"I go to a Thursday unhappy hour. That's what we call our young-widows' group. It's ten of us who look like there's no way in hell we should be widows and widowers. We look more like a PTA dance committee or a book group, take your pick. The youngest is twenty-eight, and I'm the oldest at forty-seven. We share our stories, eat crappy store-bought snacks, and balance each other out. Some of us have kids, some of us are achingly lonely, some of us have devastated parents who can't handle their child's pain, and one of us is trying to get through an oncology fellowship after his wife just died of cancer. Every single meeting we laugh, we cry, we complain that no one will ever understand us other than each other. Then I show up to your house a wreck in need of wine." Despite my attempts at meddling in her healing, Noa knew exactly what she needed to properly grieve Charlie all along.

With Noa's confession on the table, I don't know what the next best thing is to say, so I grab the low-hanging fruit. "You don't show up a wreck all the time."

"I pretty much do, we both know it, but you've always greeted me like I'm the best part of your day. My Thursday afternoon tribe is how I've come to accept widowhood. It's an ongoing process, but I'm lucky to have found some people who are living parallel lives to mine. Thursday nights are for family. I'm thankful to have found you, Marjette."

"Are you? I often worry I may be saying the wrong things to you. Starting with Charlie's shiva. Who helps a shell-shocked wife by suggesting watching *Real Housewives*?"

"You didn't?" Judy asks, shaking her head.

"She did." Noa lets out a laugh, and I'm glad that memory is not as flinch worthy for her as it is for me. "And now I'm totally hooked and watching back episodes of three different cities. Don't bother with Salt Lake. Anyway, I knew that night we'd end up friends."

"You didn't see me almost uncover your mirrors."

"No, but Max told me. We had a good laugh over that one."

"You really knew we'd end up being friends that night? I mean, you were awfully busy being sad and drunk."

"At the shiva everyone was telling me some sappy version of 'I'm sorry.' 'I'm sorry for your loss,' or 'I'm sorry this happened to you.' The pity from people was excruciating, and it kept piling up on me. There are a whole range of emotions out there you can feel when your spouse dies, but feeling pitied is the worst of them all. Pity makes you drink."
Oh, yes it does. I reflect back on my first year without Booker. There was not a bottle of Maker's Mark whiskey that was safe in Alameda County.

"When I was blathering on about Charlie leaving me, you were the only one who didn't say, 'I'm sorry.' You said, 'I know,' and that meant everything. For me it meant I wouldn't be alone with all my feelings, that maybe you knew a little something about my pain even though we were strangers."

"I can't believe you remember all that given the state you were in that day."

"That's the only thing I remember about that day."

~

Turns out Giselle got her braids done in the nick of time. The morning after our first-ever encounter at the Bombshell Bar, her twins shot into the world quick-like. It's not my fault if even in the womb kids respond to my voice. The past month since his brothers were born, Darius has been over at Booker's house for only a couple of hours here and there. The new parents needed some time and space to develop a routine, the demands of managing twins overwhelming. Having settled inasmuch as parents with two babies can, Booker invited Darius to spend the weekend with him and reminded me that the issue of our son moving in with him and Giselle was still on the table. I had been hoping Booker was suffering from the dad equivalent of mom brain.

The twice-baked potatoes are back in the oven, and now I'm seasoning Darius's favorite cut of meat, rib eye. Surprisingly, I'm looking forward to sitting down and hearing about his weekend with his brothers. Always careful not to upset me, Darius shows me pictures of the boys at my insistence, and dang if those twins don't look like two miniature versions of him. Booker and Giselle sure made some pretty babies; it might actually be fun watching them grow.

Smelling like outside, Darius saunters through the front door, his overnight bag dragging behind, bringing along debris from the yard with him. I can always tell when he hasn't had a solid eight to nine hours of sleep, and this evening, he looks beat.

I greet him at the door. "Hey, my handsome boy, I'm finishing up dinner. Come keep me company in the kitchen, and tell me about your weekend." Darius will be getting the PG-rated version of mine.

In the kitchen, Darius rummages through the pantry looking for a snack. "Don't eat anything right now. I made this dinner special for you, and I don't want you wasting my food. It's only going to be another ten minutes," I promise him.

Plopping down on a barstool and then ripping open a bag of Kettle chips, Darius tosses out, "Mom, how old was I when I stopped wearing diapers?"

"Well, we started you at around three." I didn't expect Darius to be so invested in his brothers' development, and I'm touched by his interest.

"Three!" he shouts, disbelieving. "Why's it take so long?"

"Well, it depends on the kid, but you were pretty typical. Why you asking me that?"

"Dad's whole house smells like poop, like every corner. It's nasty." Ah. So, it's not interest; it's self-preservation driving this line of questioning.

"Darius, that's rude. Every baby makes their share of dirty diapers, including you."

"Yeah, but there was only one of me. It's double the smell over there." Darius scrunches his nose like the aroma is still clinging to him.

"It's part of raising a family, nothing you can do about it."

Darius ponders this reality while I finish preparing to sear the steaks. "Not to mention, Dad and I were playing Xbox and Giselle sat down next to us in the family room and started feeding both babies at the same time. And *not* with a bottle." Good thing my back's to my son, because this conversation is starting to crack me up. I'm definitely calling Judy after dinner.

"She's doing what a mother does," I explain, opening the oven door to sprinkle some shredded cheddar cheese on top of the potatoes.

"So do it in her own room! I saw her boobs, Ma, like all of them! Why she have to do it right there?" Darius explodes, shaking his torso like an ant's crawling around under his shirt.

"It's her house, she can do as she pleases. You're gonna have to get used to it if you're going to be living over there." It's not lost on me that I'm defending Giselle—even Darius looks at me, confused by my words.

"I don't know about livin' over there anymore. I could barely sleep. Do you know babies cry during the day *and* at night? It's awful." All year I've been using Esty as birth control to minimize Darius and Simone's alone time. Who knew some oversize areolas and sleep deprivation would do the trick?

I turn to give Darius the truth. "I don't know what to tell you. That's what babies do; they eat, shit, and cry, and there's no escaping it."

"For how long?" It looks like Darius is doing some calculating in his head.

"It's going to be like that at your dad's house pretty much until you graduate from college."

Sitting there, Darius thumps his head onto his crossed forearms. "I can't do it," I think I hear him say.

This just may be my best weekend ever. Max and I are official, Noa and Judy couldn't be happier for us, and my son wants to stay living with me in my home. Before I break into a victory dance, I need to confirm I heard right.

"What's that you said? Speak up." I invite Darius to repeat what I want to hear.

"Mom, I don't want to live with Dad."

That's what I thought he said.

CHAPTER
THIRTY-ONE

"Don't try to tell me you've never thought about it," Max teases, pulling me back into him by my belt loops as I try to wiggle away. We have three days' worth of work to get done in one. All teachers must be off campus by nine o'clock tonight so facilities can start their summer campus repairs first thing tomorrow morning. The minute one school year ends, it's time to start getting the buildings and classrooms in fighting shape for the next.

"I promise you, sex on my faux walnut desk has never crossed my mind. And please don't suggest the floor." Max does a 360 around my space, hunting for a spot of industrial carpet that looks pristine. Not going to find one. "I tell you what, you help me tape up all these boxes and I'll consider a quickie in the supply closet. You can even call me Ms. Lewis." Max rips out an arm-length piece of duct tape and gets busy packing up my life's work.

The Sunday night Darius returned home, bone tired from a weekend spent with newborns, Max showed up just before we were about to sit down to dinner. I sent Darius to the door, not sure who it could be, but finding out was not worth ruining the extra-large rib eyes I had grilling.

"Ma, look who's here," Darius had announced, grinning widely. "I'm the one who told him tulips are your favorite flower, particularly orange ones."

"Well, aren't you becoming quite the thoughtful young man," I said, placing my hand on the back of Darius's shoulder to let him know he had done good, so good. Standing beside Darius, Max presented me with the largest bundle of blood-orange tulips I had ever seen.

"Did you rob a florist?" was all I could think to say.

"That definitely would have been cheaper, but no. However, I did have to go to two stands and one farmers market to patch together this many tulips all the same color."

I nodded approvingly at Max's fine work.

"There are forty of them." That better not be for my decade because if it is, this sweet moment just took a nosedive. "One for every week from the first time I laid eyes on you at Charlie's shiva to you surprising the hell out of me on Friday night."

"They're absolutely gorgeous." I could feel Darius squirming next to me. My boy had never seen a man treat me as a man should. It was about time he learned some lessons on romantic love and respect in my house. To drive the message home, I went in for some full-on lip action, surprising Max for a second time that weekend and Darius for a first.

"Ma, no, I'm out!" Darius started waving his arms back and forth like he was trying to stop a traffic accident. "And I thought it was bad over at Dad's! Call me when dinner's ready. I'm going to my room to try to unsee what I just saw."

"You think maybe that was a little too soon?" Max asked after Darius jogged away. "I mean, he just found out about us two hours ago when I texted him asking for your favorite flowers."

"It should have happened sooner," I insisted, going back in for more of Max's kisses until I remembered the rib eyes, and then flew outside to the grill.

At dinner the three of us chatted seamlessly, Max wanting to know everything about Darius's baseball season at school and schedule for summer league. He even claimed he hoped to make it to a game. I let my mind peacefully drift in and out of the conversation, as I could only care about MLB stats for sixty seconds, but turns out these two could talk on and on about it for a solid half hour. Just as we were finishing dinner, there was another knock on my front door. With my two men leaning back in their chairs, too full to get up, I went to answer it. Looking past my shoulder into the house, Noa announced Esty had baked chocolate chip cookies by herself for the first time ever and wanted to share them with me and Darius. Noa was carrying a carton of milk and a blatant lie, but I invited them in anyway.

With the front door almost closed, I heard a "Not so fast," with a push on the other side. Judy wedged herself through carrying three-quarters of an apple cake, dragging Phil with her. "Phil and I were out for a drive, and we could smell cookies fresh out the oven all the way down the street." I eyed Judy like she was fooling no one. "Okay fine. Noa texted me that Max's bike was parked in front of your house, so we all showed up as fast as we could. Sorry about the missing piece," Judy half apologized, shoving the cake plate into my chest, and beelined to the empty chair next to Max.

There we all were at my dinner table: Max, Darius, Judy, Phil, Noa, Esty, and me. At one time I may have thought the six other people sitting around my table would be my five children and Booker, but it didn't matter anymore. My dining room was full. It was too loud, there were too many tempting sweets, and it was getting too late for a school night, but it was all too good to be true, so I let it go.

As the night was winding down, Max clinked his dessert fork on his glass of milk. "I asked Marjette a question a couple of weeks back but never got a straight answer. I'm going to ask her one more time in front of all of you as my witnesses." Judy grabbed my knee so hard under the table I yelped in pain, but she refused to let go, needing me to steady her. I had no idea where Max was going with his little speech, but I knew it wasn't where Judy's mind was wandering. It sure was fun, though, watching her vibrate in false anticipation.

"Marjette, I've never had a true partner before, someone who deeply shares my interests and my sense of humor." We all laughed in collective agreement. "I have always forged my own path. But this year I've witnessed up close what a caring woman you are with your students and most impressively with my sister and niece as they've endured this trying year." I raised my glass of milk at Max to honor the kind compliment he offered up in front of all my favorite people.

"You've also shown me what a talented, skillful woman you are when it comes to cooking, and I've never enjoyed my time in a kitchen more than I have the last three months with you."

"This is way better than listening to Carole at a Weight Watchers meeting," Judy whispered in my ear, not taking her eyes off my man.

"You, Marjette, are a woman who complements me completely, so in front of your family and your friends, I'm asking you again, hoping for the positive power of peer pressure: Will you please, please join me in opening the Flour + Butter Café? I can't do it without you."

"You mean you can't do it without my soups," I teased uncomfortably, never imagining Max's first offer to join him in the restaurant was real, but this one certainly seemed so. All twelve eyes around the table fixed on me.

Max got up and squatted right down by my chair. "No, I mean I can't do it without you. We can scrap the soups for all I care. Except for the corn chowder, that one I love too much."

"That one's my favorite too," Noa, Judy, and Darius all confirmed at the same time.

"Bottom line is, I only want to do the café if you'll do it with me, Marjette." Max hopped up from his squat to dig around in his front pant pocket. Holy, no, no, no. Maybe there was a ring in there. "I believe together we can do anything we put our minds to." Max pulled out a white patch with blue cursive lettering that simply said *Chef.*

"That was better than a marriage proposal," Judy gushed sweetly to Max and me, looking like she might melt from all the emotion. "Will there be a friends and family discount for me and Phil?"

My memory of that special evening is interrupted with, "Are you sure you want to keep four boxes of LEGO? I stopped playing with mine at twelve; I doubt Darius is going to use them." Max runs his fingers through thousands of tiny parts that have sparked hundreds of hours of child-centered creativity.

"Consider it job insurance if this turn in the restaurant world doesn't work out for me."

"It'll work out," Max confirms with a confidence to be envied.

I had become a teacher as practice until my dream of a house full of kids with Booker came to be. The first decade of my teaching career, as each kindergartener passed through my classroom door, I would wonder what my own children would be like when starting their education journeys. Would they be kind or a little bit naughty? Hide behind my skirt like Darius eventually did when I dropped him off to Catherine's class, or charge in as if they owned the place like Tabitha?

While I told myself that having a healthy son was a blessing on its own, as Darius grew, I tried to heal the emptiness at home by continuing to teach and fill my arms with all my schoolchildren year after year. For so long it worked to numb the loss and pain; I had the great fortune of feeling like a member of scores of families as secrets were shared and triumphs were celebrated within my four walls. At the same time, there were milestones every year that reminded me of Booker and all that was supposed to be but wasn't. The cycle of resentment began every September with the promise of new beginnings, hope, and infinite possibilities, only to predictably end in sadness when all those children that I grew to love and care for graduated and moved on. Every child headed to their next best adventure as I looked forward to another class that might soothe my wounded soul.

In twelve months' time, Darius will be moving on, his high school journey complete, his focus set on college. And if I had gotten to have all those babies, they would have eventually moved on too, just like my students. As a parent of one or ten, as a teacher of one or twenty, as hard as it is, it's my job to let them go and urge them forward into their futures.

I now can do for myself what I've been doing for others all these years. I realize that to honestly let go of my anger toward Booker, I must let go of my job helping raise other people's children. I am long past due to release myself from the broken expectations I have been holding on to. It's not that I haven't enjoyed every year I've taught kindergarten, but it's simply come time to leave Houghton and set off on my next adventure. It will be good practice for when Darius begins life without me next year.

I have been a mother figure to scores of children and an actual mother to only one, but now it's time for me to do what I love next to a man who loves me. Max and I will be together cooking in the Flour + Butter kitchen, and hopefully more. And what's ahead of me, I'm ready for it. If I've learned anything this year from Noa, Judy, Max, and even Booker, it's that anything is possible. I've also gained a greater appreciation of my son. Darius is more than an only child. Despite my years of wishing for more, from the beginning he's been enough to hold my heart.

Ding.

Booker 5:54 PM

> Darius ended his junior year with strong grades, and he has himself a real job for the summer. Giselle wants a minivan for the twins. We got ourselves a good kid Marjette, can I please give Darius Giselle's old car for his senior year so he

can easily travel between our two houses?

Marjette 5:55 PM

That sounds all right, Booker.

I'm going to be too busy to drive Darius all over the East Bay for practices, for games, and for Simone, so I'm thankful Booker came up with a plan we can both agree on.

Marjette 5:56 PM

I won't be at Houghton next year to keep an eye on Darius, but I think he'll be just fine. I'm opening a restaurant.

My thumbs stall as I look up at Max closing the last of my boxes. I don't know if I'm ready to tell Booker about Max just yet. Or if I'm just not ready to hear Booker's snarky response to me finally being happy with another man.

"Send."

Booker 5:59 PM

That's what Darius tells me. He also tells me you're doing it with your new man. I'm glad you've found someone who appreciates you Marjette. You deserve it.

Huh. I guess Judy was right. Booker thriving on me being the hurt and angry one was a belief I placed on him so I wouldn't have to do the hard work of figuring out how to thrive on my own. I put my phone in my back pocket, release a huge breath, and decide to let Booker have the last word.

Max and I have carried all my boxes out to the sidewalk, and he's gone to bring my car around front. Sizing up the pile, I can tell it's definitely going to take us more than one trip. Darius is at home organizing the garage to make room for my things. He better be getting after it before leaving to take Simone out for her birthday. When Darius asked me and Max where he should take her to celebrate turning seventeen, we both said Barney's. I saw Max slip him twenty to buy her tulips.

My classroom is completely empty. Even the green borders and white construction paper I stapled around the bulletin boards on Labor Day are down, naked cork staring back at me. I drag my fingers over the low wooden tables and bookshelves that up until two hours ago held captivating stories from far-reaching Borneo to the history of Oakland in our backyard.

Ready to turn the lights out and exit my classroom for a final time, I hear a soft, hesitant "Marjette" behind me. For the last two remaining weeks of school following the most gossip-worthy kiss in Houghton history, Rachel and I have avoided one another. Rachel entered and exited the classroom with Char at her side, and I made sure to give Tabitha her goodbye hugs from the front of the classroom while Rachel hovered in the rear. I never imagined the last person I would be speaking to on the Houghton campus would be Rachel Ellis, but here she is in leggings and a T-shirt like she's ready to help me move right on out of her children's school.

"Hi, Rachel." There's no Tabitha with her, so I can't begin to guess what she's doing here.

"Is Max with you? I stopped by the bakery, but he wasn't there." I haven't pried into Max's finances, choosing to believe his assurances that he has enough money in the bank to cover rent for the café and pay my salary for at least a year. The rest will be left up to our hustle. Please don't let this be the moment Rachel informs me that she is silent partners with my man, thus now my boss.

"No," I lie.

"Then, um, is it okay if we sit down?" Rachel asks, pulling out a chair. She can't possibly want a parent-teacher conference now.

Technically I'm a Houghton School employee for only a few more minutes, so Rachel's going to have to talk quick.

"I owe you an apology," she says.

I sit down too. Now I'm interested.

Rachel adjusts around, trying to get comfortable in her miniature seat. I tell her it's never going to happen in a chair built for small children, and the sides of her mouth turn up slightly. Getting a parent to open up often means being at the ready with something to say first. I guess once a teacher, always a teacher.

"Roger and I have known each other since we were kids." This doesn't sound like an apology. "We actually met in kindergarten," Rachel says, looking around the room, perhaps remembering her classroom that looked much like this one. "We started dating sophomore year in high school and even went to college together if you can believe that."

"I know a thing or two about young love," I share with Rachel, but leave it at that.

"Last year would have been our twenty-fifth wedding anniversary. Thirty-fifth year dating. Forty-fifth year knowing each other. After all that time and investment in each other, instead of delivering me a happy silver anniversary, he delivered me divorce papers." Now there's a tale that just might trump mine and Booker's.

There's no significant reason for me to know, but I have to ask. "Another woman?" Old habits die hard. Or don't die at all.

Not bothered one bit by my snooping, Rachel locks my eyes dead on. "Worse, actually. He left me to be alone." Rachel's face goes weak, but I warmly smile back. Noa's taught me no one wants pity.

"I'm fifty, single, and run a company that's ninety-eight percent women. I have never dated, let alone been with, another man. I'm as rare a bird for a woman in our generation as they come." *Not so rare*, I keep to myself. "All I've ever known is Roger." Rachel's eyes are glistening, and I can tell she's trying not to blink, thus triggering a tear to trickle down her cheek.

Shaking her head vigorously to wake herself back into control, Rachel continues, "I need you to know I had no idea Max was interested in you or that you two were dating. If I had, I would never have asked you to set us up. Noa must be a good friend for you to give up your man for her. I don't know if I would have done the same for a friend, or that I have someone who would do that for me." I open my mouth to let Rachel know I had no intention of giving up Max, but then shut it and take the compliment. Rachel Ellis doesn't pass them out often.

"You probably think I'm pathetic that I couldn't find my own date."

"I don't think you're pathetic, Rachel. After my divorce I completely shut myself down, didn't even consider dating. At least you're trying."

"Did you just get divorced too?" I can see Rachel's brain churning, and I don't want to have to tell this woman that *no*, we are not going to become divorce buddies working the bars.

"Five years ago."

"You haven't had a man for five years?!" Rachel cries, horrified.

"I'm happy to report the drought is over." And that is all she is going to get out of me.

"I'm used to being able to figure out how to get what I want on my own, but I couldn't get a date to my own work party. How pathetic is it that I had to ask my kid's kindergarten teacher for help," Rachel says, her hands covering her face in embarrassment. For once I'm relieved to be hearing real Rachel return.

"Anyway, I'm here because I wanted you to know that even though my life's been turned upside down, I never meant to get between you and Max." Rachel removes her hands so I can see in her eyes that her apology is sincere. "I'm not that kind of woman. I'm just a woman trying to figure out what comes next, because it's certainly not what I was expecting."

"A close girlfriend recently said to me, maybe what's next will be better than what you were expecting."

CHAPTER
THIRTY-TWO

Ding.

Darius 5:48 PM

> Max isn't checking his texts. Tell him I dropped off the last of the 4th of July weekend orders, now I'm picking up Simone, and then I'll bring by the stuff he had me get at Costco.

"Son of a bitch!" The reason Max isn't answering his text messages is he's been battling installing the six-burner Wolf range I insisted on having. I'm going to need it to flex my cooking skills to a crowd bigger than what I can fit around my dining room table. Man vs. machine isn't going well in the kitchen, so I've been keeping myself busy on the café floor unwrapping our new Parisian blue-and-white woven bistro chairs and circular tables. I can already envision my juicy fried chicken or a perfectly plated niçoise salad with a generous hunk of warm bread sitting on the tabletops, triggering our customers to drool. I want to see mouths water at the sight of my pulled pork piled high on Max's baguettes.

At the end of May, when I finally made the decision to take a leap of faith and join Max in the Flour + Butter Café adventure, I worked on my online food safety certification while Darius built me four more vegetable and herb boxes in our backyard. First order of business, full control of the food line—dirt to dining.

Marjette 5:49 PM

Don't forget the burritos I asked you to pick up for Max and me. Also don't forget you and Simone need to be at your father's house by 6:30. He and Giselle are counting on you.

Darius 5:50 PM

I have time for one or the other, not both. Which will it be?

I've been craving a carne asada burrito going on a week now, but Darius's evolving time-management skills are not working in my favor this afternoon, and Giselle and Booker have been desperate for a date night since the twins were born. Now that the babies are almost three months old, we have all agreed that Darius, with the help of Simone, won't break them.

Marjette 5:50 PM

Head over to your father's, but if the boys get fussy don't you and Simone go bothering Giselle and Booker, just call me, I'll come over.

I tiptoe into the kitchen to fill my water bottle, not wanting to remind Max I'm the one who insisted he take on this wrestling match. As I turn on the tap the pipes *clug, clug, clug,* reminding me that calling the plumber is on my to-do list. The water does spurt out with force and a frigid temperature that is perfect for cooling my green beans.

"I give up." Max rolls onto his back in surrender. The wrench in his hand makes a thud when it hits the floor, punctuating his frustration. My man looks exhausted from us hustling day and night to get the café open by mid-July. I told Max we should give ourselves an extra two weeks and open August 1, but I'm going to spare him the *I told you so* speech I have at the ready.

"On me or the stove?" I half joke, the work of opening a restaurant amounting to more than either of us could have imagined when we shook on it naked between the sheets. It's not too late for me to get my teaching gig back. When Ernie came to the bakery to select some macaroons the other day, he told me that Houghton hadn't hired my replacement yet. I think he came by because he misses me; no doubt he misses my voice more. Looking desperate, Ernie announced that the Houghton faculty a cappella group is expanding to include alumni teachers because there's a going-away party for Frida next week and Ernie needs me to anchor the choir.

Max contemplates my question and then teases, "Never on you," and waves for me to lie down on the cool of the tile floor with him. It's hard to adjust for nineteen years of being wary of germs, but I suppose if we are going to get busy in the kitchen, better it be now before we're open for business than when we really get humming and a permanent thin coat of grime is inescapable.

Rather than lying down next to him, I throw a leg over Max's trim waist and nestle into his hip bones. "Are you sure you're ready to do this with me?" I question, a niggle of concern still present over whether Max and I have thoroughly examined what it means to go into business together. Who am I kidding? I know we haven't, but if I don't bet on myself now with Max—who has enough belief in our joint talents to carry the both of us—then when will I ever?

Max's eyes pop out of the sockets, and his hands go right to my hips, tugging at the waistband of my leggings. "Oh, I'm ready, believe me." I can feel him scooching his legs behind me, working to kick off his leather boots.

"Slow down there . . ."

"Oh my God, Esty, cover your eyes!" Noa yelps, covering her own eyes first. I leap forward onto Max's diaphragm, causing him to launch into a coughing fit that throws me onto the floor. "Are you two decent? What are you doing?" What are we doing? What are Noa and Esty doing here? It's coming up on dinnertime.

"Uncle Max, are you and Ms. Lewis playing Twister?" Esty asks, peeking through her fingers, no doubt searching for the spinner.

"I'd definitely like to twist you—" Max whispers, and I quickly cover his mouth before he can finish his thought. If anyone knows how big little girls' ears are, it's me.

"Esty, honey, I told you that you can call me Marjette now."

"Is that because you let me give you kisses when I see you?" Esty singsongs, twirling a piece of purple ribbon hanging off a package Noa is holding. All three grown-ups look at this newly minted six-year-old like *huh?*

"When Uncle Max started kissing you, he stopped calling you Ms. Lewis and started calling you Marjette. From now on I'm going to kiss all my teachers so I can call them by their first names." Noa looks at me, tickled by her daughter's logic, but also to let me know I'm the one responsible for addressing this flawed social deduction with Esty. Her conclusion is reasonable for a rising first grader, but overall a terrible idea.

Amused by the scene unfolding between the three women in his life, Max rolls up off his back and leans on his hands behind him to take it all in. I, however, hop up to properly greet Esty and Noa. This is a place of business after all.

"How did you two get in here—did I forget to lock the bakery door?" Max inquires, feeling around in his pockets for his keys, which he is always losing. Making a spare set to keep at my house, which is only a little over a mile away, is also on my to-do list.

"It was unlocked because Darius is over there unloading all the Costco stuff." Noa points behind her. Ohhhhh, I don't even know which is worse, Esty walking in on me and Max gettin' it on, or if Darius would have come across the two of us. Definitely Darius; he knows I hate Twister. "Since when are you serving bulk Cheez-Its in your establishment?" Max looks at me, since I was the one who handed Darius the Costco list.

"What? My son needs a reason to stop by the restaurant to check in on his mother," I lie. I still need to be checking in on my son even though I'll be spending most of my waking hours at the café. "Those foul things are his favorite snack."

"Not my pastries?"

"Listen, if we're working together, I'm gonna start watching your handing out free samples to any kid who looks the slightest bit hungry or cute. It cuts into our profit big-time. You're too much of a sucker for children, but lucky for you, I'm here. Their sway no longer has power over me."

"I want a sucker," Esty announces, I swear batting her eyelashes right at me. I think I have one in my purse.

"How about an Esty-clair?" Max jumps up to offer his niece.

"See?" I huff, already exasperated, and look to Noa to save our bottom line.

"Too close to dinner, Max." Noa shakes her head at her brother. I mouth *"Thank you"* back to her. Max and Esty shoot each other a look that says, *Moms!*

"We stopped by to give you two something." Noa ceremoniously hands a pristinely wrapped package with rolling pins on the paper to Esty. Esty's hands drop under the weight of the mystery gift, and then she takes a few hesitant steps over to present the gift to me and Max, careful not to stumble.

"My mommy made this for you and Uncle Max." Esty beams with pride. "You guys make food; my mommy makes books." Noa knows I love paranormal romances, but this package is too heavy and irregularly shaped to be the novel of a soon-to-be-released new series Noa was telling me about last week. And truth is, so far this summer with aiming to get the café open and tending to my expanded garden boxes, unless it comes in audio form, I've had little time for books.

Max pops up to stand by my side, draping his left arm over my shoulder. We haven't been more than ten feet apart in weeks, and I love it. Though I can't believe I spent all those years thinking I wouldn't be able to be with a man who wasn't Booker, I have to admit that line of thinking did deliver me to Max, and I'm grateful for my slow journey. Max peers down at the package and gives my shoulders a squeeze, encouraging me to open it.

"Do you have any idea what this is all about?" I needle Max, wondering if this is another scheme that he, Noa, and Judy are in on, but I'm left in the dark.

"I have absolutely no idea." Max puts both his hands up to ensure I believe him.

I unwrap the package slowly. Not being one who generally likes surprises, I want to be prepared for either public disappointment or delight. I see the word *French*, then *Soul*, then *Food* on the front of what is definitely a book. Intrigued, I pull off the rest of the wrapping quickly, no longer interested in keeping the adorable paper intact to use on a future birthday present for Judy. What I'm holding is an unfinished cookbook, or I guess a prototype of a real one. Maybe this is another celebrity cookbook project Noa is working on, and she wants Max and me to test run some of the recipes.

"Open it," Noa instructs. "Start with the dedication page."

For Darius and Esty. May you always know how much you are loved.

I stare at Noa, dumbfounded. "Wait, an author of yours is willing to dedicate their cookbook to our children? That's super nice, but frankly odd. And really not necessary."

"No, silly, keep turning the pages," Esty insists with a giggle before losing interest in what's going on in the café and skipping back through the hole in the wall into the bakery to help Darius and Simone put away the paper towels.

I turn to the title page, and Max reads along with me. "Wait, *what*?!" he exclaims in shock. I'm unable to speak, every emotion tangled in my throat.

French Soul Food
By Max Kopelman and Marjette Lewis

"Marjette, you think I didn't notice every time you slipped your recipes into my purse at Thursday-night dinners for the last ten months?" It's true, I did do that. Esty enjoyed my dishes so much that I wanted her to be able to have my food other nights of the week too. "I saved every last one. Even the fried chicken recipe you boldly left on the table at Charlie's shiva. I eventually found it lodged under the horrendous lace tablecloth my mother-in-law forced me to use. Thank goodness no one ran off with that one."

"You mean all my recipes are in here?" I stutter and start whipping through the pages of the book in awe.

"When I mentioned making a cookbook of Max's and your recipes to Judy, she contributed years of cards you have left at her house as well. I have a Tupperware full of at least a hundred index cards. The two of us worked together to sort through duplicates and then pare it down to the 'best of Marjette.'"

I sure hope they got my jambalaya in there; that one's a winner.

"Max's name is on here too—first, I might add." I can't help but use my go-to humor to defuse all the feelings that are brewing. It's too much.

Max's chest puffs up, and just as quickly Noa deflates it. "Alphabetical by last name is publishing standard." Makes sense.

"So, how'd you get your hands on my recipes? You've never shown any real interest in my cooking career before," Max pushes with a hint of hurt sibling history in his voice.

"You need a stronger password on your laptop, brother. EstyisBesty. Really? You got that from Charlie. A couple of times when you came straight from work to play with Esty, I snooped through your messenger bag, grabbed your laptop, and went digging. The file on your desktop named 'recipes' made it super easy." I guess in addition to meats, I'll be in charge of cybersecurity. "Anyway, I did some market research, and not surprising, there are no French, Jewish, southern, Baptist cookbooks on the market, so I thought the world needed a taste of our special mash-up of food and love."

"Noa, I can't believe you took the time to do this for me. For us." I finger flip the mock cookbook backward, forward, upside down, and around. It's mind blowing to think that less than a year ago I actively avoided Noa. Now here we are sharing one of the great joys of my life—my family recipes. I only wish Auntie Shay and Grandma Birdie were here to witness this—my love and my passion connected to Noa Abrams and Max Kopelman—because I'm not sure, up in heaven, they're believing it. I'm having a hard time believing it myself.

"I'm amazed by everything you've done for me this past year," Noa gushes in return. "You saved my life and Esty's, Marjette. And don't you dare try to tell me it's not true." Noa puts her index finger up to me, insisting I don't debate. Tears let loose from the corners of my eyes, turning the tables. I'm now the one unexpectedly weeping while Noa wraps her arms around me, wiggling her way between me and her baby brother to give me a tight hug.

"Hold up, Noa." Max taps her on the shoulder, vying for his big sister's attention. "This is great and all, don't get me wrong, but I have questions." Such a man, needing to put facts ahead of feelings. Max steps in front of Noa and me, looking at his sister straight on.

"Don't think I haven't noticed how lukewarm you've been with me about my career choices. You questioned me every time I chased a new idea, not understanding that while you found your passion for books in college, it took me longer to find my path. And now, what feels like out of nowhere, you're willing to publish a whole cookbook by me and Marjette?" Max runs his hands through his hair, searching for his next words.

"It doesn't add up for me. I thought Charlie was the only one in the family who was supportive of my going to Paris to attend cooking school and then coming here to open up a bakery. That's what I always assumed, but then you show up with this and . . . and I don't know what to think." Max waves our cookbook at Noa, and I recognize he's upset that the narrative he sold to himself for years about his sister's support of him is flawed. I've sold myself a few too many flawed narratives as well.

"Max, it's not that I haven't supported you, or that I haven't believed in you—I always have. I always will. It's just, well, you have to admit you've run through a lot of career aspirations." Noa reaches out to grab Max's hand. "But with Marjette by your side, I truly believe anything is possible for you. For the two of you." I grab Max's other hand so we can share Noa's compliment together.

Max nods his head, slowly taking in Noa's words. I grab Noa's other hand, forming a circle with the three of us, making it clear we are in this new adventure together. "I appreciate your support, Noa, and I'll forever be grateful Charlie believed in me enough to make a substantial investment in Flour + Butter. He's the reason I was able to open the bakery in the first place." From the expression on Noa's face, I can tell Max has delivered his own surprise.

Registering Noa's shock, Max's body tenses. "Oh no. I swore to Charlie I would never say anything to you, because he knew you were skeptical of me going to cooking school. That you thought I was running away, once again, from settling down." Noa drops her head, not willing to meet Max's eyes and admit the truth. "Plus, you know Charlie and I had our own relationship. Yes, you lost a husband, but I lost one of my best friends."

"I know you did, and I know Charlie thought you were capable of great things, even when I may have doubted you. I just don't know why he would go behind my back to give you money. It makes no sense."

"Charlie knew I would never ask the two of you, so he offered the money on his own. The bakery, this soon-to-be café, and now this cookbook, at the end of the day it's really all because of Charlie."

And here I thought my family was firmly planted at the top of the drama pyramid. We need to scoot over and make room for the Abramses.

"Noa, since we're spilling all our secrets, there's one more thing I have to tell you about Charlie. I would have told you sooner, but I haven't quite known how." Lord have mercy, this is better than the *Real Housewives* of anywhere. "Charlie was at the bakery with me the night he died." Immediately, Noa drops our hands, and I feel like we are back facing the police officer the night he delivered Charlie's keys. Back to the night that Monica delivered the truth about her relationship with Charlie. And now we are here, together, hearing the final piece to the puzzle about what truly happened the night Charlie passed.

"No, no, Charlie was out with some buddies," Noa frantically insists, having already squared Monica's truth in her head that her husband was not a cheat nor a liar. Now it seems perhaps part of her original assumption rings true.

"Yeah, I was the buddy. I gave Charlie a spare set of keys to the bakery on a monogrammed key chain my old girlfriend from Paris gave me. I wanted him to have his own set so he could come and go whenever he could spare a free hour or two to help me set up shop. Turns out he wasn't so handy with any tool other than a bottle opener." Max chuckles at the memory.

"So, the keys on the *M* key chain are to the bakery?" I light up, the only one between me and a stunned Noa registering that the mystery of the keys has been solved.

"Wait, you have them?" Max looks at me, wearing the same surprised expression as his sister.

"I don't have them, Noa does." I point to my friend, who is slowly bringing herself around to understanding everything Max has unfolded between the three of us. I hold off from inserting my two cents that I'm personally thrilled Rachel Ellis is not Max's mystery investor, and that Edwardian script seems an odd choice for a tower of a man like Max. It must be a Parisian thing.

"I wasn't going to ask you about the keys, Noa, but now that I know you have them, we could use a spare set." I mentally strike that errand off my list. "Marjette, you want to keep them?" In a blink, Max has shifted from the emotional to the practical, meaning we have shit to get done.

"Yeah. I don't want a regift from your ex-girlfriend, even if the initial fits."

"Oh God, Max, maybe you are hopeless." Noa laughs.

"However," I interject, picking up the cookbook from the kitchen counter, "in this afternoon of revelations, I do have one request." There has been enough talk this afternoon about the past; I want to refocus the three of us on the future. "I think we should change the dedication to the book."

"To what?" Noa and Max ask in unison. Neither of them can imagine who I would want to dedicate our cookbook to more than Darius and Esty.

In memory of Charlie: Without you, none of this would have been possible.

ASHA'S FRIED CHICKEN

Ingredients*:

1 plump whole chicken
seasoning salt (Johnny's Seasoning Salt is my favorite)
garlic powder
onion powder
coarse-ground pepper
hot sauce
all-purpose flour
vegetable oil

Directions:

Step 1: Place your whole chicken on a cutting board for butchering. Remove the backbone (discard or save for stock) and separate the thighs, wings, and legs, and split the breast. Cut the breast in half again to create four equal-size pieces that will cook more closely in time with the rest of the chicken. You should now have ten similarly sized portions. Rinse the pieces, transfer to a clean surface, and pat dry.

Step 2: Lay the chicken out and sprinkle lightly on both sides with the Johnny's seasoning salt, garlic powder, onion powder, and pepper. Place the meat into a shallow bowl and dash all over with hot sauce. Use a small amount for a light zing or add more for a spicier result. Toss until evenly coated and place the chicken in the refrigerator for at least 30 minutes. This is a good time to disinfect your cooking surfaces and prep your side dishes.

Step 3: Remove the chicken from the refrigerator. Add flour to a double paper bag and shake two pieces at a time until well coated. Set aside the chicken on a clean surface.

Step 4: Heat an inch of vegetable oil in a pan with high sides to 350°F (175°C) or until a pinch of flour sizzles when tossed on the surface. Give each piece another dip into the flour before gently laying them into the pan. Avoid over-crowding, as this will lower the heat of the oil and create soggy chicken. Fry on both sides until brown or for about 15 minutes.

Step 5: Remove and allow to drain on paper towels. Internal temperature should be at least 165°F (75°C) with no pink flesh remaining near the bone. Serve right away for a hot and crispy bird.

*There are many recipes and variations on frying chicken. This is a very simple one that has held up in my family over decades and generations. This recipe includes no measurements because that's the way it was passed down to me. I learned from watching the women in my family, and they learned from those before them. Cooking taught me to not fear mistakes and to keep trying until I got it the way I like it. I encourage you to do the same.

ALLI'S SWEET POTATO PIE

Filling Ingredients:

1 pound sweet potatoes (can be purple and regular mixed, or just regular; baker's choice)

½ cup butter, softened

½ cup white sugar

½ cup brown sugar

½ cup evaporated milk

2 eggs

½ teaspoon ground nutmeg

¼ teaspoon cloves

¼ teaspoon ginger

2 tablespoons lemon juice

½ teaspoon ground cinnamon

1 teaspoon vanilla extract

1 tablespoon flour

Directions:

Step 1: Boil sweet potatoes whole in skin for 40 to 50 minutes, or until done. Run cold water over the sweet potatoes and remove the skins.

Step 2: Break apart sweet potatoes in a bowl. Add butter and lemon and mix well with mixer. Stir in sugar, brown sugar, evaporated milk, eggs, nutmeg, cinnamon, cloves, ginger, and vanilla. Beat on medium speed until mixture is smooth. Add the flour for a bit of thickening. Pour filling into an unbaked 9-inch pie crust (can buy one or make the pie crust recipe below).

Step 3: Bake at 350°F (175°C) for 55 to 60 minutes, or until knife inserted in center comes out clean. Pie will puff up like a soufflé, and then will sink down as it cools.

Pie Crust Ingredients:

1 teaspoon salt
6 tablespoons unsalted butter, chilled and cubed
¾ cup vegetable shortening, chilled
½ cup ice water

Directions:

Step 1: Mix the flour and salt together in a large bowl. Add the butter and shortening.

Step 2: Using a pastry cutter or two forks, cut the butter and shortening into the mixture until it resembles coarse meal (pea-size bits with a few larger bits of fat is okay). A pastry cutter makes this step very easy and quick.

Step 3: Measure ½ cup of water in a cup. Add ice. Stir it around. From that, measure ½ cup of water, since the ice has melted a bit. Drizzle the cold water in, 1 tablespoon at a time, and stir with a rubber spatula or wooden spoon after every tablespoon is added. Do not add any more water than you need to. Stop adding water when the dough begins to form large clumps. I always use about ½ cup of water and a little more in dry winter months (up to ¾ cup).

Step 4: Transfer the pie dough to a floured work surface. The dough should come together easily and should not feel overly sticky. Using floured hands, fold the dough into itself until the flour is fully incorporated into the fats. Form it into a ball. Divide dough in half. Flatten each half into 1-inch-thick discs using your hands.

Step 5: Wrap each tightly in plastic wrap. Refrigerate for at least 2 hours (and up to 5 days).

Step 6: When rolling out the chilled pie dough discs to use in your pie, always use gentle force with your rolling pin. Start from the center of the disc and work your way out in all directions, turning the dough with your hands as you go. Visible specks of butter and fat in the dough are perfectly normal and expected!

Step 7: Proceed with the pie per your recipe's instructions. And Max is right. Wet fingers help to crimp your pie's edges.

BOOK CLUB QUESTIONS FOR

NEVER MEANT TO MEET YOU

1. This book addresses different kinds of grief and varied ways to deal with it. What were some of the types of grief you recognized? Did you relate to one character's emotional journey more than the others?

2. Anne Roiphe wrote in her memoir, *Epilogue*: "Grief is in two parts. The first is loss. The second is the remaking of life." When do Marjette, Noa, and Judy acknowledge what they've lost? When does each character start remaking her life?

3. Judy and Noa both prove themselves to be good friends to Marjette. What are some of the gifts they give Marjette? What does Marjette give them in return?

4. Did you have a favorite food moment from the book? Did the story stir up any cravings or food memories for you?

5. It is apparent that Marjette and Noa have encountered racism and antisemitism, respectively. What were some of the experiences you noticed? What did each character learn from the other's experience?

6. Although Marjette doesn't have the biological family she

hoped for, she finds family. How does this "found family" support and fulfill its members?

7. Do you think Marjette's relationship with Darius would have been different if she were still with Booker, or do you think it actually would have been the same?

8. Even at some of the darkest moments in the story, there is humor. What role does humor play in grief and healing in the book? In your familial and cultural experiences?

9. We get to see Marjette in her professional role as teacher. What do you think that role means to her? Why do you think she's ready to move on from it by the end of the book?

10. Where do you think these characters will be in five years?

ACKNOWLEDGMENTS

In *Hans Brinker, or the Silver Skates* lives the infamous Dutch boy who put his finger in the dam and kept it there all night, despite the cold, to save the town of Haarlem. As parents, spouses, children, friends, and professionals in 2020/2021, we both felt like the Dutch boy with our respective fingers in the dam holding together our immediate worlds, and we recognize our experience as universal. Fight or flight is not an ideal scenario to spark creativity, but in a culture that is simultaneously fearful of grief and humor, we found writing *Never Meant to Meet You* provided the necessary moments in our days that we could take our fingers out of our dams and feel, really feel.

A core tenet of being a writer is being an observer of the broader world. When life shut down and became very small, observation and inspiration had to come from new and varied sources. We would like to thank the following people who were profoundly instrumental in bringing the story of Marjette, Booker, Darius, Noa, Charlie, Esty, Max, Judy, and Rachel to life even though they don't know it.

- Melissa Gould's book *Widowish*

- Leslie Gray Streeter's book *Black Widow: A Sad-Funny Journey Through Grief for People Who Normally Avoid Books with Words Like "Journey" in the Title*

- Zibby Owens's podcast *Moms Don't Have Time to Read Books* as well as her aptly named book *Moms Don't Have Time To: A Quarantine Anthology*

- *Kelly Corrigan Wonders* podcast with guests Wanda Holland Greene, Andy Laats, Anna Quindlen, Anna Sale, and Jen Hatmaker

- *Rich Roll* podcast with guests Maggie Q and Rabbi Mordecai Finley

When we set out to write together in 2017 (with zero evidence we could do so), we were dedicated to the mission of bringing stories of joy, love, and laughter amid the challenging topics of race, religion, privilege, parenting, and education. In an entertainment era marked by trauma—on screen and in books—we knew it might be difficult to find our audience and have our characters heard, but we have never been deterred. We want to thank our team who believes in our mission, who believes in our dream, and who chooses joy above all else.

We'd like to thank our tenacious agent, Liza Fleissig of Liza Royce Agency. She is a force, and we are grateful every day she is our force. It has been our good fortune to be supported by our acquisitions editor at Montlake, Alison Dasho, who exudes a jubilant spirit and quick wit that matches ours, thus expanding the A-team from two to three. We are thrilled to count as a friend Tegan Tigani, who has been with us as our cheerleader, coach, and developmental editor since the early days of our first book, *Tiny Imperfections*. May we be blessed with many more opportunities to work with her. Along with every great editor is a team of people who work to bring a story from a black-and-white manuscript to a three-dimensional book for authors to hug, hold, and share with their audience. Our book magicians are the incomparable (and patient)

Kris Beecroft, Liz Casal, Jillian Cline, Kristin Lunghamer, Anh Schluep, Stef Sloma, and Cheryl Weisman.

There is a longstanding history in the United States of the Black and Jewish communities standing together from the cofounding of the NAACP, the Southern Christian Leadership Conference (SCLC), and the Student Nonviolent Coordinating Committee (SNCC), to participating in large numbers together in the Freedom Rides and marching alongside Dr. Martin Luther King Jr. We are honored to be a part of the Black-Jewish Entertainment Alliance and to have focused our creative efforts in *Never Meant to Meet You* on helping our country better understand the stories and struggles of the Black and Jewish communities in America today.

—Alli + Asha

I was reluctant to write this book, and Liza Fleissig nailed the reason for it: I was reluctant to examine what it meant to me to be a Jewish woman. While writing this book with Asha, I was also watching my oldest daughter study Hebrew and prepare for and then become a Bat Mitzvah. Between writing *Never Meant to Meet You*, supporting my eldest daughter, and living an abbreviated life from the confines of my home, I indeed came more face-to-face with my own "Jew-ishness" than I ever had before. The following women, friends, and family have been remarkable models, each in their own unique way, of female Jewish strength and power: Beth Silber, Shelley Bransten, Beth Scheer, Ally Gwozdz, Nicole Avril, Dana Berntson, Rabbi Cantor Robbi Sherwin, Stephanie Griggs, Dana Nordquist, Carolyn Starr, Cookie Glasser, Kristy Schulman, Nancy Oberman, and Lynn Stahl. And always, always, always my daughters, Lila and Lexi Pinizzotto, and my mom, Bunker Frank. Scott and Dad, you know nothing I do is possible without the two of you. Asha, as long as we keep laughing, let's keep going.

—Alli Frank

There are aspects of life that tie us together across gender, racial, national, and generational lines. They transcend religion; they are inevitable; they are uniquely human experiences. The significance of each may vary in importance to us as individuals, but the three that have had the greatest impact on me are grief, food, and love. Grief over the death of my father left my family to wrestle with emotions that were deeply personal and often difficult to convey. We gathered over shared food to alleviate our pain and reminisce about his life. We remembered how deeply he loved us and finally healed in the love we have for each other. This book is in tribute to my mother, Lynda Vassar, who showed me there are reasons to go on despite suffering a great loss and that life is beautiful when you have family around the dining table. This book is in celebration of my mother-in-law, Mary Ann Youmans, for loving me like her own daughter despite our differences in race and religion. This book is in honor of my grandmother, Eva Vassar, who taught me to cook and to believe in the power of food to lure relatives together to remember the unbreakable bonds of family love. Thank you to my husband, Jeff, who is always my hype man. And to my writing partner, Alli: you can count on me because I can count on you.

—Asha Youmans

ABOUT THE AUTHORS

Photo © 2018 J Garner Photography

Alli Frank has worked in education for more than twenty years, from boisterous public high schools to small, progressive private schools. A graduate of Cornell and Stanford University, Alli lives in the Pacific Northwest with her husband and two daughters. With Asha Youmans, she is the coauthor of *Tiny Imperfections* and is a contributing essayist in the anthology *Moms Don't Have Time to: A Quarantine Anthology*.

Asha Youmans spent two decades teaching elementary school students. A graduate of University of California, Berkeley, Asha lives in the Pacific Northwest with her husband and two sons. With Alli Frank, she is the coauthor of *Tiny Imperfections*.

For more information visit the authors at www.alliandasha.com and find them on social media @alliandasha to connect.